Shamaness of the Pride

Fur, Lust & Magic Book 2

Mary Leihsing & Aden Lewis

Published in United States of America by:

Mary Leihsing and Aden Lewis
www.newnightpublishing.com

ISBN-13: 978-1532906435
ISBN-10: 1532906439

New Night Publishing
Mary@newnightpublishing.com
www.newnightpublishing.com

Table of Contents

About the Authors

Mary started writing at a young age, and one of the first stories she wrote was about The Immortals. From then on she fell in love with muscled men and wrote about them.

Now her books are full of Numen, Shifters, Aliens, Faie and more. When we first read Mary's work we were flushed and breathing heavy.

The spicy love scenes are breath-taking and very stimulating. The action and danger filled moments leading up to those scenes make them all that more powerful.

When Mary is not writing she can be found hiking in the wilderness, or out at a local club looking for the man that can inspire her next book.

Aden Lewis really fell in love with writing while teaching medieval history at The Willow School in Kansas. When writing a period journal for the grade school class she was teaching she quickly realized that her writing was strictly for adults only.

Now she writes Paranormal romance full time. While she has dated women and men she has yet to meet one to measure up to the standards set in her books. When not writing Aden is busy getting her degree, and learning to cook. She can be found with Mary Leihsing from time to time looking for the man or woman that can measure up to the amazing characters in their books.

While writing with Mary Leihsing they quickly discovered a shared love for anything Paranormal. Throw in the spicy intense sex scenes both writers excel at and reading their books becomes a thrill ride of intense romance, sex and action.

Dedications

The Authors of this book want to dedicate it to many people. The publishers felt that the pages in the book should be put to better use. Things like their logo, copyright and legal mumbo jumbo. In consideration of this, not because the decision was out of their hands, the Authors offer the following few heartfelt dedications. They both sincerely hope that the book is as fun and entertaining to read as it was to write and that in the following volumes more dedications will be possible.

Mary and Aden would like to dedicate this book to the person who is our first real fan. – Calyie Martin.

They would also like to dedicate this book to all of their fans of their first book.

Now everyone else spread the word so the publisher will hurry up and get the third book out. Then we can put more of the people that made this series of books possible in the following volumes.

Now without any further ado read on, laugh, cry and scream as you read our book. No, wait that's what we did while writing it. And shush, the 6-foot holes in the back yard are empty.

No, we do not know where those salespeople disappeared to after interrupting the writing of this book.

Disclaimer

To protect the privacy of certain individuals the names and identifying details have been changed. Any Werecats, Werewolves, Were-anything, spirits, faerie, or humans (regular or magical) in this book are protected by the Super-Natural Beings Clause, of 2155. As time travel is common, this clause is retroactive.

And for the last time The Authors deny any knowledge of where those salespeople disappeared to. The six-foot holes in the backyard are entirely coincidental. The livestock guardian dogs like to dig.

What is also coincidental is if any person in the book has any resemblance to, living or dead, anyone in the so-called real world.

Prologue

The bumpy road and lack of shocks on the old ambulance wakes Alexis. Looking around, she straightens, hoping no one noticed her dozing off. She sits up listening as Derek and Roger continue speaking.

"Any idea why the one Werewolf gave us gifts at the Pride formation ceremony?" Derek asks.

"The Major said all the witnesses were to bring gifts. I suppose none of the others bothered, just our mange-riddled friend." Roger shrugs.

Alexis grunts, jabbing her eyes while wiping away sleep, as the old ambulance hits another large pothole. "So how far have we gotten?" She asks looking out the window. *Wow, I thought the country was supposed to be lit up with stars. The only thing out there is inky blackness.*

"We're somewhere in Arizona. At least, that's my guess since I saw a cactus awhile back. We have lost a couple different tails on this mountain tracks. Of course, with Bryan driving, we could also be in Mexico." Roger's voice is a bit louder as he finishes.

"Ouch." Alexis cries out as Bryan guns the engine as they hit another large pothole.

"Do you think the major was telling the truth?" Roger asks, holding on at the increased speed of the ambulance.

"I think he was too angry we formed our own Pride without him to lie well. Of course, I'm sure he left enough out to cause us problems." Derek pulls Alexis into his side as he finishes.

"My Grandmother's Ranch hasn't been used since I was six or seven years old. I'm not sure what condition it will be in." Alexis sighs as she feels Brother Lion's warmth spread through her.

"Amanda called while you were resting." Derek murmurs in her ear.

Alexis starts to stiffen until she sees the slow wink from Roger. "How is everything?" She finishes, not sure who to ask about first.

The ambulance careens to the left briefly going on two wheels before slamming back down. "Sorry," Bryan doesn't sound too sincere as he shouts over his shoulder.

"Amanda and Sabrina have Mrs. Collins and Aaron safe in a motel with them. His ex-wife and son went to her mom's out of state. He emptied his savings and gave her the money to move with the kids."

I'm sorry Aaron I never intended for you to have to move away from your kids. Alexis looks out the window as Derek continues.

"The moving crew will be at your house in the morning. Matteas texted that the rest of the Pride has a lead on Mr. Armstrong and will let us know more when they land." Derek squeezes her hand as he finishes.

Swallowing, Alexis nods. "Well, I suppose that's something. Tell them thank you for me."

Dad, you better be okay. When we get you back we are going to sit down and chat. Her resolve to finally know once and for all if her Dad had anything to do with her Mom's death loosens the tightness in her throat.

Roger looks away so he will not see her tears and embarrass her.

"Well, whoever was following us is not back there anymore," Bryan announces from the front seat.

"So, can you slow down before you kill us for them?" Roger's sarcasm brings another 5 mph, which is Bryan's only reply.

If I don't distract them, I might live but I will definitely be black and blue head to toe. "Derek, you never did tell me what it means when you and Brother Lion keep calling me your mate."

If Brother Lion and Derek weren't busy discussing who might have been following them, one of them might have heard the warning in Alexis' tone. Then again, being lifelong bachelors they might not have.

"I suppose, if we were just human we would be married," Derek answers distracted as he returns to the place where he and Brother Lion spoke.

"Derek Bartholomew Mathews." Derek and Brother Lion turn, eyes widening at the angry authoritative tone. Ignoring Roger's mouthing of Bartholomew, Derek looks at Alexis with raised eyebrows.

"I will have you know that one night in the alley is NOT a proposal." Alexis swings her left hand in Derek's face. At that moment, the ambulance hits another pothole and instead of showing her ringless finger she slaps him instead.

Derek growls in startled pain leaning away. "Don't you growl at me! Until I have a ring, a NICE ring, a proper date, and a romantic proposal, I will hear no more talk of mate."

"But Alexis..."

"Shut up and start looking for a jewelry store. I am sure they have one in South Dakota somewhere." As Alexis' glare moves from Derek to the chortling Roger, he gets up and moves to the front seat beside Bryan. The ambulance slows to a more reasonable speed.

Derek leans back, takes out his cell phone and begins looking for Jewelry Stores. *Where exactly did she say this 380-acre ranch is? All I can remember is the Badlands of South Dakota. Suddenly the huge ranch doesn't seem so huge or perfect anymore.*

"And Derek, I expect a honeymoon. Somewhere nice with beaches, yes beaches would be nice. Without men chasing us!"

Derek sighs looking at rings, as the ambulance gets quiet. *Priceless cut, round, oval, pear, radiant what the hell. I want a diamond ring, not food.*

Definitely not round or pear remember when you said she was nice and round? Brother Lion winces in memory.

Yeah, I remember and you said not really round

more like a pear and she threw her bowl of ice cream at us? Derek shared the memory with Brother Lion.

We need a woman to help with this. Mrs. Collins will know what kind of diamond to get. Are there any apples left? I am getting kind of hungry now. Brother Lion askes.

Chapter 1

"Three months and still no running water in the house. Decades of life and not a one of them managed to learn anything about indoor plumbing." Alexis grunts on the last word turning the pipe wrench hard. "Okay Aaron, turn it on," Alexis calls out the open door.

Aaron shakes his head as he carefully turns on the water from the well to the house. He steps back watching the shut-off valve. He hopes it won't need to be replaced. Three months of living surrounded by Werecats has given Aaron a nervous twitch to his right eye.

"Hell YES! If you want something done right, you ask a woman to do it." *Not that they asked me but that just shows how much they have to learn.* Alexis walks out the door, cobwebs in her hair, a black smudge on her left cheek smiling in triumph. New confidence puts a lift in her shoulders that has been missing before her impromptu bonding with Derek and Brother Lion.

Aaron smiles as he climbs up from the well house. "That's good. I'm sure Mrs. Collins will be thrilled to be able to flush the toilet without hauling a bucket of water upstairs first."

Derek and Bryan walk over from the chicken coop. The idea of a house for birds, even chickens, being converted to a Werecat house is worth a chuckle. Alexis' smiles in triumph as she picks up the hose running from the spigot on the side of the house and turns it on.

"I still think we just need stronger pipes. I didn't turn it that hard. The thing just twisted." Bryan continues defending his plumbing ability as they pass the well house to stop by Aaron. "Aaron, we need you to show us what we did wrong with the shingles again. It rained last night and I got a second shower. You can play with Alexis' after_."

Before he could finish, "Yiiiipppeee." A very unmanly sound issues from Bryan as the ice cold spring water from the hose in Alexis' hands hit him in the chest splashing his face and runs downward. Aaron wastes no time running around the side of the house. Derek, on the other hand, is busy laughing when the hose catches him in the mouth. Coughing and still laughing he charges Alexis, who squeals and turns to flee dropping her hose.

Derek grabs her around the waist before she gets more than a couple of steps and swings her in the air as she laughs with him. "You are not taking Aaron off to show you for the third time how to lay shingles. He is helping me with the plumbing." She would sound more convincing without the girlish giggling.

Brother Lion looks out Derek's eyes as they lower her to her feet. "You are a worthy Mate." The stinging slap as Alexis' palm hits stubbled cheek, sounds loud in the quiet yard. Aaron, who is just looking around the corner checking if it's safe, turns pale and begins to back up.

"No mate business, your furriness might get away with that with your kitties, but I will be damned if you will pull that with me! This hand has no ring." Alexis is panting as she finishes waving her hand in front of Derek's face.

Ever since the bonding of Derek and Brother Lion, they switch the reigns faster than Alexis can keep up with. She is adjusting well to being mated to a Werelion and the man who lived in the body of the Werelion. Unlike all the other Werecats that were turned by the Major, Derek and Brother Lion shared a body but distinct individuals.

Derek leaned down and silenced Alexis' protests under his lips. Bryan is shaking his head and taking off his soaked shirt looking over at Aaron. "I told you the shut off was fine, I didn't turn it that hard. Now show me that shingle overlap thing again." Bryan's wet chest is covered in gold and black hairs. The muscles ripple like waves before a storm.

"Alexis wants me to help with the plumbing." Aaron pauses as Bryan tosses his shirt on the well house cement roof to dry. "You got the water running. I am done with cold showers between that roof and Alexis." Bryan smiles as he wraps his arm around Aaron's shoulders, leading him away.

Brother Lion whispers in Alexis' ear as he sets her down. "Proud of you, but we need lunch." He turns to follow Bryan and Aaron, who is looking helplessly back at Alexis from Bryan's massive shadow.

"We got the water running! Aaron is helping me today!" Alexis protests, moving to stop Derek as he follows.

Derek picks up the hose and spins quicker than a six-foot 400-pound Werelion should be able to and douses Alexis in ice cold water. "He already helped you and the water works great." Dropping the hose he runs after Bryan before Alexis can grab the hose. As he disappears around the corner he calls over his shoulder to Alexis, "Lunch."

"Lunch, this!" Alexis flips the retreating Werecats off as she stands dripping.

"Oh, My." Mrs. Collins stands in the open door looking aghast at Alexis. She blushes at the dismay on Mrs. Collins face as she takes in the dripping, cobwebbed and smudged Alexis standing in torn jeans a size too small.

Feeling ashamed as only someone who has changed her diapers can make her feel. Alexis shrugs and looks at her feet. "I got the water working." She passes Mrs. Collins, who backs up to give her plenty of space.

"That is lovely dear. Perhaps you should use it and wash up for lunch." Mrs. Collins turns back to the kitchen where smells of fried chicken and fresh baked bread are rolling out before Alexis can see her smile.

Dammit Derek, I was going to surprise her and cheer her up. Now I'm off to take a cold shower instead. Shaking her head, Alexis walks up the stairs, eyeing the claw marks from countless Werecat feet. Then looking at the older scuff marks accrued from over 150 years of her family's feet. Amazed, as always, how natural it feels to her to live with Werecats.

Shaking her head she passes into the one and only bathroom, blessedly empty for the moment. With most of the Pride out on the Major's latest hot tip, the house and ranch have not had more than a few of the Pride home at any one time. Getting out a clean towel and change of clothes Alexis slows, bracing herself before facing the ice cold shower.

The cold water hitting her nipples brings a small groan. *Derek, we really need more time for us. In the meantime, I'm glad I brought my massaging showerhead, let's see if it can deliver even with cold water.* Alexis' hands run down her sides still marveling at the smooth skin where scars had covered half her body a few short months ago.

Squirting a generous amount of organic apple body wash she lathers her large breasts, squeezing them more than washing requires. The feeling of the tingling suds running down her shaven mons, before teasing lower past her pouting lips. Reaching up and adjusting the shower head to the thrump, thrump rhythm with just enough force to get her there, she closes her eyes leaning back.

With her body tingling and her nipples fluctuating from cold numbness to delightful bursts of sensation, a low moan escapes her. Her hands run down her sides to her thighs. Her right-hand brushes over her lips, dipping the tip of her finger in, teasing herself.

"Helllooo." Straightening too fast at the whisper in her ear she bangs her head into the showerhead.

"Ouch." Rubbing her head, she pulls the shower head back into position. *Great Alexis, now your hearing voices. Being hunted by an Alpha that kills his own pack, having your Father kidnapped, and mating with two furry men is not enough to drive you crazy. Nope, you go that extra mile and hear voices as well.*

"That sounds like you."

"Who's there?" Alexis covers her large breasts as well as she can looking into the drain for who is speaking to her.

"It's Roger, I was sent to tell you that lunch is ready. Are you okay?" His voice sounds worried as he asks from outside the partly open bathroom door.

Alexis sighs, leaning back against the wall shivering. "Yeah, you just startled me. Shut the door and let everyone know I will be right down." Alexis turns the water off as the door closes. She hears girlish giggles as the water goes down the drain and steps from the shower into the waiting towel. As Alexis dries off, she pulls the shower curtain shut. She wraps the towel around her still shivering as she squeezes toothpaste on her toothbrush.

Well, maybe Derek can pick up where the showerhead left off later....

The picnic table is complete with a red and white plaid tablecloth. The large men all sit on the right-hand side on the homemade log benches built to hold Werecats. Mrs. Collins carries out the last of the lunch and sits it on the table. Shoving the potato chips so that yet more food can fit on the already overcrowded table. Fried chicken, potato salad, five bags of chips, dill pickles from the cellar, sweet tea, and lemonade. All spread out before the waiting men.

While they all sit at the table together, their thoughts are miles apart.

Roger, flexing his arthritic fingers, tries to remember the last time he had homemade fried chicken. His bulging muscles and childish manner are dampened by his thoughts. *After the magic had worked and I became one of the Pride for the first time despite not being a Were, the disfigurement got better. Now it's getting worse again and now my memories are going. Almost 60 years as an outsider living with Werecats, but not a Were or human. Now I am losing myself.* He wipes a tear from his eye with a sigh.

Bryan is six-foot-seven with broad shoulders and topping the few scales that can weigh him over 600 pounds. The largest of the pride and the only vegetarian Weretiger in history.

He winces as Richard crows to the sun from where he and his little harem are hiding in the barn. Smiling in relief when no one responds to Richard's repeated cock a doodle do's. His stomach growls bringing a blush to his cheeks as he eyes the potato salad to be replaced with a frown. *I hope she has more of that potato salad inside. Wait, yes, in her arms, I smell it, did she finally make it?*

He leans forward as Mrs. Collins sets the last bowl down on the corner of the table and removes the saran wrap from the top. Leaning on the table with a silly grin on his face, "Pistachio, I will kiss you, Mrs. Collins!"

"You spill my food and I will spank you! Giant cat thing or not!" Mrs. Collins produces a large wooden spoon as if by magic and brandishes it before the assembled men. The Werecats lean back and fold their hands in their laps, eyes following the spoon.

Mrs. Collins nods in satisfaction as everyone sits up and remembers their manners. While most women in their fifties in her situation would have a heart attack, not Mrs. Collins. She has spent plenty of time around unruly military men while Mr. Collins was alive. After her initial shock, she decided that Werecats were not much different than any other men. They are just furrier. A firm woman's hand is what they all need.

Looking at Derek where he sits at the end of the table on a wooden chair, she looks him up and down once. "That is good Derek, you remembered to comb your hair today for lunch. Thank You, I am sure Alexis will be pleased."

Brother Lion smiles, glad that they have made Mrs. Collins happy, as Derek blushes. At the mention of her name, everyone looks around for the absent Alexis. Turning to Roger, Derek raises an eye in question.

"She was in the shower and said she would be right down." Roger hesitates then closes his mouth.

"Go on Roger, what were you going to say." Derek leans back to keep his hands from the fried chicken making his mouth water.

"She sounded frightened when I spoke to her. I think she might already know that the rest of the Pride is coming home tomorrow." Roger looks towards the house.

The large Victorian house, built in 1855 in the Badlands of South Dakota, stands out on the plains. The handful of scattered trees look small in comparison. The back porch is sagging badly, the roof is patched with different colored shingles. The flaking paint and boarded up attic window give a somewhat sinister aspect.

"Why would that frighten Alexis?" Derek asks, looking from one to another of them.

Mrs. Collins sits down, folding her napkin neatly in her lap. "You already know that Derek, or Brother Lion, whichever I am speaking to now. Amanda and Sabrina do not like Alexis and resent her place by your side." The others relax and stop avoiding Derek's gaze as Mrs. Collins speaks up and says what they did not want to.

Brother Lion eyes each of the members of the Pride present, eyes glowing. "I am disappointed in you, my Pride. Alexis has been there whenever we needed her.

She lost her home, her father, and still she pawned her Grandmothers ring to buy that cream for your swollen joints, Roger." Roger slouches looking away.

"Bryan, she helps you hide and feed those chickens that were supposed to be our dinner a month ago. Mrs. Collins, she has been like your own child. She depends on you. Ever since she lost her mother, you were there. I would think one of you would have spoken to me before this. The least you should have done was made her aware of your own acceptance of her."

Mrs. Collins pales then goes red in the face. Opening and closing her mouth several times yet remains silent. Roger gazes into Brother Lion and Derek's eyes, "You are running around proclaiming she is your mate, despite the fact that she has told you many times to stop. You know Amanda is still in love with you. Sabrina, well she thinks all humans are pathetic."

"Now wait one fucking minute!" Derek stands up trembling in anger, claws extended and his fangs growing.

Roger backs away from the table standing to confront Derek. "No! You wait, you wanted this and you got it, your furriness. Three long months we have waited for you to step up and be a real Alpha. Either court and win Alexis or back the hell off. Anyone can see Bryan is half in love with her already. Instead, you treat her like she should just fall at your feet and grovel."

Bryan lurches to his feet with a roar. "We both love her Derek, Brother Lion, and while the two of you were busy trying to learn how to adapt to sharing that body, the rest of us have been attempting to keep Alexis safe. Roger is right, you should have put a stop to this when Sabrina and Amanda brought Aaron and Mrs. Collins with the moving truck months ago."

Bryan is panting in anger that he has held in for months. "I will never regret following you Derek. But the last few months has made me ponder my decision. I never thought you would bring me to that point."

Aaron walking up brings the conversation to a halt as everyone turns to see who is approaching after the screen door slammed. Aaron has walked on eggshells for months surrounded by huge Werecats that can tear him apart without trying. As everyone turns and stares at him, he pauses squaring his shoulders he stalks to the table.

"You all should be ashamed of yourselves. Alexis is in the kitchen in tears." Derek begins walking to the house, only to be brought up short when Aaron moves in front of him and pokes him in the belly with his finger. The six-foot Werelion being confronted by the five-foot-eight, rail thin Aaron is like watching a housecat face down a lion. "Hold it right there. You Werecats hurt her quite enough for one day. She was on the phone with her father's attorneys when you all decided to start shouting. Now I am taking her out to lunch. You can sit down and think about how to make this up to her or kill me and show her what you are all really like."

Aaron swallows but stands firm, waiting for Derek to kill him. Brother Lion and Derek step back, Aaron nods once and heads to the town car where Alexis is standing in the open door watching. As the town car turns down the long twisting drive and passes out of sight, Brother Lion and Derek let out a roar that shakes the ground.

Sitting in the little cafe, Alexis notices the farmer and his farm hand, who are growing corn a few miles past the Ranch. When he smiles and nods to her, she smiles and nods back. *It is so nice to know how to react. With everything back in California happening so fast, the attacks, being suspended from school on my second day, Dad kidnapped, Mrs. Collins hurt. Not to mention falling in lust and love with Derek and Brother Lion.*

The cowbells on the door jangle as Aaron returns with a thick pile of papers in his hands. The only waitress sees him and brings over coffee. She is a large woman, three hundred pounds and looks mean. When Alexis sat down, she ignored her for fifteen minutes. Then when she did bring ice water she spills some splashing Alexis. As Alexis smiles and says she is waiting for someone, the woman rolls her eyes and sniffs.

Now with Aaron, she is all smiles. "Didn't know you would be in town today Aaron. Glad you could take time for yourself away from those Sasquatches out at the old Stone Ranch." She actually wipes out the coffee cup before pouring his coffee.

"Thank ya Daisy, this some of that special brew?" Aaron winks at her from under his new 10-gallon hat.

Daisy giggles and nods. "You want your regular?"

How many times does Aaron eat here to have a regular? That cowboy hat is the silliest thing I have ever seen. Could he actually like her? "Actually, could we see some menus please?" Alexis asks.

Daisy waddles over to the counter, leans over it and brings one back, dropping it in front of Alexis. "You going to stop by the pub this Saturday and sing for us again?" Daisy slips a silver flask from her apron and drops a generous splash in Aaron's coffee.

"Why, how could I say no to you Daisy? We just need a few minutes then we will be ready to order." He smiles picking up his coffee, sipping and sighing. Daisy grins and leans back like she will be there awhile. "Daisy, order up." The fat bald man from the kitchen scowls at Aaron as he flops two plates with fried eggs and hash browns on the counter for Daisy.

As Daisy grunts and walks away, Aaron pushes the pile of papers over to Alexis. "The power of attorney went through no problem. The house has been transferred to your name. The personal bank accounts will unfreeze as soon as you agree to leave the business closed, pending sale."

"The buyers still hiding behind that dummy corporation?" Alexis asks sipping her lukewarm water.

"Yep. Also, the charges against your Dad will be dropped at that point as well. I think it's obvious that someone wants your Dad's business pretty badly."

Aaron doesn't finish as Daisy comes back over with a refill for his coffee.

Alexis shakes her empty glass for Daisy's attention, and she doesn't even glance her way.

"I put the last piece of my fresh rhubarb pie in the back to save it just for you." Daisy winks, yet again, at the smiling Aaron, who once again tips his white cowboy hat.

"Thank You Daisy, you always take such good care of me. You better be careful, I might steal you away just for you're cooking." As Aaron finishes, Daisy gives an improbable girlish giggle.

Alexis laughs and when both Daisy and Aaron turn to look at her she pretends to be choking, waving her empty glass around. With a glare at Alexis, Daisy takes the empty glass back behind the counter. Alexis promptly sticks her tongue out at Daisy's retreating backside. "How can someone that rude manage a girlish giggle?" Alexis leans back at the anger on Aaron's face.

"Daisy is a single Mother. She also takes care of the seniors in town since hospice closed the local office, and is raising two kids on a waitress salary. Daisy bakes all night and takes in laundry to wash and mend, all to keep food on the table. Daisy's mother's medication is not on the list of approved medicines, so she has to pay for that as well. I would have had a hard time paying for all of that even back when your Dad was paying me."

Looking out the window Aaron pales, then stands and moves towards the counter to speak to Daisy.

Alexis blushes scarlet and when Daisy and everyone look her way she buries her nose in the papers sitting before her. The cowbell jangling on the door gets only a glance as Aaron leaves. Daisy walks over dropping the keys on the table and returning the still empty glass before walking away. Alexis looks out the window for Aaron and not seeing him gathers up the papers. She leaves a $10.00 on the table as she gets up.

"Well, we sure messed that up." Bryan's voice is sad as he sits back down. "Come on, Aaron's right, if we care about Alexis, and I know we do, we need to fix this."

Brother Lion, is Roger right? Have we been ignoring problems within the Pride? Derek speaks to Brother Lion even as he moves to sit back down.

Brother Lion has not been the same since the bonding ceremony where the Pride all pledged their allegiance to them and Alexis. He is no longer a four-legged lion. Now he walks upright and is a blend of all the Great Cats in the Pride.

Brother, it's been too long since I was an Alpha, and as you know, I remember nothing of those times since I joined you in your body. Since the Pride ceremony, we wasted too much time adjusting to sharing your body. It's time we stop neglecting the Pride, Alexis and begin being the Alphas they deserve.

Roger resumes his seat as well, passing Mrs. Collins on the way, she is crying in her napkin.

"Mrs. Collins, I'm sorry for what I said before." Derek reaches across the table and gently squeezes her hand. Mrs. Collins nods.

"Alright, tell me what has been happening while we've been learning to share this body." Derek and Brother Lion both look out at each of them, braced for more condemnation.

Everyone looks at each other and away several times. Sighs and fidgeting last a few moments before Bryan begins. "Roger is partly correct in his accusation. I do love Alexis. Ever since I was changed and became a monster, no one has been able to see ME. They see my strength or size and judge me on that. Not Alexis, always when I'm upset or afraid, she doesn't judge me, she's just there. I will not fight you for her. But if you hurt her, I will do my best to kill you."

Bryan's final words bring a shocked gasp from Mrs. Collins, who turns pale as Bryan, who she thinks of as her gentle giant says he will kill.

Roger, seeing Mrs. Collins reaction and not trusting what Derek and Brother Lion's reaction will be, jumps in. "What he is saying is that all of us love Alexis in different ways. We would all fight and give up our own lives to keep her safe."

Derek relaxes in his seat and gives a minimal nod. Mrs. Collins smiles for a second in understanding and Bryan does not contradict or agree with Roger. "What it comes down to is this, the Pride is divided for the first time. We all have to adjust to the knowledge that all these decades you were not like the rest of us and we're trying. While we became part animal, you remained you, with a speaking thinking Lion living in your head. The fact that you never told any of us is hard to stomach." A nod from Bryan shows his agreement.

"What else have you not told us? After the Major turned all of us all of you into Werecats and me into the Thing I am, we thought we were all in it together. Now we learn that you have been holding back all this time." Roger holds up his muscled arm that is twisted and misshapen while Bryan does the same with his furred and clawed one.

"There is nothing else I'm keeping from you." Derek leans back, his eyes lose focus. *How can the chasm that has grown between us and our family gotten so large and neither of us notice? I thought they all understood.* Brother Lion moves in the strange astral place inside Derek where he exists and speaks to Derek in the body they share.

As it always happens, since they began sharing their body willingly after the Pride was formed, their body is surrounded by a light distortion. Alexis refers to it as a heat shimmer.

His gaze traveling from Roger to Bryan and back, "We have changed and grown since the Pride formed. We had to adapt to each other before we could explain our joint existence to any of you."

Bryan shakes his head, "You are both so well suited to each other. The problem is it took you both three months to sit down and speak to us about any of this. You become fixated on a goal and lose sight of everything else."

It is our strength, but I understand now it can also be a weakness. Brother Lion we need to pull the Pride together.

Yes, but first we heal the chasm between our mate and us. Without her, the Pride is without its heart. Brother Lion projects the image of eating with Alexis

As he gets more passionate in his images, Derek interrupts the rather improbable sex on a tree limb image. *Without her, we are not a Pride, just lost Werecats once more.*

"Derek, we're still getting to know Brother Lion. Our animal sides all respond to him instinctively. While our human side still follows you loyally. Speak to the Pride." Bryan begins.

"Fuck that shit. First, get a Goddamn ring on her finger. Then ask her somewhere private if she will marry you. If she says yes, then put that ring on her finger, and explain to her that she has to stop acting like a spoiled brat and be the woman we love and respect." Roger stands up and storms into the house. The screen door breaks in half as he enters it.

Bryan and Mrs. Collins are nodding as they stare at the screen door. Derek and Brother Lion are ignoring the huge question that keeps cropping up in their minds. Bryan takes an enormous helping of pistachio salad as Roger comes back out of the house.

"Derek, Lion dude, let's go," Roger hollers as he gets in the old 1970's pickup that they had bought from the neighbor for $300 and a day's work hauling hay.

Derek rises and starts towards the pickup in a daze. "Derek." Mrs. Collins moves up behind him, as he turns toward her she wraps him in a huge hug as the tears start. "I know she loves you. If I have not told you everything I_."

Brother Lion puts his finger over her lips and leans down. "You told us to comb our hair and to not belch in front of her. When the others were here and she was uncomfortable, you always had her running errands in town. You have done your part. Thank You."

Mrs. Collins loses herself in the glowing amber eyes and nods. As Derek speaks, the glow dims but doesn't go out. "Please pack a picnic lunch, and tonight when everyone is asleep I would be grateful if you taught me to cook a Chocolate Cream Pie."

"Of course, but you don't cook a pie." Mrs. Collins speaks to his disappearing back as Roger lays on the horn.

"Trust your Alpha Mrs. Collins." Even Bryan is unsure which Alpha says that. Mrs. Collins returns to the table and sits down. They watch as the pickup rumbles down the long drive.

"This salad is delicious. You certainly outdid yourself this time." Bryan's mouth is full as he speaks and even with half a plate, he is already reaching for more.

"Don't talk with your mouth full dear." Mrs. Collins takes a slice of bread and misses the contented smile on Bryan's face.

Alexis is halfway to the door when Daisy bumps into her from the side, spilling greasy vegetable soup all over her blouse and pants. "Look at what you did! What's wrong with you? Your nose so high up in the air you just expect us to jump out of your way?"

Daisy glares at Alexis for a second before grabbing her arm and dragging her along behind her. "The mop is in here, and I will call the sheriff to get off his fat ass and get down here if you try to leave after making this mess."

Alexis' face is scarlet and she is too shocked to protest. The jangling cowbell doesn't even register when someone enter during Daisy's diatribe. Once Daisy has her in the backroom, she shuts the kitchen door.

Alexis finds her voice. "Now wait one Goddamn minute." The slap jars, setting an ache in her jaw and catches her by complete surprise.

"I don't care if your life is in danger or not, you will not speak like that about the Lord." Daisy turns to the cook in the dirty apron, he looks like he could match

Daisy pound for pound. "You get a hold of the Sheriff yet?"

Alexis is rubbing her cheek as she looks from Daisy to the cook. *I feel like I am in that bad cannibal movie, Lunchmeat. Now when the sheriff gets here, he will be wearing a mask made from human skin.*

"No, Maud said he was out snagging at 4-mile creek. She is heading out to get him and send him this way. Might be awhile before he gets here." The cook looks back out at the cafe. "I will go out and take the order, you get her moving."

He picks up a pen and notebook as he heads out the door. "Damn women, always the same time every month, and I end up doing all their work as well as my own. You need a menu?"

The door closing cuts off the rest of what the cook is saying. "What is going on?" Alexis asks as once more Daisy begins dragging her into another room. Stopping at a row of hooks, Daisy grabs a spare waitress uniform and shoves it at Alexis, "Put this on." Alexis takes the dirty uniform, her stomach turning at the smell.

"Sorry about the smell, little Peter Withers puked on it a couple of days ago, and I have not had the time to clean it yet. Come on, we don't have all day." Alexis begins to slowly take off her wet clothes as Daisy yells, "I have your keys and you are not getting them back until the sheriff gets here to deal with you."

Daisy is busy digging in a huge box labeled lost and found. "Aaron said you were too polite to leave, but men always get the amount a woman will take wrong. I wish we could have met on another day. First, when Aaron whispered that Dean Masters was in town and you were in danger, I thought it would be exciting."

Alexis stops moving, the uniform half on, staring wide-eyed at Daisy. "The Dean is in town?"

"Yes and Aaron is in trouble, hurry up already. I was supposed to keep you here until those huge men from your place got to town. Only no one will answer the phone out there. Then Aaron called saying that there were wolves in town, we haven't had wolves around here for a long time." Daisy straightens, a thin blond wig in one hand and a pack of menthol 100's in the other.

Daisy growls, setting the hairpiece and cigarettes down, she starts pulling down the uniform. When she pulls off one of Alexis' shoes, Alexis loses her balance, sitting down on the bench hard and crying out "Ouch that hurt."

Daisy, in fact, smiles in approval, "Sit down and shut up, the sheriff is on his way." She yells toward the dining room.

This woman has a voice that could be heard in China. Before Alexis can figure out which question to ask first, she is wearing a smelly puked on waitress uniform with her hair being pinned up with hair pins and Daisy is speaking again.

"Aaron is somewhere in town trying to lead the wolves away from you." Daisy shakes her head over wolves being in town. "Why the Dean and these wolves are supposedly all after you, Arron has promised to explain to me. And he will if he knows what is good for him." The last is mumbled, but the serious tone is clear.

The Cook returns looking pale. "Daisy get her out of here now! Three more just came in, bikers and they are asking about her." He nods at Alexis. "The first one is telling them to leave." Screams and breaking glass interrupt whatever else he was going to say.

"Get the shotgun Henry, act like you have some sense." Daisy lights a cigarette and shoves it in Alexis' mouth as they approach the back door. "Be careful Henry, Pa will never let me rest if you get yourself hurt." The sound of shells being pumped is the only answer she gets. From the sounds in the cafe, the shotgun might not be enough.

As more screams and breaking furniture follows them, Daisy drags Alexis, who is beginning to choke from the cigarette, into the alley behind the diner. They are halfway to the street when two men rush into the alleyway. Stopping beside Daisy, who has her small 38 in her hands. "Where is the city girl?"

"Inside." Daisy nods her head toward the café. "Her biker friends showed up and are taking her before the sheriff gets here. So we're taking a smoke break." Daisy cocks the revolver inhaling on her cigarette.

The two men look at them and hesitate, then shots ring out from the diner. "Come on, if they kill her we're as good as dead." They get to the locked door and the smaller one grabs the handle and rips the steel door off its hinges. As they rush inside, Alexis grabs Daisy and drags her down the alley.

"Thank Gods I stink like soup, puke, and cigarettes, Werewolves would have smelled me otherwise. Come on, we have to get Aaron and head home." Alexis states as she hurries down the alley.

Daisy stumbles along behind Alexis mouthing the word, "Werewolves."

At the end of the alley, they hear a siren drawing closer to the cafe, as a shotgun goes off three times followed by a scream, like a thousand cats being stepped on. "Henry."

Daisy turns to head to the cafe, but Alexis pulls her around saying, "Aaron is counting on us to pick him up and keep him safe remember? The sheriff will be at the cafe in a minute, and there is nothing you can do back there. You can still help Aaron."

Daisy frowns then turns trotting towards a Geo Metro across from the alley. Alexis follows getting in the passenger side. As they do a U-turn in the street, the sheriff's deputy cruiser swerves to keep from hitting them. Stopping beside the sheriff's deputy car, Daisy rolls down her window. "Maude, what is wrong with you? Why are you driving the old deputy car?"

"Gerald is hurt, and there is no deputy. He needs me or I would see you lose your license driving like that in town."

More gun shots ring out, this time, a rifle and what sounds like a small cannon. "I'm coming Gerald." Maude leaves black streaks behind and clips a light pole as she turns towards the diner. As the sound of motorcycles firing up reaches them, the little Geo does its best to leave its own set of rubber prints behind.

"Do you think we lost them?" Alexis asks as she and Daisy walk along the creek heading for the house that they hope will be visible soon.

"Which them? The steroid biker mutants, or the Werewolves? Don't answer, if we're really lucky, they are still killing each other back on the road."

They are both filthy and moving slower than when they started out. "Sorry about your car, I'm sure your insurance will cover it." Alexis wipes her sweaty forehead as it gets darker as they move under the trees.

Daisy snorts. "I'm not so sure they will. Hello, State Farm, I need a new car, mine was totaled. What happened? Well I slowed down to turn onto 178th Avenue, and a Werewolf ran in front of me, I hit the brakes, and his buddy ran out and flipped my poor little car upside down into the ditch."

They stand giggling like school girls, as they pause to catch their breath. "Well, you did get some revenge, you shot the one that ripped your door off in the eye." Alexis picks up the pace when she sees a glimmer of light ahead.

"Don't remind me. I never thought I would need silver bullets when I took marksmanship in school." They both start to move faster as they remember the Werewolf howling as his eye exploded when the bullet went in. Of course, the convulsions were over by the time his buddies had Alexis and Daisy out of the car.

"Do bikers usually show up and start trouble, being close to Sturgis and all?" Alexis asks, moving closer to the creek to avoid the wild blackberry bushes. *I will ask Mrs. Collins to come out here with me and pick some when they're ripe.*

"Girl bikers always cause trouble when you have more than a few. But bikers don't drool, move like some muscled mutant freak and attack Werewolves. Okay, some do drool." Daisy looks back as they hear crashing in the bushes behind them.

Those two things with the bikers were stronger than the Werewolves. She tries to block out the image of seven bikers riding into the three Werewolves. At first, it looked like the Werewolves would tear them to shreds. Until the two freaks got started. The freak in black leather shoved his arm into the Werewolves throat and kept pushing deeper until the Werewolf was frantic to get away then stopped moving. The red thing the freak pulled out could have been anything.

"There's a light up ahead, hurry." Alexis is so excited she begins running before it registers on her that the light is from the direction of the driveway, not the house. Daisy screams as something howls a few hundred feet away.

Running as fast as they can, Alexis' foot falls into a rabbit hole, and her ankle snaps with a loud pop. Then she starts to scream. A moment later a Werewolf stumbles out of the trees along the creek coming after them. The Werewolf is drenched in blood as he gets close enough for Alexis to see. "Run Daisy!" Alexis screams, wishing her purse and gun was with her.

"You want me? Come and get me." Alexis gets her leg out of the hole and begins crawling away from Daisy so she has time to get away. The tall grasses of South Dakota give way to trees along the creek and Alexis is determined to get to the trees.

A biker and freak are already there. The first shot hits the Werewolf in the gut, the rest of the bullets just keep hitting him. "Go finish it off, then carry the girl. We need to get back and report." The freak stumbles out of the trees towards where the Werewolf has fallen down.

The freak is missing its right arm and hand. The throat looks like it was chewed almost all the way through. The biker is in better condition but still in rough shape. He is limping as he moves towards Alexis and carries his shotgun slung across his forearm. "Thought your pet dogs would finish us did you? Dogs are no match for Devils, girl."

Daisy screams from the direction where she'd ran, and Alexis sags. The freak does something to the Werewolf that makes squishing sounds before he begins coming her way. *Well, I won't go with them. I will make them kill me first.*

Then she feels a twitch under her hand, a tree root moves. She jerks her hand back and falls on her side. The freak picks her up like she is a sack and throws her over its shoulder. "Bring her." The biker starts back into the trees along the creek heading the way they had come from, back toward the distant road.

Alexis hits the freak with everything she has while hanging upside down. It's like hitting a sack of potatoes. Then she hears the voice. *"I can help if you love me. It's been so long since someone could hear me."*

Alexis grows still as she twists her head seeking the voice. She begins to get frantic but still nothing shows itself except the shadowed trees and the moon high overhead. The biker doesn't respond. "I can't see you but if you help me sure, I will love you." *Okay Alexis, pull it together.*

"Shut her up." The biker barely glances over his shoulder as he gives the order. The freak stops moving and drops Alexis on the ground. Then he picks her up in his good hand by the throat. Alexis screams, or tries to, she gasps trying to get air. A gurgle is all that she can squeeze past the Freaks hand on her throat.

The biker turns back then hits the freak with the shotgun like it's a club. "Alive you fool! We have to keep her alive." The freak loosens his grip a fraction but Alexis begins to see spots.

"Say you love me and we can feed together then love together. Long since I have fed." The voice is so close it caresses her wet cheek.

"I love you." Alexis gurgles as tears run down her cheeks. She tries to focus but things are getting hazy. Then the biker hits the freak's hurt arm with the shotgun. "Let her go, dammit."

Alexis lands flat on the ground as the freak drops her. Everything goes green and fuzzy in Alexis' vision. The biker picks her up by her shirt, raising her to a half standing position.

She manages a scream from her damaged throat. Her right arm moves, hitting him in the stomach and passes through his skin going inside him. He stares down at the hole in his stomach. Stumbling back on her broken ankle gives one hot stab of agony then it's buried in a rush of adrenaline and euphoria.

"What did you do?" The biker drops to his knees, and a root comes out of the ground. Big, round and gnarled it enters the hole Alexis made. The bikers scream makes Alexis' mouth water. The freak peers from the biker to Alexis. Moving slowly, it comes towards her one step at a time.

Alexis laughs but with her damaged throat, only a horse cackle emerges. The ground opens under the freaks feet and he falls into the hole up to his crotch. His mouth moves as he struggles to get free. Mewling cries like a wounded puppy issue from his misshapen mouth.

Alexis is starving, all she can think about is eating. "Alexis!" Roger yells as he charges under the trees. He freezes in horror when he sees Alexis on her knees watching the freak slowly sinking inch by inch into the ground. The lower he sinks, the more blood begins bubbling up around him. A slurping noise is all that breaks the silence in the clearing under the trees.

Alexis smiles at Roger. "Do you love me?" She stands on her broken ankle as if it doesn't hurt at all. Stumbling towards Roger, Alexis smiles showing her red teeth.

"Yes Alexis, you know I do." Roger sways on his feet, stepping towards Alexis. She reaches out and cups his crotch. Roger moans as he cums in his pants. Panting, he tries to pull away from her touch, but his body will not move. "Alexis, we need to get to Brother Lion and Derek."

She tilts her head and Roger pauses, staring into her green glowing eyes.

"Roger, thank Gods you got her, is she_" Derek stops, staring at Alexis' hair, a tangled mess, standing on her broken ankle with the bone sticking out and missing a shoe. Her hand pressing against Rogers erect dick that is straining against his wet pants.

"Derek, I can't move, something's wrong. Help her." Roger pants each word, a struggle to force past his numb lips.

"Do you love me?" Alexis asks looking at Derek.

Brother Lion's glowing amber eyes lock onto her green glowing eyes. "We love Alexis, and she is ours." Drawing on the strength of the Pride he pushes against the spirit possessing Alexis. She moans and sways as her mates fight for her. Derek drops to his knees as the ancient spirit strikes back at him.

"Alexis, you have to accept us as your own." The words are a muffled roar as the spirit lashes repeatedly at Brother Lion and Derek. Brother Lion roars as his spirit form is slashed and his spirit bleeds. Derek crawls forward, foot by foot until he is at Alexis' feet.

"Why do you fight me? Love me and be one with me." Alexis' glowing green eyes show confusion and power as she speaks.

"We love you, Alexis. We will not share you with any other, we are yours and you are ours."

Roger drops to his knees as his Alphas draws on his strength through the Pride bond. The ancient cottonwoods and willow trees by the creek groan as they shed leaves and limbs in the spirits fury. The Willow lashes Derek across the shoulders.

Alexis turns to flee from Brother Lion and Derek in their natural form. Fur and fangs suddenly appear to be terribly cruel to her. Her body screams in terror as her heart aches to be held in those massive arms, safe from harm. Derek tackles her legs, wrapping his arms around her. Alexis cries out in rage. Her fingernails claw at his face repeatedly.

Roger crawls over and wraps his arms around her holding her arms to her sides. Tears run down his face as he holds her in his massive twisted arms. "I am so sorry, so sorry." He repeats over and over.

"We have to get her body away from the spirits physical ties. Away from the creek and trees, it will be weaker." Brother Lion speaks in Derek and Rogers mind, too busy fighting off the attacks of the spirit to use Derek's body to speak.

Roger nods, dragging Alexis along as he holds her to him with one arm while crawling. Derek leads the way on his knees, moving backward foot by foot. Alexis twists and struggles in his arms but with all three of them fighting for her, the spirit loses its control over her.

It feels like hours have passed when they are far out on the plain and Alexis cries out as her ankle bumps against the ground. "Derek, my ankle." Roger, Derek and

Brother Lion all freeze looking at Alexis' eyes. No longer glowing, tears flow as she breathes in short gasps.

"You're safe Alexis, we will get you home." Alexis is already unconscious, the warm blackness her only surcease from pain. Derek leans back, forcing his arm to release Alexis' legs. The shooting pain of blood returning to his arms cause him to drop her legs instead of setting them down.

Looking at Roger, Brother Lion feels his broken spirit now resembling his twisted deformed body. "Give me a moment and I will carry her to the truck."

Shaking his head, Roger climbs to his feet, gathering her in his arms once more. "I failed her, you, everyone. I will, at least, see her home safe."

The angry growl is smothered as Derek turns away from Roger. Fighting down the jealous rage that threatens to launch him at Roger's throat. *Brother Lion, help me! Roger is wounded and I'm losing control!*

Brother Lion's spirit form is still bleeding and in shock over the pain from the spirits astral attacks. He nods sending what strength he can, and together Derek and Brother Lion walk away as Roger carries Alexis. They follow using immense spiritual and physical effort to take each of those steps away from Alexis when she is hurt is harder than any battle.

Werelion instincts are to fight and kill for the Pride. The instinct is even stronger for their mates. Only a few Alphas in history could have fought off those instincts as Brother Lion and Derek did. As they near the truck parked in the drive, Daisy spots them once more.

Tied hand and foot, she has managed to get the gag off and roll out of the back of the pickup. Seeing Derek in his natural form standing six-foot-three, covered in golden red fur brings a shriek to her mouth. As they draw closer the blood, sweat and rage on his face terrifies her into rolling away as fast as her round, trussed up body can.

"I will sit with Alexis in the back. Put the woman in the cab with you." Derek climbs into the back of the pickup hoping Roger understands that he cannot be pushed any farther tonight.

Roger lays the still unconscious Alexis in the back. Then he turns and strides down the driveway to Daisy and lifts her to her feet with one effortless movement from his right arm. She stops screaming as she stares into his soft brown eyes. The desperate sadness and loss in them make her ache to hold him, despite his appearance.

Daisy is set in the passenger seat. Roger buckles her in while she is still roped. Derek holds Alexis in his arms as Brother Lion gathers what strength remains in them and sends trickle after trickle through the mate bond into Alexis' weakened spirit. The bumpy driveway is a slow torturous ride as Roger steers around potholes and drives at a crawl to protect Alexis.

The cell phones lie on the floorboard dead, the cigarette lighter adapter is worthless in the antique truck that has no lighter. Roger sways once, breathing deeply, tears on his face. "I'm so sorry; I could not move, she was standing on shattered bone, and all I could think about was kissing her."

Daisy looks at him and tears roll down her face as she wonders where they are going. The moon glows in the sky bathing them in a reddish cast. "Are you okay to drive?" Daisy asks.

Roger turns his head and looks at her without speaking. Daisy has a black eye and bruises but otherwise appears unharmed. When they hit a pothole, Roger turns back to face the road. Daisy does not speak again on the long drive.

Brother Lion speaks loud enough to be heard in the cab, "It is not your fault. The thing that was in Alexis is old and hungry. We could not have saved her without you."

Roger does not respond as the unnatural hardness in his pants begins to leave him. The shooting pain in his crotch is what he holds onto during the drive to remain sane.

Derek looks around the crowded dining room table. Roger is in the master bedroom with Alexis and the doctor. Daisy is sitting with a black eye and red scrapes on her wrists from the ropes. Aaron hovers near her, dirty and with torn clothes. Bryan is the only clean person present and with the stress in the room, he is also in his natural form.

Daisy is adjusting well for only having known that not only Werewolves but Weretigers, Lions and Freaks are real for only hours. Brother Lion and Derek are both at full attention and in their Natural form.

"Werewolves, Werecats any Were has two forms. The natural form is a mix of animal and man; usually upright, bigger, clawed and hairier than the human form. The human form can be held by their force of will and concentration." Aaron is speaking low, explaining about the Weres.

Mrs. Collins comes in with a pot of coffee and begins filling the waiting cups. "Derek, the call from Amanda arrived. They confirmed your instructions and are splitting up now." Her voice is steady, and everyone breathes deeper at the good news. As she finishes pouring, she begins gathering napkins and crumbs from the dining room table.

"Mrs. Collins, please join us, your one of us now and we will all help to pick up after." Bryan stands, urging

Mrs. Collins into his vacated chair, as he stands leaning against the wall. At six-foot-seven, his Weretiger form puts him close to the ceiling in the old ranch house. When Daisy shrinks back at his large form, he sighs and sits on the floor cross-legged.

"Aaron, we know most of what happened to Alexis and Daisy from Daisy. Please, tell us what happened to you after you left the diner." Derek says.

Aaron fidgets but calms when Daisy takes his hand in her own. "Well, I saw Dean Masters while I was getting the fax from the office supply store. Then I went to the café to warn Alexis but saw a pair of Werewolves hanging around the front. So I told Daisy enough to get her to keep Alexis safe and call the ranch for reinforcements. Then left to lure the Dean away. That was going pretty well until I spotted more Werewolves following me."

"How did you know they were Werewolves?" Bryan asks.

"There was one with a Mohawk and I recognized him as part of that last attack from the North Dakota pack. I also thought I could smell them but might have been wrong about that." Aaron stumbles to a stop.

"Just start from when you left the diner, and we will hold the questions until the end. For now, just give us the highlights please." Derek keeps looking upstairs every couple of minutes.

"Well, I started walking and it was only a block later that the Dean showed up. He had a couple of men in suits with him. Expensive clothes, big and I think at least one of them was armed. I began walking faster when they headed straight at me." Daisy wraps her arm around him as he continues.

"I ran to the edge of town away from the ranch. It was at the edge of town when the Werewolves showed up. They ignored me and moved in on the Dean. I was too far away to hear what was said, but the tension was high. Lots of arm waving and yelling. I called the diner, then saw the tracker alert that Amanda put on all our phones going off, so I tossed the phone in a cattle trailer and headed into the prairie north of town."

Aaron tenses nervously. Daisy rises and pushes him into her seat. "After that, I began circling the town to meet Alexis and Daisy when the bikers showed up. I jumped in a ditch and hid. Then, when they were gone, I tried to get back into town and got lost. Old Man Tucker picked me up and brought me here after he got tired of yelling shit at his dogs and came out to see what they had up the tree. He would have called the Sheriff but with everything in town." Aaron shrugs.

"Old Man Tucker's place is almost 4 miles North West of town. How did you end up all the way over there?" Derek is looking up the stairs again as he asks.

"I was running, thought something was following me. Jumpy I guess. Then his dogs found me and I climbed my first tree in twenty years."

"Thank You, Aaron. I will have more questions later. Daisy, did you get a hold of anyone in town to get an update on what happened there?"

"Most of the town is forming patrols. Maude is acting as Sheriff until George recovers. You probably noticed we're a town that believes in being armed. Once the sheriff went down, everyone in town started shooting. I know for sure that three bikers and one of those freaks died outside the cafe. Little Tony, the rodeo champ of '81, was killed. Other than that, lots of broken bones, and such."

"Does anyone know about the Werewolves?" Brother Lion's question is intense, and everyone watches Daisy as she swallows before answering.

"No, I think the one that might have died was carried off by his friends. It was that old Gatling gun that took down the freak, cut him almost in half. Don't head out after dark and make sure you let everyone know your locals now. Maude told the state troopers too, but everyone is angry and scared."

"They're also heavily armed. The docs escort has, at least, one semi-auto and several others have not completely legal guns." Bryan nods towards the outside where three locals made into deputies for the crises are waiting on the doctor.

"Alright, I have Amanda doing background checks on the corpses, she is working with Maude on that and she has the freak in a private funeral home a county away. We don't want it to disappear. They are scheduled to deliver the corpse here in the morning. The rest of the Pride is tracking or trying to track down the survivors."

"Maude mentioned that she had to pull rank and get the doc to sign off as going to perform the autopsy in conjunction with the felonies in town. Where do you plan on putting the freak?" Daisy runs her hand through her dirty hair as she speaks.

"By the time the corpse is here, the new cat house will have 11 AC window units cooling it, a stainless steel table, scales and whatever else Amanda has emptied our savings getting. She is setting up a full lab. Alexis' credit card and student loan account is almost empty after getting everything needed." Derek looks at his watch again as he finishes speaking.

Bryan snorts, "So no cat house, instead the new roof will be on a lab." When everyone turns to look at him, he blushes. "Alright, I will stay on the couch, but Amanda better get some answers."

No one says anything for a while as Mrs. Collins refills the cups. Everyone is paying close attention to the table and avoiding eye contact.

"Daisy, I think you should bring your kids out here to stay for a few days until things settle down." Derek looks sad.

"Now wait a minute, Daisy did nothing wrong." Aaron starts to get up.

Daisy puts her hands on his shoulders and looks Derek in the eye. "You're worried I will blab about Werewolves, Weretigers and whatever else you all are."

Derek nods, "You are also now known to the groups involved and might be taken, tortured or used as a hostage. The town people would die to protect you, and it would mean nothing."

Daisy draws a deep breath turning pale. "Aaron and I are engaged. He wanted to tell Alexis today, but everything went to shit. He says he has a meadow, a half days walk from here, picked out to build a house on. For me and my kids. Why should I risk my family with your lot?"

Derek sits forward, "Because Aaron is family and we take care of our family. You know about some of the monsters in the world, that puts you and your family at risk. Here, we can protect you. You know Aaron would not put you or your family in danger but it is too late you're already in danger."

She sways and has to lean on Aaron to stay upright. "Alexis loves you and Aaron trusts all of you. I trust

Aaron, so I will bring my family here. If any harm comes to them." Her threat goes unvoiced but is understood. Derek nods.

"I doubt any of us will get any sleep, but we should try. Mrs. Collins, Aaron, with us in our natural forms we're stuck in here until the Doctor and his escort leaves. We will keep the door locked from this side. Aaron, maybe you should sleep on the couch just to be sure no one goes wandering around." Derek glances towards the doorway again as he finishes.

"Daisy, why don't you come up to my room? I have a trundle that you can use until we get a room set up for you and your little ones. How old are they?" Mrs. Collins is already herding Daisy out the door. Aaron follows after nodding to Bryan and Derek.

Bryan gets up and slides the little bolt on the door closed. "Aaron is pretty upset about Daisy's eye."

Derek sighs "Brother Lion says Alexis is sleeping and breathing normally now. Daisy thought Roger was one of the freaks and attacked him. I am not even sure if it was us that gave her the black eye, she might have already had it."

Bryan moves from the door, checking that the curtains are firmly closed. "Hard to believe Aaron had time to get engaged since we got here. He works fast."

Derek rises up from his chair and settles against the wall sliding down so he can see the door to the kitchen and the hallway. "My concern is that Alexis was possessed by that ancient spirit. If we hadn't gotten there in time, we might not have been able to get it out of her. We all need to keep a close eye on her."

Bryan goes into the kitchen and double-checks that the door is still locked before sliding down beside Derek. "You think that spirit will try again?"

"We don't know what to expect. The Dean, the freaks, where her Dad is, we know less than we thought we did. Where does the Dean fit in?" Derek takes a deep breath lowering his angry voice. "I called that Witch that does work to clean up the Major's messes. She says a spirit has to be invited in. Brother Lion knew that Alexis has magic talent, but he never expected this."

"What kind of magic does she have exactly?" Bryan looks away from Derek not wanting him to see the worry and love for Alexis on his face.

"We wish we knew. Just watch for any loss of concentration, blackouts or odd behavior." Derek leans back closing his eyes to reach for Alexis again. The bond is tenuous but strong enough to reassure him that she is sleeping and safe, for now. "She is vulnerable to anyone with magical abilities until she learns to use her gifts."

"How is she supposed to learn her abilities?" Bryan asks.

"From someone with the same abilities that she has." Derek stands and paces back and forth listening to the armed men in the yard speak about the mess in town. Were's hearing is acute and over the decades Derek has learned to sort the multitude of sounds that his sensitive ears can pick up.

Bryan doesn't ask how they can find her a teacher without knowing her abilities. If Derek has an answer, he would already have gotten Alexis the teacher she needs.

Derek settles back down, dozing until creaking stairs wake him as the window is lightening with the dawn. "See that she sleeps and stays off the ankle for at least a few weeks. She should be in the hospital. If I missed any of the bone fragments she might lose the foot, or worse."

The old doctor's voice is tired and resigned. The argument to take her to the hospital already having been fought as he worked on Alexis. "Thank you for coming, send the bill and we will pay it." Aaron's voice from the bottom of the stairs brings a startled gasp from the doctor. Roger, turning to go back up the stairs is heard as the boards repeat the groans and creaks of moments before.

"You just call me if the fever comes back or anything looks off. I will be back in a few days and if I think it looks bad, she will go to the hospital." The door slamming behind him cuts off anything Aaron might have said in response. Derek waits a few moments until

he hears Aaron slide the locks on the door home before
rushing out of the dining room and up the stairs.

Chapter 3

"Derek, relax. I'm fine. It's been three days." Alexis is still on crutches, but the speed of her healing is almost as fast as a Were heals and that is very fast.

Derek, I told you for the last three days that I needed to get out for a while. Why do you make me fight you? I need you to be my partner, not my Dad.

Derek glances around the dining room and his shoulders lose some of their tension when no one is in sight. *Brother Lion, are you sure we should wait for the picnic to ask her to marry us? We have the ring it might help heal the distance between us? She is so stressed, and we still haven't told her that her Dad is probably dead.*

Alexis shifts on her feet waiting for Derek to move so she can get to the door. *Yes, we don't want to mess up again. Especially with Amanda here, we need to ensure that Alexis is safe. She is not telling us the truth, about something. I smell her fear.* Brother Lion's fur is raised and his tail is lashing as he speaks to Derek.

She is afraid of whatever she is planning. Why does she keep pushing us away? Derek runs his hand through his hair trying to calm his fears.

When Derek stands in front of her unmoving, Alexis swings her right-hand crutch up and over, knocking the pitcher of iced tea off the table. Brother Lion uses his lion reflexes and moves fast to catch it, only splashing a small amount. While he is out of the way, Alexis walks through the door into the kitchen and past Mrs. Collins. Exchanging nods with Mrs. Collins, Alexis passes out the already open door.

Pausing outside in the sunshine Alexis inhales with her eyes closed. The sunshine seems to have a smell of growing things, with a hint of rain despite the lack of clouds. Alexis opens her eyes squinting in the sunshine. Tommy and Peggy are running around playing while Aaron tries to get the old swing set into usable condition.

Come on Daisy, before he catches up with me and tries to keep me home and safe. Alexis waves at Daisy sitting in the driver's seat of the Armstrong's town car.

Daisy sees her wave and starting the car drives right onto the grass, stopping in a cloud of dust. She swings open the passenger door of the town car from the driver's side.

"Aaron, watch the kids. We'll be back in a couple of hours," Daisy calls out her open window as Alexis struggles into the car cursing the crutches as she shoves them into the back seat.

Great, here he comes. Mrs. Collins must not have been able to delay him after all.

Alexis rolls the window down and calls out as Daisy drives away. "Derek, I have to get some pads and tampons the ones you got are the wrong size."

Derek is still walking toward the car, frowns as they turn off the lawn and start down the long drive toward the road.

Derek notices the stares from Aaron and the kids, turns and heads toward the old chicken coop. It was going to be a Werecat house but is now an impromptu morgue. *Tommy and Peggy should be afraid of us, shouldn't they?*

Human children today grow up with monsters on TV. Besides, do you really want little Tommy with his blond hair and blue eyes scared of you? Brother Lion sounds as sure as stone, which usually means that he is repeating something from a book or television show.

The hum of the eleven window air conditioners grows louder as they near the entrance. "Derek, let Brother Lion roar for us!" Peggy shrieks as her brother picks her up and swings her in a circle, her feet almost clip Derek's leg.

"I'm sorry kids, but I have to check on Amanda right now. Maybe Brother Lion will play with you later."

Derek is about to open the door when Tommy calls out, "Derek's a virgin. A big fat virgin!"

Brother Lion's laughing in his head is enough to push common sense aside. "How about I let you see a real dead body instead?"

Brother Lion shuts up as the kid's eyes grow huge. "A dead body?"

Before Derek can reply, Aaron is there herding the kids away. "What's wrong with you, Derek? They're only kids."

Sighing, Derek opens the door and gets one leg inside when "Shut the door! He's already decaying too fast!" is yelled at him.

Derek jumps to get all the way in and close the door. Amanda moves briskly, obviously in her element, in her natural form she is almost six-feet tall with sleek beautiful fur. On her face, the velvet fur covers her cheeks, her claws are neatly trimmed so they will not interfere with her work.

"A lab coat Amanda? You do know you're not a Doctor right?" Derek asks, still angry with the way she had treated Alexis while his attention was elsewhere the last few months.

Amanda ignores him, as usual. She continues cutting the clothes off of the Freak laid out on the stainless table. Derek shivers as his body tries to adjust to the sudden drop in temperature.

"I still think you should have done more to get the body here faster. This long and I might not be able to learn everything it has to tell us." Amanda moves in precise, measured movements. No wasted motion as her graceful movements take her around the Freaks left side then his right, little scissors snipping away his clothing.

"We were lucky Maude agreed to this. Dr. Michael had to go sign papers and get the retired circuit judge to approve the autopsy. This is not exactly legal in the Mundane's world you know." Derek walks to the foot of the stainless steel table his eyes wandering around the room.

All these new shiny toys and Alexis' scholarship money gone. This better not be a scheme to hurt Alexis.

Picking up what looks like a pie scoop but is serrated down one side, Derek's eyes open wide at the $359.00 price tag still hanging from it. "I have already learned some important things from my work. You should hear them if you finally have time to listen." Amanda's attention shifts to Derek as her hand rests on her hip as she speaks.

Derek places the shiny tool back on the table as he and Brother Lion stare at her, drawing on the Alpha power their eyes begin to glow. "Yes, we have some time now. Be careful you do not waste any more of it."

Amanda steps back, lowering her eyes in submission. "Yes Alpha, I will share what I have learned. His blood is only mostly human, we know that from the lab work that was done by Dr. Michael. It also has three other species in it. It will be days to confirm this because of the lack of a Supernatural lab, but I suspect it's Vampire, Were, and Coven."

Derek frowns "The Coven is the group of humans that want to control all use of magic. Why would their blood not be human?"

Amanda shakes her head no. "I spoke to the Major, he says that the longer one does magic, the more the body changes. The blood is one of the first changes. He is being close-mouthed, as always. I think he knows more than he is telling us. Magic changes everything, anatomy, spirit, and the stronger the magic used the more drastic the changes."

Alexis' body will change as she learns magic. Will she still love us? We do not know enough about the rest of the Supernatural community. All these decades and we trusted the Major to deal with other Supernaturals while we played Soldier. Brother Lion shares Derek's worry and frustration.

We will not allow magic to take her from us or anything else either. Brother Lion speaks to Amanda as his claws probe at the corpse. "We need answers, the Major is not the source of information we need. It's time we find answers elsewhere. The Supernatural community knows about us, but we only know what the Major has told us about them, and it is almost nothing."

Amanda steps back as the raw rage and power shimmers around Derek and Brother Lion. For a moment, Brother Lion seems to be about to step out of Derek.

Wide-eyed Amanda says, "Well, we will know more as soon as I am done here, late tonight or early tomorrow."

"Good. Make sure to find as much information as you can. We need answers, fast." Derek is already moving toward the door before his rage leads him to begin rending the corpse and ruining any chance of getting the answers it offers.

Amanda turns to measure the fingers on the right hand of the Freak. "Wait! Didn't you come out to help me?"

Derek, already breathing heavy, knowing he needs to get away before he loses control replies, "I didn't know you needed any help with this." His gesture takes in the new equipment, body, and everything neatly arranged and waiting to be put into use.

"I need an assistant. Someone to hand me things, charge the batteries on the recorder, make notes in case the recorder doesn't work or misses something." She steps toward Derek reaching out, eyes flashing, her breath speeding.

Derek leans toward her not sure if he is going to kiss her or slap her. Blinking, he turns away from her. Opening the door he steps out before he can find out. "I will send someone to help you."

Amanda steps into the doorway watching him hurry away. "Not Bryan!" She slams the door shaking the frame.

Aaron stops pushing Tommy on the now repaired swing and looks at Derek. Waving to Aaron, Derek walks across the yard and steps into the kitchen. Once out of the bright sunlight he blinks in the dimmer light of the kitchen. His breath slows once he stops moving. *Alexis is our mate, why would we be so attracted to Amanda? It has been over a decade since we were with her and then it was not more than a physical need.*

Brother Lion, for women, even Weres, it is never just physical, even when they say it is. At least, not when another woman shows up.

Stepping away from the door, Derek notices Mrs. Collins is busy washing dishes. "Mrs. Collins, Alexis went into town and I need to follow her to be sure she is safe. Do you know where the truck is?"

"Roger took it to lay some new booby traps farther out. I was not sure Daisy would be able to keep the kids from following him. They are never far from Roger if they can help it." Mrs. Collins sounds fond as she speaks of the kids.

Derek looks hard at Mrs. Collins back since she is facing the sink and has not turned off the water since he entered. Her shoulders are a bit stiffer and she continues washing the same glass she has been rinsing since he entered.

How do you think the other Were Packs will take the information that a little seven-year-old boy and a six-year-old girl know about the existence of Weres? Brother Lion voices the question while sharing the image of the kids falling asleep in his lap after fighting to see who could claim the lion pelt as their own. Mrs. Collins saves Derek from answering for now.

"Oh, Derek can you please try and get the washing machine cleaned out? When you told the kids how the washing machine worked, you should never have told them that it needs to be fed. They did not have any dirty clothes to feed it, so they fed it their peanut butter and jelly sandwiches instead." Mrs. Collins smiles as she speaks but Brother Lion can feel the question of why he keeps doing things like that. The memory of a DVD player and a grilled cheese incident is firmly pushed down by Brother Lion.

"Of course, I will see what I can do. I don't suppose you knew that Alexis was planning on going to town today? The day we only have one car because Roger got up before dawn to lay traps at the edge of the ranch?"

"Of course I knew Derek, she has been yelling at you for two days that she was going to town with Daisy. Didn't you hear her?" Mrs. Collins doesn't turn away from the dishes in the sink as she speaks but as Derek leaves the room, the muffled giggles escape from her, fueling the red on his face.

"I thought Alphas were supposed to be big, mean and scary?" Derek speaks out loud before he sees Bryan.

"I'm sure the two of you will be okay as an Alpha, eventually. After all, until Alexis, I thought you were both still virgins. Of course, it has been awful quiet in your room lately. Could be that you are still virgins?" Bryan doesn't bother to hide his grin as Derek walks through the dining room.

"Oh Bryan, since I'm going to be busy cleaning peanut butter and jelly from the washing machine, you can help Amanda dissect that freak. She needs someone to hold the body still while she cuts it up and weighs all the pieces." Brother Lion laughs in Derek's mind as Bryan blushes before heading out the kitchen door.

Well Brother, we know where the virgin jokes are coming from now. Brother Lion sounds amused instead of angry.

That serves him right, besides he needs to get over his squeamishness at the sight of blood. Whoever heard of a vegetarian Weretiger? As they step into the laundry room their eyes move over the washing machine and the mess waiting for them. *You know, perhaps it's not too late to help Amanda and make Bryan clean this mess up. I am sure he had something to do with this mess. After the grilled cheese and DVD player I was sure we had gotten through to the kids.*

How did they get it on the window and walls? As too often of late, neither of them had any answers.

Alexis' sigh sounds louder in the car than she expected. A moment later her stomach chiming in with a low growl brings a shocked glance from Daisy. Alexis looks back at her with wide eyes, and then the two of them are laughing out loud like school girls.

"Watch the road, are you trying to kill us?" Alexis forces out as she catches her breath. The release of tension has both women grinning as they drive down the country road, taking their time to get to town.

Daisy snorts, "I'm not the one in love with a huge Werelion. She's mine, me big tough man, lion, thing." Daisy, speaking in that deep voice, is so close to Derek's that Alexis jerks upright, some of her tension returning.

Shifting in the seat trying to get her foot in its cast comfortable proves impossible. Alexis sits back up crossing her arms as she gazes out the window as the prairie and scattered trees of South Dakota pass by. "Sorry, he spoke to you like that. He really is sweet when he doesn't_"

"Fuck it up?" Daisy asks glancing at the once again tense Alexis. "Relax, he was just trying to protect you. To be completely honest, I'm not sure this is the best idea myself."

"You know, the first time he and I made love was against a dumpster in a dirty alley." Daisy doesn't look at Alexis as she shakes her head in disgust.

Alexis hurries to explain, "No, we were being hunted by bikers then too. I didn't know if I would survive the night or not. I threw myself at him and he took my virginity. It was all surreal, I am not sure why but it was the best sex we've ever had."

Daisy grunts, not trusting herself to not say what she thinks of that. "I have never had any friends I could talk to, not since my Mom died. Hell, you know my life story now after being locked up with me for three days. You know Derek and Brother Lion both love me."

"Who are you trying to convince you or me?" Daisy asks.

Alexis sighs. "Ever since that first time we have made love at least once a day, sometimes more. Since that spirit possessed me, he has barely even kissed me." Her voice grows softer as she finishes. "He doesn't look at me the same, there's a distance between us that wasn't there before."

"Girl, it has only been three days. Not to mention he has been kind of busy trying to keep us alive. Hell, with the kids, work and Aaron always on call, we're lucky to hop on the washer during a spin cycle twice a month. Of course, before Aaron entered my life it was my trusty battery powered friend in the nightstand"

Alexis blushes as the image of skinny, short Aaron having sex with Daisy on a washing machine tries to take form in her mind. "How would that even work?"

"Well, Aaron is short, so I lie over the washing machine, and he stands on a little pink step stool." Alexis chokes a little as Daisy continues. "Or if I'm on top he is on the washing machine and the motion of the washing machine with an imbalnced load, that's important having an imbalanced load."

Alexis stares at Daisy open mouthed.

"The vibrations do the most amazing things while he is inside me. I tell you what, I never thought any man could compete with my battery powered friend but Aaron and an imbalanced load in the washer on spin cycle, it gets me there and then some."

"So tell me again about the meeting." Alexis' voice is strangled despite her throat being healed, other than a faint yellowing that if you look close is finger prints. She turns her head to look down the road. *I wonder if Derek and I can get some time alone in the laundry room?*

"Well, this Dean of yours really wants to speak to you. He gave a thousand dollars to my brother Henry to get a message to you. I'm sure you remember it. Hell, you only read it a dozen times an hour since I handed it to two days ago."

Yes, I remember it, I am not sure I trust it. I never realized how much I needed a friend. In three and a half days Daisy has become the best friend I always wanted.

Alexis, you know now

That you're a Shamaness.

I can help you.

Meet me in person in town.

I tried to save your mom,

But your Dad interfered.

Hurry, others felt you wake the spirit.

The Lion cannot protect you.

Spencer

Saying the words out loud to Daisy does nothing to calm the woman driving. "Great, so you're a Shamaness, you don't even look Native American."

Alexis laughs, "Give me a chance to get a tan and a wand, do Shamaness have wands?" The women laughs for a moment but it is forced. "You sure this is safe?"

Daisy looks at Alexis, eyes lowering in anger. "No. I keep saying it's not safe, you are the one that keeps insisting we do this." Looking back at the road, Daisy continues. "Henry will be inside with a double barrel shotgun. My cousin Luke and a couple of others will be in plain sight but out of earshot if we keep our voices down."

"Thank you for doing this. Going with me and," Alexis shrugs, "well everything." Alexis bends over in the seat trying to scratch her leg, but the cast keeps her fingers away.

"Well, the friends I had moved away to one city or another. You're not the only one that needed a friend." Daisy and Alexis both have tears to fight down as the silence lengthens.

"Well if you were a real friend you would have found a way for me to scratch this damn leg." Alexis is pretty sure she is not serious, but the itching is getting worse.

Daisy frowns. "Dr. Michael said he has never seen healing like this before. He almost fainted when you came out on those old crutches to sit at the table with him."

"I don't understand it all either. Brother Lion says that Pride magic speeds healing. He ignores me when I point out that I am not a Were. That usually means he has no clue either." Alexis leans back crossing her arms across her chest to keep from hitting her leg in frustration.

"Well, I have a message out to the reservation, but I have no idea if Mad Coyote is still alive or not. He was the only one I could think of that might take this all seriously. Of course, he is aptly named and is always a little crazy. After the last few days though, I'm inclined to think he might be the sanest man I have ever met."

Alexis turns on the radio. The rest of the drive to town is full of static and occasional bursts of bluegrass music on the only AM station that comes in every once in a while.

You know Alexis, you might just be the dumbest person alive. You have a huge Werelion to protect you and you leave him home to babysit while you go out to meet with dangerous men. Leaning against the new window of the cafe gives Alexis a great view of her protectors.

Henry, one arm in a cast and one leg heavily bandaged, is sitting in black and blue splendor on the other side of the glass. His grandfather's double barrel shotgun is on the table under his good hand. "Hey Daisy, what happened to Henry's pump action shotgun he had the other day?"

Daisy throws her unlit cigarette on the ground in disgust. "The Werewolf he was shooting holes in took it from him. After throwing Henry through the window, the Werewolf broke it across the back of a Freak killing another Werewolf."

Alexis swallows, returning the nod to Henry through the glass. Turning to the right and looking towards Plum Street she can see Daisy's Cousin Luke all of sixteen years old on the street corner. The antique 50 caliber, single shot pistol is held in a two-handed grip pointed at the ground. "Great. Do you really think Luke should be out here? Does that antique he has even work?"

Daisy glances over at her cousin. "Yeah, it works. He blew up a watermelon last summer when he shot it."

Alexis' gaze returns to Luke with new respect. "Really?"

"Yeah, he broke his wrist from the recoil when he fell down, so he hasn't used it since. Pa told him how to hold it right this time though."

Great, one shot kid, two shot walking wounded in the cafe, and the other two never showed up. Alexis sighs, considering calling it all off when Dean Masters turns onto Main Street, walking her way. The two big men with him stay at the corner across from Luke, as he continues toward them.

"He's here." Alexis pulls on Daisy's arm to get her attention.

Daisy turns and reaches into her purse while standing beside Alexis. She looks inside at Henry, then pulls Alexis over a foot to be sure they are not blocking Henry's view or aim. A second glance shows Henry has nodded off at the table. Groaning she knocks loudly on the glass to wake him.

"Alexis, I see you have brought protection with you." The sarcasm in Spencer's voice is thick. Before Alexis can respond Daisy knocks again louder. Henry jerks awake, reaches for his shotgun and promptly knocks it on the floor.

He catches the barrel, but the butt end hits the tiled floor. The resulting gunshot makes a hole in the cafe ceiling. Henry finally manages to aim the gun out the window in Spencer's general direction. The drywall dust falling on and around Henry brings a laugh from Spencer.

"You really do amaze me Lexi. You have an entire Pride of Weres, and even in this cesspit, a spirit or two that could aid you. Instead, you call on the hillbilly brigade." He reaches for Alexis' arm possessively.

As Alexis steps back, Daisy pulls out her new 44 magnum. Spencer's eyes widen as he feels the cold barrel jab him in the side. "I don't know what you are but I can pull this trigger three times before you can kill me. Now, back the fuck up."

With each word Daisy jabs harder and on the last one she cocks the hammer. Spencer backs up all of two steps. "I mean you no harm Lexi." His mouth is open to continue but Alexis pulls her hand from her purse holding her engagement present.

The shiny intra tec 9 mm is polished until it glows. "My Mom and Dad call me Lexi, no one else. This is my engagement present from my fiancé. Three months ago, I asked for a ring and after a day of shopping, he brought me this.

This is a full auto with 9 mm hollow point rounds mixed with silver and sawdust. Oh and 32 rounds in the clip, one in the chamber. I can fill a cast iron pan at 11 feet in half a minute with 30 rounds."

Good thing the Sheriff is not around, this has not been legal since the nineties. Of course, with the modifications, it would not be completely legal even

*then. Fuck, around here the sheriff would probably
want to borrow it.*

Daisy is looking from the little submachine gun to
Spencer and back. "No wonder you had no room in your
purse for your sunglasses," Daisy mutters but Alexis' fast
grin shows that she heard.

Spencer glares at them both. "Foolish children. You
think to threaten me with these toys?" His voice grows
louder, as the wind picks up as he speaks. "Alexis Marie
Armstrong I will show you power."

Alexis and Daisy step back, his last words are howled
into the gusting wind. Thunder roars across the clear sky.
Spencer's eyes flash bright silver than blue. His foot goes
up in slow motion then slams down full speed. Daisy
stumbles as the street rocks and a foot long split opens
between them and Spencer almost seeming to point at
them.

*You are too far for me to help you much. And you
did not pay me.* Alexis' head jerks around looking but she
knows the spirits voice is inside her. It must have been
hiding, waiting for her to pay the price agreed.

Speaking with only her mind as she does when she
speaks directly to Brother Lion she focuses on the space
the voice originates from. *If Spencer takes me, he will
kill me, and I will never be able to pay you.*

Alexis feels the ancient rage boil and then she is lightheaded as it takes all her strength and energy and slashes Spencer. Slash is not exactly right, it was more of like the cutting of a thick band running from Spencer to his men. The world sways for a moment and Alexis almost goes down. Leaning on Daisy for a second as Spencer cries out in shock. His hand reaches toward the two men who begin walking their way.

Alexis straightens, glaring at her crutches on the ground where they fell when the street shifted. She is able to stand unsupported, balancing her weight on her good leg. Spencer's attention shifts to her again. "Fool! You let a wild spirit ride in you for days."

Luke shoots one of the men in the side. The 50 caliber round spinning the big man half around as he falls. Everything seems to stop as the thunder echoes. Alexis and Daisy both raise their guns. "Stop!" Spencer speaks with power but with less than he had before.

"I mean you no harm. I can teach you to use your gifts. Come with me and learn your birthright." Spencer is sweating, even as his wounded man stands leaning to one side but standing all the same. Luke is reloading and Alexis can see his lips moving, but no sound reaches her. The two men stand halfway between Luke and Alexis waiting.

When Alexis doesn't respond, he continues. "With my training, we can rescue your father. You will be safe and in time if you desire the Lion, you can have him."

"If you mean all this, come with me to the ranch and teach me there. Now." Alexis watches Spencer and can see that he is about to agree when a rape whistle sounds from the old three-story brick bank building across the street. Then the noise of motorcycles reaches them.

"I cannot, your Lion would see me as a threat. I must go. I will contact you again soon and ask one last time for you to join me. If you do not, neither of us will be alive for me to ask again."

As he finishes speaking, the first three motorcycles roar onto Main Street. A Marlin .357 magnum caliber rifle fires five shots in rapid succession. Two of the motorcycles crash onto the street and the last one continues on.

Spencer turns, trotting away he yells something lost in the gunfire coming from other parts of town. The last biker leaps off the bike and begins to walk toward Alexis. More shots are fired from the roof of the bank building across the street. Henry shuffles out the cafe door to stand beside them leaning against the cafe window as the biker draws closer. Then, as if at a signal, all three of them begin shooting round after round into the biker.

He barely slows, the double barrel shotgun hits him in the face and his head whips back then forward. The recoil from the shotgun breaks the new cafe window. Daisy is trying to reload while Alexis is trying to get the spirits attention again. *Hey, more bad shit coming to get me! Need some more help!*

Then the bleeding man that Luke had shot tackles the thing wearing biker leathers. The other two bikers leap on them moments after. The resulting shrieks bring blood from Alexis and Daisy's ears and noses. They drop the guns, hands covering their ears.

As they hear a thousand chalkboards being scratched at once. Then they are pulled off their feet towards the pile of bikers as all the air is sucked in. Then, only ten feet from the pile of bikers, men and things the air explodes outward. The windows all up and down Main Street for a block shatter.

When the cloud of dust clears, the bikers are gone and the new pothole is large enough to lose a small car in. Alexis and Daisy stay on the ground coughing and catching their breath for a while.

It's only when the police siren stops across from them that Daisy gets on her feet. Bending, she helps Alexis stand. They lean on each other, bloody from flying glass and gravel. Alexis is still weak from what the spirit took from her to attack Spencer. Maude looks up and down the street before approaching them.

"I suppose your men will be around later to tell me how to do my job again." The anger and strain on her face almost takes away the ridiculous way she looks wearing her husband's uniform. The shirt, three sizes too big, and her pink belt holding up the pants.

"It is not your job, and you know it, Maude." Daisy begins patting her pockets for a cigarette, forgetting for the moment that she has given them up at Aaron's insistence.

Maude stalks up to Daisy and slaps her. "My husband is in intensive care, Little Tony is dead. And today we have another gunfight with a gang of bikers that left Sheryl dead and Jessie flashing back to desert storm. Right now, he is walking around town looking to kill the thing that got Sheryl."

Daisy's eyes widen as she steps back, looking down. "I'm so sorry Maude."

Alexis sways, tears streaming down her face making everything blurry. Maude notices the tears and dismay on their faces, sighs and runs her hand through her hair. "You better get back to the ranch. I don't want any of you in town for a week or two. People, even without Jessie stirred up, are looking to lynch someone for what was done here. I will be out to take statements in a day or two."

They gather up the guns as the street begins to fill with muttering people carrying guns. They help Henry get inside and settled before heading out the back. "You know, I worked in that cafe since I was 11 and until this week, never once did I leave through the alley."

Alexis walks along without replying using the one crutch they could find. *More people died because of me. I should have told Derek about the meeting. He would have tied me up to keep me home and then come himself.* As they drive back to the ranch, they ride in silence.

Halfway home they pass the old pickup full of Weres and Aaron all driving to town. The screeching brakes tell them that they were seen. They speed up and keep going. The truck turns around and follows them back. The honking horn finally stops as they turn onto the driveway. Looking back at the truck as they start up the drive they see Aaron flipping them off.

"You know, after this they won't let us out of their sights again for months." Daisy looks back again, Aaron is driving so close behind them now that the old truck can keep up on the rough gravel driveway.

Alexis faces straight ahead as she replies, "I think that is probably a good thing."

Daisy sighs as she nods.

Chapter 4

The tension in the room is high as Derek paces at one end of the living room. Alexis and Daisy sit on the couch side by side. Despite the large couch and lack of seats, no one is sitting by them. "I feel like I'm in the school nurse's office for having lice," Daisy mutters to Alexis.

Alexis shrugs, never having had lice she is not in a position to comment. Glancing around, Aaron, Bryan, even Mrs. Collins all sit facing them like a tribunal on the hardwood dining room chairs.

"You know we have had a long day and would like to go shower. Is all of this really necessary?" Alexis tries not to whine, but her voice is still a bit shrill as everyone stares at her.

Derek and Brother Lion turn to face them directly. "Yes, this is necessary and long overdue. People are dead, the town people could show up here for answers. If they get violent, more people will die."

Alexis and Daisy both lean back from the glowing amber anger in his eyes. *This isn't like him. I have not felt Brother Lion speak to me, mind to mind, since we got back. He has always greeted me when I return home from town.*

Daisy motions for Aaron to sit beside her and he shakes his head no. Her eyes widen and her lips go thin. The kids playing upstairs sound more subdued than normal as well.

The door slamming takes the attention off of Alexis and Daisy for a moment as everyone turns to see who came in the door. Alexis coughs covering her face as she begins breathing shallowly. The stench of formaldehyde, bleach, and rotting meat arrive moments before Amanda walks in.

Her hair is mussed, and a red smear on her left cheek is unusual for her. The white lab coat is stained, filthy and the stench from it is nauseating. "Well, I hope this doesn't take long. The body is already telling me so much_"

Derek interrupts her, "Take the lab coat off and leave it outside."

Already turning away from her he whips back around as she snarls, "What, the rest of us have dress codes now? While snow white sits there filthy before she goes out to get more people killed?"

Brother Lion and Derek move as one. The roar fills the minds and ears of everyone there. "She is my mate, and if she kills every person in this state, you will crawl on your hands and knees to clean it up." Amanda's eyes only have time to widen before she is dangling from his hand as his claws dig into her neck. "Unless you have decided to challenge me to be Alpha."

Amanda drops her eyes in submission and tilts her head to the side showing her subservience. Once Brother Lion drops her, she looks at the floor as he stands over her. "You are my Alpha, and I serve you and your chosen Mate."

Derek nods once before he turns back to face the others gathered in the room. Everyone looks away from him except Roger, who is standing on the stairs with the two kids clinging to his legs in fear. "I think we need to begin with some background on Weres." Roger picks up both kids and sets them on the couch beside Daisy.

Mrs. Collins leans away as Derek moves past her to the center of the room. When no one says anything, Roger continues, "Weres are not really human, once they are turned into a Were. The animal is always there. The wildness of a wolf, lion or any carnivore is always waiting, ready to take over."

"Like in science, where we watched the wolves fight for the bitch." Tommy cries out as Daisy smacks the back of his head. "Ouch! Mom, it's just a female dog."

"I don't care, you speak like that again and I will wash your mouth out with a bar of soap." Daisy holds both kids in her arms rocking them gently.

"Ahhhh Mom." Tommy leans away from her crossing his arms. Daisy glances at Aaron, and she can see the concern for her and the kids in his expression.

Roger nods to Tommy, "Exactly, only wolves don't have fingers, or the ability to use guns. If a Werelion or Werewolf loses control it is dangerous. That's why Weres that don't have a pack or pride are hunted by the Weres that do."

"So they just kill them because they don't have a family?" Peggy's eyes are huge as she watches Roger.

"Yes." Roger agrees nodding.

"We don't have a Daddy since he left us when Mom got fat. Will they hunt us to?" Peggy's voice cracks as a tear runs down her face.

"Of course we have a Dad, Aaron. Besides Uncle Roger picked up the pickup all by himself, remember? You had to give him your apple from lunch. He won't let anyone hurt us, will you Uncle Roger." There is no question in Tommy's voice as he promptly wiggles out of Daisy's arms and runs to hug Roger's legs.

Roger gives a half smile as he tousles Tommy's hair. "Well, it was only the front half."

"Tommy, come here and sit with me. Roger is talking to us right now." Daisy says.

"That's okay Mom, I'll sit with Dad." Tommy is already climbing into Aaron's lap. Aaron and Daisy have tears in their eyes as they share a look across the room. After a quick hug, Aaron sits back, calmer than he has been in days. Tommy leans against his chest.

Roger clears his throat as he continues. "You see, in a Pack or Pride there is a leader, an Alpha. It is his job to make sure the Weres in his family all stay in control. A weak Alpha will not have the dominance needed to keep them all safe."

"Derek and Brother Lion were our military leaders for many years and we managed to stay in control of ourselves with their help. It has only been a few months that they have really became our Alpha and all of us a family." Bryan inserts with a look at Derek.

"That is a good place for me to say what I have to then. I am responsible for all of you. Alexis is my mate and as such she is second only to me in leading the Pride." Derek moves to the center again as Roger goes to stand against the wall with Amanda, who has returned, without the lab coat.

"N'unh unh! Alexis says you have to give her a ring first." Peggy shakes her finger at Derek as she speaks. Daisy turns bright red trying to pull Peggy back but Peggy scoots over into Alexis' lap. Daisy glances around before leaning back and crossing her arms.

Brother Lion begins as Derek walks forward to kneel in front Alexis, who has to lean around little Peggy to look in his eyes. "That is part of the problem. Everyone in a Pride must know who is in charge all the time or people get hurt."

Derek reaches into his pocket and pulls out a jewelry box. Looking into Alexis' eyes he opens it. The lid tilts a bit, one of the hinges on the box is broken. Alexis and Peggy both lean forward to see the ring sitting inside the box. "The box is broken."

Derek and Brother Lion pale at Peggy's words but ignore them. "Alexis, three months ago we gave you our hearts and asked you to be ours. You said to put a ring on this finger." Derek extends his ring finger and waves it as everyone watches.

"Here is the ring, you already have our hearts, now

will you make it official and marry me?"

Alexis opens her mouth but before she can say anything Peggy scoots forward. "It sure is a small diamond. That the best you could do?"

Choking sounds issue from Derek as his eyes widen looking from the silver ring with its small, slightly cloudy diamond to Alexis' eyes.

Daisy reaches over and pulls Peggy back into her lap. "Shhhh."

Alexis straightens and presents her ring finger to Derek and Brother Lion. "I will marry you both."

Brother Lion roars in triumph as Derek slides the ring on her finger. Everyone in the room exhales after what feels like an hour of holding their breath. Tommy hops down, leaving Aaron's lap, and walks over to see the ring.

Looking at it, he turns to Alexis and whispers loud enough for everyone to hear, "You sure you want to say yes? It really is SMAAAAALL." The drawn out small brings a gasp from Mrs. Collins, who is patting her eyes.

Trying to keep a straight face, Alexis looks Tommy in the eye. "You know, you might be right. You think I can do better?"

Tommy tilts his head and squints in deep thought. "Maybe. If you say you have to think about it, he might cough up a bigger ring."

"I already waited three months I think I better just take it."

Tommy shrugs as Aaron scoops him up and carries him back to his chair. Tommy sighs dramatically. "You are supposed to kiss her now!"

As the laughter erupts, Derek and Brother Lion scoop the laughing Alexis up in their arms and carry her up the stairs.

"I think it's a good night for us to set up the kid's tent. They can sleep in the yard with us." Aaron says walking over to the couch and kissing Daisy's cheek.

"Ooohhh," is all that Derek hears as he closes the master bedroom door with his foot.

"Derek, you're supposed to kiss me now." Alexis is still smiling as she looks up into his glowing amber eyes.

He stops a foot in the room leaning down, his lips hesitate an inch from hers. She stretches, pulling herself up to meet his mouth. The first brush of their lips is lingering, stretching into a slow exploration.

Derek breaks the contact as their breath is beginning to speed up. Walking towards the bed, he tosses Alexis in the middle of it. She lets out a squeal as she bounces twice. Brother Lion stretches at the foot of the bed. "You are ours, and we will take you as ours."

Derek begins unbuttoning his dress shirt. "Alexis, this should have been completed three months ago. We must claim you, mark you as our Mate. I love you, and I am sorry if it's rough." Derek swallows dropping the shirt on the floor.

Alexis' eyes narrow at his tone. She opens her mouth but no words emerge as the heat shimmer surrounding Derek thickens. The red gold downy hair down his cheeks thin, as the fangs and claws retract. A roar of pain and lust fills the room. Derek's cry echoes around the room at the same time.

Alexis blinks rapidly trying to clear her eyes. The heat shimmer around Derek moves to the left. A wet sucking sound is followed by a wet snap and the heat shimmer fades. There, at the foot of the bed, breath slowing is Derek Mathews.

The pants he has been wearing are shredded and the pieces are thrown around the room. His boots are missing, sweat cooling on his body as the air conditioning clicks on. His muscular chest gleams free of hair, his pink nipples are hard little points.

Rolling his neck, then his shoulders results in a series of pops. His belly ripples as Alexis licks her lips seeing her human fiancé for the first time without Brother Lion. As her eyes move lower, a moan draws her eyes to the right where the heat shimmer has returned.

Then Derek gasps, his body jerking to the right. Then a bang like a gunshot echoes around the room. With a little growl of pain, hunched over is Brother Lion. Derek and Alexis watch in awe as he straightens.

The fur that has covered Derek's body is now revealed in its fullness. The golden red hair is more of a mane, standing out six inches, framing his face. His eyes are closed as he masters breathing for himself for the first time in centuries.

His cheekbones are high, and the tips of his fangs hang over his lower lip. The nose is three inches wide and flattened spreading to his cheeks. A small slit spreads out from each side of his nostrils.

This is no mere animal but the ultimate expression

of the best of both man and lion. The inch long fur running over his body in a rainbow of colors. Red, blond, ash, and brown. The rippling muscles match Derek's as does his six-foot-three height.

Alexis' eyes travel down his chiseled chest. His arms flex, then his fingers move. Long claws are moving in and out on each finger. Then his eyes open and the amber glow is the same as it has been when in Derek's eyes.

"Alexis, holder of our hearts, we asked you once if you would accept us as your mate. Now, before you, I show you my full form. One last time, I ask you if you wish us as your own. If you say yes, we will take you, mark you and be yours for as long as time exists."

Alexis is breathing fast as pheromones fill the air. She pulls her shirt off and unbuttons her jeans. "Alexis, be careful, we are barely in control of ourselves here. The pain of separating and the animal lust is overpowering."

She wiggles out of her jeans and tan hip huggers lying half on her back. She sits up on her knees, holding her hands out to the side. Her love handles and belly roll on display. Shaking her hair, small bits of gravel and shiny little pieces of glass glinting in it.

"This is what you get. It's not perfect, but it's me. I love you both. Do you still want me?" Alexis thinks she is prepared for any response, but she is wrong.

Derek moves a fraction of a second slower than Brother Lion. Leaping from the foot of the bed to land beside her, he wraps his large hands around her ass and pulls her up against himself.

Alexis draws in a breath as her knees are raised off

the mattress. The long delicate whiskers on his cheeks tickle her face as his mouth reaches hers. Brother Lion's smooth dry lips run over hers. Moaning into his mouth, she exhales her breath into his mouth.

As her breath leaves, his tongue runs over her lips, asking, then pushing in. Demanding more of her as a low growl builds in his throat. Alexis' lips open wider, her tongue brushing the tip of his.

As his rough tongue slides over hers, his growl shifts into a steady, vibrating purr. His breath enters her mouth when she would have pulled away for air. The wild tang of the air from his mouth makes her mouth water.

His hands squeeze her plump ass, his claws extending with each squeeze kneading her ass. Then the bed shifts and Brother Lion growls tensing, drawing her closer. A challenging "Mine." Rumbles from behind her on the bed.

Feeling Derek behind her, his muscled, smooth chest tense against her as Brother Lion pulls her tighter against him his claws extend and stay out. She feels his fangs as she darts her tongue into Brother Lion's mouth. His growl lowers almost back to a purr.

She reaches behind her with her right hand, sliding it over Derek's smooth hip, her fingers brushing his ass. Then Derek's mouth closes over her ear as his hands move down her arms caressing. Alexis' head is light as she draws back from Brother Lion, breathing her own air again.

Derek's lips and teeth tug teasingly on her ear lobe. Her gasp brings a small growl from Brother Lion again.

Now her left-hand lowers from around his neck as he eases her onto her knees. Leaning down, his mouth slides over her right breast.

His rough tongue, gentle as it circles the aureole before flicking the erect nipple. Her ass bucks as his lips hold her nipple and his tongue darts against it, fucking her nipple. Slow, hard jabs that send blood rushing from the nipple to her wet pussy.

Her moan deepens as her left-hand finds Brother Lion's shaft. He growls at her pressing himself against her palm. As her fingers circle his uncircumcised shaft, he thrusts against her hand. The sensitive moist head is pressed into her palm.

Then Derek presses his hard cock against her ass cheek. His right-hand slipping between her legs from behind. His thumb presses against her asshole firmly, his fingers slide between her thighs, parting her lips as they slide forward.

The clean musky smell rising from her wet pussy releases a low moan from both men. Then Brother Lion releases her breast and takes her other one in his mouth. Her hands strokes both of their hard cocks. The long thick shafts with swollen heads, one circumcised and one not sends another tingle of desire through Alexis.

Then Brother Lion kneels in front of her spreading his wide rough tongue, he laps her pussy. Sending shooting jolts of pleasure through her, his rough tongue slurps up her love juice. Derek growls, drawing his fingers out from between her thighs. Worried that they will hurt each other, Alexis spreads her legs wider. Using her now empty left hand to support herself on Brother Lion.

Derek pulls away from her and Alexis tenses, but before she can move to stop the fight, Brother Lion's tongue spreads her lips and curves around her clit. Her moan turns into a gasp as Derek kneels behind her, his tongue fucking her pussy as his hands spread her lips.

Alexis instinctively leans back. Pressing the back of her pussy against Derek's mouth as he lies under her and forward where Brother Lion is busy working over her clit and moans as his hand squeezes and plays with her nipples.

When one man brings a moan or gasp of pleasure out of Alexis, the other redoubles their efforts. Moaning, Alexis rides Derek's face faster and harder. Brother Lion sucks her hard clit between his teeth. Then swirls his tongue around and around it.

The orgasm begins in her nipple as Brother Lion pinches and twists it. One hot electric jolt shoots from nipple to clit. Gasping, shuddering as she starts cumming. Derek grabs her ass, forcing his tongue in deeper and harder.

Brother Lion's tongue stops swirling and begins jabbing and flicking her clit, hard. As one wave ends and another builds Alexis' breaths are ragged gasps. She barely notices Brother Lion's hips moving up and down against the mattress. She feels the bed moving behind her and knows that Derek is dry humping air.

As she draws away from their mouths to catch her breath, she collapses on her side gasping. The men sit up and glare at each other. Tensing, growling, moments from attacking each either.

"No! Please no." Alexis gasps, lying on her side as a smaller tremble runs down her legs. Alexis reaches for Derek tugging with the tips of her fingers. Her foot runs down Brother Lion's side, her toes trying to draw his attention back to her and away from fighting.

Brother Lion lies down in front of her, the smell of fresh wet pussy filling Alexis' nose as he leans forward. The kiss begins slowly but in seconds, it evolves into a panting, demanding kiss. Brother Lion is scooting closer and closer.

Derek presses up behind her kissing, then nibbling her neck and shoulders. Her body spasms as the stimulation from the kissing ignites a new fire in her loins. Then it is too late to stop.

Her eyes fly wide as first Brother Lion's hard throbbing cock slips from the foreskin and rubs past her clit. Derek's long, hard cock slides past her ass and hovers, brushing her dripping pussy lips from behind.

Then both men push into her at the same time. Pain at being filled and stretched blurs as another orgasm swamps her. Two massive hard cocks working in and out of her, bringing one long rumbling orgasm or a multitude of small ones, one after another. All Alexis knows is that she is filled fuller and deeper than she ever thought possible.

She becomes lost in the rhythm of in and out. Claws roaming, grabbing, pulling. Softer, human hands every bit as demanding. Then when she thinks she will faint, the

98

men's thrusts become less controlled. More ragged as they hold their breath.

Alexis screams "My Goddess!"

Derek cries out "Alexis!"

Brother Lions roars is wordless, all-consuming animal lust. The twin burning volcanic eruptions inside her push Alexis to the fine line of where pleasure and pain blur. The bed sways one last time and the frame breaks down the middle as does the box springs. 780 pounds of pumping grinding bodies is too much for it.

Sandwiched between the sides of the mattress the three lie gasping as spirits and flesh meld. Where three bodies lie, one spirit stirs. With a soft caress to each, it floats away back to the tree clearing by the creek.

Unable to pull out, they stay cocooned by the folded mattress. Alexis relaxes fully for the first time in what feels like years, her body going boneless. She is held between the Lion and the man that love her.

Chapter 5

"I don't care if she is in there with The King, Elvis Presley himself. She is my patient and she missed her appointment for her x-ray."

The voice from the other side of the door wakes Alexis enough that she tries to sit up. Groaning as her stiff body protests, she only manages to shift her head. Blurry eyed from sleep, arms numb beside her, held in place by warm men, she lays her head back down.

As her eyes are closing the door thuds open into the wall. "Wait! I said_." Whatever else Daisy was going to say is left unsaid as Brother Lion in his own form glares over at the two humans in the doorway. A loud roar that could never come from a human throat, not even Derek's, brings a gasp from Daisy.

"Holy Mary mother of God." The doctor, being a practical man, does not put all his fear into prayers. Sideburns, 70's sports coat on, he wastes no time reaching into the black medical bag in his hand.

"No!" Daisy yells grabbing his wrist and pulling the Dirty Harry 44 off its target of Brother Lion.

Unfortunately, the gun fires, the window blows out and Derek, naked as the day he was born, is halfway to Daisy and the doctor. The kickback from the large gun, coupled with Daisy and the doctor struggling over the gun, ends up with them falling backward into the hallway.

Derek drops to his knees as Brother Lion gasps in pain. Alexis stumbles out of bed looking from Derek to Brother Lion both are on the floor in agony. Blood is trickling from their eyes and ears. Alexis shivers as the air turns cold. She gasps but does not get any air, then the room begins heating up. The shifting atmospheric pressure causes Alexis to fall on her side, struggling to breathe.

From the doorway, Daisy is stuck under the doctor watching along with him, eyes wide as Derek slides across the floor to Brother Lion. Alexis cries out "Brother Lion, Derek!" But no sound issues from her mouth. The lack of air begins causing black dots to dance in her vision.

The heat shimmer around Brother Lion condenses, sweat forms on Alexis' body as she crawls toward the men she loves. Then the pressure releases and her lungs fill with air, her ears pop and the cries of pain reach her.

Roger stumbles to a stop in the doorway standing over the doctor and Daisy looking in. Alexis reaches Derek's side afraid to touch his trembling red and bloody body for fear of hurting him. *"Close the door."*

The command is mental from Brother Lion and verbal from Derek. The force behind the mental command brings a grunt from Roger as he steps back, pushing the legs blocking the door out of the way with his foot. As the door closes, the sound of running feet and shouted questions reach Alexis.

"That man is in pain, let me help him." The doctor's voice is shrill but firm.

The sound of scuffling, followed by grunts, as Daisy regains her feet are cut off as Bryan lifts her up and holds her for a moment. "The man you are worried about is the one you almost shot." With Daisy's announcement the murmurs and questions outside the door cut off.

"No! I was going to shoot the limmikin. The bullets would not do it lasting harm but might have allowed the man and woman to escape." The doctor's words open the floodgates as more questions begin, one on top of another. Thankfully, they are all on the other side of the door.

"Derek, what can I do to help you?" Alexis is crying as Derek remains curled in a fetal position. One side rug burned, the nose and ear bleeding has stopped. Now he just lays as still as he can.

"Just let me rest, in a few hours, I will be okay." When Alexis doesn't move Derek forces one eye open. "We were planning on a slower rejoining. All we need is sleep and being away from mental touch while the sensitivity fades."

Flinching as if he has slapped her, Alexis gets to her feet turning to the bed, she grabs the sheet hanging half on the floor. Something is rolled up in a knot in it. She shakes the sheet until it falls out. Then walking stiffly to the door, her side and shoulder burning, the tears and pain of rejection hit.

"Lexi, we love you, you're ours." The verbal words
are a half grunt of pain. The mental one tries to be a soft
light breeze but is more of a hurricane. The emotions of
love and longing for her in their arms washes over her.
Acceptance, already a stirring desire in the loins, takes her
breath away. Understanding dries her tears as she
understands, inside and out as no other lovers could ever
show her. *They love me and want me always.* When they
claimed her, they were also stating that they were hers.

As she opens the door, just enough to slip out, she
becomes the object of intense scrutiny. Standing stiffly,
one leg numb, wrapped in a sheet, drying blood on her
face and neck from her ear and nose bleed, she looks
around at the assembled Pride and doctor watching her.

"Aunt Alexis, your cast is gone, are you all better
now?" Peggy in her pigtails, tugging on the edge of the
sheet, is looking up at Alexis with large brown eyes.

Alexis and everyone else looks down at her bare leg
where the sheet stops at her knee. The skin is red and
irritated where the cast had been. The image of the cast
rolling out of the sheet as she fought it off the bed
surfaces in her mind. Flexing her ankle a little, then
rolling it when there is no pain, Alexis nods. "I guess so."

Amanda reaches the top of the stairs with a final leap
from the middle of the stairs. Seeing the doctor standing
in the hall she hides her fangs and retracts her claws, but
the fur still covers her face, arms and the rest of her slim
body.

The doctor glances at her, stepping out of Roger's
reach. "Do not move that ankle! Daisy, get over here and

help my patient. I need a place to examine her before she does herself any lasting harm." When everyone stands still staring at the doctor, Alexis, and the closed door, the combined spiritual and mental pressure brings an agonized command from the other side of the door.

*"**Move! Care for our heart, we love you.**"* The mental command leaves them all swaying and with a pounding headaches. The next sending is warmth, love and strength. The pure rush of Pride magic would be felt by all in the hallway for years to come.

"The kid's room is down here. You can examine her there." Daisy inserts her shoulder under Alexis' arm and gets her moving. Busy holding the sheet in place, Alexis stumbles along in a daze.

Amanda is next, following behind Alexis after a quick word of instruction. "Mrs. Collins, I think we will all need lunch outside today." Mrs. Collins nods and turns to get started. Roger, Bryan and Aaron all follow the command of the Alphas and head downstairs.

The two little heads left in the doorway to the bathroom across from the master bedroom are unnoticed by almost everyone. The shock and daze left behind in the mind of the adult members of the Pride are not to blame. There is no blame, it simply is. These little things, like radioactive spider bites, are what legends are made of.

"Save your stories for those young enough not to believe their own eyes. That is not the first skin-walker I

have seen. The second one being so beautiful is a shock."
The doctor stops rubbing the cream into Alexis' irritated
skin as he loses himself in Amanda's eyes again.

Daisy and Alexis share a startled look. "So Dr.
Michael, the ankle is fine now?" Alexis asks.

The distraction worked, Dr. Michael takes his eyes
back and looks away from Amanda's glowing chocolate
brown eyes.

"Other than a rash that would likely go away on its
own in a week anyway, yes. With the cream, a couple of
days and even that will be gone." He sounds disgusted as
he puts away his cream, leaving Alexis to finish rubbing it
in by herself.

Alexis sighs as she feels another pain from her
feverish side and shoulder. Frowning, Dr. Michael
reaches for the sheet and exposes her neck before she can
stop him. Daisy gasps. *Great, I knew I should have
bought more turtle necks, the way they like to nuzzle my
neck. I probably have a huge hickey, and everyone can
stand and stare at it.*

"It's just a hickey, I'm sure even you Dr. Michael
have had one." Alexis gasps as Dr. Michael touches the
feverish spot on her shoulder.

"No young lady that is not just a hickey. No, I have
never had a hickey, my Pa sent me to boarding school
and not being interested in boys, I never played the usual
games of the young." Alexis looks from Dr. Michael to
Daisy frowning.

A glance at Amanda shows that she has tears in her
eyes as she turns away from Alexis' shoulder. Alexis

stands up and moves to the closet and opens the door. The squeak of a stuffed clown the door bumps is the only sound in the room. Turning her shoulder to the full-size mirror hanging on the inside closet door, she inspects her shoulder.

A large red hand print is pressed there in her flesh. "The detail is amazing, I can see every line of his fingers." Alexis pulls the sheet up, modesty forgotten in her need to see her burning side. Amanda's gasp is so pain filled and full of loss that Alexis turns to look at her. Amanda's eyes meet hers once. Her eyes are large, red, full of torment and overflowing with loss.

Amanda turns, opens the door and walks out of the room pulling the door closed behind her. Gasps and harsh breathing moves down the hall, getting quieter as Amanda reaches the stairs. Turning back to the mirror, Alexis looks down for the first time at her side.

The red print is a bit bigger than the one on her shoulder. Three Darker redder patches inside the palm area. At the end of each finger is a piece of healthy skin then a raised puckered scar where something had pierced deeply into her.

"They took away my scars, now they give me new ones." Her voice is filled with shock. Then the chills begin, sending shivers through her.

"She's in shock, help me get her in the bed." Dr. Michael moves as he is speaking, pulling the bedspread and covers back before he is finished speaking. "There now, on her back, I need to put something on those brands."

Alexis' eyes widen as the word brand penetrates her shock. "Brand?"

"Yes. I imagine that female skin changer knows what they mean better than I do." He reaches into his doctor's bag and pulls out the ointment once more. "This is not ideal for burns but it is all I have on me. I will call in a prescription for someone to go to town and pick up."

Daisy stands staring at the brands and inflamed skin surrounding them. Alexis looks at her and asks, "They're really not that bad. They told me they would mark me, and I said yes." Alexis smiles as her eyes go dreamy. A hot breeze flows in and around Alexis. The smell of Lion and prairie mixing with clean sweat of Derek after working outside surrounds her before fading.

Dr. Michael stands frozen as he watches the hair on Alexis' head blow. After the breeze leaves, she finishes rubbing in the cream. "I understand that the skin changers here will find it hard to allow me to go. Now that I know their secret."

Daisy sits on the end of the bed. "I think we can convince them you're to be trusted. I'll make sure you are safe and free to go." Even as she finishes speaking Dr. Michael is already shaking his head no.

"But you see Daisy, you are wrong. I delivered you all those years ago and you are still as stubborn now as then. Maude and the others know that strange things are about. You can go around claiming those Werewolves in town are just drugged men in costumes all you want. We are not like city folk. We old timers still remember the spirits and worse things that were taught to us by our

Grandparents, even if they are scoffed at today."

Dr. Michael moves to look out the window as he speaks. Daisy and Alexis share a look. "That sounds like your threatening us Dr. Michael." Alexis' voice is firm as she speaks, sitting up on the pillows.

"Don't be silly. Everything will be all right." Daisy stands looking flustered when no one responds. "Dr. Michael tell her you will not stir up trouble, please."

"Oh but Daisy, I will do far worse than that." He gazes at Alexis as she swings her legs off the bed. "You see, moments ago she was in shock. Now, already she prepares to stop me physically. Her ankle should have taken weeks to even be ready for a walking cast. Within a week, she is walking."

"They will kill you! Don't you understand that?" Daisy is moving to stand between Alexis, whose eyes have a glow around the edges that they have never had before, and Dr. Michael.

"He knows that Daisy, he wants something from us." Alexis had grown up wealthy and privileged. Her father, a wealthy businessman. She is used to being in charge of drivers, housekeepers and bodyguards. The command in her voice is not new. Just more powerful and more sure of herself than before.

"Daisy, even if they kill me it will mean little. I have less than six months left to live. The cancer is eating me up from the inside." The silver hair and gray bushy sideburns are a testament to his long life. "I will be 76 next month."

His announcement brings a wave of shock to Alexis,

who looks at him again. A few lines mar his weathered and tan face. His arms are thin but corded with wiry muscle. Standing erect and proud he appears to be a man in his 50's or early 60's. Not a man dying of cancer in his 70's.

"Whatever you have seen on TV, just biting you can't make you a Werecat. I'm sorry but even if they could, the other packs would all swarm them and kill all of us." Alexis sounds sad, but her body is still tense, ready to fight for her Pride.

"Oh, I have no desire to be bit and half killed. Even if it would work, I do not wish that. I want to live here, among the legends that caused my Pa to be institutionalized." The doctor finishes watching Alexis calm with acceptance. Death or the chance to live with the creatures and magic that has brushed his life so often and destroyed his parents and grandparents. It was no question really for Dr. Michael, he would do anything to live knowing that his Grandparents and parents were not crazy.

Alexis relaxes slightly, her head moves to the side as she considers. "Everyone works here. I'm not sure what care your condition requires, it might not be feasible."

The excitement of a much younger man fills his face, "Oh, I need no care and I'm not dead yet. You see, I know that your taxes are due and the trust is no longer paying them. In fact, all of you are in need of money and a lot of it."

Daisy looks at Alexis shaking her head no. "Daisy didn't tell me. Since your father disappeared, you have had legal problems. We do read here and on the west coast your Dad's arrest, loss of his assets and then disappearance made headlines for weeks. After you suddenly turn up after almost twenty years to your Grandmother's ranch, which has seen better days, it was inevitable that we would all dig."

Alexis moves to the bed, suddenly tired all over again. "It's not as bad as you make it sound."

Laughing, Dr. Michael replies, "No one here except Daisy has a job, and the cafe will need to replace her soon if she misses any more shifts. Shawn at the food mart says you lot buy three or four hundred dollars of food a week. I can help."

Does the entire town know how much food we eat? I know we ended up with a few hundred pounds of beef a time or two also. If people start connecting missing cattle with our food bill, it will mean trouble. Alexis closes her eyes as she reaches out to Brother Lion. Closing eyes always makes the mental touch easier on her.

You see the balls disappear when you lose concentration. Brother Lion closes off his other conversation from Alexis as he turns his attention to her. *"Alexis, we are not safe to contact yet."*

"The Doctor wants to move in with us. He's dying of cancer and only has six months to live. We either kill him or give him a room." Alexis is sweating as her body temperature spikes from even the brief connection to Brother Lion.

"Allow him to move in, we can always deal with

the problem later. Now go before you get hurt." Brother Lion pushes her away and locks the metal door to keep her out.

Sighing, she opens her eyes, sweat soaking her, the sheet sticking to her sore body. "You can move in, for now."

Frowning, the doctor moves forward and presses his hand to her forehead. "You are burning up! Daisy, ice water and lots of it." Digging into his bag, he barks at Daisy, "Move girl, she could stroke if we don't get that fever down!" Following Daisy to the door he calls after her, "And warm broth with sandwiches." Shutting the door, he turns to Alexis.

"I think the fever is already going down." She is sweating less, but groggy.

Moving closer he nods. "I'm sure you will be fine. Daisy is a good girl but always has had a big mouth. I have no family, and while you do not need to hear the whole story now, I want you to understand. I am not crazy. More importantly, I have proof now that my parents and grandparents were not either. I will never be able to tell anyone that and the ones that I would tell are all dead."

Alexis shifts waiting.

"I will be changing my will and cleaning up my legal matters tomorrow. Putting my house on the market, bringing the few things I care about here. The Robertsons are desperate in their single wide, it will do fine by me to be out here. Then I will transfer the bulk of my assets to you. A small amount I promised to the church and county museum but the rest will go to you."

"Why?" Is all Alexis can think to ask.

"Because they are real and always have been. Drink and eat then shower, you will be all right." Dr. Michael walks out the door carrying his doctor's bag. Leaving a more confused Alexis behind despite his explanation. Unable to reach Derek or Brother Lion for advice she paces waiting for Daisy.

"Alexis, I saw Derek and a Werecat I have never seen before when I went in your bedroom. I want some answers while we eat." Daisy says.

Turning, Alexis sees Daisy setting a tray of sandwiches, a pitcher of chilled milk and steaming broth on the kids play table. Sitting across from Daisy on the floor she takes a sip of the chilled milk in the glass and then downs half of it.

Daisy sits across from her shoving the small blue chair with the teddy to the side. "Well, last night Brother Lion separated from Derek into his own physical body so they could both take me."

Daisy mouths the words "take me," nodding, Alexis continues, "I will be sore for a month when they are in Derek's body with one cock they fill me up but last night......

The teddy bear, a clown laying by the open closet door and Daisy all sit at the kids table listening as Alexis tells them of her ménage a trois with a Lion and a man. It's safe to say that after that day the children's toys will never be the same. Good thing they can't talk.

Later that night Aaron will be ordering a large supply

of his new cologne 'stud.' Shhhh don't spoil it for him, he thinks the hours-long workout Daisy put him through was all about him. Well, it was, partly.

Chapter 6

"So her Dad is still missing?" Dr. Michael asks as he studies the autopsy report in the impromptu lab.

"It seems like forever but has only been a few months. The Werewolf pack in North Dakota is claiming this as their territory and using it as a reason to attack us." Amanda moves the fat tissue to the scale and jots down the weight.

"Now Roger seems to have the same over hypertrophy syndrome as these Freaks as you call them. What other symptoms is he displaying?"

Amanda shakes her head no. "It is not hypertrophy syndrome. That is what I thought at first but it simply isn't the same. The uncontrolled muscle growth and reduced body fat is the only similarity. The Major gave us all injections for months. Then he dumped us in the jungle to kill some terrorists."

"When was this?" Dr. Michael has stopped working and is just watching Amanda move in her natural state.

"Around 1965. You see, the Major is a Werewolf who got his pack killed. To replace them fast he used their blood and pure blood from wild wolves. I have not been able to figure out how or why it worked like it did. Instead of a new pack of Werewolves he ended up changing a bunch of soldiers into Werecats. Roger never became a Were."

"This Freak's brain has atrophied and has massive lesions beyond even the worst case of MS I have ever heard of. Does Roger show any signs of developing similar problems?"

"No, other than muscle mass and almost no fatty tissue he has no other similarities. Derek, he never became a Were like the rest of us. He has the same Werelion form, but Brother Lion is a Werelion with his own personality that lives in the astral plane of Derek's aura. Until last night, none of us knew he could manifest a body of his own."

Amanda takes off her special made rubber gloves that allows her to move specimens with the tips of her claws. Turning from Dr. Michael, she wipes her eyes. Dr. Michael removes his gloves as she asks, "Is that why you're crying? Because Derek is not the same as the rest of you?"

"No, it's silly. Derek and I were together once and then we drifted apart. I was fine until he marked her and then I knew he was hers." Amanda chokes out the last word fighting for control.

Dr. Michael slips up behind her and wraps his arms around her. Amanda stiffens in shock but he doesn't let go. She pulls away and turns to face him, her shock on her furred face. "You're not used to Were's Dr. Michael.

You should never touch one without invitation, it is a good way to die." Her growl is forced and rough.

Stepping up to her his mouth even with her chin, "Good, I need a good way to die." He places his hands on her ears and draws her mouth down to his. She doesn't resist, but her lips do not respond at first.

As his left-hand slides over her shoulder to the lower middle of her back and pulls her closer against him, a little gasp of surprise opens her lips. Dr. Michael runs his tongue over her lips. Then her arms enfold him and her mouth opens as her tongue moves over his lips. Dr. Michael's tongue brushes the point of a fang. A small cut drips blood into her mouth.

A low rumbling purr begins deep in Amanda's chest. Dr. Michael moans as he pulls her tighter against him. His growing erection presses against Amanda through their clothes. Her claws run down his back leaving small cuts in the fabric of his shirt.

"Hey Doc, Alexis is asking if you_." Whatever else Aaron was going to say ended in a choked "Sorry." As he stands in the open door staring at Amanda and Dr. Michael in each other's arms.

Pulling apart, Amanda glares at Aaron for a moment as she fights down her lust. Dr. Michael steps back, breathing fast as Aaron pretends he never saw the bulge in Dr. Michael's pants. Then his eyes dart back to the blood dripping from his mouth. "Dr. Michael, your bleeding, are you okay?"

Amanda turns, walking away toward the walk-in closet sized room she sleeps in, "I warned you, I'm sorry, but I did warn you. It would be better if someone else helped me from now on."

"Stop." Dr. Michael steps up behind Amanda again. "No one else here has the medical knowledge to be able to help you. And I'm still alive and feel more alive than I have in decades."

Amanda spins in anger her clawed hand grabbing his throat. The tips of her claws just pressing against his skin. "I'm dangerous you foolish old man. Claws and fangs to rend and kill with. I am no man's plaything."

Dr. Michael ignores the clawed hand gripping his neck. His hand runs over her cheek as he gazes into her warm chocolate eyes. "Yes, and I have guns in which to kill. We are both old enough to know when to use them. I need to go to town tomorrow and wrap up my affairs. We can have an early dinner afterward. Be ready around 5 pm." He runs his hand over her arm until it reaches her hand.

Aaron makes a gasping sound as he lets out the breath he can no longer hold. Dr. Michael's hand draws the hand from his neck and kisses each claw, then her palm. "Wear something sporty and fun, we might go dancing after dinner."

He looks in her eyes and waits a moment until she nods once. Then he turns and walks to Aaron, "Alexis sent you for me, yes?" Aaron nods. "Then we should go and see what she needs. I hope the fever has not returned."

Amanda stands staring at the closed door they had gone through for a long time straining to hear his voice long after it has faded.

———————————

Alexis is waiting outside the back door alone as Aaron and Dr. Michael walk up. Alexis looks from the slight smear of red on Dr. Michaels chin to the pale, rigid look on Aaron's face and frowns. "I thought you might like to walk with me this evening Dr. Michael. With everything happening of late, I'm not supposed to go anywhere without an escort."

Aaron clears his throat. "You should really have more than just Dr. Micheal with you if you go far." The reproving tone is clear in his voice.

Alexis reaches down beside her and picks up the dirty harry 44 that Dr. Michael left upstairs. "I'm sure if Dr. Michael shoots this, even once, everyone here will come to my rescue. Relax Aaron and don't bother Derek, I will not be far."

Handing the gun to Dr. Michael, she turns and begins walking away. Dr. Michael follows her putting the gun in his ever present doctor's bag.

Daisy steps out the back door, "Aaron, have you seen the kids since lunch?"

"They took food up to Derek. Brother Lion said that the kids had enough manners to keep their emotions to themselves. Did they not come back down afterward?" Aaron is looking around the yard. The deserted swing set, and scattered toys mixing with the ever present dust blowing in the breeze.

Alexis and Dr. Michael are already halfway to the

creek that runs through the back forty acres behind the house when the sound of the truck driving up the driveway draws Daisy's attention. "Maybe they went to town with Roger and Mrs. Collins."

As the truck pulls up in another cloud of dust, Mrs. Collins climbs out while Roger grabs a screwdriver from the toolbox in the truck bed and pops the hood. "Aaron, Daisy, can you give me a hand with the groceries please?"

As they head over to the truck, Aaron stops by Roger, "Have you seen the kids since lunchtime?"

Roger is trying to get the dipstick out without breaking it. "They took food up to Brother Lion then a while later they came down saying he wanted ice cream. I imagine they're sleeping off the half gallon that Mrs. Collins sent up for him."

"You think they lied about it?" Daisy demands, arms full of groceries as she returns from the pickup bed.

Roger glances at her and smiles, "Derek is allergic to ice cream, gives him the hives. The only person in the world I know of that is. So if he and Brother Lion asked for it, they intended it for the kids."

Daisy turns and stomps toward the house muttering. Aaron follows behind her nodding in thanks to the chuckling Roger as he hurries to get his share of the groceries. As he passes Roger, he hears a cursed "Ouch! Damn radiator." Aaron smiles to himself as he hurries back to the house, groceries in hand.

"Derek, you seen the kids?" Aaron calls into the bathroom holding the door cracked open as steam rolls past him.

"They went to play, we told them it was okay. They brought us lunch and distracted Brother Lion while I slept. Then they got us ice water and sandwiches. Worked hard running up and down the stairs and are probably sleeping now." Derek's voice sounds horse but more normal than earlier.

"Thanks, I'll look in their bedroom." Aaron closes the door and moves down to the kid's bedroom at the end of the hall. Arron looks inside and he spots the kids sleeping in their beds, surrounded by stuffed animals. Shutting the door, he goes back downstairs to find Daisy and lets her know they are fine.

———————————

"Derek, you okay?" Alexis sticks her head in their bedroom door. The bed is a mess, all the covers are thrown on the floor. The cast is split down the side and sitting up ready to slip on beside the bed. Derek is sitting up in bed surrounded by papers.

He doesn't look at her but nods. Brother Lion speaks in her mind. *"I missed you."* His mental voice a sleepy murmur that tickles the back of her neck.

"I love you." She sends to Brother Lion.

Closing the door behind her, she walks over to Derek. The papers scattered around him are rumpled, and some have soup stains. "Those are the legal papers from Dad's lawyers." Picking up a pile by his foot, she can't resist giving the big hairy foot a tickle.

"Yeeeiiiee! Don't do that." Laughing, he leans forward and grabs her in his left arm, pulling her in for a

quick kiss. It lingers too long for a quick anything and
leaves them both a tad breathless. "These were in the
mail from Henry. He's not sure if they are all here, but I
doubt it. His note said he was going to give them to you
the other day when you met with Spencer Masters but
things got out of hand."

Alexis blushes, glancing at the papers in her hand.
"Dr. Michael says the entire town knows we're broke and
are talking about how fat we are."

Sitting beside Derek on the bed, some of the papers
shift. "Small town, with all the shooting and such I'm
sure they won't worry about how fat we are for months
or longer."

Still sorting and stacking pages with his right arm he
holds her in his left. Feeling warm and safe Alexis leans
into him. "Do you think I should just sell the company
and be done with it? Maybe they will even let Dad go."

If she hadn't been leaning into him, she might have
missed Derek's inhalation of breath. "*Tell her.*" The voice
floats to them from the mostly asleep Brother Lion.

"Yeah, tell me." A hard note in her voice matches
the hard jab in his side.

Setting the papers in his hand down, he looks her in
the eye. "Matteas and the others tracked the bikers that
attacked the town the first time. They were hired for big
money by a front man the Major claims is high in the
Other's pack."

Alexis tenses, holding onto her anger, at his not
telling her sooner, to fight the fear. *Don't be dead. Don't
be dead.* Her mind keeps repeating as she listens to

Derek.

"The trail lead to Sturgis as you might expect. They tracked the Other's front man to Chicago where they met up with Sabrina. She and the others found a Freak Factory. Or what was left of it. They got there a few hours after the Major's men hit it."

Alexis feels the first tear escape as Derek wraps her in both his arms as he finishes, "Your Dad's wallet and DNA were found on the body of a partially turned Freak. There was not enough left for a visual ID."

Alexis leans back and hits him in the chest, the pain in her hand feels so good; she hits him again, over and over. Until Alexis collapses into his waiting arms and sobs. "No, No, they took Mom, it's not fair that they both be dead."

Derek holds her in his arms as she cries, curses, and denies that her Dad could be dead. Brother Lion wraps his warm love in a warm blanket of emotion and subtle anger at those that did this to her. That kernel of rage is all Alexis can hold onto while the pillar of her world since she was born teeters, possibly already dead.

Mrs. Collins knocks and looks in when Derek answers softly. Alexis flees from the bed into her arms incoherently telling her that her Dad is gone. Then saying it is all a mistake and he is fine. She goes with Mrs. Collins to her room, and they cry until both of them fall asleep.

———————————

Derek walks down the stairs carrying a box while it is

still dark outside. Looking into the kitchen, he sees the dishes, all still dirty from the night before. Leaving the lights off in the other rooms he shuts the dining room and kitchen doors. Then turns on the lights and sets the box on the counter.

Taking out a knife he opens the box and unpacks the under counter AM/FM radio CD player. Looking around, he finally spots a clear place to set it and plugs it in. He leaves the screws and mounting bracket in the box for Aaron when he gets up.

Derick tunes the radio, finally finding the oldies station. As Blue Suede Shoes starts he turns on the water, beginning to fill the sink with suds and hot water for the first round of dishes. Washing and rinsing, then stacking them to dry keep his hands busy. His mind refuses to think, having already sat up all night worrying about what to do about Alexis' Dad, the Major and all the other problems demanding his attention.

Singing along to the radio, he finishes the dishes when Brother Lion stirs. *Matteas is here, almost to the door. His aura is splotchy and ill.*

Thank You. Derek and Brother Lion are careful around each other after almost fighting over Alexis the other night. Brother Lion is still recovering from exhaustion after manifesting a physical body.

Opening the back door off of the kitchen, in the side yard, he spots Matteas heading for the front door. Walking, head hanging and disheveled. Whistling, Derek gains Matteas' attention and motions him over. Not waiting for him, Derek returns to washing dishes.

Matteas stops in the door glancing around the kitchen in a disinterested way. His human form looks stretched and unhealthy. Derek tosses a dishtowel to Matteas and points to the wet dishes waiting. Catching the towel he moves over and begins drying dishes.

"Bad?" Derek asks.

"Worse," Matteas says.

Nodding, Derek continues washing, waiting for the right song.

"Red, red wine, Goes to my head. Makes me forget that." Derek bumps into Matteas' hip when he doesn't respond. Matteas ignores Derek and keeps drying the glass in his hands.

"Red, red wine, you make the girls look so fine." Derek picks up the wet dishtowel from the counter and flicks the corner at Matteas ear.

"It's up to you. All I can do, I did." Matteas' words are an animal growl, and claw tips are clinking against the glass as he holds it.

"Memories won't go, so the bottle this soldier will swallow whole." Derek's voice is cheerful and teasing.

"I'd have sworn that with time, you would be less of a slime." Matteas finishes with a wince.

Shaking his head in disgust, Derek continues, "Thoughts of you would leave my head, your sisters are still in my bed." Derek counters.

"I was wrong, now I find, you have lost your mind."

"Just one thing makes me forget: Red, red wine" They sing out together smiling.

"Stay close to me, for family we will always be." As

Derek finishes, Matteas shivers as they hug in the kitchen.

Tears run down Matteas' face. "They had little kids, like when Sophie lost it, half eaten."

"We stopped her and we will stop this psycho also. Now we have to cook breakfast for a bunch of Weres and a few humans that eat like us." Derek picks up the next song and within minutes, they are singing together and laughing as they cook pancakes, eggs and much more, breakfast for an army, or a half dozen Weres.

A little over an hour later, breakfast is ready and set out on the two picnic tables in the yard. "Grub in the mess hall in five minutes! Shake your willies once, any more and it's a pleasure. And that's not the business we're in, move it!" Derek and Matteas roar at the top of their lungs waking the entire house.

The neighbors dog, half a mile away, starts yapping so loudly old man Hinckle fires his shotgun once and yells "Shut up."

The kids are first on the scene, as usual. "Hey Uncle Derek, who's the new Werelion?" Tommy asks.

"This is Matteas, he is the Pride's only other lion beside me. Matteas, these are Daisy's kids, the one's I told you about." Derek is dishing up bacon and scrambled eggs.

"I don't care who he is Aaron, speak to him or I will!" Daisy hisses louder than she intended as everyone stops speaking to stare at her.

Aaron looks like a kid that has just learned that Santa isn't real. Alexis and Mrs. Collins both arrive in the clothes they wore yesterday. Bags under their eyes, and faces puffy from crying. Or the bottle of Johnny Walker Blue label they had finished off.

Dr. Michael arrives dressed in a pressed pair of Dockers, polished loafers and with his doctor's bag smiling. "Well it might not be a cure for cancer, but if this is how you all eat every day, it sure is a good start on one." Without waiting for an invitation, he sits down and starts dishing up food.

Bryan and Roger arrive about the same time both grinning and in good spirits. "Trust two lions to ruin a tiger's dreams of a beautiful_" He coughs as Roger whacks him on the back of his head pointing at the kids and a glaring Daisy. They both sit down and concentrate on dishing up food.

"Uncle Bryan, what beautiful thing were you dreaming about?" Peggy asks.

"A beautiful princess. She was running away from an ugly, wart-covered Weretiger named Bryan. Uncle Derek and Uncle Matteas saved the princess by waking up your wart covered Uncle Bryan here." Roger winks at the kids who erupt in gales of laughter.

"Payback is a bitch," Bryan mutters.

Daisy's elbow hits Aaron in the side, and he sighs. "The kids have been repeating the swear words and Daisy," a glance at her convinces Aaron to rephrase that. "We, I and Daisy, I mean, Daisy and I, oh hell. They are just words Daisy. I'm too tired after last night's workout to do this now. Here, have some coffee." Aaron pours her a cup and adds three sugars.

Alexis manages a small smile and a wink at Daisy.

"Mom, is that what you and Dad were doing last night? Working out?" Peggy asks. The murmured hellos and how is Sabrina? is cutoff as all eyes and ears turn to Aaron and Daisy.

"Go ahead Aaron, perhaps you feel it's time my kids heard the talk. You know they're only words." Daisy waits.

"Oh, when will our new brother be here?" Tommy asks.

"You have a brother?" Aaron asks looking from the surprised Daisy to Tommy.

"Well, I hope it's a boy, we have enough girls anyway. He sticks his tongue out at his sister.

"Stop making up stories Tommy." Daisy sounds tired as she takes a drink of her coffee.

"You and Aaron had sex last night, so you're going to have a baby, it's not a story if it's true," Tommy says. He watches as Daisy chokes on her coffee and spills most of it.

"I think your Mom would like to know who had that talk with you. Perhaps you should tell her before she hurts herself or Aaron." Roger is busy fighting the grin on his face as he speaks.

"At school, Mr. Pierre had to move away after he taught health class but he had pictures of flowers and bees. You remember mom, you wrote a letter about him to the principle last year."

Everyone except Daisy and Aaron are laughing. The kids are smiling, thrilled to be the center of attention. "I'm not pregnant. This is not something we will discuss at the dinner table," Daisy says, drying her shirt.

"Mom, this is breakfast," Tommy says, rolling his eyes.

"Kids, let's let the adults talk for a while okay," Aaron says in a firm voice. The kids sigh but begin eating.

Alexis is sitting beside Mrs. Collins. Both of them eat very little and are subdued. Brother Lion sends love and concern to Alexis but she is so hung over and depressed it doesn't even register with her. Brother Lion could have pushed harder for her attention but doesn't want to make her feel worse.

Matteas grows more subdued and withdrawn as the meal continues. What had started as a happy family meal with conversation and jokes, becomes a quite apprehensive one. Everyone's eyes are drawn to Matteas and Derek waiting for the bad news.

With a sigh, Derek pushes his plate away. "Alright everyone, as you all seem to have guessed, Matteas has some news for us. It might be better if the kids went to play while we discuss things."

"No." Alexis words are firm, clear and when Derek begins to speak she hits her glass with her spoon cracking the glass. "No. Until we know for sure, there is no news. The Major has done nothing but send us to do his dirty work and lie to us."

Mrs. Collins wraps her arm around Alexis, hugging her against her side. Both with wet eyes. Derek looks surprised and swallows. "That's all true. Before we share all of the new information, I think the kids should go upstairs and play."

"They need to clean their room anyway. You both get up there and clean it. I will be picking up your school work today and you go back to class on Monday." Daisy shoos the kids, looking relieved.

As everyone fidgets among themselves, Amanda rises. "I really need to finish the last of my examination and I already spoke to Sabrina."

Derek nods and she returns to the lab. The shock on Matteas' face shows he hadn't known that Amanda and Sabrina are in communication with each other. Dr. Michael half rises to follow Amanda but sits back down with a sigh, pouring a glass of orange juice and taking the last slice of toast.

Derek begins, "I won't go into the specifics here and now. The facts, as far as we know them, are as follows. The Freaks were being created in Chicago. The factory where they were being made was hit by the Major, hours before the agreed time. When our team got there, it was half burned and the human authorities were already arriving. Matteas please just tell us what we know for sure."

"The trail of money from the bikers led to Chicago, so I followed it. The Freaks left a trail of witnesses that led first to Denver then to Chicago. We don't know for sure why the two biker gangs both fight each other and the freaks. The Werewolves seem to be split with some on both sides. Then some of the bikers appear to be working with the Freaks."

"Someone is making more of them on a scale large, enough to be a factory?" Dr. Michael sounds alarmed.

Matteas nods. "Someone is trying to make an army of them. They are using children because the lesions and loss of cognitive function are slower in them. The condition of their remains was horrible." Matteas sits back down looking ill.

Derek rises to finish, resting a hand on Matteas' shoulder for a second, as everyone adjusts to the shock. "I believe they are looking for a cure to the loss of thought and speech that occurs with the increase in muscle, speed, and dexterity. The only person we know that has ever developed anything like this is the Major."

"Wait a minute, you said the Major attacked and destroyed the factory before our people arrived." Dr. Michael has already begun thinking of himself as one of them.

"Yes but Sabrina contacted him for help to deal with the security in place there. He claims his people acted early because the factory was being moved and there was no time to contact us. At this point, we don't know if that's true."

Matteas looks out at them, his eyes bleak as he speaks still seated. "We're aware of only two other things for sure. One, the reason Mr. Armstrong's business is so important to the military is that they've been working for private contracts on perfecting the formula developed by the Major. We know that from a partially burned folder."

Derek closes his eyes for a second and finishes for Matteas, "The other thing we know is that the Major never intended for us to be Weres at all. We were to be Freaks; ferocious, rational, eradication, attack, kill, specialists. The transfusions were altered by a group we suspect are Weres of unknown origin without the Major finding out until we were too far gone in the change to stop."

The silence is complete all around the table. "That's why he suddenly sent us on the suicide mission and then when we lived he tried to have us killed. We were all mistakes." Bryan closes his eyes as the pieces fall into place.

"His excitement at each new transfusion and increased abilities in the Unit. The constant mental testing to see if we were losing cognitive function. Then when the fur, fangs and claws began showing up the Major knew what was wrong and abandoned the project."

"And I was his only success. That's why he is always contacting me. Offering me cures if I would come in for more testing." Roger sounds sick.

As everyone lets this sink in, Dr. Michael is taking notes for questions to ask later. When no one speaks for a long time, Alexis suddenly stands up. "Dad knew about this. Maybe not all of it but back when he and mom first started fighting, I remember parts of their arguments now."

Derek turns to look at her, pale and trembling as she continues. "She used to work with him. I thought it was in his office paperwork or something. But now I think it was music related. Then she refused to help him, and she wanted him to close the business and move overseas."

"Are you sure he was aware of what he was helping

to develop?" Derek asks concerned.

"He knew it was for military personnel, to make better, safer soldiers. I have to know for sure. I have to go back." She looks at Derek lost.

Mrs. Collins is trembling. "I remember when she used to work with Martin. They were so excited, inseparable. Then almost overnight they started fighting all the time. She refused to go with him or look at the paperwork he brought home for her to help him with."

"The police and feds emptied his business of everything, there won't be anything left." Derek tries to sound reasonable.

"Not at the business. In our secret room. 'Never go to the bottom of the stairs, Alexis. I will show you when your sixteen, I promise. Now go color, Mommy has work to do to save Daddy.' That's what she used to say all the time. She was still working on the project but without him, from home."

Alexis is rocking back and forth. "Your dad's safe room? The police emptied it also, remember?" Mrs. Collins asks sounding gentle and lost.

"No, Mom and I have a secret room. They never found it. Derek, I have to go back. I have to KNOW!" She grabs him and shakes him.

"Okay Alexis, I will make the arrangements. A few days, just a few days for everyone to get here and we will go. I promise." Derek holds her, feeling lost and confused. Brother Lion wraps himself around Alexis crooning until she falls asleep in Derek's arms.

Derek turns and carries her inside. He stops once

looking out at his Pride. "Sabrina is to infiltrate the Major's network. I want his secrets. Contact the North Dakota pack Alpha we will pay the $500k for South Dakota Territory by the end of the year. We have enough enemies."

Bryan and the others sit looking at each other for a long time. Then Dr. Michael walks to the lab to get more information. Mrs. Collins begins gathering dishes. Roger says he has a headache and is going to lie down.

Bryan helps Mrs. Collins clean up. Daisy leads a stunned Aaron to the kid's fort, where they had gone instead of cleaning their room, so they could sit and watch the kids play. All of them understand that if the Major and this Other Alpha, that has been terrorizing Alexis and kidnapped her Dad, are working together that war will be fast, furious and some, maybe all of them, will not survive.

For now, they are all determined to live and enjoy each moment they have before Alexis and Derek go back to the Armstrong Estate and find out what the hell is really going on.

.

Chapter 7

Sabrina walks past the milling group of Weres, humans and the handful of freak bodyguards with contempt. *I could be pass them and kill the Major before they even knew I was here.*

"Take two teams and find the truck with the biosamples. I would like some prisoners alive if possible, but the samples are the priority." The Major stands six-feet tall, and while dwarfed in height by many of the Weres and Freaks around him, he somehow manages to seem the right height while everyone else is too tall or short.

Well, I could kill him maybe, if he is having a really bad day. Sabrina grimaces, remembering the humiliating sparring session from when they first met up with the Major's group.

He moves like a Goddamn dancer. How is he so fast? Dark, ruggedly handsome with Playboy streaks of gray on the sides of his head. The only Were Sabrina has ever heard of who can be relaxed, fangs and claws out and remain clean shaven.

A Were and a human merc salute and move away, a smattering of the milling Weres, freaks, and humans split away following the two lieutenants. The Major turns his hard gray eyes on her and she instinctively straightens and has to force her arm down, already halfway to saluting him.

A slaughterhouse and he dresses like he is ready for a General's Ball. Pressed uniform, boots polished to mirror brightness and not a hair out of place. As the Major's eyes move over her, the slight frown and head shake at her appearance stiffens her spine, while embarrassing her.

"I assume Matteas is back with Derek, so you have decided to tell me the truth of where he is." As he speaks, he begins walking through the throng surrounding him. Ignoring the body parts, smoking electronics and the occasional scream or burst of gunfire.

Ignoring the stench is the hardest thing for Sabrina. Unlike Matteas, the bodies of children, pregnant women and some in the middle of C-sections, when they died, do not bother her. Humans are fodder, she was a firm believer that they should all be rounded up and kept in zoos.

"Matteas is with Derek for the moment." Sabrina draws to a stop at the nursery beside the Major. "Dead children, even human ones, are hard for Matteas to deal with."

"An Alpha should help his Weres to overcome such weaknesses. I would have done so, out of family loyalty for Matteas." The unsaid, if you would have come to me instead of Derek, rings louder in Sabrina's ears than if he had come out and said it. Doubtless, why he left it unsaid.

Looking at the bodies of Freak babies, most dead even before the Major's forces attacked, allows Sabrina to ignore the Major's disappointment in her. The rows of incubators, cradles with steel bars, and assorted deformed children hold an immense interest for the Major. "Sharon, be sure to send all of these specimens for dissection. Perhaps we can still learn something from this fiasco."

The human woman nods before directing the careful bagging of the Major's newest specimens. "We have been running around attacking these labs, factories and research stations for three months. Not once have we gotten any closer to the Other." Sabrina follows the Major as he tours the area.

"I suppose Derek has told you that this means I am in league with the Other?" The Major waves his arm, dismissing the question before she can respond. "The sad fact is, that the few of his famous Unit he has sent have performed below the standard of even my human soldiers."

"You sent us into traps three times, yet you are surprised we have stopped rushing in wearing the targets you give us?" Sabrina snorts but it turns into a swallow as the Major turns to look at her. The disappointment in her was plain on his face.

Shaking his head,"Of all of the Unit, I thought you would be the one to understand that I am the only chance any of you have to survive. Despite my good faith and repeated offers to send my Freaks, soldiers, and specialists to aid you, I am lied to."

Sabrina swallows as she notices that five freaks, three Weres and a couple of Specialists are closing in around them. "Where is Felix? He has not reported back to me since he came to see you." Sabrina steps away from the Major, giving herself room to fight.

Felix steps out from behind a pair of freaks. "I'm right here Sabrina," Felix smiles his too handsome smile. His swimmer's body is always gorgeous. Even Sabrina, who loves Matteas and worships her mate, enjoys watching the Wereleopard. Moving or standing his perfectly sculpted body is a delight to behold.

"Why didn't you report in on time?" Sabrina demands. Never comfortable being in crowds, since becoming a Werepanther, she hates it. Her eyes flash in her black-furred face as her body tenses.

"Don't be too hard on him Sabrina. We both have you and the entire Unit's best interests in mind." The Major is watching with that fatherly, I know best look, firmly in place.

"I would have been an Alpha with my own pack long ago under the Major's leadership. I have never liked Derek's leadership." Felix's lips wrinkle in distaste on Deeks name. "He is not even a Were. He allows that dead Werelion ghost to say and do what it wants. If he cannot even control his animal why should we follow him?"

Sabrina hides her shock, as well as she can. "Derek would never stop you from leaving to join the Major. We will all be sad to see you go." Sabrina steps back again, legs tense, ready to spring.

The tranquilizers hit her in mid-leap. Unlike animal tranquilizers, these are loaded with synthetic, magic and charm driven force. The debilitating cramps hit her muscles in seconds of entering her body.

Falling to the cement floor, Sabrina curls in a fetal position. Her eyes are tracking the Major as he walks away. Felix saunters over and kneels beside her. "The problem, dear Sabrina, is that Derek and the sorceress bitch he is fucking, have something the Major needs."

Felix runs his soft hand down her cheek. "The fact that he betrayed the Major by claiming the Alpha spot just made it easier to convince the Major to put the blame for making all of us on him."

"You are a fool, Derek already knows the Major has been using us for months." Sabrina's eyes open in shock as she bites her tongue to stop babbling.

Smiling, Felix's hand runs over her left breast fondling, squeezing until her body reacts. Disgusted at her body's betrayal, she whips her head forward and rips into Felix's cheek. Her fangs raking over and over. Felix screams, trying to push her off him. Laughter is the only answer to his cries for help.

Then the Major's voice roars out "Get her off him and double the dose of the serum." Sabrina gasps as a Freak picks her up by her treasured Dreadlocks and holds her off the ground as the Major stands glaring at the bleeding Felix.

"You want to be an Alpha? Then you better start

acting like one. Get cleaned up. I want you on the way to meet up with Derek as soon as Shawn is dead." The Major turns to Sabrina looking at her bloody face, as convulsions shake her body. Dangling by her hair, each uncontrollable shake tares hair free and causes stabbing pain.

The Major steps up with a large hypodermic needle. Sabrina swats at him but he moves her cramped arms like she is a child. The needle slides into her carotid artery and the warmth spreads through her, leaving behind a partial paralysis.

"Lower her to the ground." When the Major commands his freaks, they obey better and comprehend more. "Sweet Sabrina, I did not want it to come to this. Perhaps if you survive the transfusions and I get the key to makig the transformation stable you can be saved. If not, you will make beautiful babies with my Freaks. Shame you will never be aware enough to see them."

Sabrina spits blood and saliva in his face before losing consciousness. The Major calmly cleans his face with a monogrammed handkerchief. "Load her in the truck. Tell the witches to give the fire an hour to take hold then release the illusion spell. Make sure they are well paid."

The merc nods and moves to inspect the detonators personally. Everyone present remembers the fate of the Were that failed to destroy all evidence of the Major's ties to the Other. Thinking of the man being used as a breeder for the Major's Freaks speed his feet.

Armless, legless, tied to a bed and fed Viagra until he

stroked out over several weeks, Freaks that were once women use him in ways that can only be called evil.

———————————————

"Sabrina, you fool, I told you they wouldn't let me leave." Shawn stands talking to himself as he waits for the bus. Looking at his phone again hoping to see her message that all was well and she is on her way to meet him.

With his cutoff jeans, gray hoodie and school bag it fools most people. At five-feet tall he can pass as a high school or short college student most of the time. Unless someone looks in his eyes and sees the hard glitter that comes from war or prison.

Moving back inside the terminal he takes out his cell and hits Derek's number from speed dial. "Hello Shawn, missed you this morning at the get-together." The Major's voice is reproving.

Looking at the cell phone display, Shawn confirms that he dialed Derek's number. "Sorry about not being there. Sabrina thought I should go check on that lead. She was going to tell you about it, she not there yet?" Shawn sets his backpack down, easing his hand inside and holding the 38 as he scans the mostly empty bus terminal.

"Oh Sabrina made it but we're having some heavy resistance and, as always, she is in the thick of it. Seems we might have finally cornered Cornelius, the Other's third in command. Could sure use your help."

Shawn watches as a blue station wagon and Dodge

pickup pull up outside. "Oh I think I have some bad guys here on my doorstep, have to go." Hanging up he begins walking toward the only bus loading passengers.

Three Freaks and a Werewolf from the station wagon enter through the glass door and look around. Three Werewolves from the pickup head for the bus, warning Shawn off. Seeing a security guard Shawn walks up to him. "Those big guys that just came in said they have a bomb. You should call the police and evacuate the building."

The guard puts his hand on his taser looking from Shawn to the now approaching Freaks and Werewolf. Shawn frowns, watching the large blond haired blue eyed man speak into his walkie-talkie. "Got some gang trouble here at terminal F."

From the walkie-talkie, "You need police assistance? Have Gerald on his way."

The big security guard smiles as he watches the Freaks get closer, ignoring the Werewolf. "No, Gerald can have any I leave." He pats Shawn on the head. "Go stand over there and watch the show. Don't do drugs." The last is said like a rote line as he draws his taser from his belt-holster and from under his shirt a second larger taser.

The Freaks are ten feet away and Shawn is moving away shaking his head in disgust. "Dumb ex-jocks, still have the blood cut off by wearing those dumb jockstraps. Bomb they have a bomb! Raid, run the fuzz is here!" Shawn yells as he starts walking faster, half looking over his shoulder.

An older couple and a single mom head for the door at the cry of bomb. The two homeless and a man in a suit all head for the exits as he yells raid and fuzz. Over the years, Shawn has learned that two types of people take the bus. The ones that are afraid of almost everyone else on them. And the ones that are afraid of the police for one reason or another.

"Hold it right there! Put your hands on your head and drop to your knees." The guard backs up when the Freaks do not even look at him. "Stop!" If it was anyone with a working brain they would react, speed up or slow down. Freaks do not have working brains. The person they view as their Alpha or who is put in charge by that person gives an order and they follow it.

At five paces the guard realizes the three Freaks are not stopping. He shoots his first taser, hitting one in the chest. The resulting scream is from the guard, not the freak that was shot. The freak just stumbles and then keeps on walking.

The second taser hits the same Freak again and the Freak does drop to the ground. Unfortunately for George Smith, winner of the Polk High award for most touchdowns in one football game, the other two keep coming.

George could have run and they would have ignored him, only caring about getting Shawn. Instead, he backs up and runs at them like they are the opposing defensive line. That is as Shawn is going out the door into terminal B and Gerald is coming in.

"Watch where you're going, slow down you."

Whatever else Gerald was going to say freezes in his mouth as his eyes go round. Shawn squeezes between him and the door as Gerald yells, "No!" Looking back, George is down, well, what is left of him.

The two freaks had each grabbed an arm and pulled. A freak is as strong as a Were that can lift, on average, 600 to 800 pounds. The human body is not built to stand up to that much force. Screaming as his life bleeds out, he looks at his friend from high school and screams. Unlike George, Gerald never played football. He was in the Glee club, he did win a medal though.

"Run kid. Call the cops and evacuate now!" He screams into his walkie-talkie before dropping it. He reaches into his pant leg and pulls out the snub nosed 38 that is a twin to the one still strapped to Shawn's leg and starts shooting.

Shawn runs and never looks back to see if the gun does him any good. If Shawn had time to think about it, he would have said no, the guard was dead from when he decided to go to work that day. He should have agreed to call in sick like George wanted and gone to the nudie bar.

As Shawn is running, the Werewolf that has been with the Freaks runs at Shawn from the exit to the outside. He goes around the outside and comes back in terminal B while the Freaks have all the attention. Three more guards are running towards them, all holding real guns. Security guards take a lot of flak so they tend to stick together. Hearing the screams of George and Gerald convince them that tasers will not cut it. Not all of them have permits but that won't matter this day.

The Werewolf slows until the guards are pass. The freaks are in the terminal with Shawn and the second group are now entering from outside as well. The Werewolf starts running and so does Shawn. The first dart gets Shawn in the back of his arm. At first, he doesn't even notice it, then the second dart hits him in the back of the thigh. The hoodie and jeans do nothing to protect him. That's when things start to get fuzzy around the edges

---

Shawn runs as fast and hard as his short legs will carry him. He has surprised the first Freak that catches up with him with his strength. They always seem to think that short means weak. He grins, remembering ripping the femoral arteries in both its thighs, then his knife severs the Achilles tendon in the left leg. As the Freak goes down it is a seconds work to shred the carotid artery and run.

The smile fades as the stitch in his side doubles, he collapses against a brick building somewhere near downtown. The two darts they have shot him with must have been poisoned. His muscles keep trying to cramp and despite sweating he cannot stop shivering.

Taking out his cell, he hits Derek's new number and waits. He hears the clomping, booted feet of the remaining freak and the softer tread of the three Weres approaching.

"Shawn, you need to come home now."

"Derek?" He asks.

"No, it's the Major, you will be safe here." Shawn doesn't bother hanging up, instead, he just drops the phone. *I must be worse off than I thought. Why else would I keep calling when I already know that the Major has all my calls forwarded to his phone.*

Stepping away from the wall, he stumbles a few feet down the alley, his vision blurring. There, he sees five Weres he has never seen before. All in their natural form, a couple with shotguns and another with chains.

Turning, he sees the Freak and three Werewolves behind him and closing. Smiling, he takes out his last knife and slices his throat before they can stop him. Dropping, he sees the strange Weres firing into the Freak. Why are they attacking each other?

Then he remembers how the Major deals with failure. In the Major's pack or employ, you serve one way or another. It leads to intense effort and constant betrayal, as blame is shifted from one faction or person to another.

Smiling, content that he will soon be reunited with his love, Cherise. "Cherise, I did what you said, I lived for as long as I could. Now I'm joining you, like I should have when we were changed into Werebobcats." His gurgle is unintelligible. Even a Were's body needs a will and reserves to heal. Poisoned, shot, and bleeding, Shawn has done his best to ensure he will never end up in the Major's breeding dens.

Chapter 8

The chill air, that always seems to arrive before dawn, might be why people, especially men, speak in a hush at that time of morning. The dew forming on the picnic table and oak tree hanging over it shimmers, reflecting the light from the kitchen window.

"I haven't felt this alive in decades." Amanda's voice is flushed with excitement as she stands looking out over the sprawling ranch acreage that has become the first home the military Weres have had since becoming Weres.

Dr. Michael slips his hands around Amanda, bringing a gasp as they slide under her shirt. Her blouse is loose, silk and a vibrant red. Still in her human form, from the night out on her date with Dr. Michael, she is struggling to remain in control of her form. She can stay in human form for 36 hours before she begins to have problems.

Her surprising attraction to Dr. Michael and his attention is making it hard after only 16 hours in human form. Keeping her head up, looking east as the first pink glow is lighting the clouds.

"Maybe we should go in and see if there is any news." When Dr. Michael doesn't respond she looks down at him gazing into her eyes. Stepping on his tip toes, he is able to reach her mouth. She moans and then jerks back from him as her fangs slide out a half inch and she begins breathing hard from the effort of staying human, she shakes her head.

Dr. Michael grunts and nibbles her chin, tugging it with his mouth. "I know you have fangs and claws Amanda. I was fascinated by your form the moment I saw you."

Anger is coloring her face as she turns away, she allows herself to relax. The intense itching, as all the soft fur grows covering her body, lessens as she relaxes. The tearing pain as her claws extend from under each fingernail feeds her anger. "I do not want to be ogled by some freak that is into animals." The single tear that escapes is the only way she allows the pain out.

Stepping up behind her, Dr. Michael slaps her ass, as hard as he can swing his arm. A single undignified "Yelp" escapes from Amanda as she spins around eyes flashing.

"I am not some bestiality freak, and you are not some animal." His voice holds the anger and authority of a Doctor that has seen over 70 years of life. Many of them sewing up people dumb enough to get themselves hurt or dead.

"Don't ever touch me again!" Her face flushes under all the fur. Her heated skin grateful for the fur hiding her excitement from the thrill that slap has sent through her.

Stepping up to her, Dr. Michael peers into her eyes.

"If you insult me, I will take it for a while." He grabs her shoulders, his lips running over hers and his teeth pulling, nibbling her lower lip when she does not respond.

Her clawed hands run over his ass, then as his tongue darts in her mouth, her slap against his ass pushes his pelvis against her. His hands roam over her back, fondling and gently squeezing the skinny ass he had slapped moments before.

They draw apart, breath coming fast. Arms holding them only inches apart. "We need to feed you more girl. That ass is as thin as a bone." Dr. Michael says.

Brows lower as Amanda runs her knee under and against the hard boner in the Dr. Michael's pants. "For a man dying, your body seems to be working exceptionally well." Her breathing speeds up as Dr. Michael's hand squeezes her upper breast.

Her low moan encourages Dr. Michael, who reaches his hand under her loose shirt before she can stop him. They both freeze as Dr. Michael feels first her small B cup breast and then above it, her fuller C cup breast both with hard nipples. Trying to pull away, she is met with firm resistance from Dr. Michael.

"Amazing, there must be karma after all." He continues playing with the one breast and slips the bra under it so he can lean forward and take first the smaller one and then the bigger one in his mouth through her shirt. She moans, her hands frozen on his shoulders. Wanting him to continue and afraid he is doing it for the wrong reasons.

"Karma? Were you evil in another life?" Her sarcasm

brings a not so gentle bite and tug on her nipple. When he pulls his mouth away, two large wet spots are sticking her shirt to her left breasts.

"No. I never held or kissed a woman's breast in almost 76 years of life. Now, the woman I love has four, so I can begin making up for lost time with each of them." Dr. Michael is looking into her shocked eyes. They both begin leaning forward until their breaths are mixing.

"You love me?" She whispers.

Dr. Michael reaches up drawing her down to him as she leans down he breathes into her ear, "Yes." His simple heartfelt answer sends a spike of adrenaline through her.

While they hold each other tightly, the back door opens with a squeal of rusty hinges.

"Yes Mrs. Collins, I know it is my turn to take out the trash." Roger slams the new screen door off of the kitchen, it echoes around the yard. They both step back smoothing their clothes and standing still hoping he will not see them.

Of course, his eyes work fine, almost as good as a Weres. "You two are up early." Then Roger stops, looking harder from one to the other and he begins laughing. "Or up really late. By all means continue. I love a good porn in the early morning."

"Roger, we need milk and eggs again." Mrs. Collins' calling out the back door is followed by a click and the porch light was lit. Then another and another and the yard lights were on. Mrs. Collins steps onto the porch staring from Amanda's shirt to the bulge in Dr. Michael's pants. The bulge is beginning to leave a wet spot on the slacks Dr. Michael is wearing. Luckily, Mrs. Collins being only human, never sees that.

"Well Amanda, I hope you will allow me to call on you again. I had a lovely time." Dr. Michael speaks at the top of his voice, bringing a chuckle from Roger and a creak from the screen door as Mrs. Collins leans forward to hear better.

"Yes, please call on me soon," Amanda speaks in a hush and then kisses Dr. Michael on the mouth. A brief, hot, moist meeting of their lips that for all its brevity makes up for it with a heartfelt tenderness and longing. Then she is on her way to the lab where she sleeps.

Dr. Michael waves to Mrs. Collins. "Roger the truck is too loud it will wake the kids. My Cadillac is still warm, I will drive you to the market for those eggs."

Roger still chuckling heads for the Cadillac after dropping the trash bag in the burn barrel. "Don't forget the milk! Three gallons, whole milk organic, if they have it, or Alexis won't drink it!" Mrs. Collins calls out. She watches them both wave and get in the car.

———————————

The market in Eisworth is not open until 1:30 pm on Sundays. The gas station sometimes opens on Sunday, by appointment only. The next nearest town is Burlingame, a fifty-minute drive each way.

Dr. Michael is both ashamed that it takes the first 15 minutes of the trip for his wood to soften and also proud of the hardness. *They have mentioned Pride magic several times. I wonder if I could ask if that might account for my renewed sexual responses.* While Dr. Michael has never lost his desires, even at his age, he has noticed a decided lack of rigidity, that the last couple of years since his cancer had gotten worse, has begun to lessen.

"Roger, do you know much about Pride magic?" Dr. Michael asks.

At the same time Roger says, "Dr. Michael do you know anything about Alzheimer disease?"

Then they both say "What?" then chuckle.

"You go ahead first Roger." Dr. Michael says.

"Well, I was wondering if you had any experience with Alzheimer disease." Looking out the window, Roger is tense.

"Well I have never been diagnosed as having it, and personally, I feel I have an excellent memory especially for my age." Dr. Michael is confused as to why anyone would think he has it.

"No, that is not it. Never mind, what were you saying?" Roger says, waving his hand in surrender.

"Are you having some problems with memory Roger?" Dr. Michael perks up turning off the radio that has been playing a blues cd. The sky is lighting up with the newly risen sun.

Taking a deep breath, Roger begins, "I have always been careful, you know, since I was changed into this." Roger gestures to himself. "Then when we started seeing the Freaks and learning more about them I figured I was just lucky."

"Go on Roger, I'm a Doctor." Dr. Michael glances at Roger waiting, not wanting to scare him into clamming up.

The car swerves, narrowly avoiding a deer in the road. Staring down the road Dr. Michael feels his heart beating faster but not racing as it would have been a couple of months ago.

Roger smiles, "No need to kill me doc. I'll spill." Rogers' joke brings a smile from Dr. Michael that leaves as soon as he glances over and recognizes the dread on Roger's face.

"My memory has been getting worse, it's harder to remember things. I carry a notebook and try to write everything down. That helps some but the simplest things are escaping me these last couple weeks." Roger watches Dr. Michael with the corner of his eye as he takes out his notebook.

"I forgot the groceries yesterday, the trash and I'm not sure if I ate lunch or dinner but I remember breakfast so well I can still taste the char from where the last strip of bacon had fallen on the burner." Roger swallows holding his pen to write down what Dr. Michael has to say.

"You had lunch with us. You played with the kids, starting a food fight that ended with Daisy yelling at Aaron for joining in." Dr. Michael slows as he turns down old highway 16.

"I was always good at food fights in school." Roger's voice is low and lost.

"What other symptoms are you having?" Dr. Michael slows to drive around the curvy country road at 15 mph as another deer races the Cadillac. When the clock on the dash moves from 5:11 to 5:15 he asks again. "Roger, what other symptoms are you having?"

"Sleep, I can't sleep. I toss and turn or just stare at something in my room. I know I don't sleep because I'm aware that I'm supposed to be sleeping. I'm tired, exhausted even but can't sleep."

Dr. Michael is silent for a few minutes while he considers how to handle this. "That could be a big part of the memory loss. Sleep deprivation can affect memory, cognitive function, even basic motor functions."

Roger sits like he has not heard a word and stares into space. The next 40 minutes pass very slowly for Dr. Michael. As he puts the Cadillac in park at the Corner Market and Deli, he looks at Roger who sits immobile.

Once Dr. Michael is out of the car and going inside to get the groceries, Roger gets out following Dr. Michael. "You really think it could just be sleep deprivation? I thought this market was further than this. You should slow down Doc going to get a ticket with that lead foot."

Dr. Michael stumbles "I will do that Roger." After getting the 3 gallons of milk, one organic, the last the market has, and two regular they get back in the car.

"Roger, maybe Amanda and I should do a few tests, just to be safe." Dr. Michael watches the clock to time the response.

"Sure thing Doc. and that will give you more time

with Amanda, wink wink." The completely normal, no delay reply worries Dr. Michael more than if there had been a delay.

The ride back to the house is filled with the sounds of 70's country. Tear in your beer type of tunes that grates on Dr. Michael's ears. Since Roger has shut off the CD and played with the radio. This might have something to do with his speed up on the long winding driveway to the house. Speeding around the last 90-degree curve before the house comes into view "Shit!"

Roger grabs the dash, bracing himself as the car swerves to the side. The tires spin on the gravel trying for purchase with no success. As the Cadillac slows to a stop, it is 500 feet off the drive. Dr. Michael has a death grip on the wheel and Roger is waving the dust from his open window trying to see what exactly had been in the road.

As the dust settles, Dr. Michael's grip relaxes on the wheel. Rolling the driver's window down to match the passenger side window they hear frightened voices from the drive. As the last of the dust settles, they saw Tommy and Peggy pulling on a large wolf trying to get him to go with them.

Roger and Dr. Michael get out of the car and begin walking toward the kids. With a sigh, Tommy straightens stepping in front of the wolf. The wolf, a beautiful silver black with the deepest blue eyes Dr. Michael has ever seen shoves his nose into Tommy's side. When Tommy begins scratching behind the wolf's ears, the tail begins a steady thumping on the ground.

"Kids, step away from the wolf and Roger will deal

with it. Walk slowly towards us." Dr. Michael speaks slowly to not scare the wolf and endanger the kids.

Peggy stops hugging the wolf and joins her brother. Both kids are covered in the dust from the driveway. Tommy has torn his jeans and has tears in his eyes. "She's ours, and you can't hurt her!" Tommy's fearful declaration brings the wolf to its feet.

Stopping ten feet away, Roger begins to circle around, trying to get behind the wolf. When the wolf shoves between the kids to see who or what is going on, the bright pink and a purple scarf wrapped around its neck becomes apparent.

"Sapphire is our friend. Roger, you said you would talk to Dad so he would make Mom let us have a dog." Tommy looks betrayed as he glares at Roger.

"That is not a dog, it's a wolf. A damn big one too." Roger says freezing when the wolf growls at him.

The wolf's head is just over four-feet high when sitting on its haunches. As she stands up, an impromptu pair of saddles are visible, tied on her back. A pair of jeans used as a cinch strap and a sweater as a saddle blanket. The wolf shakes her massive head looking from Roger to the kids and back confused.

"See Peggy, I said we couldn't trust Uncle Roger, he is just a grown up and only pretends to understand. Get Sapphire hidden and don't let her come back or they will kill her, like Old Yeller." Tommy draws a deep breath, closing his eyes for a moment.

"Now wait a minute, you know you can trust me." Roger sounds lost and dismayed.

Peggy is crying and shaking as she climbs on the back of the wolf. Tommy turns, opening his eyes and ties her feet to the "stirrups" a knotted hole in the leg of the jeans. "Sapphire, take her to the hideout and stay hidden."

Once she is firmly on her back, she grips the ends of the scarf in both hands. "Wait, we don't want to hurt her." Dr. Michael begins, but it is too late.

Tommy yells, "Go!" The wolf starts walking toward the tree line along the creek in the distance.

"Roger, you distract the wolf. I'll grab her off its back and take her to the car." Dr. Michael begins moving up parallel to the wolf as Roger lopes past it to cut it off.

"Peggy, you have to do it! She won't run otherwise!" Tommy cries before he closes his eyes and begins breathing deeply.

"Yippee Ki Yay Scumbags!" The girl screams around her tears. Roger spreads his arms to block the wolf. Dr. Michael runs in to grab the girl. The wolf takes off like a jet. One long graceful leap and her back legs catch the shocked Dr. Michael on the back of his head and pushes off.

Dr. Michael stumbles, his forehead bleeding where the scratch from Sapphires claws had dug in. The wolf falls and lets out a yip and half howl, almost matching the yells from Peggy.

Roger runs after the wolf or begins to. Tommy opens his eyes that have started to glow a dull silver. As he moves his hands, his lips move in concentration. Roger draws to a halt, swatting at colored balls zipping around his head. When his hand catches a blue one it bursts, covering his hand with water so cold it freezes as it touches his skin.

Dr. Michael, oblivious to Roger, colored balls and everything is in hot pursuit of the wolf and Peggy. Roger stumbles to a halt trying to get the ice off his hand.

Tommy turns to look after Dr. Michael and drawing in a deep breath moves both his hands up and then spread them out. The sudden burst of wind hits Dr. Michael's back, knocking him down. The wind dies and Tommy passes out. Already to the creek, the faint howl of Sapphire is fading as she continues running.

––––––––––––––––

Daisy is pacing, dried tears staining her cheeks. "I never should have moved out here. Werecats, wild animals, she isn't speaking to anyone, just continuing the ongoing condemnation of herself, the Pride and especially her fiancé Aaron.

"Brother Lion says Tommy will be fine, he just over exerted himself and his body is resting," Aaron speaks slowly, trying to sound reassuring while his worried eyes say otherwise.

Dr. Michael walks in drying his hands. "Well, Roger shouldn't lose any of the fingers."

Daisy stiffens, "How do you even know it was Tommy?" She holds onto her anger as her only defense to fear.

"I was there, remember." He speaks calmly, having experience in dealing with traumatized parents as a doctor. "Also, Brother Lion and Derek confirm that the children have been learning to use Astral Magic." Dr. Michael stumbles over the words. Learning that Werecats, Werewolves and such are real is less troubling than that magic is all around them.

The living room is not as crowded as it has been in the past. Bryan is left without a room and with everyone wanting to watch over Tommy as they pass in and out, a constant flow of traffic was inevitable.

The couch is threadbare and the blue roses are faded. The blankets are all tucked around Tommy who is propped up on several pillows. Mrs. Collins is busy, as usual, in the kitchen.

This time, she is baking the kid's favorite triple chocolate fudge cake. The gummy bears on the top are all red and orange. Peggy swears they taste better than the others. Despite her eating the others that don't make the cut. Mrs. Collins sniffs as she remembers the kids playing under foot and learning to bake from her over the last couple of weeks.

"Aaron, you be sure and get those steaks to Brother Lion and the others. I don't care if the wolf is not an ordinary wolf, it will still love the prime rib." Mrs. Collins calls from the kitchen.

Aaron calls back to Mrs. Collins. "Thank you." He is too choked up to say more, worry about Peggy lost with only a wolf. The fact that the North Dakota Werewolf pack has accepted the sale of South Dakota to the Pride, doing only a small amount to reduce the dangers that Peggy could face alone.

Mrs. Collins turns back to sorting gummy bears for the top of the cake. "You tell her to get home safe, or there might not be enough cake left for her." Mrs. Collins tries for gruff but her voice is a bit shrill towards the end.

Aaron nods, heading out the door with a bag of sandwiches, a ten-pound prime rib roast and a pink and purple coat with faux fur that matches the scarf last seen on the wolf's neck.

Walking at a fast trot, he follows the trail towards the creek, where they think the wolf might have run to. It is past noon and Aaron is hurrying back out to help look again. Halfway to the creek, he spots Bryan in the distance working his way parallel. Nose working overtime trying to catch a scent of wolf, Peggy or anything that might lead them to her.

When Bryan smells the food and Aaron on the breeze, he waves and they begin walking toward each other while still heading in the general direction of the creek. Bryan is dressed in his coveralls and still has the tool belt on, which he was wearing when Roger stumbled into the dining room holding Tommy in his arms.

Dr. Michael has already been following the wolf and Peggy but a wolf running over prairie leaves a slight trace of its passing in the dry soil. Even with the added 60 pounds of Peggy.

Aaron and Bryan are out of breath as they pause beside each other. "Any luck yet?"

Bryan shrugs, "Brother Lion and Derek think the wolf went into the creek but we haven't found where they came out again."

Bryan eats two of the ham and cheese sandwiches while they stand looking around. "What about scent? Don't Werecats have a good sense of smell, you know, to track them by scent?"

"Yes we do, not as a good as a Werewolf but better than humans. The problem is, we spent all morning looking for a scent of the wolf. Found a few of Werewolves but they were older, from when the North Dakota Werewolf pack was trying to scare us."

A low whistle from across the creek and south reaches them. They both begin walking in that direction. "Then everyone met up at the Cadillac where it was stuck in the sandy soil beside the drive. Roger and Dr. Michael swears the wolf was all over in the drive. Rolling around and playing with the kids."

"So you have the scent now, what's the problem?" Aaron sounds frustrated and confused.

"That's just it, there is no scent of a wolf or Werewolf anywhere around there." Bryan seems angry. "Then we all split up again looking for any sign we could find."

Aaron grunts in disbelief and shock as they both move into a trot as a second louder whistle reaches them. They cross the creek in three large steps, the water only reaches their knees but the mud sucking at their feet only lets go with loud slurping sounds.

A few minutes later they spot Derek, Alexis and Roger all in a cluster, looking at the little clearing where Alexis had been possessed by the ancient wood spirit.

"I know what it told me Derek and no matter what

you or Brother Lion think, it is the only option I see."
Alexis is pale even for her. The pale complexion and red
hair leaving her unable to tan even when the Werelion
that is her mates lets her outside long enough.

Derek shakes his head no. "It's too dangerous. Even
with Brother Lion and me pulling on the Pride magic, we
are unable to get it completely out of you."

"What's going on?" Bryan asks, the hair on the back
of his neck rising as a breeze blows through the tree
covered spot by the creek. The scent of blood is still
fresh, almost three weeks after the Freak and Werewolf
had been killed here.

"The Spirit says it will part the veil and show Alexis
where Peggy and the wolf are. In exchange, it wants to
ride with her again." Roger explains staring at the wooded
area.

"Is that such a big deal? Can't Brother Lion and
Derek just force it out again like last time? Peggy has
been gone for almost the entire day; it will be dark soon."
Aaron's fear and frustration are thick in his voice.

"No, it's not that simple. Last time Alexis made an
offering of blood. This time, we don't have a Freak or
Werewolf to give it. That means a blood and life sacrifice.
If Alexis gives her own blood, she might never be free."

"I will offer my blood then." Aaron begins walking
toward the trees, determined to save the girl he considers
his daughter.

Alexis tries to run after him but Derek grabs her and
holds her off the ground. "Put me down! It will kill him!"
Alexis beats at Derek's arms but all she accomplishes is

new bruises on her hands.

Roger runs after Aaron, who is reaching the shade of the towering trees. "You can have my blood if you show us where Peggy is." Aaron uses his pocket knife to cut his finger letting drops of his blood hit the muddy creek water.

The trees shake and Roger reaches Aaron as the ground opens under him. Roger drags Aaron by his collar and heaves him back away from the creek. "Tell Derek I can't live as a Freak." Without looking back, he steps towards the hole but it closes before he sinks in.

"No! Take me and help Alexis find Peggy." Roger demands, striding under the trees. He strips the bandage off his damaged hand. The patches of missing skin where the ice had been drip blood and ointment as he strides under the trees. A low moan reaches out from the trees.

As he steps completely into the thickening shadows, they reach out and fold around him. Then, he is gone from sight. Aaron stands staring into the clearing where Roger had been. Alexis stops struggling in Derek's arms and he sets her on her feet but doesn't let go of her.

"He chose to go, Dr. Michael said he is having problems with memory lapses and the arthritis pain is getting worse. Tell me when the spirit shows you Peggy so we can get her. Then Brother Lion and I will try and bring Roger back from where the spirit took him." Derek speaks confidently but his eyes have tears barely held back as he looks where one of his best friends for 60 years has disappeared.

Alexis relaxes in his grip nodding. "She is over there

under the crab apple tree."

Derek turns to look as does Bryan. "I don't see anything, are you sure Alexis?" Derek leans forward straining to see what Alexis is pointing at.

"Right there, are you blind?" Alexis demands, pointing again. This time, when Derek leans even farther out, his hands loosen on her arms. She twists, welcoming the spirit in and using its strength to break free. She runs for the creek. "It won't work without me! I can't have more people die for me!"

Derek races after her but the ground opens under her before she even reaches the creek. When Derek gets there, the hole is already filling up. He screams in rage. Digging with his claws hysterically, the hole fills faster than he can dig. Then with a sigh, the sandy dirt blows into his face knocking him back.

Bryan runs under the trees screaming "Alexis!"

Derek joins him a moment later and attacks the first tree he comes to. Stripping it of bark in seconds. His claws and fangs eager to rend and kill to get his mate back. Then an intense pain filled gasp fills the clearing. "Derek why are you attacking me?" The shock and betrayal in Alexis' voice has the effect of ice cold water thrown in his face.

"She is in limbo, between worlds where spirits dwell. Not fully in this realm but tied to it as is the spirit of this place. If we kill the trees and grass that anchor the spirit to our world, it will fade into the other." Brother Lion speaks in Bryan and Derek's minds.

"I will try and reach her to bring her back. Be

patient Brother, in limbo, time is all one piece. An hour here might be a year there or the opposite. Care for our Pride until I return."

As Derek feels the presence of Brother Lion leave, he looks in that place within himself where Brother Lion lives and sees the Werecat body of Brother Lion sleeping.

"Yippee Ki Yay!" Turning, Derek and Bryan see Peggy riding on the wolf across the creek coming to a stop looking at them. "Can we come home yet? Sapphire is tired and I'm hungry." Aaron rushes, from where he is standing in shock, to her.

Chapter 9

"It's been five days Derek. Matteas is sick with worry over Sabrina and attacked Amanda yesterday. Dr. Michael almost got killed jumping in to protect Amanda." Derek sits in the clearing where Alexis had disappeared with Roger. His clothes are stained, he stinks and has refused to eat since Alexis disappeared. Bryan is once more standing in front of Derek trying to get his attention.

"You are in charge until I get my mate back. Deal with it." Derek does not even look up from where he sits unmoving, glaring at what he considers is Alexis' tree. The one he had attacked and stripped of its bark.

Bryan closes his eyes, one black and blue, and takes a deep breath. Looking at the tree, he shakes his head. The first day Derek had demanded tree salve. An expensive, organic mixture that helps trees heal after being pruned. Nurseries use it on the most expensive trees. Derek had used it to put all the stripped bark back in place.

"Derek, if you do not come back now_." Bryan steps back at the rage on Derek's face. He looks homicidal before he closes his eyes.

"I will come back with my mate, soon. Be sure everything is ready for the trip I promised her." Derek sighs as his shoulders relax.

"This then is the great Derek, reduced to a pitiful remnant of himself." The sneering voice is standing by the creek. "I have defeated Bryan and that makes me acting Alpha."

Derek turns to peer at who else has come to interrupt his vigil. Felix is wearing satin and silk. Blues and greens to better show off his creamy skin. He is wearing long sleeves which is unusual. He prefers to show off his toned body too much to wear sleeves. His jeans are designer skinny jeans that, like their name, are skin tight showing every inch of his six-foot body.

Derek frowns, turning his back to Bryan. At six-foot-seven, Bryan towers over almost everyone in his natural state. Today, his shoulders are hunched. His black and blue eye is only the first of his many bruises. His arm is held across his chest as if it pains him, or his ribs do. Looking at the red soaking through his clean jeans, he is hiding worse wounds.

"He challenged you for leadership?" Derek asks as he once more returns his gaze to Felix. The real question that was left unsaid but that Bryan replies to was if he had defeated Bryan.

"He beat me, and would have killed me, as is his right, if Matteas and Amanda had not interfered. I am here to ask you to take back leadership. Then I can leave the Pride without having to live knowing that I left him as Alpha over my family." Bryan speaks the last sentence

166

sounding lost and alone.

Derek sighs, shifting shoulders that have not moved much in days. "Felix, this is odd, even for you. Have you finally lost the last of your loyalty to the Pride?"

Felix shakes his head angrily with rage. "No! I have been hunting the Other. The one that wants the Major and all of us dead. While you have been here catering to a human and when I come home, what do I find? A strong Alpha preparing our Pride for battle?"

Bryan turns red and steps toward Felix. "You wish for me to finish you? End your pathetic life that you wasted on a possessed man that failed as Alpha?"

"I accept your challenge, Felix. I will meet you at noon tomorrow. Until then, you are only a challenger to the Alpha, no more than that. Now leave this place, a challenger may not stay with the Pride the night before their challenge is answered." Derek lowers his head breathing deeply as the exhaustion he has been holding back swamps him.

"Why wait? Face me now or admit you are no more than the cur I thought you were." Felix steps into the creek spitting and hissing in anger. The two feet of muddy red swirl around his feet, the mud begins to pull him in. "Yiiieee! Trap, you cheat!"

Derick staggers as he gets to his feet, his legs have cramped from not moving for so many days. He almost falls but Bryan catches him and half supports him from the side. "She lives." The relief in Derek's voice is echoed in Bryan's grin. "Felix, for the years we were as a family, go and prepare for tomorrow. Before the Heart of the

Pride destroys you." Derek's voice grows stronger with each word.

Felix manages to get out of the creek. One shoe is lost in the mud, his designer jeans now stained with mud, and black muck that stinks of rot and dead things. Getting out of the water his makeup is smeared from wiping his face, the scars on his cheek are revealed. Without a word, Felix turns and walks away only glancing back once, his face is uncertain as he stares at the creek.

"Help me to the house Bryan and explain how you lost to Felix," Derek says walking stiffly away from the clearing.

It's a long walk back to the house. Even with his burst of energy it has been over five days and nights since he has slept. Over four since he has moved out of his sitting position. If he had not felt Brother Lion push him to deal with the threat to the Pride, he might still be sitting there.

That touch, as brief and light as it was, reminded him that he is not alone. His heart and his Brother are still alive. Brother Lion's body shares space within his aura still. The claws, fangs and fur show that Derek is still a Werelion.

"He came the day before yesterday. Said the Major and Sabrina are moving in on the Other. He would not give details only that we needed to prepare to go and help the Major." Bryan walks along beside Derek, still limping from his humiliating defeat at the hands of Felix.

"Enough about that. Tell me about our family, the Pride. Did Tommy wake as Brother Lion thought he would?" Derek asks walking along unaided but going slow as his muscles threaten to cramp if pushes too far too fast.

"Well, after we all left you to wait for Alexis….

…The house looks the same but feels emptier. It seems silly but Bryan thinks the grass and house are already missing Alexis. His heart is shattered, never having gotten the courage to tell her how he felt about her before Derek and Brother Lion claimed her. His ancestors in Gaul would have said he is soul sick.

Carrying Peggy in his arms, limp and sound asleep, as her wolf walks beside him is probably not the best way to return. "That mangy thing killed her! My baby, oh my baby." Daisy comes a few steps out of the kitchen door only to turn around, reach back inside and grab the shotgun kept beside the door in case of trouble.

"Daisy, no, wait, she is sleeping." Aaron hurries forward putting himself between the gun and the wolf.

Daisy is normally a practical woman and not prone to rash or impulsive behavior. In the last three months, her life has been turned upside down. Falling in love and getting engaged to Aaron is possibly the best thing she has gotten in her life since her kids were born.

At the same time, Aaron brought bikers, Weres of all kinds, magic and now her worst fears have been realized. One of her children missing all day, possibly dead, with a wild wolf. Her other child passed out after doing magic that she still thinks might be the work of the devil, as her Pa taught her at church when she was small.

All of this pushes Daisy over the edge. She pumps

the shotgun once and fires. The wolf has circled out from behind Aaron to check on Peggy. The shotgun blast hits it full in the side, knocking it down. Peggy wakes up, saw her beloved wolf down and screams "No! Sapphire no." Bryan lets her climb down from his arms. He is still numb with grief and not thinking clearly.

Daisy, seeing her daughter hysterical on the wolf she has just shot, drops the shotgun and begins shaking. The back screen door opens and Tommy sees the wolf down and his sister hysterical. Tommy screams "No!" then runs to the wolf as well.

Aaron steps up and holds Daisy but the look on his face is grim and filled with sadness. He is reproving himself for not being faster and saving the wolf before Daisy could shoot. The kids are inconsolable.

Mrs. Collins runs out the door to see what is happening. Her hands still wet from washing her hands after using the bathroom. Looking from Bryan, standing with a dazed look on his face, to the children Mrs. Collins goes to Bryan and drags him to the picnic table pushing him down until he sits….."

Bryan continues speaking to Derek on the walk back, "You know, Mrs. Collins might look like a frail old lady but when she gets her back up, there is no budging her. I think she and Alexis have a bond like we do in the pack. Alexis told me once that Mrs. Collins was like a favorite Aunt to her even before her mom was killed, then after that, she was an aunt one minute and replacement mom the next." Bryan stops, looking around the deserted yard.

Derek walks over and sits at the picnic table. "Go

on, what happened after Daisy killed the wolf?"

"Well, Daisy did and didn't kill the wolf......"

... Once Mrs. Collins heard about Derek and Alexis she sits down beside Bryan and holds him. "I know you love her. You also love him like an older brother, go ahead and cry."

Bryan had gone to war at 17, like Derek, when the Major recruited them from the streets and forged the paperwork to get them in. Even as a child, Bryan was not one to cry. Hold other weaker children while they cried yes, but not cry himself.

Maybe that is why when Mrs. Collins held him he starts and can't stop crying. "He is my brother. How can I be in love with his wife?" The fact that the wedding hasn't happened yet makes no difference, Derek and Alexis are mated and in the Pride, that means more than a human ceremony anyway.

"You never did anything dishonorable and why shouldn't you love Alexis? She is a warm-hearted young woman that has been there for you since you met her." Mrs. Collins holds him while he cries himself out. It seems to be hours but is only a few minutes.

It would have probably lasted longer if the kids and the wolf had not interrupted his cry.

"Run Sapphire, hurry, before they try and murder you again!" Tommy cries out as he and Peggy are pushing at the wolf to run. The wolf seems unconcerned with her earlier encounter with a shotgun. The wolf is standing, licking Tommy's face after not seeing him all day.

Daisy and Aaron are standing staring in shock at the

beautiful Wolf. A wolf with no sign of ever being shot. Bryan leaves Mrs. Collins sitting at the picnic table watching. He moves around to approach the kids and wolf from behind.

The wolf, seeing Bryan turns and tilts her huge head to watch the Weretiger approach. It is not until Peggy sees Bryan walking up and yells, "Run Sapphire, he will kill you!" The wolf doesn't react other than to look at Bryan.

The wolf stands in one fluid motion and puts her body between Peggy and Bryan. Her growl is deep and rumbling. The ice blue eyes seem to absorb light into their azure depths and swallow it. The fangs are as long as a Weretigers and being one, Bryan should know. He stops moving and backs up two steps.

Daisy, meanwhile, is calling, "Come away from the animal it's scared and might hurt you." She speaks in an almost normal voice that speaks well of her as a strong woman. It is just as well that Aaron has the shotgun, and she cannot reach it at the moment, no sense testing her limits.

Mrs. Collins shocks everyone by walking right up to the kids and wolf. "Oh, Pffsh! Stop that, he's not going to hurt the kids, now stop or no more of my hot dogs and pork chops for you." Her tone is firm but exasperated rather than threatening.

The wolf sits down and looks abashed of all things. The kids look at Mrs. Collins waiting for her pronouncement. "So, this is where all my leftovers have been going?"

The kids nod their heads yes. Peggy, through her arms around the wolf. "Sapphire needed the food Grams, she was ever so skinny."

"Malarkey, she looks as fat as a bull calf." Whatever else she is going to say we will never know. For that is when she realizes that Peggy has called her Grams. Her eyes fill with tears and both kids hug her.

"Please don't let them hurt her. She's a very good dog and we will keep taking care of her, honest we will." The Grams or the wolf licking her face while she cries cinches it.

"Of course you can keep her, and no one will hurt her, or they will not be eating at my table." Grams is jostled as Daisy joins their little group.

Once Daisy sees the wolf is uninjured and has gotten her share of licks from Sapphire and hugs full of promises and begging, she makes her pronouncement, "This is our family wolf, and that is that. I'm sure Aaron will make a dog house for her."

Aaron frowns, not sure when he will have time for that with Alexis and Roger going into limbo and Derek sitting in vigil waiting for them to return. Not to mention the roof leaking, old wiring in the house blowing fuses because it needs to be switched to breakers or the power company will cut them off next month. His list of things that needs doing just keeps growing.

Amanda and Dr. Michael drive up in the old truck, which is splattered with mud. Seeing the crowd around the children and the wolf, Amanda runs over to them. Dr. Michael hurries to Bryan since he is the one that looks hurt.

Bryan has not moved other than to look over the wolf and breathing in and out deeply a few times. When Amanda is standing with Aaron on the other side, he asks, "Amanda, do you smell a wolf at all?"

Frowning, Amanda sniffs and shakes her head. "Neither do I and I saw it get shot with the shotgun."

"Did the kids heal it?" Dr. Michael asks remembering the colored balls, Rogers frozen hand and the wind knocking him down earlier in the day.

"No, we didn't heal Sapphire. I don't think she can be hurt by things like shotguns and stuff." The boy says shrugging, only pausing for a moment before rubbing Sapphires belly, who promptly rolls over so he an get the itchy spot under her front arm pit.

Swallowing, it is Aaron who asks the next question, "Why do you think she can't be hurt by shotguns?"

Tommy and Peggy look nervous but sigh as they turn to face Aaron. Sapphire, no longer the center of attention, stands up and puts her nose in Daisy's face to get an ear scratch. That exact moment, as Daisy is looking into Sapphire's azure eyes, seeing herself fall into them as she reaches to scratch the ears that Peggy says. "Oh because she's a ghost wolf. Watch. Sapphire fade."

Sapphire winks her right eye at Daisy whose hand is scratching behind her ears when she fades. Her hand passes through where she used to be. "Ahhhh." Thunk is the only sound anyone hears or makes as Daisy collapses after her loud sigh, out cold. A wolf, she has come to terms with, her kids learning magic from a Werelion okay, bikers shooting up her town, she has dealt with and is pressing on with all of that. Yet, a ghost wolf is more than she is ready for.

What happens next is not really anyone's fault. The kids are worried they will be told that they can't keep Sapphire after all. Bryan is having a really bad day with his brother, woman he loves and one of his best friends Roger all gone, one way or another.

Dr. Michael is reassessing rather it could have been his dead father's ghost that spoke to him years ago.

And Aaron, well Aaron has been blamed for everything that has gone wrong with the world since the dawn of time. Don't get me wrong, he is divorced, so he knows that is what to expect when he got engaged again, and right then he is enjoying a moment when no one is calling him names or telling him to fix something. Or at least, that is the way he feels right then.

Of them all, only Sapphire seems to want to wake Daisy up. After all, she had been getting that spot right behind the ear that was itchy. So Sapphire reappears and licks Daisy in the face a few times until she wakes up. She is looking in Sapphire's eyes, still half asleep when Mrs. Collins stands up and backs away looking uneasy.

Bryan moves up behind her and reaches for Sapphire's back. Daisy came all the way awake as Bryan touches Sapphire. She screams bloody murder and Sapphire whines and fades out. This time, Bryan goes along for the ride……

"I don't want to think about that time. I couldn't breathe and it was black, not dark black but the complete absence of all light. That is all I'm saying about it. Anyway, when Sapphire finally brought me back everyone else was gone from the yard. The kids swore to everyone that I would come back with Sapphire they just didn't know when."

Derek can think of nothing to say in shock over the news and he feels Bryan's trembling at the mere thought of where ever he had gone with Sapphire. "Bryan, I'm exhausted, can you help me get to my room? I want to smell Alexis and then I can sleep. After I nap, you can tell me how Felix beat you."

Bryan sighs in relief that Derek will not press for details of his trip with Sapphire. He helps Derek upstairs and tucks him in. Derek inhales the scent of Alexis and is asleep in moments. Bryan stands guard outside the room, turning the rest of the Pride away after telling them that Derek and Felix will fight to see who will be Alpha the next day at noon.

———————————————

"I can take him, Major. He is lost without Alexis, and if the others are right, his vaunted Brother Lion is gone now too. Thanks to your help I can kill Derek and lead the Pride." Felix smiles relishing the image of Derek begging for his life at Felix's feet.

"No, the timing is wrong, I need Roger and the only ones that might be able to bring him back are Derek and Brother Lion. Wait until Roger is back and in my hands, then I will give you enough serum that you will be able to kill both Brother Lion and Derek. You will never really

be accepted as the Unit's Alpha until they are both dead."
The Major's voice is commanding, and as usual, he says
all the right things to get Felix to do his bidding.

What the Major doesn't know this time is that Felix
has already taken a double dose of the serum so he can,
not only kill Derek but humiliate him. "Okay sure, but
soon, I won't wait for long, it has to be soon. Remember
you get Roger but nothing is to happen to Amanda, she is
under my protection."

"Of course Felix, I know how much your half-sister
means to you. Now remember what you are to say. Don't
let me down." The line goes dead and Felix stands
shivering and sweating at the same time as he moves in
jerky starts and stops. A smile covers his face as he heads
for the meeting with Derek as the sun moves closer to
noon.

The sun is close to its peak, in no more than fifteen
minutes, noon will be on them. Derek looks like a new
Werelion. Sixteen hours of sleep where he could smell
Alexis and Brother Lion has done wonders for him. He is
wearing a clean loose pair of jeans and a canvas shirt that
Mrs. Collins has selected for him. It is blue and thick
enough that it might slow Felix's claws.

Ordinarily, Derek and Brother Lion would wipe the
floor with Felix without breaking a sweat. Of course, the
same is true for Bryan, who is still a little sore from
having his ass handed to him by Felix. No one, Derek
asked, had a clue of why Felix is suddenly so much faster

and stronger than he has ever been before.

Derek had spent a long time on the phone with the Major's lieutenant demanding answers about Sabrina and Shawn's whereabouts. Again, with vague reassurances about them being with the Major as they move in to capture a top lieutenant of the Other's.

Everything sounds right, all the answers are in line with his last instructions to Sabrina and Shawn. Infiltrate the Major's command structure and stick with him until they find answers. No matter how many times Derek says everything sounds fine and Felix has indeed returned better than ever in fighting ability, if not in brains, it still feels like he is missing something.

Derek stands, waiting in the hot sun, using the time to stretch and exercise. Everyone is dealing with the stress of the day differently. It is hard for everyone not a Were to understand that even if Derek wins, Bryan cannot stay in the Pride any longer.

He had been acting Alpha when Felix challenged him and he accepted on Derek's behalf using the authority Derek entrusted in him. Then he had failed the Pride and worse, he is still alive. He is pushing the limits of the Pride magic that guides and rules the Weres in so many ways. He has a headache from ignoring the urge to leave.

Amanda is sharpening her claws and preparing to kill her half-brother herself if he manages to win. She hopes no one else knows how they are related. She has tried to love her half-brother but he always takes the easy way out. Now, since she suspects that he has cheated somehow or he could never have beaten Bryan, it was worse.

The fact that he has tried to get her in bed since they were teenagers is a deep part of her shame. No matter how nice she tried to tell him that they are related and she will never think of him that way, he never seems to understand. He always says the right things and pretends everything is normal but she still catches him staring at her when she is swimming or watching her as she walks away.

Dr. Michael is hurrying back with a trunk full of bandages, antiseptic, cauterizers and anything he thinks he might need to patch up Derek after the fight. Weres heal fast but they also deal a lot of damage, and Dr. Michael is determined to be prepared.

The kids are supposed to be in the house but have snuck out and are hiding under the picnic table where anyone looking can see them. Today, everyone is too busy looking down the drive for Felix to notice they are not where they are supposed to be. Except Mrs. Collins, who understands their need to see firsthand their family fight for all their lives.

It is the kids who jump up and announce, "He's almost here. He just stopped at the last curve."

Derek turns to look at the kids at the picnic table. The ghost wolf is standing by them getting a good scratch. Apparently, the kids had the wolf out scouting, good thinking. It reminds Derek of how much he misses having the extra senses of Brother Lion.

Sure enough, as Daisy makes a beeline for the kids,

Felix walks into view. Derek remains leaning against the cottonwood watching him approach. Felix's normally neat attire is wrinkled like he has slept in it. As he stops 15 feet from Derek, the sweat staining his shirt and ruddy complexion is obvious.

Despite being an arrogant pain in Derek and Brother Lion's ass for decades, Felix has always been loyal to the Pride. Never fond of Derek or his leadership he has saved the lives of Amanda and others several times. *Major, you have burned what little goodwill I had left for you by using Felix's weaknesses to get him killed.*

Shaking his head in sadness Derek steps forward. "Felix you are ill." As if to prove Derek's point, Felix turns and pukes for a full three minutes. When he is done, he can barely stand. Glaring at everyone looking at him. Puke splatter on his pants, even wiping his mouth and hands on clean grass doesn't get rid of all of it. The rage reflected in his eyes is only outweighed by his weakness.

"Go on then Derek, get on with it. Kill me and be done with it. We both know if not for me, you would still be on your ass by that creek while the Pride fell apart with no Alpha." Felix finishes and while trying to spit at Derek he goes into a seizure falling on his back.

Derek and Dr. Michael rush forward. Amanda grabs Dr. Michael's arm, "He's dangerous, stay back." Her eyes are wet but her voice is steady.

Nodding, Dr. Michael pulls free. "I'm a Doctor. I have to help, it's part of who I am, not just a job." His voice is gentle even as he moves forward with his little black doctor bag. The bag won't close because of everything he has shoved in it to be ready for the fight.

"Derek, he's swallowing his tongue, try and get a hold of it." Dr. Michael is cool and professional as he fills the syringe with Phenobarbital sodium. He has tripled the dose to compensate for Werelion's denser bodies and resistance to drugs of any type. Amanda has been educating him about Were anatomy, verbally and physically.

Felix hisses at Derek, his eyes dilated from the overdose of the drugs the Major has given him. Cursing, Derek manages to get the jaws unclenched and tongue out of his mouth long enough to shove a thick stick in his mouth. "Got the tongue Dr. Michael, how long for that stuff to work?"

Dr. Michael is taking Felix's pulse. "Amanda, get the defibrillator! Derek, sit him up and hold him so we can get the nitro pill in him."

Derek's eyes widen as almost before Dr. Michael finishes speaking, Felix goes into cardiac arrest. The seizures stop but so does his heart. As they get the pill into Felix, he stops breathing.

Derek begins CPR as Amanda rushes out with the defibrillator and Dr. Michael takes the paddles as soon as Amanda has the conductive gel applied to them. "Clear. Derek stop." Amanda pulls Derek back away from Felix.

Amanda rips Felix's stained silk shirt, exposing his furred chest and then leans back. Dr. Michael wastes no time, he places the paddles and releases the charge into Felix. Unlike on television, Felix's body does not jump off the ground. Nor does his heart start beating.

"CPR." Dr. Michael instructs Amanda and Derek as he hits recharge on the old portable unit. It is over a minute before it is ready again. "Clear."

Derek hears the defeat in Dr. Michael's voice. "NO. The Major does not win this one, not today." Without a word Bryan and Matteas approach, ready to lend their strength to their Alpha.

Derek draws in a deep breath and holds it. Reaching for the strands of life, of each of his Pride close by him, he feels them all as they, in turn, reach for him. Bryan strong, resolute, Matteas streaked with worry over Sabrina, even Mrs. Collins, and Daisy register as family, Pride.

When Dr. Michael places the paddles, almost the second he releases the stored voltage in Felix, Derek drops to his knees and places his hands on Felix's shoulders.

He goes rigid as the voltage passes from the paddles into Felix then up his arms from where they are gripped on Felix's shoulders. Then back down into Felix, connecting him once more with his Alpha. Through Derek, he is attached to the rest of the Pride as well.

Dr. Michael's eyes are huge as the defibrillator smokes and partially melts. It seems like hours but is less than three minutes in total. Then, Felix's eyes open and he draws in a breath. His eyes lock on Derek's and for one moment they are a family again like they had been in countless jungles, surrounded by enemies betrayed by the Major.

Then the moment passes and Felix is swallowed by the black sleep of the dreamless. Derek falls back on his back, his breathing harsh. Dr. Michael is unpacking an IV unit. "Amanda, set up the autopsy table and get the IV stand, Dobutamine and milrinone ready. Bryan, can you carry Felix into the lab please?"

Bryan nods, walking over and picking Felix's smaller form up and carrying him to the lab. "Dr. Michael, he shit himself, is that normal?"

Dr. Michael doesn't answer as he slaps Derek in the face. Mrs. Collins gasps seeing it. Aaron is just coming out from helping Daisy drag the kids inside and goes pale. "Never interfere when I am working on a patient. I don't know what you did but I felt something akin to my grand Pappy working his medicine. You will sit down and explain what you did in detail. But first, I have to see to my patient."

Dr. Michael shhh's Derek when he would have replied. Taking Derek's pulse must have shown that he is not harmed because Dr. Michael gathers his black bag and heads after Bryan and his patient. "Easy with him Bryan, we just saved his life, no reason to take it away so soon."

Derek watches them for a minute before dropping back on his back and exhaling. Aaron walks over and crouches over him. "You going to be okay?"

"Not until our family is home and safe." Derek groans, getting on his feet to begin once again being the Alpha. He has never felt less capable of his families trust than he does right now.

Brother Lion, find her and Roger fast. I need you brother, we're in deep water here and the sharks are circling.

Chapter 10

"It won't work without me! I can't have more people die for me!" *Please understand Derek and Brother Lion everyone is in danger or hurt because of me.* Tears fall down her face as she runs as hard as she can for the trees.

Looking back she can see Derek running after her and almost to the creek. *Come on, those kids are counting on you. Daisy only agreed to move out here because you said they would be safe, now move girl. He is catching up, the energy from the spirit calls her name.* "Alexis, come to me and the child will return."

"I'm trying dammit." Then five feet from the creek the ground opens up under her and she falls in. When you imagine falling in a hole deeper than you are tall, you would think it would be scary. The hole closing over her swallows her screams.

The hole is lit by a dim green light that fuzzes to brown around the edges. Warmth and the scent of clean earth and living plants rise around her. The warm air runs up her arms then tickles her neck, and breathing deeply from the spirit she draws the spirit-rich air into her with every breath.

The fall slows until she feels like she is floating. Just floating like she used to imagine astronauts did when she would watch them on television in space. Warm, lassitude fills her, and her thoughts grow thick. Holding onto her fear for the children and Roger keeps her conscious despite the growing difficulty in focusing her thoughts.

"Return Peggy, I'm here now." Her words slur like they had the time she drank her parents $1,000.00 bottle of wine when she was eleven.

"The ghost rider has returned as promised, the man is safe." The spirit whispers, nuzzling her ear.

The spirit is playful and curious about her memories. "What did they do when they discovered you drunk?"

Alexis smiles as the memory envelopes her. She does not tell the spirit. Instead, she relives those moments as the spoiled girl she had been then while the spirit rides along savoring every moment.

"You both said you would be home in time for the play. Then you both worked late. Again." The formal living room is lit up with every light on. Mrs. Collins is standing wringing her hands in shame over Alexis sneaking into the wine cellar.

Alexis loves the wine cellar, it is cool, damp and smells of the cedar hung around to keep bugs away. She lies on the floor for hours daydreaming. She is not allowed to go to her Dad's work anymore. So she spends more and more time alone or with Mrs. Collins.

Her Dad looks more amused than she remembers and her Mom, "Gods Mom, I miss you so much!"

Grown up Alexis runs to hug her Mom and the memory bursts. Crying, she stumbles to a halt, "Mom?" But the memory is gone and as hard as she tries to bring it back, all she has is just a memory again.

The spirit croons to Alexis, cradling her in the warm moist air that solidifies around her. The room tilts and she tenses. Then she is lying on her back as fear, tears and the effects of the spirit-ridden air takes her into a dreamless slumber.

Roger stops moving and looks around. He is in the Armstrong estate living room, but it is different than he remembers it. Where the LCD big screen television should be is a twenty-seven-inch tube TV. Turning to look at where the door should have been he is confronted with just a bare wall.

Stepping up to the curtains that hang on each side of where the door should be, he moves them aside. Revealing no windows and more wall. Walking around the sofa, he pauses looking at the delicate crocheted afghan in blues and greens draping the back of it.

"Hello, anyone home?" Roger shivers. His voice seems to travel a couple of feet in front of him and stops. Moving farther into the house, he looks up the stairs not seeing anything up there, he continues on down the hallway. The formal dining room, where he has shared meals with Derek, Alexis, Mr. Armstrong and Mrs. Collins brings a gasp.

He stands unmoving, watching the ghostly images

from his memory act out his memories. "Derek, how did you get here?" Stumbling forward, he passes through Mrs. Collins, who is leaving for more coffee. As she passes through Roger he shivers, his temperature dropping ten degrees.

The images all disappear from Roger's view as another migraine begins. Stumbling from the room with his hand held to his head, he walks down to the kitchen. A quick glance inside shows no windows like all the other rooms. This room, especially, looks out of date. The appliances are all twelve or fifteen years old.

Feeling thirsty, he goes over to the refrigerator and tries to open the door. It will not open. He pulls and pulls until the handle breaks off in his hand with a snap. Roger drops back onto his ass, dropping the broken handle as a pained moan echoes through the house.

Looking over his shoulder and scrambling to his feet he turns back to the fridge and sees the handle back in one piece again. Going to the sink, he attempts to turn on the faucet but it will not turn. Roger's shoulders sag and his migraine is getting worse. Roger walks back to the couch and sits down.

"Derek, I wish I could have told you goodbye. I know you of all people would have understood and accepted my decision not to go on living, becoming less and less me, and more of a drooling Freak." Closing his eyes seems to help the nausea if not the pain of the migraine. Roger breathes deeply for a few minutes, he opens his eyes and watches himself, laughing and joking with Alexis and Mrs. Collins. But this time, the images are even fainter and he has to squint to make them out.

The images do not match the house he is in, close but where a window should be full of sunlight or a door open there is a doubled image that blurs what he remembers should be there and what he sees now. The more he tries to see past the blurred spots, where the memories he is viewing doesn't match the house he is in, the worse the migraine gets. Finally, he closes his eyes, sprawls out on the couch and covers himself with the afghan.

As he keeps his eyes closed, he realizes what else is odd ever since he ended up in the house. The only sounds he hears are made by himself. He is never sure if he sleeps or just loses track of time. He gets thirsty and hungry, only to watch memories of himself in the other Armstrong estate eat and drink. As his memory of himself get full, his hunger and thirst go away.

Wandering through the house, he soon learns if he has not opened or done something in the real house he cannot do it in this house now either. "Is this what it's like to be dead? You spend eternity watching yourself do things over and over? Wishing you had done more so you would have more to watch in death?"

The upstairs is not stable, he learns this after his one and only trip up there. He goes to look in Alexis' room and sees Alexis as she had been the day he ran into the clearing and ended up in the house. The same blouse with the unicorn and moon on it. Her hair wavy and free as an unfelt breeze blows it. Then he shouts "Alexis!"

Once he steps into her room, she is gone, and he

falls through the floor breaking the couch. He hits his head and passes out on the broken couch looking up at the hole in the ceiling. When he comes to, he is black and blue and has a knot on his temple the size of a robin's egg.

The couch and ceiling, of course, are back as they were when he first entered the house. He avoids the upstairs after that. There are no clocks in the house, where he remembers clocks he sometimes sees a flicker but that brings on another migraine, so he trains himself to avoid looking for windows, doors, or clocks. He gets tired and lays on the couch under the afghan and rests.

As time passes, he gets into a routine. He wakes hungry and thirsty and goes to the dining room and pulls up a memory. Watching himself eat and drink fills him up. He never tastes anything or has to go to the bathroom. He just stops being hungry and thirsty.

The few books around the house are all sealed closed because he has never opened them when he had been alive. With nothing to do but think and watch memories of himself in the house, he soon begins to find the pattern of when he began to lose his memories, dexterity and himself.

He stops counting after nine of the times he gets tired and falls asleep on the couch. Once, he stays awake despite being tired. A migraine starts mild but increases moment by moment until it is so bad he has the dry heaves. Then he passes out, when he wakes up, Roger is on the couch and so hungry that he knows he has been out longer than normal.

With his stomach in knots, he staggers to the dining room. This time, while he watches himself eat, the image of himself is more stable, almost glowing with a green tint. "You know Roger old boy, you never told Mrs. Collins how much you enjoyed her cooking. You really should of, it's odd thinking back but her apple pie is one of the high points of the last ten years of your life. Look at you shoveling it in, not even treasuring each bite as it deserves."

When he first starts feeling the need to speak to someone, he thinks of telling Derek, or the memory of him, about his fear of becoming a Freak. Somehow, he never brings himself to look at Derek directly. A part of him is too ashamed of his grabbing the chance to sacrifice himself so he will not have to kill himself to avoid becoming a mindless, drooling Freak.

As more time passes he begins to feel the urge to talk to someone, anyone, it grows like his hunger does if he sleeps too long. Roger is never sure when he begins to speak to the memory of himself, it just starts one day. Then it becomes a habit until he seems to always be talking to his image. "Roger, you know many intelligent people talk to themselves, you, however, have to be the only loony to talk to the memory of yourself."

This day in the dining room starts ordinary enough. "Roger, slowdown. That is a damn good batch of BBQ ribs. Look at that, you ruined another shirt." Then everything changes. Derek and Mr. Armstrong fade, Alexis continues eating and speaking to people who are no longer sitting around her.

The memory Roger with the green glow turns and looks at Roger. "If you could go back and never have to worry about becoming a Freak, would you?"

Roger stands up from where he has been sitting in the corner and swallows. "Now, don't be changing the rules on me. I'm just getting used to this crazy shit. You just go back to doing what I remember you doing."

"It is my house, and I make the rules Roger. If you knew how it would end, would you still follow the Major and join up?" Memory Roger that is no longer acting out a memory watches, waiting.

Roger sighs and thinks back all those decades ago to what his life had been like before the Major faked some papers and recruited him. The nights watching his uncle get drunk and beat his mom before sleeping with her. The ways she always makes sure he has his headphones on so he will not hear.

"I miss my Mom, still do I suppose, I just never slowed down enough before to realize it. Uncle Ray was not a bad man unless he was drunk. I think Mom knew I would have killed him if I stayed. I was becoming a man and that is what men do, they kill to protect their family."

"I disobeyed the Major back then. I told Mom, showed her my fake enlistment papers showing that I was eighteen instead of not yet sixteen. She said she was proud of me." The tears he had not shed all those years ago, thinking it would make him less than a man, falls as he relives being that boy. Roger is hugging his Mom one last time.

Shaking, Roger continues, "She died while I was in

my third year overseas. Derek and Bryan got me a ticket and took turns bribing a nurse to say that I was sick and quarantined. I was going to kill Uncle Ray."

Then he was there, out of the house, watching as he carries the beaded necklace a man had tried to garrote him with while he was losing his virginity with a whore. He had killed the man, and had to kill the woman too, but that was an accident. He had never gotten around to being with a woman after that. It was just over a year later that the Major poisoned him, which left him with immense muscles and a deformed man.

Roger pulls the necklace, exposing the piano wire that will not just strangle but, if used correctly, can slice a larynx silencing the victim as well. The long climb up that dirty staircase with the bare bulb casting shadows is even more detailed as he relives it. There is a cockroach waiting on the side of the third to top stair. All of it is like a high definition of the first time he had experienced it.

The apartment door is open, as always in August. No AC in the 60's for anyone in that neighborhood. Everyone would open the doors to the hallway and the windows in the apartment to create a breeze. All the kids would run from one apartment to another. Those days are colored golden in Roger's memory.

Laughing, playing, being a kid. It is like everyone on the third floor are related. Then, his Dad is a delivery laborer for a furniture store. He sneaks home to be with his mom and him for his lunch breaks, never minding the run to be back on time. His Dad always has a smile on his face. Never enough money but life is rich in love, friends, and laughter.

Once Roger's Dad is killed by a driver that fell asleep, everything changes and his Uncle Ray moves in to help them pay the rent. There are no jobs anymore in the neighborhood and everyone but them has moved away. His Uncle was hurt in an accident at the dairy he worked in. They have no insurance and just gave him some money, and that was it. There are no lawyers on the TV back then begging you to let them sue someone for you.

So his Mom goes to work dancing and Roger hopes that is all she has to do. His Uncle gets more bitter as his stump gets infected and they have to take more of it off. They can't afford pain pills, so his Uncle drinks. Then he becomes the monster Roger is there to kill.

Apartment 303, end of the hall, door open and TV playing like the old days. Except back then the hall and little area where it widens out was always clean. Now it is filthy and all the doors are closed on all the empty apartments, except 303.

Roger knows how to move silently and he doesn't make a sound as he walks to that open doorway. Looking in he sees a gray head where he expects brown almost black sticking up above the old gold swivel rocker. The black and white TV is playing a Laurel and Hardy rerun. A board creaks as he shifts his weight and the gold rocker proves threadbare and filthy but it still swivels.

Roger steps back from the doorway looking at the creased visage of Uncle Ray. They have finally removed the arm at the shoulder. His body is thin as a rail and the smell of sickness wafts out of the apartment.

"She died Rog, you should have stayed and taken care of her instead of dying. All those years, she said she couldn't decide. You had the job and were in school. Goddammit, you had everything to offer her! I left so you could give her everything that I couldn't. Then you died, and I failed her just like I knew I would." At fifty, Uncle Ray looks closer to 90. The tears aren't fake, the cup in his hand is tea, not liquor.

"Ray, who are you talking to?" The woman's voice is old and frail. Roger turns and walks away, dropping the garrote on the way out.

"No, I would not change it if I could." His Mom had used the money he sent her to get Uncle Ray's arm removed so it could heal. He quit drinking after that, and started dating an older woman, a nurse I think." Roger trails off as he steps from the stairs in the apartment into the dining room again.

Roger stops looking into the glowing green eyes of himself in his memory. Then the glow gives it away. "You are the spirit aren't you? The one that possessed Alexis."

"I bargained with her. You know your brain is dying, I can feel it from here." The spirit sounds curious.

"I have also talked to you about it thinking I was alone." Roger sighs, sitting at the table not caring anymore if any of it is real, he is just so tired.

"I'm dying as well. The land is sickened, they spray poisons and fewer animals and plants survive each year. I have been alone for a very long time Roger. Your company in my last days have been a blessing." The spirit looks less like Roger, more gnarled and deep tan but the shape is still true to Roger's memory.

"You're welcome, if you have let Peggy go as you promised." Roger has not thought of Peggy, the wolf or the events that led to his being in the house for a long time.

"I never had Peggy or the wolf. I simply parted the veil between worlds, so they ended up near your friends. I am not strong like I once was. Your body will not sicken or die quickly here." The house shimmers and fades in and out for a moment.

Roger stands looking around in alarm. The spirit waves for Roger to sit. "We have time, maybe. I would like to see the world again before I fade completely away Roger. To do that I need to be in a host. I would be weakened to the point of being almost useless."

Roger sits up listening as alarm bells ring in his head. "I would have power for a time to stop and reverse the mental degradation. In return, I would see, hear and feel what you do." The spirit looks at Roger waiting.

"How long would I have before your power stops working and I became a Freak?" Roger fights the hope but the idea of helping Alexis and the others to be safe is overwhelming. A chance to say goodbye, perhaps borrow enough money from Bryan to hire a woman to take his cherry, even as deformed as he is, all the things he has been telling himself he should have paid more attention to. Apple pies, conversations, the feeling of cold milk going down his throat and it is so tempting.

"Not long, I am not good with your time." The spirit pauses, calculating before going on. "The trees would bud no less than 100 times but no more than 300. Probably somewhere in the middle if you take care of the body."

Roger swallows, a hundred years of life when he thought this life was over. Before his time watching himself and reliving all the things he has not paid enough attention to the first time, he might have said no. Roger wants everything he misses, things that are so fresh in his mind and he wants to live, actually live.

"You would see, hear and feel but you would have no control? It would be my body and my decisions, not yours?" Roger wants this but he does not want to end up just giving up his body and being possessed.

"I will not even be a voice in your mind. Perhaps a thought might pass between us once a season, no more than that." The house fades for a longer time and, this time, everything is washed out looking when it solidifies again. Like it has been left out in the sun too long.

"Decide now Roger. Also, know this, if you agree and we do this then the union must be cemented in love by a Shamaness of great power." The spirit stands to wait for Roger's decision.

"I agree but where will we find a Shamaness?" Roger asks.

The spirit shakes its head, "One period of sleep and we will go to her in a moment. First, understand this, during the cementing of our bond I will be as one with you. If you stop us, we will both die. The joining must be of our free will and she must give her part willingly or we will all die here together but separate."

"As long as it will not hurt whoever it is and I remain in control of my body then I agree." As Roger finishes the spirit steps up to him.

Roger blinks and once more the spirit is a mirror image of himself. The spirit reaches out and Roger mimics the gesture. The fingers touch, then merge, rising above their heads the arms merging as well. It is like stepping into his own reflection.

As the spirit steps into Roger and Roger steps into the spirit, everything seems more real. The colors that have seemed so fade a moment before are now vibrant and alive. Yet the opposite is true of his memories, they grow foggy, and he cannot remember who he is or where.

Roger knows he has to go upstairs to tell someone something that he has almost waited too long. Not wanting to miss this chance, he hurries to the stairs. Half way up he pauses uneasily for some reason about going up the rest of the stairs. Then he hears a sigh from upstairs and he forgets the unease as he smiles. "Now I can finally tell her."

Chapter 11

Alexis wakes up in her old bedroom, the small one at the end of the stairs that had been hers while she was growing up. Sitting up in her old daybed, with the purple and gold comforter surrounded by her stuffed animals, feels right. She is a long while just sitting there before sighing and swinging her feet onto the floor.

Where the door should be is just more wall. The window is gone as well. She hears someone walking down the hall, smiling in excitement she calls out, "Mom, Dad I'm in my room."

She is so thrilled to see her mom again. For some reason, she gets really sad whenever she thinks of her since she woke up in her room. Remembering things is harder than it should be. No matter how hard she concentrates, she can't remember anything except that she loves her mom and dad. Her name is even eluding her.

Alexis stands up and goes to where she thinks the door should be. Running her hands over the wall results in nothing except a headache. "In here! The doors are missing."

The house shakes and she stumbles, falling onto the floor. While she's sitting on the floor, everything goes fuzzy and dim. When she looks up again, a man is standing in the open door that wasn't there a moment ago.

"Alexis, I have so much to tell you." The man smiles

child-like in his enthusiasm at finding her. She smiles back as he reaches down and helps her up.

"Alexis, yes that's who I am, Alexis Marie Armstrong." Saying her name makes her so happy she hugs this big man who hugs her back laughing.

"Of course, you are Alexis, and I am." He pauses, frowning as she steps back looking him up and down.

He is tall and covered in muscles. Not like an athlete, more like a body builder who's gone too far and the muscles have melted and flowed into odd shapes then became solid again. Her eyes move down to his fingers and hands. Each sausage sized finger is misshapen and swollen in advance stages of rheumatoid arthritis. Moving her eyes past his hands and up his arms she shivers.

The arms are covered in muscles, his biceps and triceps can swallow a football easily. His chest is slanted, one side higher than the other. Everywhere she looks she feels sympathy for his pain. Even the hug she realizes in horror has been painful for him. Then her eyes meet his.

The warm innocence and trust in them welcome her hug, accepting the pain as worthwhile. Then she sees the love, deep abiding love as she falls into his treasured memory of her…

"Mother fucking crap, work goddamn you or I swear to god I will cut you off. Work." The last words are filled with frustrated pain.

Roger is standing hunched over, his finger swollen even more than normal struggling with a bottle of pain pills. The childproof cap is too much for his misshapen painful fingers to open the bottle. Tears are filling his eyes when he looks up and sees Alexis. Standing horrified in the doorway.

Alexis, seeing herself as he remembers her. Almost seeming to glow, she turns and leaves the room without saying a word. Alexis cries out as she feels the terrible self-loathing that he feels when she walks away. Feeling his misshapen body has repulsed her so badly she will never be able to look at him again.

Then the blinding rage, filling with the desperate need to punish someone for the way his body is, he grips the bottle in his fist and slams it against the cement floor of the garage. Hating his body is something he has lived with since he was changed by the Major at eighteen.

Alexis returns carrying a small jar. He looks up at her from where he is kneeling on the floor catching his breath from the pain. The pill bottle falls broken, open and misshapen, like his hand, onto the floor. His fingers refuse to open all the way, and several drops of blood and gravel are stuck to his hand.

At first, he thinks she will just run away like before, but instead, she does what no one has done for him since his change. Her eyes flash as Alexis sees his hand. "Roger, you dumb ass! Your hand is not bad enough you have to make it worse?" She waits for him to apologize.

"It's my fucking hand. What do you care?" Then in a lower sullen voice, "Not like you helped me to open the fucking bottle." He glares at her, in turn, breathing deep to expand his wide muscled and deformed chest.

For the first time, Alexis realizes how good her guess at how to react has been. She feels his shock when she marches up to him and slaps him. His complete shock fills her now as they share the memory.

"My garage floor, is that none of my business? Or how about the fact that you work for me? That any of my fucking business?" She glares for a moment then goes for broke. "Sit down so I can see if I can keep you able to, at least, look threatening since with your hand messed up you're not much good for protection in any other way."

Together in his memory, they sit, him holding as still as possible. Alexis is hiding her nervousness in a brisk manner. She pries the lid off the jar and right away the smell of fresh crushed mint, lemongrass, and rosemary begins filling the air. "I will fix the floor," Roger mumbles, watching her from the corner of his eye.

"Hummfff doubt you would know how. I will have Dad hold the cost of hiring a professional out of your pay." Even as her gruff voice and dismissive manner allow him to put his guard down, her gentle hands catch him off guard.

She pulls his hurt hand down first. She brushes off the dirt and pieces of grit. Then she dips the tip of just one finger in the jar. He is expecting cold then burning painful heat like he gets from asper cream and the like. Instead, the ointment goes on warm and soaks in without heat or cold.

His eyes water as the swelling eases within moments. He is shocked by the lack of throbbing pain. He doesn't notice Alexis humming as she moves her fingers over his hand. There are no words, just hum music. The more she hums, the less pain he feels. She moves to his other hand

and he braces the one with the ointment on it, still afraid to move it and reawaken the pain.

After she finishes the second hand they both look at each other realizing how close they are sitting. "Thank You, I uh hmm, Thank You." He stutters, almost saying I love you, but catches himself at the last moment.

Alexis opens her mouth to say something, but he leans forward and kisses her. At first, she stiffens, but as he begins to pull away, she leans into the kiss and her mouth opens to him. His hands warm, tingling and pain-free for the first time in decades, stroke her cheeks softly as they both sit back breathing heavy.

Once they sit all the way back, he feels awkward and almost starts to apologize. She speaks first, "My mom was a healer, herbs and stuff. I only have this jar left that she made before she was killed. Dad took the rest to his work. I snuck into his room and took this one. I was so scared he would find out, but I wanted something of hers to hold onto."

Roger nods and who knows where things would have gone if at that point Mrs. Collins didn't call for Alexis from the kitchen window. They both get up and Alexis looks back at him before walking back into the house. "I really like Derek, but if things don't work out with him, you could ask me out sometime. But only if they don't work out." She hurries away blushing.

Coming out of the memory, Roger notices how close they are standing and tries not to move or startle her. "How are things going with Derek and Brother Lion?" He is proud of how stable his voice is.

Then it hits Alexis. All the memories that have been dimmed and buried while she has been in the house flood back. She stumbles back, just making it to the edge of the bed before her feet give out as she remembers losing her mom to a car wreck that was intentional.

Then she relives the whirlwind courtship with Derek. Brother Lion sliding down the handrail yelling "Yippee Ki Yay Mother Fucker" with her in his arms to cheer her up and show off for her. Derek, buying a chocolate cream pie to celebrate her first day of school and getting locked in the janitor's closet.

Then the heat and lust as he relaxes and lets her see him as he really is. Furred, in reddish gold fur, fangs, and claws. Then she moans as she feels him once more take her in the alley with her against a dumpster as he takes her virginity and then they give her all of themselves, swearing they were hers. Proclaiming her, as the heart of the pride.

Then Roger falls down to his knees as something green and brown flows out from him leaving him gasping. She stands to go to him but the house shakes and everything goes dark. Warm, black darkness that muffles sound is all around her. "Roger?"

Her voice receives no echo or response. Then a golden glow fills the void as it moves toward her. Her heartbeat quickens, straining for breath in a place with almost no air. Then he is there, claws grabbing her shoulders looking at her up and down. Painful pricks as he breaks the skin in his fear for her. His amber eyes are glowing fiercely, asking, and demanding an answer. "Yes,

I'm fine."

Then he pulls her into his arms and holds her, his warmth filling her body inside and out. "Don't ever leave me like that again." Half arrogant command half pitiful begging as only a cat can accomplish. Her breathing eases as she smells the fresh scent of the prairie after a spring rain with just a hint of lightning nearby.

She doesn't promise but wraps her arms tighter around his shivering body. She can't get any words out, the relief at having one of her men with her is so immense, all she can do is hold him and send "*I love you.*" Mentally the way he has taught her.

They never knew how long they floated in that black void only lit from Brother Lion's glowing astral body. Moments or decades might have passed, then they both feel the pain as the bond between them and Roger reaches them.

"Roger's trapped in my house, but not." Alexis struggles to explain but words fail her when she doesn't understand how she has been in her bedroom, watching her parents and younger self-repeat her memories of them in that house. On purpose or accidental, she broadcasts enough of the mental images to Brother Lion that he understands.

"If we go to him we might all perish and never get back to our plain of existence." It doesn't seem odd to either of them at the time that Brother Lion, who has no physical body 98% of the time in that plain of existence, can still refer to it as his.

"We have to help him, he's family." There is no

hesitation in Alexis' voice. She feels the silent agreement from Brother Lion.

"Concentrate on Roger as you last saw him, felt him. Not just what he looked like but how he felt in your spirit. The smell, taste of him when you breathed near him." Brother Lion's low voice has a hypnotic effect almost immediately on Alexis.

She relaxes as he leans his furred forehead against hers. Their breathing is slowing as they begin breathing in and out in time. Alexis breathes in as Brother Lion breaths out. Brother Lion breaths in as Alexis breaths out.

Her mind fills with Roger. The shock of the kiss, mouths meeting, hearing in his memory the "I love you" he is too afraid to say. Uncertainty in her, if she could step back from Derek and Brother Lion, as if he has said it. Knowing that now, she will always love Roger but can never be with him in that way. Then Brother Lion stiffens as something of her emotional kiss with Roger begins to pass from her to him.

Then she is pulling her memories back and burying them. She leans away from Brother Lion and everything is flickering around them. She feels the heat, surprisingly it hurts, and not the anger she expects from Brother Lion. Since falling in love with Derek and Brother Lion, she has learned that the territorial male lion is ready to kill not just to protect her but to ensure no one else will touch her either.

"You and Roger were together?" Brother Lion shuts his mental self off from her completely, something she has never experienced since her bond with him in his own astral body. She is shocked at how cold she feels without his presence inside her, warming her with his love.

"Just a kiss back when we were in my house. Before everything went crazy. We had just started getting to know each other, I didn't even know you were a part of Derek." She fights tears, afraid she is losing Brother Lion. "It was only a kiss." She whispers.

Brother Lion remains still, he doesn't take away his arms but he is no longer holding her close. The void flickers again and again. "If it was back then and not since why do you hide it from me? Am I so terrible that you fear to trust me with something so treasured in your memory?"

Alexis shudders, not sure of the answer. *Am I afraid to share things like this with Brother Lion and Derek?* "I don't know. This is all so new and in the house with my Mom and_." She stumbles to a stop, fighting tears as once again she relives the loss of losing her Mom.

He pulls her against his furred chest and begins the rumbling purr that vibrates all through her being. Pulling another memory to the surface. "You know when we were first making out in Sexy Kitties, I thought you were growling when you began to purr. It was kind of scary but also exciting." She leans against him holding him as tight as she can. "Now I can't sleep unless I hear it beside me."

Brother Lion sighs, "Roger is running out of time, we will discuss this with Derek when we get home. But never doubt our love, even here, cut off from almost all awareness of him that is the one thing that I can still feel, our shared love for you."

Alexis nods her head against him, hearing the unspoken if we get home. "Now begin again, focus on Roger and the room and anything odd, or that didn't make sense when you were there before I brought you out."

That took her by surprise. *He brought me out of the house.* "You left Derek to come and rescue me." Then the fear hits her and she hits him on the back of his shoulder as hard as she can while still being held close to him. "You said if you left Derek for long you would lose the connection between you and might never be able to return. You promised me that you would never do that."

"The most important part of me was already lost in limbo, my heart. Now concentrate on the room, we must hurry." The urgency in Brother Lion's voice is not just for Roger.

Alexis feels it as well, something far away has noticed them and is beginning to drift closer. She has no idea what it is but her instincts tell her it is a predator, and they have to get away. She refocuses on the room.

It should have been easy, that room had been her sanctuary and haven growing up. Everything about it is so familiar. The worry for Roger and the threat drifting closer all makes it harder. "Calm, focus on the breathing and let the memories float up naturally."

He sounds so sure of himself and in control when she feels so hopeless, which is a bit much for her, she smacks him on the ass in irritation. "It might help if you tell me you can kick that things ass that is coming this way."

Brother Lion begins a deeper purr. "As we prize peace and quiet above victory, there is a simple and preferred method….. run away."

"Master Tae really? You are quoting an 80's TV show now? What did I do to be stuck with a Werelion addicted to TV?" She smiles oddly, more relaxed as she concentrates on her room and Roger who is left behind in it.

When her thoughts turn to the missing door that is only there long enough for Roger to come in then goes away again. Brother Lion tenses, "That's it. Concentrate on the moment the door was open."

She feels a wave of cold and hunger as she feels the thing getting closer. She can't see it, even if her eyes were open, which they aren't. It is merely a darker black than everything around it. And hunger and empty waves of cold start her shivering, dimming even Brother Lion's warmth inside her.

Then inside her mind she feels a click. Then a moment of dizziness and falling. She lands on her bed, bounces and rolls off onto the floor. "Ow! Watch those elbows girl. Eiiihh, there goes my chance to ever have kids."

Turning her head to see what she has landed on, her eyes widened. "Roger, we made it in time. Are you okay?"

Alexis is sprawled on Roger, breathing heavily as she waits for the dizziness to pass before she tries to move off him. "I was fine until your fat ass landed on me. What do you mean, WE, we're the only ones here, remember? Even the spirit left me after you disappeared."

Alexis moves as the dizziness fades to nothing. As she wiggles to get off Roger, she feels his body react. "I think your equipment works just fine." She can feel his equipment responding to her wiggling as she tries to get off him.

"You never said who 'we' are," Roger says sighing as she finally gets on her hands and knees beside him.

Before she can reply, "Kow wa bunga." Looking up, Rogers's eyes widened as Brother Lion, all six-foot-three and 350 pounds of him, hang for a few seconds before he plummets and lands on Roger, missing the bed by inches.

"Ooofff, get off you fat oaf!" Roger says.

As Brother Lion climbs off Roger and leans close "Never kiss our mate again." As he finishes speaking, Brother Lion bounces his knee once more, hard into Rogers's groin.

Alexis' eyes widen but she looks away as Brother Lion turns his attention to her and asks, "Are you okay?"

Alexis nods, hiding a smile as Roger says a prayer for his unborn children. Brother Lion limps to her side and she takes a closer at him. "Are you hurt?" She asks, grabbing his shoulders to hold him still. The right leg is burned and the acrid smell of burned hair and flesh is filling the small room.

Brother Lion smiles "Sadly, I could not kick its ass. But we are both alive and here." Turning from Alexis he walks the room.

Shaking his head, Roger climbs to the edge of the bed and sits. "So now we are all here. The spirit is gone, I guess it changed its mind on the deal."

Brother Lion turns to Roger frowning and steps closer. As his foot comes down, the house flickers, going dark for a long minute before returning. "I have not changed my mind about our deal. I have simply realized that I do not wish to share you. The SheMiTali may bless us or not by her actions."

Everyone turns to the corner of the room, startled by the voice. The spirit is clothed in flesh, and a comely flesh at that, if not human then certainly very female. Stepping from the shadows is a short five-foot woman. At first, it appears she is wearing brown and green clothes but as she steps into the light, they see she is indeed very naked.

Brother Lion's loose pants are not sufficient to hide his reaction to the spirit. Her hair is the green of oak moss and hangs down to just past her shoulders. Her breasts are D cups and dark brown with green bud shaped nipples.

Her skin ranges from warm chocolate to faded silver and runs in ridged patterns over her body as bark on a very old tree. "Roger Stanton, we have made an agreement to the benefit of both of us. During your stay with me here I have grown very fond of you and your memories. I would honor our bargain, will you take me now in my own flesh to seal our bargain?"

Her voice is like the breeze through the leaves of a tree. Musical and vibrant, leaving trickles of goosebumps behind it. Roger stands swallowing, "I would be honored to be with you in your flesh." For Roger, there was no one else in that room until the spirit turns to Alexis.

"SheMiTali, will you honor our bond with your flesh?" The spirit's face shows less expression than humans do as she speaks. Her voice shows her fear that Alexis will refuse.

Brother Lion speaks before Alexis can. "She is our mate, spirit of the earth." He steps beside and half a step past her as he speaks. His husky breath and stiff legged walk shows that his body is very aware of the sexual pheromones filling the room. There is no whiff left of the acrid smell from his already healing leg. Weres heal very fast.

Smiling at Brother Lion with brown outer lips that expose green inner lips she replies, "You are his Alpha, and your blessing is fitting, I accept your offer."

Brother Lion doesn't move as he mulls over the spirits words. Alexis elbows Brother Lion hissing, "What are you staring at?" However much she tries to act upset her words lack any real anger. In fact, they sound downright distracted as her nipples hardened and she feels herself getting wet.

Roger stands up beside the bed and watches as the spirit walks toward him. "I stand before you in my natural form, will you not share yours with me as well?" Her voice manages to sound hurt and be sexual at the same time as very few females of any species can.

Alexis draws Brother Lion back as the spirit poses before Roger. Spreading her legs to shoulder width, she turns in a circle before him. Her hair, that upon closer inspection, is thin, new growth limbs like you would find on a willow tree. Each is covered with new growth leaves. As she turns, they swirl around her as if dancing in an unfelt breeze.

Roger stands mesmerized by the stunning female spirit. It is a full minute and several swallows later that he begins unbuttoning his shirt. It has been decades since he has allowed anyone outside of Bryan or Derek to see him without any clothes. With the spirit, he feels no fear of rejection. Somehow knowing that she has been inside his body with him more intimately than any woman ever had before gives him the confidence to drop his shirt.

His chest is almost hairless. The stomach flat and showing not just the six pack bodybuilders strive for but the full eight-pack. One side of his chest is higher than the other but his pale body is so heavily muscled that the odd muscle patterns are lost in the chiseled body.

Alexis' mouth drops open as Roger drops his pants. The muscle growth brought on by the Major's transfusions have affected ALL of Roger's muscles. His dick is erect and pointing straight out at the spirit. Brother Lion pulls Alexis back a step this time but neither of them can take their eyes from the unfolding scene before them.

"My Goddess, how big is his cock?" Alexis asks out loud without intending to.

Brother Lion shifts his feet before he replies, his eyes still on the spirit who is running her hands down her sides as she watches Roger undress. Her fingers move around to cup her own breasts, squeezing each of her hard nipples. The low moan from the spirit makes Rogers hard dick flex.

"Just over 10 inches long and over two inches around last time anyone measured it." Brother Lion glances at Alexis to see how taken she is with Roger's muscle.

Smiling mischievously, she looks up at Brother Lion, "Do soldiers go around measuring all the boy's toys or is that a special hobby of yours?"

Brother Lion laughs low, relieved to have Alexis looking at him for the moment. "When we all changed, it took months for our new bodies to stabilize. Everyone kept a record of all the changes, not just fur and fangs."

Roger's loud gasp draws their attention back to him and the spirit. Roger still has one sock on but he and the spirit are breathing heavily and are tired of waiting. The spirit is standing in front of Roger, her right hand running up and down his cock while her other hand explores his chest.

Roger's large fingers find a dexterity that they have not had in decades as he runs them over the rough skin of the spirit. The skin is rough as his hands first pass over it, but as her breathing speeds up, it softens and warms under his touch.

Roger leans down, running his tongue over the dark brown areola. The rough outer areola soon warms to a warm moist bud in his mouth as he sucks on her nipple. His hands grip her ass cheeks and squeeze, pulling her closer as his mouth opens, sucking in the entire aureole as well as the nipple.

The spirits moan is louder and her hands are squeezing and stroking Roger's shaft. When precum wets the end of Roger's dick, she pulls her breast from Roger's mouth and kneels before him. She swirls her tongue around the tip of his dick, the drop swallowed from his dick as his breath whooshes out. Her hand's soft, sensitive palms are running up and down his sides. Her hair rises and begins caressing his stomach, and any part of him it can reach.

"If you don't stop_." Rogers warning brings her left hand to cup and massage his tightening balls. Her mouth and tongue swirl around the head, nibbling and sucking. Her right hand is rubbing herself and she moans onto his cock as two of her fingers slip in.

Alexis' eyes are glued to Roger and the Spirit. She runs her hand down the soft downy fur on Brother Lions arm. His breath catches at the light touch, his hand rises and slides down her back. Turning her body sideways, she runs her hands under his t-shirt and plays with the downy fur covering his nipples.

Brother Lion turns, facing Alexis and slides his hand down her back, between her legs and slides two of his fingers between her legs. Raising her up onto her tip toes, he applies pressure and moves them to the side, pulling her labia aside so the fabric of her panties slides against her open, wet pussy.

Their eyes lock, glazed with mounting passion. Watching Roger and the Spirit has excited them beyond any foreplay. Brother Lion's hard cock is pressing against

Alexis as their mouths meet. His wet tongue darting in as her lips part. The rumbling purr is vibrating all through Alexis' body.

Alexis tugs on the button of his pants but it won't budge. Brother Lion has no patience for clothing so he runs his razor sharp claws down her back, cutting through shirt and bra in one pass. Leaving thin trails of red marks on her pale flesh.

Moaning at the feel of cool air flowing over her sensitized back brings a moan from Alexis. She grabs Brother Lion's pants by the pockets while they are still buttoned and pulls down with all her strength and weight, dropping to her knees with them.

Roger moans louder, his hips thrusting as the spirit moans around his dick. Her hand has three fingers rubbing herself in fast jerking motions as her body trembles. Then she moans, her fingers sliding in and out quickly, her clit sandwiched between two of them as she gasps and sputters as her orgasm sweeps over her.

Roger gasps, shudders, and moans as the spirits mouth takes all he has and sucks for more. As the spirit leans harder, sucking him and her fingers still spasming in and out, a second smaller orgasm building on top of the first. They both lose their balance, Roger falls back onto the bed, the spirit half climbing half falling on top of him.

The spirit lays on top of his chest, her juices dripping onto him. He draws her hand up to his mouth and savors each lick of her dripping fingers. The fresh musky scent is keeping him hard. The spirit slides back until the tip of his huge dick is pressing against her lips, and she rocks brushing the head, getting it wetter and teasing Roger. The sound of Brother Lion falling as Alexis pulls his pants down draws Roger and the spirit's attention.

Alexis climbs forward, thankful Brother Lion is going commando. Her eyes drink in the sight of his eight and a half inch hard dick. Leaning forward, he tugs her by the hair drawing her mouth to his. Alexis gets her button jeans undone in record time and wiggles out of them. Her wet panties slip to the ground with her jeans. Smelling Alexis' wet and ready pussy brings Brother Lion up into a sitting position.

The spirit slides herself slowly onto Roger's shaft when the sensitive, swollen head slides into her she and Roger moan. They both watch Alexis and Brother Lion as the spirit slides lower, impaling herself on Roger's throbbing cock.

Brother Lion draws Alexis into his arms kissing her then his mouth slides down. His mouth is nibbling and sucking on the back and side of her neck as her hand strokes him. Brother Lion thrusts his hips up, pressing himself into her hand. Then he begins to lean forward, to climb on top of her.

Alexis growls deep in her throat and pushes back against him trying to get on top. Brother Lion's purr deepens at her attempt to be on top but he is too hard and eager to bury the animal instinct and allow her to fuck him.

As Alexis feels him pushing her onto her back, her hand lowers down his shaft and grips his balls in her hand. Then she slowly begins to squeeze. At first, this brings a moan of pleasure from Brother Lion and a renewed eagerness to get on top of Alexis. As Alexis squeezes harder; his moan becomes shrill.

"You're mine." Her voice is low and husky. He falls back as her grip tightens even further, sending shooting pain up from his balls to the tip of his dick where it flexes harder. Once he is on his back, Alexis throws her leg over him. Sitting up with her hand still gripping his balls, "Are you mine and only mine?"

Brother Lion's eyes run over her heaving breasts stopping at her dazzling eyes, "Yes Lexi, I am yours."

Alexis slides onto his shaft, releasing her grip on his balls. She is not slow or gentle. She slams down on him taking him all the way inside. Her eyes close, savoring the feel of him filling her. Up and down she fucks him, hard and fast, satisfying her own need.

She looks over at a moan from Roger to see the spirit sliding forward and back onto Roger's cock. The spirit is leaning forward, her nipples brushing Roger's chest, her back arches as her pussy slides over his cock over and over in rhythm with Alexis' movements.

Alexis leans forward to slide her nipples over Brother Lion's chest but instead, Brother Lion leans forward and begins sucking on her nipples. She moans and starts fucking him harder. Up and down as the Spirit begins speeding up as well. Then Brother Lion nibbles and tugs a little rougher, sending jolts of electric pleasure from nipple to clit and back.

The spirit is leaning all the way forward on Roger, rubbing her clit against him with each backward thrust.

All four of them are moaning louder. Roger reaches around, grabbing the spirits ass and grinding her against him. His hips are thrusting to meet her as she slides back. When her moans get louder and faster, her legs begin to twitch with each thrust, he slides his finger inside her pussy, wetting it. Then when she slides forward and back onto his cock he slides his finger an inch into her asshole. The spirit begins to jerk and quiver as she comes.

Roger thrusts his hips, fucking the spirit as his balls tighten. The spirit is leaning forward and biting Roger's nipple hard. Roger gasps in pain as he explodes inside her.

Alexis is riding Brother Lion hard and fast, then she feels his cock head expand inside her. She moans as his dick flexes against her, hitting that special spot. As her orgasm builds she begins to only lift half off of Brother Lion's cock, going faster and faster. His mouth leaves her nipples and begins nibbling and biting her neck.

Alexis has no warning, the scalding hot cum shooting out of his dick inside her, his hips thrusting him deeper into her as he moans into her neck. Then her climax is on her, waves of pleasure traveling down her. She stops moving as the pleasure overwhelms her muscle control. Brother Lion grabs her hips and thrusts in and out furiously. Her orgasm intensifies with his pounding in and out of her, drawing out one long orgasm until she collapses on his chest.

The breathing and small sighs and moans of orgasms are all that can be heard in the room. The smell of sex is thick in the air. As pleasure fades to contentment, no one is in a hurry to remove dick from pussy, as they all drift into a well-satisfied slumber.

Chapter 12

"Do you really think there is any chance they will come back, it has been three months already." Felix is sitting at the inside dining room table watching his words sink in. He is healed from his overdose of the serum the Major had given him. He is still thinner than he has ever been before and doesn't have the endurance like he did before.

They are all sitting inside at the dining room table since there are fewer of them than before. Derek is thinner as well. As each day passes, Derek has less inclination to eat. He is fighting a battle the likes of which he has never been trained for. The battle to keep hope alive in himself and the Pride.

Bryan looks drawn and haggard as well. He hasn't lost weight but sleepless nights and nightmares when he does sleep are taking a toll on him. "Shut up Felix. You already drove Daisy, Mrs. Collins, and Aaron away, just shut up."

The food before them is frozen lasagnas that are burned on the outside and cold in the middle. It was the constant complaints and threats when Derek or Bryan were busy that drove the humans away. Felix is an expert manipulator. Knowing instinctively how far he can push them before they retaliate.

Leaning back, Felix ignores Bryan since he has beaten him in a challenge, he is now of higher rank than Bryan and has more status. Derek could have put a stop to it but spends much of his time on the phone and internet looking for a way to go after Alexis.

"You know, the sad thing is if this had happened in a year or two instead of right after she moved here, she might have found her way home by now." Felix sounds disappointed but has to hide a grin behind his wine. Never water for Felix, always wine, and always spending the money they got from Dr. Michael on expensive clothes, food, and drink.

Derek sits up looking at Felix, a light sparking in his eyes. "Say that again."

Felix chokes on the wine and sets the glass down while he dabs at the already spreading stain on his shirt. This is the first time Derek has shown such a strong emotion since Matteas left to hunt for Sabrina with Amanda and Dr. Michael.

"No offense Derek. Just repeating what the old Indian said." Felix is careful and very aware of how unstable Derek has become. Despite the Major's assurances that Derek's rages are a good thing, Felix is not convinced. Too vividly he remembers the last group of three Werewolves that had attacked the ranch to scare Daisy into taking her kids and going.

Derek goes out the window when the first gunshot rings out. Felix has been watching from his window excited to see the show the Major has arranged. Instead, Felix sees Derek going berserk, letting his animal run free. He tears two of the Weres to pieces while Bryan watches after knocking the first one out.

Derek would have killed that one as well if Bryan wasn't standing his ground. Felix has to climb out his window and shoot that Werewolf himself and claim it was waking up and was about to go in the house. Bryan doesn't believe him but in his lowered status is safe to ignore. At least, as long as Derek is depressed and not taking action.

"Yes, I know, just the way you said it, I had an idea but now it's gone." Derek stands up, his food untouched and walks toward the kitchen. "I need some air. Felix, clean up, Bryan go check on Aaron and everyone in town."

Derek walks out through the kitchen and outside picking up speed as he goes. He doesn't have to think about where to go, he has made the trip so many times in the last three months there is a trail all the way there.

Bryan smiles in triumph at Felix. "He's not dead yet, you sure you want to be around when he wakes up to what you have been doing?"

Felix pushes down his shock, glaring at Bryan. "Are you sure you want to be here? You shame the Pride by not leaving after letting them down in a challenge.

Perhaps I should finish what we started before he gets back to save him the trouble of getting rid of you."

Bryan stands, looming over the smaller Felix who bristles at the insult but remains seated. "Whatever the Major gave you is long gone. I think when I get back from town, perhaps I should challenge you. Or we can go outside now." Bryan's normally joyful eyes are alight with a fire and hope he had thought gone.

Felix sneers. "There's not enough of us left to waste fighting each other. The Major says."

Bryan threw his water in Felix's face. "The Major is a traitor and coward. Do not mention him again." Leaning forward, using all of his six-foot-seven height he draws on the Pride magic and pushes at Felix. Felix is more dominant and only Roger has ever been able to come close to dominating him. Other than Derek and Brother Lion who, when together, are dominant enough to go toe to toe with the Major.

Felix resists but gives in with a nod. Bryan turns and walks out, taking the keys to the truck as he goes. The old truck is still running but without Roger's constant tune-ups and babying it is hit or miss if it starts or not. Something in the air makes Bryan believe it will start easy this evening.

Bryan's good mood dims as he thinks back over the last three months. Derek had held it together for about a month. Then Felix finally managed to get Matteas and the others to go out to the Major to look for Sabrina and Shawn, who no one has heard from.

Without the support of his Pride, the loss of Alexis

and Brother Lion really took a toll on him. "Felix, you are a traitor and when I have proof, I will kill you." As always, thoughts of the oily Felix pushes Bryan to red hot rage.

Even without the Pride looking after the kids, the human members of the Pride has kept Derek moving, planning. Then, when he lost control while fighting those Weres, Felix used it as an excuse to separate Derek from the rest of the Pride.

The only one he has been unable to move is Bryan. Pulling up in front of the small house in the center of town, Bryan shuts off the truck and watches the kids play. They have run off and gone back to the farm house to see Uncle Derek a few times and Derek has been about to suggest they all come back home when Felix announces that the Major has word of an attack being planned against them.

Getting out of the truck, Bryan shakes his head. No attack had come, and that was three, almost four weeks ago now. No contact is to be made with the human Pride members so as not to draw an attack to them. "Uncle Bryan!"

Bryan smiles as the kids run to him, tugging his arms and pulling him toward the house. "Is Uncle Derek better?" Tommy asks.

Peggy speaks right after, "Did he finally kill that mean Felix?"

Mrs. Collins' gasp is still the same. Bryan tries to hide his shock at the way she looks. Mrs. Collins has always looked like a woman in her early fifties. Now, since

Alexis and Mr. Armstrong have gone missing, she has aged. She walks with slumped shoulders and her hair has gone gray almost overnight.

"That is no way to speak about someone, not even that slimy bastard, Felix." Mrs. Collins looks at Bryan for a long moment before she opens the door for him to enter.

Bryan's mood has sobered at the cool reception from Mrs. Collins. The children hide grins and lead the way into the small house.

Mrs. Collins is sleeping on the couch since the house only has two bedrooms. Aaron and Daisy have one and the kids the other bedroom. Despite the cramped quarters, the house is immaculate. Mrs. Collins cleans when she is nervous. Daisy cleans when she is stressed, since she gave up smoking for Aaron and the kids. With both of them in the house, dirt has no chance.

Bryan stops inside the doorway looking around the small living room. The window is facing the street. The couch has a pair of knitting needles and yarn on it. "Have a seat, Bryan. Daisy and Aaron are at the market getting a few things."

Bryan nods and sits on the couch that takes up most of the room. The kids sit in front of him on the floor giving him their full attention. The kids keep smiling and are bouncing around. "If you two have so much energy, perhaps you should go back out and play." Mrs. Collins says, putting away her knitting needles and yarn.

Tommy grins looking from Bryan to Mrs. Collins. "But you will need our help to pack."

Bryan looks up at Mrs. Collins. "Are you leaving?"

Mrs. Collins sighs shaking her head no. "Where would I go? These two had a dream last night and are convinced that Brother Lion found Alexis and we need to go back to the ranch." As she speaks her eyes get wet at the thought of Alexis.

Bryan flinches, looking away from Mrs. Collins and instead focuses on the kids. "Well, Derek sent me to see how everyone here is doing." Bryan looks at the kids and waits for some sort of answer while Mrs. Collins blows her nose into her handkerchief. "Well, how are you? Glad to be back in school?"

The kids have never taken to him the way they had Roger and Brother Lion but he has grown fond of them during the time they lived with them at the ranch. They have always seemed to like him but he isn't as much fun as Roger. The silence is beginning to make him uncomfortable.

"They will be here in a minute, then you will know it's time to pack," Peggy says, looking at the front door as if she could see someone no one else can.

Mrs. Collins shakes herself, shaking her head as Bryan looks at her in question. "They do that now. Announce things they shouldn't know. It's not natural for kids to know such things." She stands, moving to the kitchen to put on tea. "You still take two sugars in your tea Bryan?"

Looking from the kids to the door Bryan answers, "Yes please." When he is looking at the kids, both watch the door while sitting very still, it flies open and bounces off the wall. Bryan jumps and Mrs. Collins lets out a squeal from the kitchen at the bang.

"Bryan, get off your ass and help us carry him in." Aaron's voice is annoyed.

Getting up, Bryan steps toward the doorway and once he is clear, he can see that Aaron is holding up a very drunk old Indian. Stepping out of the door to where Aaron is half sitting half leaning against the handrail, Bryan scoops the Indian up in his arms. Then turns his head away at the smell of vomit and tequila.

Daisy is busy talking on her cell phone while sitting in the town car. Carrying the Indian inside, Bryan pauses not sure where to put him. The Indian becomes more alert after they enter the house. "Put me down skinwalker! Have some respect."

The kids stand up as Mrs. Collins walks in carrying a tray with a tea pitcher and 6 cups. Bryan stands the Indian on his feet, who wobbles but remains upright. "You know why I am here don't you?" The old man speaks to the children in an ominous voice trying to stand straighter.

The kids giggle, bringing a sullen look and a wave of his wrinkled brown hand their way. "I am Mad Coyote, the great medicine man. I have drunk the sacred Peyote and spoken to the spirits." If he didn't belch and sway, as the room spun, while he spoke he might have been impressive.

"We already told them it was time for us to go back to the ranch but they didn't believe us. They will dink around until Derek gets here and then it will all be a rush and hurry." Tommy speaks in a loud whisper to Mad Coyote but everyone hears him.

Daisy steps through the door getting off the phone. "If you puke in my Pa's house, you will need medicine when I am through with you."

Mad Coyote flinches at Daisy's loud threat turning to Bryan and speaking to his chest, "Beastly woman, if she had fought the Whiteman with us we would have driven them back to the salt water." Then he blinks realizing he is speaking to Bryan's chest. "Spirits man, you must be a tree."

Aaron stands behind Daisy waiting with a grim look on his face. "Bryan, I'm glad you're here. That means Derek is at the clearing where Alexis disappeared. We might as well wait until he gets here. I will go ahead and order pizza and beer."

Aaron takes the cell Daisy holds out to him and walks back out onto the front stoop. Mad Coyote looks at Daisy and smiles, "Beer would be good. Speaking to spirits is hard work."

"You only get sick because you get drunk before you speak to them. You know better, Running Crow taught you better." Peggy says.

Mad Coyote flinches turning away from Peggy. "Stay back, child of stars. You tell Running Crow he should not have left me to do his job. Or marry his fat Granddaughter." Despite his declaration to stay away Mad Coyote goes past the kids into the hallway and out of sight.

Bryan shakes his head looking to Daisy for an

explanation. "Have a seat Bryan. I told Aaron we should just pick up the pizzas on the way home, but he had to see you before he believed Mad Coyote."

Bryan returns to his seat on the couch. As Daisy looks at her kids she looks overwhelmed and tired. "You might as well go finish packing."

The kids smile, get up, run to her and hug her. She hugs them back after a second then they are heading to their room. Tommy pauses in the hallway and is looking back. "Mom, May the force be with you." His voice is so low and serious that Bryan looks at him, not sure if he is serious or not.

Then Peggy's laughter brings the giggles out of Tommy. Both kids flee when Mrs. Collins throws a throw pillow off the couch at them. Daisy and Mrs. Collins laugh as they sit on either side of Bryan. Somehow, the joke has broken the tension.

"They know what is going to happen sometimes now. Other times they will be playing catch with colored lights. Sometimes it seems like they stopped being kids. Then they prove that their just kids to relax us." Mrs. Collins explains.

Daisy sighs, sipping her tea as Bryan passes it to her. "I used to worry that they only did it because they knew how freaked out I was and that it would relax me."

Aaron walks back inside after closing his cell phone. "Now we know better than to ask or think about it. How you been Bryan?"

Bryan is no longer sure how he is. "I thought I was pretty good. Now I feel like I'm in the twilight zone."

"Don't worry tree man. Wise Coyote will share secrets from the spirits with you. For a drink." Mad Coyote walks back in looking and smelling better even if he still looks dirty. His jeans have holes, his plaid shirt is faded and has a patch sewn crookedly over a tear.

"Malarkey. You can't get drunk anymore. Ever since you married Running Crows granddaughter, you can't get drunk." Daisy scoots over, making just enough room for Aaron to half sit in her lap.

Mad Coyote goes red in the face and he stands up straighter, all pretense at being drunk gone. "You tell Running Crow that Mad Coyote got the last laugh. Everyone knows his fat Granddaughter drove me mad and none will send me a young brave to teach. He has no Great Grandchild either; his line ends with me."

Daisy and Mrs. Collins look surprised, "You mean, you really can't get drunk? Then why do you puke after you drink all night?" Daisy asks.

Mad Coyote's eyes widened as he sits down on the floor crossing his legs. "You didn't believe them?" he laughs until tears run down his face. "I suppose you believe now?" Without waiting for an answer he continues. "I was a going to be a great warrior until Running Crow decided he could no longer stand the hen pecking of his Granddaughter."

He sits up straight to tell the story, stories are serious business. "The spirits would not let him go until he trained a replacement. He went to everyone on the reservation, yet no one would the spirits accept. That is when he set up a trap to lure an innocent young man away from his intended bride."

"That is not true Mad Coyote. You were in bed with Moon Doe when Running Crow caught you. If the spirits had not spoken to you, he would have killed you." Tommy says, looking around the couch.

Mad Coyote shifts, "Ruined a good story you did. You might as well as finish it." He leans forward taking away Bryan's tea after he finishes stirring in a third sugar cube.

"Since your obviously not packing you might as well join us," Aaron says.

Tommy walks into the room grinning. "Running Crow agreed not to kill him if he admitted who his Dad was and married Moon Doe. He got drunk and tried to run away every day for the first two weeks. Each time he was drunk, and the spirits led him back home. Finally, they got tired of it and cursed him to never get drunk again."

Mad Coyote spits on the floor, "They did nothing about the hangovers and puking, though."

Mrs. Collins and Daisy both are about to lay into Mad Coyote for spitting when Derek steps through the open door. "I know where she is and we have to hurry. I need all of you to get her back. Will you come with me and help me bring Alexis and Brother Lion home?"

"Of course we will Derek. The pizza should almost be here. Kids go get the bags and take them out to the truck. We bought you some clothes in town Derek since we won't be stopping at the ranch before we leave town."

Derek's mouth drops open. Looking around the

room prepared to explain everything and convince them to go with him.

"I told you it would hurt his feelings if you didn't let him explain it all. Uncle Derek, we told them to let you tell us your story." Tommy says, looking sad for Derek.

Peggy walks up and hugs Derek's legs. "It's okay Uncle Derek, Running Crow said that your speech was beginning to sound better after you said it in front of the mirror at the gas station. He still thinks it would have been more dramatic if you had not stopped running to take a dump on your way here."

The big wolf walks past Derek and out the door wagging her tail. Aaron takes pity on the bewildered Derek. "Get the bags or no pizza." The kids go and get the bags, almost knocking over the pizza boy who is standing in horror as the wolf eats the pizza, box and all, it had taken from him. He is still holding five pizzas.

Chapter 13

Alexis is in no hurry to move from Brother Lion's arms. She sighs as she twirls his chest fur around her fingers. "You know, if Derek was here I think I could stay here forever. The three of us making love and not needing to eat."

Brother Lion's purr stops then begins again. "You do need to eat though Alexis. There is no telling how long we have been here and despite the illusion of not being hungry, your body will be weakening."

Almost as if to emphasize his words, the house shakes like a bell has been struck. The spirit sits up pulling on Roger. "Someone is trying to get in, we must leave before they catch us."

The house flickers and dims like before, only when the light comes back it is not as bright as before. Roger gets up and begins pulling on his clothes. Alexis gets up, dragging on her pants as fast as she can. "What is happening, are we in danger?" Alexis asks, breathless as she wrestles into her clothes in record time.

"Yes, great danger, those that are hunting, are after you and my sodalis vitae." The Spirit is tugging on Roger's arm, trying to get him to hurry. She is actually slowing him down by only leaving him one arm to dress with.

Brother Lion looks around the room and spots a door that wasn't there before. "Spirit, do you have a name?"

Alexis growls under her breath, "We are in danger and you are worried about what to call the naked spirit woman?"

Brother Lion smiles for a moment as he squeezes Alexis' shoulder. "We need to be able to trust her, I can feel her in the Pride bonds now but without a name, she's not entirely part of the Pride." The lingering suspicion over the spirit's loyalty jolts Alexis.

Why am I trusting the spirit? Goddamn magic spirits, get out of my head! Pushing with her will at what feels like cobwebs sticking to her has no effect.

The spirit looks over at her with wide eyes. "My sodalis vitae must name me in my new form. Sister Alexis, there are numerous clouds marring your aura. If we do not cleanse them from you, they can take control of you and make you do their bidding, as well as find you."

The spirit steps up to Alexis and before anyone can move or protest leans down and kisses her. At first, Alexis stiffens, ready to pull away, then her body reacts to the soft, warm lips against hers. As her mouth parts, allowing the spirit's tongue to enter, Alexis feels a spike of desire flow from her mouth to her nipples, then lower.

As her tongue tentatively touches the spirit's, both women moan. The house lights dim, not like before, this time, more like mood lighting. Alexis' arms move around the naked spirit, she can feel the spirit's nipples harden as hers follow suit.

Then she feels the spirit's energy mingle through her and in her mind where Brother Lion speaks to her when

he is in Derek, she hears, *"Push while I freeze them."*
That fast, Alexis pushes and she feels the cold of deep
winter as only a tree whose sap has mostly frozen within
can pass through her and into her aura.

The lights go out and a hundred screams echo
around the room. Then Alexis pushes harder and it's like
a moldy blanket is removed from a window. Her breath
catches as she feels clean for the first time in so long, she
has forgotten what it's like.

The spirit steps back as the lights return brighter
than before. Everything looks more vibrant. Brother Lion
steps up and wraps his arms around Alexis, hugging her
tightly. "I am so sorry, I have failed you." The heartbreak
and despair in his voice scares Alexis.

"Failed me, how? Would someone speak English
and tell me why I feel like I just took my first bath since, I
don't know when?" She gets shrill toward the end,
hugging Brother Lion back.

Brother Lion looks to the spirit but she only shakes
her head. "I do not know why she is not protecting
herself. She has the power to spare but uses it to call all
to her." The spirit looks confused and Alexis
understands, that within herself the spirit simply is not
human enough despite her form to explain.

Brother Lion looks into Alexis' eyes while Roger
draws the spirit back, whispering to her. "All this time I
thought you simply were shielding yourself so well that I
could not see your aura and power clearly. Instead, it was
all the orphan spirits and pieces of forgotten ones that
you had called to yourself."

Alexis steps back, running her hands through her hair, "That is so not helping me to understand." She is tired of being confused and frustrated.

"You're a power and those with power leak it into the world around them. Normally, ones with power, like you, shield themselves so that only more powerful or very talented powers can recognize what you are. But you shine like a beacon in the night." Brother Lion looks at her and sees that she still doesn't understand what he's trying to say and growls in frustration.

The house rocks, almost knocking Alexis off her feet. The lights dim again but stay on. "It's like you are wearing sugar water all over your body in a fucking swamp. Mosquitoes and leeches stick to you and are drinking your power until you are a dried up husk. Marie_"

Roger nods to the spirit, "I helped you clean them off but already new ones are circling. If you do not learn to shield yourself, you will not live another year."

Roger and the spirit walk out the door heading for the stairs. Brother Lion hugs Alexis for a moment then drags her behind him following Roger and Marie. Alexis feels better than she ever has. Her whole body thrums alive with energy. It is also affecting her body in other, more alarming ways.

Whenever Brother Lion brushes against her as they go down the stairs, a thrill of desire shoots through her. *Concentrate, you're not in junior high! Lives are at stake here, focus dammit.* At the bottom of the stairs, they all stand staring at the front door that wasn't there before.

"I am sorry. When we cleansed Alexis' aura, we sundered the ties to my clearing. I cannot take us back home." Marie looks more like a child expecting a spanking for something than a thousand-year-old spirit.

The house rocks again and the door splinters, allowing darkness to come in through the cracks instead of light. "What exactly does that mean Marie? We need to leave now, how do we do that?" Brother Lion sounds reasonable and calm. Alexis can feel his fear through the Pride and Mate bond where before she was deaf to the feelings of the other Pride members.

The house rocks again but Alexis barely notices, exploring her new sense of Brother Lion. *This is what they all feel when they are near each other, no wonder none of them accepted me as a member of the Pride. I couldn't feel them and was not connected.* While she is reaching toward Derek, a link that is vague because of distance, she can feel that he is alive and that is it.

"Dad? My Dad is at the door, we have to let him in!" She rushes to the door, Brother Lion reaches for her but a second to slow. Roger, who is already moving the couch to barricade the weakening door, catches her in his arms. "Easy Alexis, your Dad's not here, it's a trap." He speaks soothingly to her while holding her.

Brother Lion stops a step behind Roger. "Let her go." Brother Lion's voice is low and a threatening growl. Alexis knows that it's hard for any Were to allow their mate to be near other males. During times of stress, the males, especially Alphas, are even more territorial. The

fact that she has kissed Roger and her life is in danger
from so many threats makes it impossible for Brother
Lion to be rational about her.

Marie understands her mate is being threatened and
moves up behind Brother Lion, ready to attack him. The
green glow around her shows that her attack will not be
all physical. Roger, while he does not have Were instincts,
understands Brother Lion is holding onto his control by a
thread and slowly lets go of Alexis and steps aside.

Alexis has not seen her Dad in the flesh in months.
Everyone else has accepted him as dead. After watching
her memories of him from when she was a child play out
she can't ignore the feeling that he is in pain and at the
door. In so many ways she is a victim of her power. She
has almost no control of it, so it controls her. Right now,
it is calling her to open the door for her Dad.

She dashes away as soon as Roger's arms release her
and in six steps has the door swinging open. Her smile
turns to horror as she sees the Other is the one waiting
on the front porch. He is not like any Were she has ever
seen. His fur is matted and filthy, what he has of it.
Patches of baldness that look like mange covers much of
him.

It's hard to tell exactly what kind of Were he might
be. He is crouched down clawing at the door with a claw
glowing black. His eyes are not black, they are the
absence of any color. The light that hits them don't
reflect or shine as it should. It simply is absorbed into the
pitiless dark abyss behind his eyes.

Alexis has never believed in evil, real evil. Looking at

the Other, she understands that this thing before her is not just bad it is evil. Weres can be cold, mean and often the animal in them take over leaving pain and death behind. This thing before her is always in control and relishes the pain and destruction it causes.

Time freezes into one long agonizing moment stretched into eternity. Then she begins falling, slowly picking up speed the farther she goes into the abyss. Her screams echo in her mind, the terror separating her from her body as part of her feels her bladder release. Then the stabbing cold pain of the things voice speaking in her mind cracks her mind-body connection.

"Greetings Lexi, I have a job for thee." The thing's voice in her mind is so powerful that each syllable echoes inside her. Blood begins to flow from her mouth and ears as the pressure builds inside her. She feels her sanity tearing. Her sanity is splintering under the force of its will.

She feels Brother Lion and Roger pulling at her body, trying to get her back in the house. Even their combined strength is failing and the Other hasn't even moved.

"Lexi!" The cry is from the side and in it is all of her childhood memories rolled into one. She turns to see the man who has defined what man and Father mean. The mixed martial arts competition she has insisted on when he wants her to play T-ball. He still goes and cheers her on. Missing meetings at work when she has a competition just to see her.

The savage roar of rage from the thing in front of

her shakes her free for a moment. Brother Lion and Roger manage to pull her inside the doorway. Marie sends something that looks like green acid into the Other's face when he goes to step in after her.

He shakes his head as his flesh melts but raises his foot to follow. Then from the side, a gale force wind and a flash of lightning hit the Other on the side. Alexis is blinded by the flash of the lightning and is blinking tears from her eyes as she falls on Brother Lion and Roger from the force of the wind and the lightning hitting the Other.

Then the door is closing even as smoke is billowing in. "The deadbolt won't go in, it's melted. I told you to wait until she was clear!" Her Dad's voice is recognizable in its anger. Even with the hoarseness, she knows that voice.

The voice that answers it is ragged and filled with pain, but it's still familiar. "Fool! Why did she choose you, a damn mundane human? Bolts mean nothing." Then as Alexis' eyes adjust and she is picked up and handled like a doll from Brother Lion's hands to Roger's as they gain their feet and move to protect her.

A low buzzing like a hive of insects fills the room, making Alexis scratch her arms looking for the insects. Then light appears around the door in orange and red hues. When the light goes out, the buzzing dies away and the door is solid again and melted somehow to be part of the wall.

Her eyes are adjusting after the flash of light but things are still blurry. "Dad, is that you?" Alexis squints, shrugging free of Roger's grip, but he steps half in front of her ready to pull her back if she takes off again.

Then her father, Martin Armstrong, stumbles past Brother Lion to wrap his arms around his only daughter. "Alexis, you foolish, foolish girl. Gods, you should not be here." His crushing hug is returned by a suddenly crying Alexis. "But I'm glad you are, I love you. I never said it enough before, I love you."

The sound of a body hitting the floor draws Alexis' attention. Brother Lion moves forward and picks up the man that has collapsed in front of the door. Growling he carries him to the couch and lays him down on it. Alexis' eyes widened as they clear enough for her to recognize the man passed out and bloody on the couch. "Dean Masters?"

Her Dad lets go of her as she steps around him. "What's he doing here?" She asks, the tears gone in a flash of anger.

The house rocks like it has been hit by an explosion. The door flexes but the orange and red glow holds steady. She turns, looking closer at her Dad. His right hand is in a crude, blood-soaked bandage. Burns, cuts and part of his left ear are missing. "Oh Dad, what did they do to you?"

He sighs, sounding old and tired. "Less than they would of if I had told them what they wanted to know. And if I had known the answers I would have told them."

Brother Lion is standing over the Dean, who looks even worse than her Dad and has smoke coming off of him in places. His breathing is shallow and labored. "The Other did this to you?"

Martin laughs harshly. "No, I believe it was that Major you mentioned. I was taken by the Other's Weres at first. But before they got me to him they were ambushed by what I believe you call Freaks and Weres loyal to the Major. The Other would have killed me when I didn't answer him fast enough."

The house rings like a bell, everything goes black, and Alexis falls into her Dad. When the lights come back on, one of the new orange bands Dean Masters has put on the door is black and broken in half. Smoke begins filling the room. "We need to go now. The anchor is burning and when it's gone so will this place be. If we are still here, we will perish with it." Marie sounds anxious as she stands to face the door, waiting for the next band to break.

"We don't understand, what anchor? What's burning, I see the smoke, but nothing feels hot." Brother Lion looks from Marie to Roger, who shrugs looking confused.

Marie stomps her foot, a very human gesture for a spirit. "I am telling you, the house is the anchor and it's being destroyed! We must get out of the spirit reflection or we will be taken into death with it."

Alexis closes her eyes, counting to twenty to keep from screaming. "We are trying to understand but we need more information."

Martin puts his hand on Alexis' shoulder. "Our home is burning in Sacramento. This is the shadow of it in the spirit realm or limbo. It's held together this long because you are here with your memories of it. It's a long story and I don't think we have time for all of it now."

As if to prove him right the door shakes as something massive hits it. Everyone turns and looks at the bars on the door that Dean Masters has put there. None broke this time but the sound of gunfire and screams is entering from outside the house. The house groans as if in pain.

Alexis' eyes widened, "Our house in the real world is burning?"

Dean Masters opens his eyes with a groan, "Yes, and if you do not get out soon, it will be too late for you. The Major plans on blowing it up and then retreating." The Dean is pale and his nose is bleeding a slow trickle.

"That sounds great, except none of us know how to get from here to the real world," Roger says, standing beside Marie who is watching the door, waiting for it to break and allow the Other in.

Mr. Armstrong walks over to the couch and looks down at the Dean. "How long will the wards you placed on the door keep it out?"

The Dean laughs but it turns into a wet cough. Brother Lion helps him sit up so he can catch his breath and continue. "Until I can no longer hold them. Once I lose consciousness, he will be able to walk in as if passing through cobwebs."

Alexis walks over to stand by Brother Lion and looks down on Dean Masters. "You said you could teach me to use my gifts. Can you teach me now so I can help?" She is tired of running and not being able to fight back.

Dean Masters shakes his head no. "If we had a few years then I could teach you and together we could rend the Other. But I will be dead before the hour is over." He looks at Mr. Armstrong. "I have given my life to keep our bargain. Now keep yours, let me hear you tell her the truth."

Alexis' heart speeds up, and she steps away from Mr. Armstrong and closer to Brother Lion. "Dad?"

Mr. Armstrong looks angry but that fades and he just looks tired and old as he begins. "Your Mom, Spencer and I all grew up knowing each other. You know how beautiful your Mom was, is. It was inevitable that we would both fall in love with her."

Brother Lion wraps his arms around Alexis, holding her while her Dad continues. "Master's and I both courted her. I had money and could help her with her work. Spencer had magical abilities that complemented her own. She refused to choose, she insisted we could all be together, or all remain friends. We were both desperate and did things that hurt your Mom and us."

Mr. Armstrong swallows, "I framed Spencer so it looked like he was in a plot against your Mom's family. He used his magic to cast a glamor on a call girl, so I thought it was your mom. Then he recorded the whole thing and sent the tape to your mom, only she didn't see the glamor, just the call girl."

Spencer speaks with his eyes closed. "We were both fools and have suffered for it. Your mom forgave Martin his whore, but never got over the harm done to her family in my name." He leans over spitting bile and blood on the floor.

The door groans and the house flickers. When the lights brighten the room is filling with smoke and one of the orange bands sealing the door is dimmer. Spencer grows paler and his breath is coming in short gasps. "The Major must have given up and retreated. The Other is not distracted anymore." He looks at Martin. "Get our daughter out of here, keep her safe. Then tell her everything."

"People, that door is bulging in the center, we need to do something fast. We still don't know how to get out of here." Roger is pulling Marie from the door where she has been standing, ready to slow down anything that comes through.

Martin and Spencer both gasp as they notice her for the first time. Her willow branch hair is covered in white and pink blossoms. Her naked, exotic, very female body displayed before them. Spencer shakes his head, "You need an anchor to the real world. Then follow it to the real world." He passes out when he finishes speaking.

Martin looks from Alexis to Brother Lion, "Spencer is fading fast. When he got me away from the Major he used more magic than he has and it tore something inside him. Then when we saw the Other about to get Alexis he gave what he has left. Do either of you have a tether to the physical world?"

The smoke is getting worse and the temperature is starting to rise. "Tether? Dad speak English, what are you talking about?" Alexis moves to the stairs where the smoke is thinner.

"He means a tie to the physical world if the Alpha is not here, the connection to him might be enough to guide us out. If he is close to the anchor's reflection here."

Brother Lion and Roger look at each other at the same time, "Derek."

"Is he near the house in the physical world?" The spirit asks, dragging Roger toward Alexis and the stairs.

Roger's shoulders sag "No, he would not leave the place Alexis and Brother Lion entered. That is over a thousand miles away."

The door splits down the middle, black inkiness oozing through to puddle on the floor. Mr. Armstrong moves away from the door, joining everyone at the stairs. "What do we have to lose? What do we do to try and use Derek as our anchor?" Mr. Armstrong asks.

"Wait a minute, Dad you said the house in the real world is burning? What about the fire department, they can't just burn our house down!" Alexis looks from Mr. Armstrong to Brother Lion for reassurance.

"Honey, the Major is planting C4 all the way around it, then he plans on blowing it out of existence. The Other and the Major have magic being used, so no one even knows there is a fire or battle going on. There is no way to save the house."

Alexis sags against Brother Lion, coughing as the smoke continues to rise. "I was so close to finding out what I am, who I am. If the house is destroyed, I will never be able to go to the bottom of the stairs."

Brother Lion holds her as everyone else looks at Marie. "I cannot even save myself. I gave up my anchor when I bonded with Roger." Marie turns to the door and gestures, wiggling her fingers. The pale green light grows from the floor into the red and orange bars, brightening them again. A howl of rage from the other side echoes back.

Brother Lion whispers to Alexis, "All your things are in South Dakota at the ranch already."

Alexis' eyes widen, "Marie, if this is a reflection of our real house is it a complete reflection? Are all the rooms here?"

Marie shrugs, "This is limbo built and sustained by your memories and longing. I helped you form and shape it so you would be comfortable. It has whatever rooms you created."

Mr. Armstrong looks from Marie to Alexis. "You mean the safe room in the master suite? I don't think it will do us much good."

Alexis is already walking up the stairs. "No, Mom and I have a special room. I think Mom left a message there for me."

The house rocks and the door cracks. Spencer groans, sending a weak flow of light to hold the door from where he is lying on the couch. "Whatever you're doing be fast, he will be in here soon."

Everyone follows Alexis upstairs and into her adult room. As soon as everyone is in, Brother Lion and Roger begin moving furniture in front of the door. The bedroom is crowded with everyone in it. "It's here, everything is here." Relief fills Alexis' voice as she moves the picture and begins punching in the combination.

The room dims and for a moment, it feels like they are floating. The floor no longer holds them up and everything is pitch black. The cold makes breathing painful. As the room becomes solid around them again, they all hear Spencer screaming in pain. Then everything goes silent, all they can hear is their own breathing.

The sound of the passage opening draws all eyes. Alexis moves to the open door and takes a deep breath. "You must follow me exactly and step where I step. There are traps all the way down, and you must be silent." As she begins the descent into the dark passageway the sound of furniture being thrown and broken reaches them.

Chapter 14

"Just stay put and work on finishing the new wrap around porch. We'll be back soon." Derek pushes his orders with the Pride magic into Felix. It will fade as Derek and the Pride gets farther away, but for a few more days it will keep him at the ranch house. Hanging up, Derek walks away from the pay phone.

"I'm still not sure if it was a good idea to leave all the cell phones behind. It took us until New Mexico to find a pay phone." Daisy passes out more napkins to the kids. The outside picnic tables at the tasty freeze empty when the odd group pulls up in the town car and the old pick up.

Mad Coyote is busy eating his burger as fast as he can. Sapphire is sitting watching him, with her tongue hanging out.

"Hey Coyote, do you want anything else before we head out to the res?" Bryan asks as he fills the five-gallon water bottles they have for the trip.

Everyone pauses to see if this time Mad Coyote will acknowledge Bryan. After the bottles have been filled and

Mad Coyote is done with his burger and working on his fries, it happens again. Sapphire leaps, her fang filled mouth closes around Mad Coyote's hand holding his large French fries.

"Eiiiehhhh!" Mad Coyote yowls as his hand and fries disappear with Sapphire drawing everyone's attention. As Mad Coyote grabs his wrist with his hand, his missing hand reappears. With a vicious oath, he runs to the bathroom to run hot water on his frost covered hand. Sapphire materializes on the table Mad Coyote is running past, eating the fries.

"You know, I wonder why she only does that to Mad Coyote. She never steals anyone else's food or body parts." Bryan tells Derek.

Aaron answers, "I think it's because Mad Coyote is convinced that Sapphire is actually sent by Running Crow. From what the kids have said, they have a long history." Aaron takes the chance to get away from Daisy and the kids by walking over to help Bryan load the water bottles in the back of the truck.

Derek is eating his Rattle Snake burger with extra cheese, chilly, extra jalapenos and three slices of meat. After barely eating for three months he has lost enough weight that he looks sick. His clothes hang loose on him. "Bryan, we need to get more answers from Mad Coyote. This detour to the Jicarilla Apache Reservation will slow us down by several days. They need me."

Sapphire is done with the fries and looks at Derek for a long moment then goes into the bathroom where Mad Coyote had gone.

Bryan hands the last water bottle to Aaron with a nod and walks over to the tree where Derek is leaning. With his lost weight, he has lost some strength as well. A Werelion has to eat ten to fifteen thousand calories a day to be healthy. Derek hasn't been eating nearly that much.

"You should eat another five or six burgers. A few days to speak to this woman whose ancestors come from below will give you time to start getting in shape." Bryan watches Derek to see what effect his words have. Everyone is afraid to say the wrong thing around Derek and send him into the black depression again.

"Maybe I should take the truck and go on by myself. The rest of you can take the car and go to the reservation then catch up with me." Derek nods to himself as he begins walking to the truck before he finishes speaking.

Bryan hesitates a moment then begins hurrying after Derek. As Derek reaches the truck a loud wolf howl echoes from the bathroom followed by growling. "Alright, alright! I'm going already." Mad Coyote stumbles out of the bathroom with Sapphire growling and snapping at his hind quarters.

Derek pauses beside the truck and looks back at everyone else. Mad Coyote is red in the face and hurries over to Derek. Bryan joins them as Mad Coyote arrives hobbling quickly with a large tear in the back of his jeans exposing his tighty-whitey underwear.

"If you go to the house without visiting the reservation first, you will die." Mad Coyote speaks in a flat voice while looking at Derek.

Derek tenses, stepping towards Mad Coyote. "Speak

plainly, what do you know that you have not told us?"

Daisy follows the kids and Aaron over until Mad Coyote is standing surrounded. He looks around at the faces of the people he has traveled with the last few days and sighs. "I don't know much. The spirits have told me that you need to visit the reservation and speak to the people who have descended from those who come from below. If you go to the house without hearing what they have to say, none of you, except the children, will survive."

Derek moves without thinking, the animal surging out of control with Brother Lion's continued absence. He grabs Mad Coyote by the throat and would have shaken him hard enough to break his neck if Bryan didn't grab Derek's arms.

Straining against Derek's animal strength. "Control! Damn you, control the animal!"

Derek's eyes widened as he drops Mad Coyote and starts shaking. "Brother Lion has been gone too long. The animal is all that is left and it's stronger than me."

Mad Coyote is half on his back, his hand holding his bleeding throat where Derek's claws have scratched him. "You need to be one with the animal or it will destroy those you love." Aaron helps Mad Coyote get to his feet.

Bryan stands in front of Derek waiting for the shaking to stop so he knows that Derek is in firm control again. "This is happening more often every day. I can feel the animal in you, it's not like any of the animals in the rest of us. You must control it."

Bryan braces himself, almost backing away as

Derek's eyes flood gold. Sapphire runs by from nowhere and leaps onto Derek knocking him back, into the side of the truck. Sapphire drops down off him and stands looking up at Derek.

Derek draws in a deep breath as he returns the stare of Sapphire and nods. "Let's get going, the reservation is several hours away. I'll ride in the back with Mad Coyote. He can tell me more about what the spirits have said along the way."

———————————

Derek and Mad Coyote ride in silence in the back of the pick up watching the desolate landscape slide by. *Brother Lion, I'm coming. Keep her safe until I get there. And keep yourself safe also.*

After exhausting threats and demands, Derek finally admits to himself that Mad Coyote doesn't know any more than what he has already told them. They have been driving on dirt and gravel roads for a few hours. Going from place to place looking for the one woman who Mad Coyote says has answers.

They are drawing up to another single wide trailer. This one has several pickups, one new and three beat up, waiting across the road. Mad Coyote shakes his head no as he stands. The town car slows to a stop and the pickup rolls to a stop behind them.

The men standing around and in the trucks are all armed with shotguns, rifles and one with a large knife. "Wait here, they are suspicious of outsiders other than tourists. They have little reason to trust anyone." Mad

Coyote jumps from the truck with the agility that looks odd in the sixty-some-year-old man.

Derek breathes deeply, managing, for now, to remain in control. The last few days have been up and down for Derek. He is more alive now than he has been since Alexis and Brother Lion went into limbo after Roger. Every day though, he has to fight more and more to remain in control. His Were half has always been controlled by Brother Lion. Without him, Derek is losing control too often.

When Derek looks up again from staring at his boots, concentrating on breathing, he sees two of the men shaking their heads no at Mad Coyote. The wind is picking up again and the dust is making it harder for Derek to see. A shotgun goes off and the trailer door slams. Derek inhales, "Werewolf!" He roars in challenge as he jumps on the cab. From here, it's a single leap to bring him charging at the smaller Werewolf in natural form running out from the trailer.

Bryan is running after him yelling something lost in the wind. Aaron is holding his Spencer rifle at the man holding Mad Coyote. Everyone is yelling except for Derek, this one time he and the Werelion inside are in agreement. They shrug, stumbling as their bones break and realign in seconds.

Changing from their human form into their natural two-legged lion form is usually stretched over ten or fifteen minutes. This time, they do it in the time it takes to close on the Werewolf. The pain from the fast change has dimmed whatever control Derek might have had.

Blood roars in his ears, he is deaf to everything but the Werewolf. The Werewolf doesn't hesitate either. He is reddish gold and about 50 pounds lighter than Derek was three months before. In his emaciated state, they are close to the same weight. The impact as they collide in mid-leap is heard and felt for miles.

It's not just the collision of two Weres, each over 300 pounds, it's the clash of Pride magic hitting Pack magic as two alphas with nothing to lose collide. The windows on the front of the trailer blow into the trailer. The vehicles rock, glass explodes everywhere sparing no one. The first swipe of Lion claws opens the Werewolf from left waist to right shoulder.

The Werewolve's fangs rip half of Derek's ear off and opens his cheek to the bone. Then they are pass each other rolling and springing to their feet already turning to attack again. Then gunshots ring out hitting Derek, one, two, three high caliber rounds punching him in the back and knocking him off his feet.

Bryan leaps onto Derek's back when he is half on his feet. Bryan's eyes are glazed, fighting for control as he fights to keep Derek down. "Derek! Stop this! He's not your enemy!" His shouts are inches from Derek's ears but he goes unheard.

The Werewolf is on his feet and moving to attack again. More shots ring out, hitting the Werewolf this time, but he doesn't go down until Sapphire runs in from nowhere and hamstrings him before blinking back into limbo taking a huge chunk of flesh from the back of the Werewolve's right knee. The Werewolf howls in pain and rage but goes down as more shots hit him.

Derek throws Bryan off and leaps on him, his fanged mouth closing around Bryan's throat. Bryan freezes, holding his breath, reaching out to Derek with the Pride bonds that have only strengthened the ties that have bound them as teenagers in a war they didn't understand.

Derek breathes harshly as his body struggles to draw strength from him to heal the damage from the Werewolf and the gunshots. Weres of any kind heal fast, and when they're hurt too badly, the Were body forces a coma onto themselves to speed up the healing. Derek is still weak from almost starving himself for three months. His body begins shutting down, no matter how the animal rages for blood, for their mate, for Brother Lion.

"It's alright Derek. We're here, this is where we need to be to save Alexis. Rest, I will be here, rest." Bryan catches Derek in his arms as they both collapse flat on the ground. Derek nods once as his eyes are closing and his breathing deepens with sleep.

The other Werewolf is being helped to his feet, his body is healing already. An old woman walks out of the trailer with a cane. A young girl, no more than 10 or 11, steps fast to keep up with the old woman. "What foolishness is this?"

The Werewolf bows to her as she stops half way between him and Derek, where he lies in Bryan's arms. Bryan sets Derek down and stands looking from the Werewolf to the old woman noticing her eyes are all white. "We mean you no harm."

The old woman laughs harshly and spits in Bryan's

direction. The Werewolf tries, "Grandmother, these Werecats have invaded our home."

The old woman waves her hand at her Grandson, and he flies back several feet, landing roughly. But her eyes are all for the old man walking toward her with his shoulders back and his head high. "Grandfather, been a long time since you paid your family respect. Now you will pay what is owed. Take them, tie them. Use the charmed bracelets on the children, they are astral walkers."

Mad Coyote doesn't resist as he is restrained, his hands tied behind his back with glowing cast iron manacles. Bryan turns to fight but Mrs. Collins, Daisy, and Aaron are already being tied and lead forward by the Werewolves that have joined the men by the trucks during the fight. Bryan growls but allows himself to be tied and blindfolded.

Brother Lion, have you found Alexis? Derek reaches for his best friend and brother. For a moment, he thinks he feels an answering thought from far away, but then it fades. He opens his eyes and looks around. The room is small and smells of earth and incense. The only light is entering from a frayed blanket hanging as a door and stopping four inches from the floor.

"It has been too long since you last served the people." The old woman's voice is firm with no sign of frailty or age.

"So much of your Mother is in you. It makes my

heart ache to see her in you and remember all that I have lost." Mad Coyote sounds more lost than Derek has ever heard him.

Derek swings his feet off the bed and sits still as his head swims. His body is still soaring but the gunshot wounds are almost all healed. The slashes in his face are held shut with stitches that are itching something fierce.

"Faghh, who do you think you are fooling Gramps? I remember you too well. Mom was the one always left to clean up your messes. Grams still visits the speaking chamber once in a while. She warned us you were coming and that trouble would be coming with you. Do not play the sad old man with me."

Mad Coyote replies with no sign of sadness. "If she warned you then you know what a dangerous game you play by delaying us. And don't call me that!"

Derek manages to stand and walks toward the doorway. His feet are bare and his shirt is missing. The pants he's in are ragged and stained like he has been dragged along the way. When he touches the blanket, a cloud of dust and pieces of the rotten blanket fill the air. Coughing and waving his hands to clear the air he stumbles into the larger room.

Mad Coyote and Grandmother are sitting on the dirt floor with a small flat-topped boulder between them. A hole is emitting smoke, heavy with the smell of sage and rosemary. Derek's eyes water as he stands shoulders tense and knees bent ready to move.

"Derek, stop gawking and join us. The sooner we get the formalities out of the way the sooner we can get to where we need to be." Mad Coyote sounds aggravated as he takes a long swig from a dented steel flask.

"Forgive my Grandfather, Alpha Derek, he lacks common courtesy. He is correct in the lack of time we have, please join us. I have much to tell you and then you must make a decision. More than your Pride's or my families lives rest on your decision." She gestures to a spot between them. Despite her all white eyes, they follow Derek as he joins them dropping the last foot when his legs give out without warning.

The woman is on her feet and holding her head to Derek's forehead before he has time to protest. "I am not feverish." The woman sniffs his breath and then steps back, sitting in her place again.

"Foolish men! Half-starved with all lives at stake and no word." She shakes with anger, even Mad Coyote turns red at her finger shaking at him and then at Derek. She is wearing a homespun shirt with rosebushes with viciously long thorns and very few blooms along the hem.

"Mad Coyote, what is going on here?" Derek asks, looking from the hold man to the old woman. *Are they both insane? I should be in California by now.* "Where are Bryan and the others?" He tenses, about to stand again.

"You stay put or I will switch your ass as your Pa should of." The old woman pulls out jerky from a pouch tied around her waist and tosses it at Derek. "Eat while we explain about the people who came from below and how we have bound our fate to their descendants."

Derek begins to stand, ignoring the jerky on the flat-topped boulder. The old woman slaps her hand on the boulder and the room tolls and jerks like a giant bell has been rung. "Your mate and Brother's life will end within 72 hours if you leave here now."

When Derek hesitates, half turned away looking for the exit. Looking around the still swaying room, he sees the only way in or out other than the room he woke in is a hole in the roof of one corner, 20 feet in the air. "All of our families will be dead, yours included, within nine turnings of the moon if you fail to save the SheMiTali." She speaks to Derek softly, he barely hears her words as the ringing from her slapping the table fades with the last of her words.

Derek looks to Mad Coyote who is holding his head in pain. "She is telling the truth, sit and listen." The old woman nods in Mad Coyote's direction. "It's the only way to deal with old women, let them have their say or they never allow you any peace."

Derek sinks back down, his ears ringing. He braces for the animal to fight for control, then he sinks, his muscles going loose in shock. "The animal is gone. Brother Lion's body is gone." His momentary relief turns to fear as the reason, after all this time, his Brother's body would suddenly be gone. Looking to Mad Coyote, he demands answers with no words.

"I sent him to limbo for a short time. Without Brother Lion's spirit to control the power of his physical self it is too dangerous to leave him loose. Now eat and listen, we have little time."

Derek picks up the jerky and begins to chew, being

thankful he still has his lion's powerful jaws and teeth or the rubber disguised as jerky might have ruined his teeth. His eyes never leave the old woman's face as she begins to speak.

"The Jicarilla Apache are the descendants of the first people to come from the underworld. When they passed from that realm to this, some among us changed. Spirits were rampant across the lands, back then they were not yet displaced and almost made extinct by the people of the machine. In that time, those that were changed were still accepted as family."

As she speaks, Derek can see the long row of people climbing from a smoking chasm into a night lit by the red glow from the chasm. Two by two they crawl and climb out of the ground and spread out in different directions. Some are staying together, others spread out. Among them are Weres of all kinds some winged, some furred and other things that are not Were but some other being that once might have been humanoid.

"This is not the story of the large group who came from the nether world. We are but a forgotten remnant. They have never considered us to really be of them. Their own histories do not match ours nor do they include us in them. They allow us to stay and live near them. Now as time goes by, we're forced to make decisions that drive us farther apart from them."

Derek witnesses horrible atrocities befalling the People. Time after time they go from prosperity to famine, happiness to despair. The centuries pass and the people survived. Then the Navajo with the white people's weapons made war against them, and they fled. The once proud people are a scattering remnant across the southwest.

"They knew we had the power to help them in their war. They didn't want to hear that if we drew attention to ourselves, they would see the end all that much sooner. How do you explain that whatever power, the strengths we have, is but a part of the power that flows all around the world?"

Derek watches as a group of widows and old men beg for help, only to be offered a few supplies and turned away. His eyes fill as he sees women and children selected to be taken by the Navajo, then the rest being cut down. The years pass and the Weres and strongest of those that are different draw more distant. Sending warning to save a few when they can. But mostly hiding and hating the edict that they do not help in the war.

"The Ancients walked the land then and hunted Weres and all beings with power for sport. They were betrayed by their descendant's and now slumber the sleep of the dead."

Derek watches as Anubis, Hades and what could only be Persephone hunt Weres and great magic users as his Pride hunts deer, but with more cruelty. Then time passes and he sees them seal themselves away and sleep at the urging of their descendants, the Numen.

"Now we are few and less powerful than we were, but we will not stand aside from the war that is coming. Fight, though we are fewer and weaker than we have ever been. Now we will face the threat we were told to save ourselves for."

Derek sees the people glowing with power, begging with a being so filled with power that he can't look directly at it. He feels the people's anger at being told to save themselves and draws attention to themselves. The people; Weres, Shamans, and Sorcerers all powerful in their own right will go and fight to save their distant kin. He hears the being speak:

**When the people of the machine
Are desecrating the land.
Then you will be needed,
Every man woman and child.
Even then, alone you will not survive.
The one you will face is the Other.
A demon from the abyss,
In a body of a Numen.
Held together by people of the machines magic,
And ancient power he will destroy all the earth.
Only the last SheMiTali can make him vulnerable.
Or make him a God.**

**Will you see the world a scorched ruin and ALL the people dead?
Or are you worthy enough of my regard to live and fight when it matters?**

Derek gasps his breath, the first he has taken since she began speaking. His eyes still have spots from where he tried to look directly at the glowing being. "Time is up Alpha Derek. Your mate is the last SheMiTali. The Other waits, closing in on her as we speak. Alone, you will not stand a chance."

"You cannot defeat the Other until the SheMiTali is trained in her power. For that to happen, you will need all the help you can get. With our help, you might be able to rescue her and your Brother. But first, you and your Pride must become allies of the Lost Remnant."

As she finishes speaking, the Werewolf that Derek had fought drops into the room from the hole in the ceiling. "They will be here by tomorrow. There is more of them than we thought there would be."

Derek looks at the Werewolf, missing fur like he had mange, scrawny, then Derek's eyes grew wide. "You gave us the gifts at the Ceremony when we became a Pride."

The Werewolf smiles at Derek. "Yes, I hope you have them somewhere safe. If we survive the battle tomorrow, you will need them to save the SheMiTali."

"You mean the battle to save Alexis?" Derek asks.

The old woman shakes her head no, and Mad Coyote closes his eyes. "No, the battle here is to save what we can from the one you call the Major. His abominations will attack us in force sometime in the early morning tomorrow. If you fight with us, those of us that survive will journey with you to save the SheMiTali."

Derek rocks, trying to find the way out of the mess he is in. *Brother Lion, what do I do? If they are right, and I cannot win without their help, do I stay and fight? Or rush off to try on our own?* "I must speak to Bryan and the others. I want to help you, but Alexis needs me."

The old woman shakes her head. "You do not understand. Either you fight with us and help a few of us live, or you do not leave here."

Derek jumps to his feet but she is already floating away toward the hole in the ceiling. "Think carefully Alpha Derek, you were promised to aid us a century ago. We have learned to shape prophecy to our purpose rather than to be used by it."

The Werewolf looks at Derek in disgust before the old woman gestures and he begins floating after her. Mad Coyote shakes his head, watching them disappear. "Sit down Derek, there is no way out until you agree to swear a blood oath to them and become kin. As well as to swear your pride, those of it here anyway, to fight tomorrow."

Derek leaps but comes up short every time. He tries climbing, but the walls become glass-like after ten feet. Breathing heavy, he collapses beside Mad Coyote. Several baskets of food and jugs of spring water are lowered by ropes. Derek springs, catching one and is up several feet when the other end is dropped into the cave, where it unravels.

Mad Coyote opens a basket and takes out a piece of fried chicken. "Come and eat. They're not bad people, they're just trying to survive and protect their families. No different than you."

Derek glares at Mad Coyote, tensing as he considers who led them here. "You know Sapphire told the kids the same as the spirits said to me. I ignore them as often as I can, but they would not shut up until I swore to help you rescue your Alexis. Now, come and tell me about her, and I will tell you about the women I have known."

The light coming through the opening to the outside shifts to a new angle and grows dim. Derek is sprawled out beside the still smoking pit. Mad Coyote is pacing from one place to another, muttering to himself.

The light still flowing in is blocked as the Werewolf from earlier looks down at them. "Have you made a decision yet? The others from your Pride grow restless."

Derek stands, stretching, aware as he does that the animal is waking inside him. He isn't sure, but it feels like it will be awhile yet before the animal is fighting for control. "Is my Pride safe?"

The Werewolf snorts, "They are being treated as blood kin. We need the alliance with you and yours to survive. You also need our aid to rescue your mate and spirit brother."

The Werewolf jumps into the room, his shadow stretching across the room. He lands with a grunt and rolls to the side to absorb some of the impact. Standing, he nods to Derek and spreads his hands in front of him showing them to be open and empty. "I am Shane Shovel, Fist Alpha of the Peoples Pack. I offer you shade and water during your time among us."

Derek looks at Mad Coyote with a raised eyebrow. "Well get on with it. You and I both know we either help them or we sit here until the Majors Freaks kill them and then come for us." Mad Coyote waves his hands in agitation for Derek to get on with it.

Brother Lion, we really need to discuss etiquette when one Alpha visits another Pride or Packs territory.

"I am Derek Mathews, the lost Alpha of the Unit Pride of South Dakota. I accept your offer of shade and water." *Great, why did I say lost? I am sure that slip up will come back to bite me in the ass.*

Shane's eyes widened as he looks from Derek to Mad Coyote. "Yes yes, you are both mighty Alphas." Mad Coyote steps up to Derek and drags him by his arm to stand in front of Shane. "Now, as the spirits witness, I ask you Shane Shovel, Fist Alpha do you wish to shed blood with Derek, the lost and his Pride as a family?"

"Uhhmm Grandma I mean Priestess Shulah Tiere_" Shane is cut off in mid-word.

"She's not here and the first family is already dead. The Major is only hours away. Now get on with it boys." Mad Coyote pulls a huge bowie knife from somewhere, grabs Shane's hand and slices his palm.

"Derek, the Lost and dimwitted, do you want to save your mate?" Mad Coyote doesn't wait for an answer but grabs Derek's hand and when it doesn't open fast enough slices his wrist instead. "Boy, do you love your Mate?" Mad Coyote drops the knife and it fades from sight before it hits the floor and grabbing both of them, he shakes their arms.

"I do." *Did I just get married? What the hell is happening here?* Derek's thoughts stop as Mad Coyote shoves his bleeding wrist against Shane's bleeding palm.

"Abra Cadabra!" Nothing happens as Mad Coyote frowns and begins running the palm and wrist together harder.

"Great Gramps_" Shane is cut off when Mad

Coyote with eyes huge, shove the wrist and palm across his mouth.

"Drink, you have to drink the mixed blood. Yes, I know it's here!" Mad Coyote continues muttering to himself as he rubs it across Derek's mouth as well.

"Blah. What the hell?" Derek shuts up as his body goes rigid. Every muscle is frozen in position. All he can move is his eyes and by the odd posture of Shane, the same is happening to him as well.

"One last time, I ask the Lost and the shovelnose, will you live and die as Blood Brothers before spirits, man, and beasts?" When neither speaks fast enough, he kicks each of them in the shin, one after the other while still holding their arms together.

Wincing, Derek manages to get out a low "I do." Without being able to take a deep breath, it's barely a whisper.

Kicking Shane in the shin again, Mad Coyote manages to get an "I do" grunted low but audible from Shane.

"Then fight as one family. Deal with the mad animal inside Derek, I will slow the Freaks." Mad Coyote lets go of them and darts to the side with his knife once more in his hand as a Freak falls into the hole. It lands on its side and the wet crunch of breaking bones fills the cavern.

Derek misses what happens next as his body temperature spikes. Shane moans as his temperature plummets. His hand is wrapped around Derek's wrist, and blood is moving between them. As the blood flows from one to the other, the temperature goes up and down.

The animal in Derek, which was left behind when Brother Lion astrally left, roars in rage. Derek gasps as he feels his control eroding away once more. *Gods, why is it so strong? The others have no trouble controlling their animals this way.*

Fuck man, this is not a normal Were animal, it is much more powerful. Shane's mental voice shakes Derek as he realizes that he can feel Shane's body as if it is his own.

He has no time to ask questions as the animal body left behind by Brother Lion's spirit attacks both of their minds. Claws are striking astrally across the ties that bind their spirits to their bodies. The rage from both of them surge, sealing the bonds as mere words can only begin to do.

Together, we do not want to kill or maim it. Shane's voice is stronger than before as new energy hums between them. Derek can feel his Pride nearby in battle. Then he staggers with Shane as he feels a tearing away as one of Shane's pack dies.

The lion body attacks again while they are reeling from the loss. The wound bleeds their spirit into Limbo. Why is it attacking now? Either we kill it or it kills us.

Shane attacks from the left, his body shifting into the space where Brother Lion lives while riding in Derek's Aura. *We beat it down to prove we are worthy of its obedience. Just like any challenge to the right to be Alpha.*

There is no time for Derek to consider the words,

he is busy fighting a Lion bigger, faster and tougher than he ever realized Brother Lion was. He and Shane fight as one. When Derek moves into slash the flank of the Lion, Shane just knows what he intends and moves to distract him.

It seems to take hours, but in reality, it's only minutes before they beat the Lion into submission. There is no thought or words to announce when the Lion submits to their leadership. One moment, Derek is slashing at the exposed belly while Shane is on the Lions back clawing with Werewolf claws, only slightly smaller than a Werelions claws.

Then the lion is lying on its back, exposing its throat. Breathing heavily Shane and Derek lean against each other, feeling the lion bond to their Pride just like any other Pride or pack member. Then the Lion heaves, shoving them apart and back into their physical bodies.

Derek opens his eyes, crusty with sleep in a room no longer recognizable. Mad Coyote is covered in blood and gore. His knife is now covered in black and red so thick it is impossible to see where the arm and knife separate. All the way to his shoulder he is dripping blood.

Spread around the ground, Derek stops counting at seven freaks, some dead some still struggling to rise. Mad Coyote is backing up with three Freaks, one wounded and two unharmed hammering at him one with a club and the other two with rusted swords.

Guns lie discarded and broken around the floor, some still in the hands of dead Freaks. Derek is reeling from the astral wounds that still seep parts of him into limbo. When his body moves to attack with a roaring challenge, Derek is dragged along for the ride in his body.

He notices Shane moving a moment later to attack a newly arrived Freak as he closes with the one on the left of the trio forcing Mad Coyote back. Derek's body moves in a whirlwind of claws and fangs. The stabbing pain in his side as the wounded freak stabs him is swallowed in the rush of adrenaline.

Mad Coyote uses the moment the Freak is turned stabbing Derek to slice its throat with his bowie knife, stepping stiffly, he's not quite fast enough to avoid the club swing by the last of the trio that takes him in the shoulder. He cries out as his collar bone breaks and he falls back.

Shane is moving to attack a Freak that has just jumped in and slipped in blood, falling belly first on a knife pointing up. Shane kicks the Freak rolling it over and grabs the knife in its stomach wrenching upward gutting the freak as he moves past it to leap at the next one that lands on its feet and swings a club at his head.

Derek pulls his mouth from the throat of the Freak he has just finished and grabs the one with the club, who is about to smash it into Mad Coyote, by the head wrenching it back and around. The Freak's frantic swings clip him on the head and shoulder. Any one of which, if better aimed, would have finished him.

Mad Coyote switches hands with his Bowie and rams the knife into the groin of the Freak. As the Freak leans forward, Derek manages to twist and snap the neck of the freak.

Derek stumbles as the lion steps back into the back of his being and leaves him in control. Shane is leaning against the wall looking up and out to see if any more freaks are coming. When he looks back at Derek, he shakes his head no.

Derek turns and helps Mad Coyote up from his knees. "You took too long, the battle went poorly with the Alphas here. My Granddaughter is gone." The sadness in Mad Coyote's voice and tears in his eyes are shocking. When his eyes roll into his head and he goes limp in Derek's arms it shakes Derek and Shane to their core.

Shane limps over as the sun begins entering the cavern again. "It's dawn. The spell to float out is not working."

Derek nods, watching the light slowly fill the cavern.

Chapter 15

Matteas crouches on the roof of the old farmhouse waiting for Amanda and Doc to come into view. *When this one is over, we are going to discuss who gets to be a distraction.* He shifts his weight but the roof creaks and he has to stop moving and hold his breath again hoping no one inside hears him. It was around three am when he climbed onto the roof while it was still dark. Amanda and the Dr. Michael are running late.

"I told you to check and make sure the spare was aired up!" Amanda yells as she and Dr. Michael walk up the drive. The front door opens, a man wearing black military fatigues and dark sunglasses steps out. "This is private property. Turn around and leave now."

Doc ignores him as yells back at Amanda, "Who the hell rents a car without checking for a spare and that it is aired up?"

The man on the porch blinks then steps down the three steps leaving the door open a foot behind him. "Now listen here, you need to get off this property." He reaches Doc and Amanda, his hand on his holstered gun.

Matteas swings off the porch roof and onto the porch, already in his natural form. For once, he's glad to be a smaller Werelion than Derek. He lands with a light thud and slips inside shutting the door behind him.

"Hey, you can't_" reaches him as the door closes. Looking around at the dim room, he sees a broken down couch with a man reading a magazine sitting on it. "Did you send those fools packing? Should have kept the woman, she could have been entertaining." He turns the page of his magazine without looking up.

Matteas shoots the guard with his crossbow now slung off his back. A wet gurgle and thump as the man slides off the couch with the bolt through his back and out his front. "Amanda would have killed you painfully. You owe me."

Matteas reloads the crossbow with another bolt from his back case and walks over to the dead man. Leaning down while listening, he searches the man. Transferring keys, wallet, and cell phone to his pockets he straightens, kicking the dead man in the ribs.

Then he moves to the desk set up in the corner with three monitors. Amanda is dragging the first man who went outside towards a pile of trash. A fridge missing its door sitting on its side works as a coffin. Then she moves the camera, looking toward where the barn is.

The other two monitors show the Cadillac at the end of the drive complete with a blowout. The last monitor is fuzzy and shows a part of the area behind the house. A swing set, a lawn mower missing the motor and some brown patches that might have been grass.

"Should have paid attention when that camera got fuzzy around three am," Matteas mentions as he passes the dead man heading for the hallway. The hallway is dark, only lit by the light escaping the curtains in the living room.

"Lucky for me, I have Werelion vision." Matteas' voice is low as he moves up beside the first closed door. Leaning against the door, he holds his breath listening but not hearing anything, he sprays a penetrating oil on the hinges. Putting away the oil in his waist pouch, he holds his crossbow in one hand and swings the door open in one silent move.

Breathing out, he closes his eyes for a moment as he considers the empty metal coat hangers before closing the closet door. The next room doesn't have a door, it's just an open entry to an old fashioned kitchen. The stainless steel appliances are out of place. The double sized commercial subzero refrigerator is blocking half the cabinets and is gleaming.

Walking through the kitchen, he looks into a sunny dining room with a large wooden table and a matching china cabinet against the wall. At the table are three men. One is a specialist with a patch bandage over one eye and a metal arm from the elbow to his fingertips on his left arm. The other two are wearing the black fatigues and are ordinary looking middle aged men. One balding and one with long hair and a beer belly that shows he is not career regular military.

Matteas shoots the specialist first with the crossbow but he is already moving and the bolt takes him in the right shoulder instead of the chest. Dropping the crossbow, Matteas leaps on the table drawing the scimitar he is wearing strapped against his right leg to keep it quiet.

The balding man doesn't move as fast as his buddy with the beer belly and with one flick of his wrist and bend of his knees, Matteas opens his jugular for him. Beer belly gets his 9 mm out and might have gotten Matteas if the specialist had not grabbed Matteas' leg in his cyber arm and yank him off the table.

As Matteas falls he twists and he cuts off beer belly's hand holding the 9 mm. The specialist is crushing his ankle. The specialist drags Matteas off the table and throws him out the window. "Fuck!" Is all Matteas gets out before he crashes onto the ground, once more outside the farmhouse.

The specialist follows him out the window, holding a small cannon in his cyber hand. "Who are you?" He demands of Matteas, who has gotten to his feet only to collapse when his crushed ankle won't support his weight.

Thunk, Thunk. "What?" Is all the specialist gets out as he falls with two crossbow bolts in him.

"Damn, about fucking time. Let me guess, the barn is empty so you two were playing hide the salami." Matteas lays back breathing heavily and pulling out little slivers of glass from his arm and cheek.

Doc goes over to help him up while Amanda fires a bolt into beer belly's back as he is running into the kitchen shouting for help. "Barn's empty. There're signs of a few transport trucks leaving in the last few days." Doc looks over his scrapes and whistles as he pulls up Matteas' pant leg.

"Yeah, damn cyber head crushed the bone, be a day or so before I can use it right again." He leans on Doc until they reach the side of the house and then leans against it.

Amanda hands him her crossbow. "Stay here, shoot any that get past us."

Matteas drops the crossbow pulling a pair of 50 caliber desert eagles, shiny and gold. "I smell Freaks in there and if anyone heard us, they already know we're here. My guess is, this lot is all that's left. The others are gone off into the sunset."

"If she's not here, we'll head for California or New Mexico, that's where they all seem to be heading. Either way, we will find her." Doc squeezes his shoulder as he follows Amanda through the window. Matteas nods, fighting down his worry with rage at what they had found over the last two months as they hunted for where the Major has his mate Sabrina. Matteas watches, leaning against the side of the house as Michael follows Amanda into the kitchen and out of sight.

Dr. Michael pauses by beer belly and searches him. After almost a month of hunting for Sabrina, it's second nature now. Keys, key cards, communication devices move on. This time, he only finds one key card, a pack of menthol lights, and 67 cents. Shaking his head he moves to follow Amanda.

His feelings for Amanda have grown stronger as he spends more time with her. The frustration of not being alone for long enough to consummate the growing relationship also puts an awkward frustration to the moments when they can make out.

Damn it, man, you know to keep your mind on business. Last time your mind wondered you got shot. Running his hand over his right ass cheek brings a twinge. Three weeks is not enough time for a 45 caliber gun shot in the ass to heal, especially without leaving a scar. The sound of gunfire brings his 44 magnum up and ready as he slings the crossbow on his back.

Moving out of the kitchen, he sees the open door and stairs leading down in the middle of the hall. Amanda is out of sight. Moving in a half-crouch, he had made fun of seeing actors do this on television only a few months ago but now it feels natural. *Lower, sideways, present less target area. Bullets are relatively small, limit the number of targets you present.*

Looking down the stairs he sees Amanda crouched at the bottom of the stairs waiting for a clear shot while using a dead woman in a lab coat as a shield. "Clear!" He grabs a flash grenade and throws it blindly from the top of the stairs toward the area where shots are coming from.

Amanda ducks behind the body when Dr. Michael yells. When the grenade goes off, Dr. Michael runs down half the stairs that are open on the left with just a handrail and a solid wall on the right. When he is half way down he sees the man that is shooting at Amanda duck into a room that might have been a bedroom at one time.

Dr. Michael looks at Amanda wondering why she's still at the bottom of the stairs and sees the blood pooling around her while she struggles to get the handcuff connecting her to the obese woman's body off. An animal rage at Amanda being hurt fills him and he leaps over the side of the handrail and lands in a roll.

"Michael, wait!" Amanda curses as he ignores her and charges after the man that has gone into the bedroom.

Dr. Michael glimpses two more bodies, both human in what used to be a family room but is now filled with computers and lab equipment. The lighting is hospital bright and the stainless steel gleams. He ignores all of this as he charges into the room blindly.

He fires two shots at the man in black who is closing a stainless steel door behind him. He rushes at the steel door but it slips shut and he hears bolts sliding home. Amanda runs in the room. "What's wrong with you? I've told you over and over not to enter a room blindly!"

Michael looks Amanda up and down holding his breath, "You're okay?" He asks.

Amanda frowns, "When will you learn, I'm a Werejaguar, it's almost impossible to kill me. You're the fragile one." She leans around Dr. Michael examining him, like he's her patient, backside and front. When he snorts and turns away to examine the door the man had escaped through, she slaps him on the ass hard enough he takes a step forward to keep his balance.

Amanda looks around the small room. A hospital bed with straps to restrain the patient is on the left. The white sheets and pillow are crisp and clean. "Looks like they were just getting set up here. No sign of any patients being made into Freaks or Specialists." Amanda doesn't mention the breeding dens they have been forced to destroy. The men and women with amputated arms and legs chained to beds so drugged that Freaks can use them in the hope of creating a breed of mutant Freaks that won't lose cognitive mental function.

Dr. Michael shivers as the same train of unspoken memories of gassing then burning the poor doomed creatures that once had been human. Thankfully, no fetus have resulted from the breeding experiments. Dr. Michael feels Amanda become aware of the mingling of their thoughts at the same moment he does. They both stumble as they see out of each other's eyes for a confusing moment before pulling back into themselves.

Turning her attention to the rest of the room, while she concentrates on breathing, she notices a pair of waiting room chairs and a computer screen and a small stainless counter and sink. Turning to the open door to the family room as a shadow runs by, Amanda raises her 9 mm and fires three shots, one after the other.

Dr. Michael turns from the examination of the sealed door in time to see Amanda stumble and grunt as a rapid staccato of shots enters the room. "Amanda!" He moves to her side dragging her out of the line of fire despite her growls and resistance.

As they both fall beside the bed, the gunshots stop.

"Damn you! Get off me. I can catch him." Amanda struggles to pry Dr. Michael's arms off, they tighten in answer.

"You're shot, be still." Amanda heaves upward, dragging Dr. Michael along with her. "Dammit woman, listen to me for once! He's going to run right into Matteas sitting with those cannons of his." Breathing heavy, he trips her and they both fall again.

Looking into each other's eyes, chests heaving, heart beats beating in sync, they begin to smile. "It wouldn't be fair to keep all the fun for ourselves would it?" Amanda half speaks half thinks to Dr. Michael.

Before he can finish his return thought, there's a click. They both turn as one and look toward where the sound came from. "Fuck!" Amanda thinks it and Dr. Michael speaks it as they struggle to get to the closing door before it seals them in.

Amanda might have reached it if she hadn't been hampered by Dr.Michael in his own effort to reach it. As it is, they both slam into the door as the bolts slide home. A whirring sounds from under the door and is followed by three inches of Plexiglas sliding up along all the walls and doors.

Amanda roars and rams her shoulder into the stainless door. A crack fills the air as one of the bolts holding the door splits. Before she can ram it again, the plexiglass slides into place. She turns to Dr. Michael, eyes flashing, claws moving in and out. "That's why I should never have taken up with you."

Dr. Michael rubs his nose as his nasal passages begin

to burn and itch. "You ungrateful whore, without my money you all would have been helpless."

"Gggggrrrr!" Amanda swings her clawed paw at Dr. Michael, who is connected mentally with her and is already moving out of the way. His punch misses by inches as she leans back. Over the last few months, as they have grown closer, the barriers between their thoughts and emotions have become blurred.

"Get out of my head!" Amanda grunts, managing to knick Dr. Michael across his right cheek when she moves faster than before, and he doesn't quite lean back far enough. They had discussed going to Derek for advice but with his other problems they kept putting it off.

Dr. Michael's eyes widen as the sting of the three scratches from her razor sharp claws burn his cheek. Panting, they stop swatting at each other, both rubbing their noses. "What's wrong with us? Do you smell something?"

The thoughts are on top of each other, both of them frown, not sure which thought is their own and which is the other persons as their ideas mix worse than before. "Does she really not know how hard it is for me not to kiss her?"

Amanda's growl deepens nearing a purr. "I hope he doesn't notice my nipples hardening around him again. His arms look thicker than when we met."

They step closer, almost touching, breathing faster. Thoughts are mingling until neither of them knows who is thinking what. It's not a thought, it's not desire, the meeting of their lips is a need. Amanda leans down, her

fangs fully extended, rough tongue sliding over his lips
before sliding over his smooth tongue tracing hers. The
swirling sensations as each feel what the other does is
disorienting.

Feeling his tongue move in her mouth exploring,
while experiencing the sensation of his smooth hot
tongue brushing over hers, the highly sensitive feline taste
buds swirling with a mixture of sweet and spicy that
evoke a flood of heat from her and the pure animal
emotion, "Mine."

Her cheeks flush as she feels him respond to her
claiming him. The rush of blood to his swelling cock and
fierce pride that she would claim him as her own. The
fatigues and boots fly off them. Her shirt falls to the
ground a moment after his. His button is stuck, hung up
on loose threads. Growling animally, he rips the pants
open, the button falling free as the zipper tares.

A moment later they look up, he has on his plaid
boxers and one black sock. She has nothing on but fur.
His eyes trail over her and all four of her breasts. The
instant fear of allowing anyone to see her second smaller
pair of tits is swallowed by the feeling of wonder and awe
that has his mouth hanging open. "Beautiful."

Her orange block spots are almost hypnotic in the
patterns as they run over her body. The fur is short,
covering her skin in such a way that when his hands run
over her smooth rippled belly, it startles him all over
again at the thick richness of her fur. Leaning into her, his
tongue swirls around her lower left nipple.

His nipples harden painfully as he experiences the

warm moist tongue swirling her sensitive nipple and aureole. When his hard cock pokes out of his boxers and brushes her furred leg, she gasps. The sensation of her velvet fur running across the swollen head sends an electric jolt of pleasure from her nipples to her clit.

As Dr. Michael's hips jerk as the electric zing hits her clit, his cock slips between her thighs brushing the underside of her lips. "Aaahhhhhhhmmmm." The moans fill both of them. Amanda feels the Jaguar swarm over her, having been denied the consummation with her chosen mate for months she will no longer be denied. A fleeting fear that Dr. Michael won't survive a mating buries as his hands grabs her ass and squeezes.

Her claws run down his shoulders leaving trails of blood behind. The warm wetness brings a heightened pleasure to both of them as Dr. Michael loses himself in the moment and his nibbling of her nipples turns to an insistent tug and flick of the tip of his tongue.

"Raaawwwrrr!" Dr. Michael is flung onto the bed and bounces. Then Amanda is on him. The mating urgency is increasing, the ache in her loins rise to a heated need to be filled. She straddles him, her hips moving instinctively. As his pale hardness enters her, they both shiver.

The flood of sensations is filling Amanda as she feels the hot wet silkiness of her pussy flowing over and swallowing his cock, rocking in time to the fullness and pleasant pressure of him pressing that spot inside her. She isn't sure if she is feeling her cock sliding into his pussy or his cock into her pussy. The flow of physical sensations from one to the other is too fast to know who feels what, drowning them in animal lust.

As her four nipples brush across his chest, her claws slide down his sides, cutting skin like paper, marking her property. He rakes his fingernails down her back, and it isn't enough! His teeth find her shoulder and bite down, breaking the skin. Her orgasm builds, his balls tighten painfully, need overflows every part of them.

He twists, heaving with all his strength and is on top. His hips thrust hard, slamming into her again and again. Biting, clawing, mixing with licking and kisses. Then she can't take it anymore, he has to take her like an animal, mating with her like the male he is.

She grabs his arms rolling under him and she half falls off the bed. Then she pulls him onto her back. Dr. Michael half stands on the floor and is half leaning on her. Her hips push back, grinding against him. He thrusts harder and deeper inside her. Her hips are rearing back to meet his with each frenzied stroke.

His long throbbing cock jerks, spasming as he feels the point of no return passing. Feeling the pressure filling his hard dick as it pummels in and out of her, the strain as he fights to hold back the ocean of his seed fills them both.

Amanda's nipples brush the hard polyester sheets. Then Dr. Michael grabs her hips, his balls slapping wetly against her clit and his hot seed shoots into her. He bites her shoulder as he feels the hot wetness fuel her next orgasm. Trembling as his aching balls and her trembling legs flood them both with orgasm after orgasm.

Then, when they can't take anymore, they collapse onto the floor, his cock buried deep inside her quivering pussy. His arms are wrapped around her, holding her tightly to him. Breathing harshly, they both jerk as a breeze of fresh air flows over their sweat drenched bodies. There's an almost audible snap as they separate back into their own minds and bodies.

"Goddamn it! Get dressed, Sabrina was here just two days ago!" Matteas stands panting in excitement in the doorway, blood covering one of his arms and part of his chest. When neither of them do more than groan, he snaps, "I'm going after my mate, either get dressed and come with me or stay here." He turns and heads for the stairs.

Walking out of the bathroom with his pants held up with a safety pin, Dr. Michael drops the towel in the hamper after giving his hair another brisk drying. Shirtless, he follows the voices down the dim hallway.

"Looks like you worked him over pretty well, you think he's lying to just stop the pain?" Amanda asks.

Dr. Michael stops halfway down the stairs, looking over the rail where Amanda is rolling over the body of a specialist with electric wire connections coming out of one side of his head. Matteas' voice draws him down another couple steps until he can see him sitting at the row of computers in the family room.

"No, he thought I would keep him alive to open the door and release the two of you. With the amount of cyber hardware in his head, I'm not sure how much he actually felt of what my knife was doing. It was his excitement over watching the two of you rape each other."

Amanda straightens, the snort freezing half released as her eyes find Dr. Michael's. She reaches toward him with her thoughts and the snort releases as a gasp. He returns her look, nodding as he conveys that he can't reach her thoughts either. For the first time in months, they can sense each other but no more than any other mated pair of Weres.

Matteas looks up from the screen at the gasp and shakes his head after a quick glance from Amanda to Dr. Michael and back. "You two should have spoken to someone months ago. The mating bond is magic and can have funny effects when mundane humans are involved."

Dr. Michael continues down the stairs, focusing on the specialist's corps with effort. Matteas speaks while clicking through screens. "The Major is on his way to California, he thinks Roger is there for some reason and he's determined to have him no matter what." A large laser printer begins printing as he finishes speaking.

Dr. Michael kneels to examine the specialist. The dark hair is thick on the left side of its head and gone on right. The row of bundled wires end with a mix of HDMI, and what appears to be audio video cables, as well as an optical triangular plug that Dr. Michael is unfamiliar with.

Matteas gets up, turning to the printer but stops as his eyes widen on Dr. Michael's back, sides and shoulder.

"Damn Amanda, I wasn't paying much attention to the mating but he looks lucky to be alive."

Dr. Michael stands up from his stoop, stepping over the body to stand beside Amanda. "He had to be marked as mine. Now any female that poaches him will know why, when I kill her." She speaks in a low growl.

Matteas walks to the printer and removes a thick stack of printouts. "You two are newly mated and a disaster waiting to happen." He turns back around, walking past them to the couch with a limp, but his Were body is already healing the crushed ankle. He will be able to use it normally in a day or two. "When did your age begin reversing Dr. Michael?"

"I didn't tell him." Amanda squeezes Dr. Michael's hand.

"I know, we aren't sure ourselves." Stepping toward Matteas, "How do you know my age is reversing?"

Matteas begins unpacking explosives from the large duffel on the couch. "The cuts from Amanda's claws are already healing and look like they're a week old. The same as if you were a Were. I thought you were dying your hair, but now I can see the gray is all but gone." Matteas turns, carrying the large clay looking explosive with wires coming out to fit. "I haven't seen you without a shirt since we left the ranch. You looked like a man in his late fifties that worked out regularly. Now you look like an athlete in his prime."

Dr. Michael turns to Amanda as Matteas walks out of the room after installing the first explosive onto the row of computers. He walks through the bedroom where

Amanda and Dr. Michael had been locked in and out the other side where three more identical rooms and a small half bathroom are located, carrying the black duffel bag.

"I'm sorry, I didn't mean to endanger you." Amanda's voice is soft as her arm wraps around him hugging him to her possessively.

"I might become a Were or develop some latent magic ability or go crazy and have to be killed. I told you before, I love you." His fierce smile sets her heart racing as he steps away from her to follow after Matteas and learn more about setting explosives.

Amanda takes the other duffel full of papers and DVDs up the stairs. Her heart is beating to a slower beat than it had since she changed, half way between a human's and a Werejaguar's. Her step is confident and her mind is alone in her head once again. Yet strangely, she feels less alone than she can ever remember feeling. That small cloud of emotions and sense that part of her is that way shows the direction where Dr. Michael is and that he's enjoying himself.

Chapter 16

The pillars of flames and smoke filling the sky in the rear view mirror is an odd contrast the peaceful fall day. The two-lane rural highway is filled with rolling hills and farmland that spread across rural Illinois.

The radio is playing light Jazz since it's Dr. Michael's turn at the wheel. Matteas is in the backseat looking back at the growing red tinged black sky. Amanda glances in the rear view mirror from the front passenger seat. "Are you sure the major didn't keep her with him? He has dragged her around the country with him up until now."

Matteas turns to the front as Dr. Michael moves the car to the side of the road and slows. The passing red and blue lights are accompanied by blaring sirens. "The files said she was to be a witness or something like that. The online translator is not that great but the Major is convinced that this prophecy can make him the Alpha of all Weres everywhere."

Dr. Michael snorts from the driver's seat. "We have enough psychotic politicians without adding an immortal lunatic Werewolf to the mix."

Amanda smiles as she squeezes Dr. Michael's thigh before turning back to Matteas. "Explain it again, just the high points. We spent an extra three days there for this information without hot water." Both males sigh again as she once more finds a way to complain about the lack of hot water and other amenities. "Not all of us need cold showers like the two of you."

Both men blush at her reference to finding the pair of them watching her mating with Dr. Michael on the surveillance recordings. In his defense, he had been very proud of her claiming of him. With Weres, it's all about who is more dominant. Amanda and Dr. Michael, both having dominant personalities, have a potential problem for a future together. On top of his being just human.

"Well, the gist of the prophecy is that a Skinchanger will save the SheMiTali and then go on to be Alpha of the world. Like all prophecies, it is full of little signs or things that need to happen before the grand finally. The Major has decided that Alexis is the SheMiTali." He picks up his notebook and jots down 'check with Brother Lion on what SheMiTali is.'

"I understand that part but where does Sabrina come in?" Dr. Michael asks once more, moving over for the third fire engine to roar by.

"The Major has more of the prophecy than I do. His notes refer to blood kin of the SheMiTali being present at each of the signs. With Mr. Armstrong still in the hands of the Other, he is trying to get blood kin to equate to a member of Pride or pack." Matteas circles the note he has just written.

Amanda whistles, "Seems like he's grasping at straws."

"The Major has been unstable since he got his last pack butchered. Some of the portents have already occurred and the Major missed his chance to be part of them. Now, he is getting desperate, and that is fine with me." Under his breath, he says, "Hang on Sabrina. I'm on my way."

Dr. Michael and Amanda both reach for each other's hands as the idea of being separated sprout an intense fear within them. "I remember reading many books on prophecy. They all contradicted each other. The only thing any of them agreed on was that it was a very bad idea to try and force a prophecy to happen." After Dr. Michael speaks, the car is silent, as all of them hope the black and red sky behind them, from the burning farm, is not a portent of things to come.

"Gods, it's nice to finally have a hot shower." Amanda walks into the restaurant smiling as Dr. Michael is turning from the table with three to-go boxes in his hands as Matteas hurries to the register.

"Glad to hear that. It will make you having breakfast in the car easier to swallow." Dr. Michael heads for the door out of the restaurant. After a moment, Amanda turns and follows.

Amanda catches up to Dr. Michael as he's placing the three Styrofoam to-go dishes in the back seat. "What's going on?" she asks as she stops beside the open door.

"Get in, I'll explain on the way." Matteas hurries past her to the driver's side as he slides behind the wheel. "Let's go already!" He says when she doesn't move fast enough.

Dr. Michael gets in the front passenger seat before she can protest. Getting in the back seat, her shoulders stiffen as the smell of fear and excitement flood the small SUV from the two men in the front seat. Matteas' fur begins to grow then recedes leaving him in a constantly agitated state. Weres have to concentrate to look human. Stress or too long without relaxing into their natural state and they lose the ability to assume human form.

"So let's hear it. What's going on?" Her hunger wins out over her agitation and as she digs into the large stack of pancakes in the first take out container.

Matteas pulls onto the interstate and accelerates to 75 mph before answering. "I can feel Sabrina. Not just know that she's alive but really feel her." His clenched hands are leaving permanent marks on the steering wheel. "Whatever magic was keeping her hidden from me disappeared as your food arrived."

Amanda eats faster as the SUV gets up to speed and hits 90 mph. "Close?" After months of not being able to feel his mate, she is suddenly there again in his mind. A warm ball of sensations. Scared, hurt but alive and he is getting closer by the moment.

Dr. Michael opens the duffel at his feet and pulls out Matteas' gold 50 caliber Desert Eagles. "There's more, for a second I could swear I could feel Derek again, then

294

it was like I was doused in ice water." He shivers as the thought of the mental shock and brain freeze pain returns his attention to the lingering effects.

Amanda stops moving and closes her eyes. She frowns as her sense of her mate in the front seat keeps overwhelming her efforts to feel any of the rest of the Pride.

Breathing deeper, she reaches past the distractions. They're closing fast, Bryan is enraged beyond anything she has ever felt before. His attention registers on her then blinding pain in the kidneys, and she doubles over in the backseat.

Dr. Michael jerks and moans as he shares her pain. Undoing his seat belt he turns in his seat. Before he climbs into the back with her, Amanda straightens and shakes her head. "Bryan is only minutes away and hurt badly."

She shoves the mostly eaten food to the floor, as Matteas takes the closed for construction ramp, the thump thump, of orange cones announcing the road closed sign before they hit the plastic sign. The SUV jerks to the right before Matteas gets it straightened out. "Left, he's to the left."

Sitting up and reaching into the back seat, Amanda grabs two duffels and drags them into the backseat. "Heat mirage is ahead, closing fast," Matteas announces grimly as once more he loses the contact with his mate Sabrina.

They fly past a partial sign 'welcome to vation' sign most of it in pieces and scattered across the road. They pass a small school house, which has smoke coming out the windows then they all gasp as a wave of heat passes over them. The next moment, the sound of gunshots and screams of people and Weres in pain fill the air. "Big Magic. It's almost 5 am, wasn't the sun peaking up before we passed into here?"

Three pickups are burning alongside the road. What looked like an armored personnel carrier is on its side where the old pickups had rammed it together. The bodies scattered around are a mix of Native Americans, Weres, and Freaks. Lots of Freaks.

"There!" Amanda cries out pointing ahead as she shoves the last gun into its holster. Ahead of them, a Weretiger is fighting a specialist and three Freaks. Behind him in a minivan are two kids one staring wide-eyed the other flicking what looks like a whip made of fire at the faces of the freaks to keep them from flanking Bryan.

Matteas floors it, taking them off the rough dirt road and heading at the combatants. 50 feet, 30 feet, he hits the brakes and spins the wheel. On pavement the SUV would have rolled, in the sandy New Mexico dirt, it slides sideways, right into two of the freaks knocking them down and rolling over them. The Specialist with two cyber arms, one holding a machete and the other a dagger, gets out of the way and Bryan stumbles back into the side of the minivan.

Amanda fires into the specialist while the SUV is still moving. Dr. Michael rolls out of the door, his 44 Magnum and his new 9 mm firing into the freaks under the SUV that are already lifting it. Matteas fires out his open window. Moments after the SUV slides onto the scene and the freaks and specialist are down and not moving. The kid with the whip moves from one to another jabbing a dagger with a wicked smoking blade into each of them.

Bryan is bleeding heavily from his side, and the fact that he's not healing is alarming. "We have to go, they pushed the others back to the village." Bryan and the kids head for the car. One kid is a Native Amercian the other is Peggy. Her pigtails are frazzled, she has dirt and blood over most of her, but her eyes are bright and face grim. Amanda looks back at her eyes and sees the glow, lighting the area in front of her, it makes Amanda swallow.

Bryan climbs into the driver's seat, his left side moving stiffly. Peggy guides the young Native American boy, a couple of years older than her, into the back seat. Dr. Michael gets in the back. Bryan starts the SUV and puts it in drive. Amanda has to scramble to squeeze into the crowded backseat holding her arms and gun out the window. Matteas leaps into the front passenger seat as Bryan hits the gas and fishtails the SUV onto the dirt road.

"Where are your guns?" Matteas asks, watching the road and reaching desperately for Sabrina, yet feeling nothing other than that she is alive.

"Guns wouldn't fire. Then a few minutes ago whatever magic was in place began slipping or at least we started hearing gun shots." Peggy helps the still silent boy over the back seat and into the cargo area. "Big Magic, not astral, blood and earth mixed. Bad mojo man."

Amanda shivers at the adult voice coming from the little girl. "How many of them are there? Where are Derek and the others?" There's more room in the backseat after the Native American boy goes in the back, she is able to reload her gun and holster it.

Bryan shivers, "I don't know, they snuck past the perimeter guard. Burned the school and would have finished us if we had been where they expected us. I was cut off and ran into Peggy. It's bad Amanda, several hundred Freaks, specialists, and Weres. If they had used guns, we would all be dead by now."

Dr. Michael uses his handkerchief to clean Peggy's face. "They got Mrs. Collins, Tommy and I tried, but they were too fast. Then it was just us, and we could feel the bad mojo magic building. We thought we could stop it but they were too strong." She sounds like a disillusioned child as tears run down her cheeks. If her eyes hadn't still been glowing and the hard lines around her mouth speaking of rage, that children should never feel, she might have been just another little girl lost in an adult war.

The sudden lack of gunfire draws everyone's attention to the sun finally rising and the smoke clearing ahead of them as they roll to a stop, unable to go farther. Dozens of vehicles, some wrecked some still running. They form a massive parking lot, one cluttered with bodies of Freaks, specialists, Weres and worse.

They all get out as Bryan shuts off the SUV and begins walking. The bleeding has stopped, but he's still listing to the side. The sound of fighting from the west draws their attention. Looking down at the bodies is something you learn to do when fighting in a war. Otherwise, one of those bodies, not ready to die alone, might take you with them.

Amanda's voice in his mind from the first battle scene doesn't make him look down again after seeing the first child crushed under a military jeep. That's why he is the first to see the woman. "Jesus, Mary and Joseph it's Armageddon." He slows, staring open-mouthed, gun pointed down.

Bryan and the others stop as well. Flying from the roof of an RV to a jeep and then a pickup is a black feathered Angel fighting with a five-foot long scimitar. Peggy struggles and gets past the frozen adults as the reason she is flying from roof to roof catches up with her. Seven freaks charge from behind the vehicles and walking behind them is a tall, thin man in a hooded robe.

"Samantha! Help her, she saved me." Peggy doesn't wait, running at the freaks not seeing the tall thin man. The freaks are all armed with clubs, and a couple have large axes.

"Peggy, get down!" Matteas yells after her, but she ignores him. Unable to shoot for fear of hitting the winged woman or Peggy, the others charge after her. Then when Dr. Michael has a clear shot, his gun doesn't fire, pulling the trigger again the hammer thuds down with a dull clack instead of the bang.

"Guns aren't working again!" He drops his gun, drawing his survival knife as he reaches Peggy, pulling her back as she is swiping with that odd smoking knife. Then, he's on his back as black specks fill his vision. His chest is sending sharp pains through his body. A heavy thud landing beside him draws his eyes from the sky. The Freak that hit him with its club is boneless beside him, smoke rising from where its eyes used to be.

Amanda sees her mate hit and hears the cracking bones, before she can avenge him, Peggy stabs the freak in its privates with her smoking dagger. When she draws it back, it leaves a spreading inkiness behind. The Freak takes two steps toward Dr. Michael, its mouth open in silent screams as its eyes drip from their sockets leaving burned streaks across its cheeks and smoke flowing from its emptying eye sockets as it falls beside Dr. Michael.

Amanda loses sight of Peggy as she watches the end of the Freak. Bryan runs and leaps into the pickup bed with two freaks, one swinging an axe at the winged woman who stands as tall as Bryan at six-foot-seven and is using her scimitar with her left hand. Her right arm and wing are broken and bleeding.

The one with the club turns to swing at Bryan before he has his balance. He catches the club with his hands, digging in with is claws, he throws his weight in the direction the club is going. The Freak is pulled along by its momentum and the almost 400 pound Weretiger now attached to the end of its club. Bryan and the Freak go over the side.

Bryan lands on his back getting his feet up just in time as the freak crashes stomach first onto him. His legs heave, tossing the freak several feet away. Matteas' claws open the specialist from groin to neck as it stands over

Bryan with a short sword in its metallic hand. Bryan blinks as the blood and bile fall on his face and chest as he rolls away. "Dammit Matteas, you did that on purpose!"

Matteas' smile is still on his face when the lightning strikes where he was standing. Bryan is knocked down again, blinded by the flash. No thunder rolls after or before the strike. Bryan rubs his eyes trying to restore his vision, something shiny flies past him. Then he's on the ground sneezing as his face is buried in feathers.

"Look out, it's moving again!" the voice sounds like rocks being crushed and is only inches from Bryans' head as it shouts.

Amanda leaps to the side as something bright white and liquid flies past her and hits a red Ford pickup. She watches as the half of the truck that is hit goes from a bright white to a rainbow and then is mist. Half of the truck is simply gone. She swallows as she crawls, holding onto the short sword she has picked up from a dead specialist.

The tall man thing is damn fast. *Where the hell is it? What the fuck is it? Goddamn magic!* Amanda spots its legs on the other side of a blue station wagon looking out of place with the military vehicle, pickups, and SUVs. Crawling under the station wagon, she swipes at its feet, smiling the moment before the sword hits the leg above the ridiculous brown loafers he is wearing. Then her smile turns into a grimace of pain as her hand tries to drop the sword but refuses to obey her. Her whole body vibrates as if she has struck a metal beam with the sword.

Laughter reaches her as the white liquid drips into a pool beside the silly shoes and begins to flow in her direction. Not fast, like when he threw them but slow as they dissolve the sword and creep up the hilt.

"Now Tommy! He's ready, Sapphire hurry!" Peggy's cry is followed by a wolf's howl, a shout from Tommy, "Die!!!" Then the station wagon is flying up and away from her. The concussion shoves her sideways. Bryan and the winged woman are once more knocked down and into each other's arms.

Amanda is trying to get to her feet and has made it to her hands and knees when her hearing returns, "You dumb bitch move!" Her face flushes red at the insult, then her eyes look up and widened at the station wagon falling back down from where it has been blown into the sky. She scrambles away but it's Matteas, burned and bleeding, that drags her to safety.

When he tries to help her to her feet, they both fall and just sit panting. The sun is now halfway up in the sky.

And if the Star Children dispatch the Damned.
Dawn will shine once more on the descendants of
those from below.
Then the World has a chance,
If the two once more join now being three by blood.
Then the blood of the sacred will flow as the rivers,
And a Sirens song shall curse or save
A world of desecration.

Everyone turns to stare at the rock crushing voice.

Bryan is holding and is being held up by a beautiful woman. Her one good wing is held out beside her, the black feathers all have one streak of either blue or red. Her face is chiseled perfection. High cheekbones, proud green eyes, and pale alabaster skin. Somehow her perfection is such that it makes the bloody crushed wing, broken arm, and blood soaked leather corset all seem to drape her in radiance.

No one speaks as they gather around Matteas and Amanda. Dr. Michael is sitting up against a car watching. Amanda looks at him to assure herself that he will make it. He gives her a thumbs up sign and a grin. His accelerated healing, like his reversed aging, defying explanation, magic is like that.

It is the sound of singing that finally pulls them onto their feet and leads them to the ancient Pueblo dwellings. The people they pass all bow their heads as they pass but never stop the low, mournful song.

After climbing several ladders, and passing into a basin surrounded by taller dwellings, they see where everyone is going as they continue to sing. An old woman is being laid on a bier. Derek and a Werewolf are walking toward the bier as they stop, watching from the crowd.

The Werewolf looks at the woman and howls, his voice is joined by a dozen other Werewolves scattered amongst the hundreds of people scattered around. Then the flames go up by themselves. Flames in all colors of the rainbow soar fifty feet in the air.

"Our priestess is gone! The Gods will not speak to us again until our blood debt is paid." He turns to the tired looking Derek. "Brother, we will follow you to save the SheMiTali that she may save and curse us."

There is no cheering, no response other than the singing stopping. The people, all dirty and wounded in body and spirit, watch as the priestess who has protected and guided them for decades, moves on in the colorful dancing flames.

Chapter 17

"We have to go today, no more delays." Derek sits with his shoulders hunched, tense claws out.

The large wooden table is polished a deep dark walnut color. A table intended to sit 16 attorneys comfortably feels crowded with just a fraction of that number when it's angry, grief-stricken Weres, and a few other things as well.

"Our folk ar' not leavin wit' out, carin fer our kin." Darrel sits, every bit as tense as Derek. Standing as he speaks, knocking his wooden backed chair over with a crash and leaning on the table as his thick hands clench, each word bitten off with a glare. 4'1 is tall by Delver standards. The fact that he is three feet wide and wears his long reddish blond hair in ponytails is the reason why Bryan is not at the meeting.

The Werewolf Alpha of those who come from below looks like he has aged fifty years since the battle of tears. "We will leave by sunset Derek, you have my word. I will not be able to bring all my people but I'll do what I can."

"The Coven will not commit our resources without a full commitment from you. We are fewer than Werekin. Perhaps I should seek the council of the Prime before risking the lives of the Enlightened." Sebastian Rinoldo Carmichael is an average man. Unremarkable really, from his beige shirt and slacks to his clean shaven face and light brown hair combed into the most popular style. All designed to blend in.

"If he dost not commit, I will not send e'en one of the growers from the cavern, not a one!" Darrel's barrel fist slams the thick table making it jump, the echo stopping everyone.

"The Coven has agreed to clean up its part in this mess." The flashing eyes in the Werewolf Alpha's face loosens some of the tension in Derek's shoulders. *Yes, he is a man of his word, he will not delay me further. I wish I could tell them all to stay and grieve, Gods know they deserve more time. But I need them to save Alexis.*

Derek crushes the guilt again as he knows he will take all of them into the hell he knows is waiting for them in California, even if Alexis and Brother Lion were not at stake. The memory of walking through what had been a small community on the edge of the reservation where the misfit Weres, gifted, and ancient races have lived would give him nightmares for the rest of his life. Children were killed like animals in that battle. They had fought, and even the younger ones had daggers in hand.

A human woman slams the door open, her wide-eyed visage covered with dirt and worse. "Demons! They have come from the abyss to take us back down where our ancestors should never have left!"

Derek rises, motioning Amanda to stay. "I will check it out, you deal with these." He sees the brief irritation flash across his blood brothers grim visage before he feels the amusement through the blood bond.

"Thank you Derek. Please be patient with our people, they have had a hard week." Without waiting for Derek's response, he turns once more to Sebastian. "Your damned Enlightened killed my people." The hard edge and glowing eyes as he draws on his Alpha power would have stopped anyone with any sense. Unfortunately, the Enlightened are not known for their sense.

Sebastian laughs, head thrown back, loud and wild then he stops between one breath and the next. Derek shakes his shoulders to hide the chill that sound sends down his spine. "Those that did trespass here are forsworn and sentenced to death already. This is really a matter for Werekin only. They do follow a Werewolf as you have already admitted."

Derek begins to close the door, only to have Matteas slip past him before it's all the way closed. The howl of rage and surge of adrenaline from his blood brother staggers him a moment. Matteas pushes him from the doorway and closes the door pointing to the trembling woman who has given them the excuse to escape the political bickering.

"Tell us about the demons." Matteas' calm voice draws her attention from Derek's glowing eyes and flexing claws, sliding in and out in time to his rapid breathing. Even for people that grow up living with fallen angels, Growers that look like the dwarves of legend and Werewolves, Derek and the wild animal part of Brother Lion are intimidating.

"A big round demon made of mud, a skeleton of a man, and a banshee came out of the ground near Pedro's trailer while the work crew was cleaning up the_." She trails off as the horror of bodies and carnage return to her.

"Do we need a vehicle to get to Pedro's trailer or should we walk?" Matteas asks, his hand on the woman's elbow guiding her along behind him.

The walk out of the building is short, the community center has not been affected by the battle because it is out in the middle of nowhere. Thirty minutes from the village and even further from the main area of the reservation.

"We can drive most of the way, it's over by the wash behind the village. I brought my truck, I can take us back."

Moving out into the empty parking lot, the neighing of horses and bright desert sunshine pushing the horror of the last few days back. The three of them climb into the shiny new blue Silverado, content to listen to the 1990's hits station.

Brother Lion, did you know that Angels, dwarves, and other things live in the world with us? In all our decades we have never met any of them other than an odd vampire now and then. Derek sighs looking out the window. *I wish you were here, keeping the Mundanes out of this is getting harder.*

They drive past watching the desolate landscape, going by brings back the question of what they are heading out to deal with. "You never said your name," Derek asks the middle-aged woman driving the new truck with more care than it really needs.

"I'm Barbara, but everyone calls me Barb." Her hands tighten on the wheel at the reminder that Derek is in the back seat of her truck.

"I'm Matteas, the goon there is Derek. You want to tell us more about what we are dealing with?"

Barb's shoulders relax at the soothing tone of Matteas' voice. While he is not high on the dominance ring, he is no Omega either. Derek shakes his head in wonder, yet again, at the way Matteas has with women.

"If guns would work properly again I would say bring big ones. But since Shane says it will be months before fire works reliably again, I suppose you two will have to do."

Matteas smiles, flexing his claws and rolling his shoulders. "Oh, I think we can deal with a mud demon and skeleton man. Eh, Derek?"

Derek snorts as they turn past a rundown trailer and slow, pulling up beside a green Honda Civic and a beat up white Blazer. No people are around as Barb shifts into park. They sit looking around. "The sink hole opened up a few years ago, a few hundred feet down as near as anyone can tell. Took a shed and anything or anyone dumb enough to get close to the edge." She points ahead into the distance where what looks like a dark stain hovering above the ground is.

"That's where the mud demon came out of?" Derek's voice is soft as he shifts in the back seat, eyes roaming the deserted trailer and vehicles.

Matteas opens his door and gets out, leaving it open for Derek to follow. Derek crawls out of the half backseat with a grunt and rolling of cramped muscles. "Whose cars are these?" he asks as he inhales, sifting for scents. The wind that never seems to stop for long defies even his Werelion sense of smell.

"There were only four of us this morning. Dumping trash and freak's bodies down the sink hole is slow because you never know how close you can get." She hesitates before following Matteas and Derek as they walk toward the sink hole. "They all jumped on Pedro's old saddle horses and rode off when the cars wouldn't start."

Derek turns to look from her to the Silverado and back. She blushes, "I'm not as young or thin as I used to be. By the time I caught up, they were almost out of site and my truck started right up." She moves closer to Matteas as they draw closer to that inky area that seems lower to the ground the closer they get.

Up close, the sinkhole is larger than it appears from a distance. Derek can see the far side, or thinks he can if he squints. *That is the other side isn't it?* "Fuuuuuuck!" is all he gets out before the edge of the sinkhole collapses under his weight and he slides down into the sink hole.

Matteas approaches the new edge of the sinkhole cautiously. Gravel and dirt still sliding down in a cloud of dust. "Derek?" Matteas' voice is low as he looks over the edge.

"I'm here, for now." Derek is crouched on all fours on a large yellow school bus that is wedged where the sinkhole dips out. When Derek moves, the bus shifts, threatening to fall the rest of the way into the sinkhole.

Matteas' breathing deepens as he squints to see Derek, almost 40 feet down on the top of a bus. Despite the bright sunlight all around the sinkhole, almost no light makes it into the hole itself, except at noon, which is still several hours away. "Hang on I'll get some rope." Matteas retreats from the site calling to Barbara, "We need a rope!"

"Where am I going to go Matteas?" Derek's sarcastic reply didn't leave the sinkhole.

"Well, you could have brought some food and water with you." A cracked voice says from under Derek. He spins around looking for the voice and the bus slides another half foot deeper into the sinkhole.

"Be still! We have waited for two days for rescue now that it's here don't kill us!" This voice is deeper but every bit as horse as the first one.

Crawling on his hands and knees, Derek creeps to the edge of the bus and looks over the side. The sinkhole runs down into inky blackness with no visible bottom. Everyone's voices fall into the hole and never echoes back. Looking up from the open windows along the side of the bus are Aaron and Daisy. Filthy, bloodstained but alive.

Derek's relief is short lived as he glances into the

abyss waiting for all of them if Matteas doesn't get back with a rope in time. "Everyone said you died in the battle. I haven't felt you in the Pride bonds since then." *If only Mrs. Collins had made it through as well. How am I going to tell Alexis that she is gone?*

"We're not alone in here, Sabrina and Mrs. Collins are here also." Daisy's voice breaks as tears cut new tracks in the dirt and blood caked on her face.

"They're in real bad shape Derek, I'm not sure they will live the hour. It's a miracle they've lived this long." Aaron looks away, face tight as he pulls his head back in the bus and squeezes Daisy's hand.

"Tommy and Peggy, are they safe?" Daisy chokes out, unable to keep from asking any longer, yet the fear of the answer makes her repeatedly swallow not to be ill.

"They saved the day, Tommy appeared from thin air on that wolf and stabbed the leader of the battle, then Peggy castrated him with that huge smoking knife of hers. If not for them, most of the Pride and I would be dead." Derek speaks over the edge of the bus, a warmth spreading through his body. *Hang in there Mrs. Collins and Sabrina, one of the magic folk will heal you or will need their own healing.*

The front of the bus makes a piercing shriek of metal as it slides a few inches, tilting the bus at an angle when Daisy thrusts her head out the window and part of her shoulder, "Are they alive, hurt, what?"

Derek holds onto the roof of the bus with his claws, "Yes, they're fine, running around with the wolf, scaring people."

Daisy sinks back into the seat and breathes, her body shaking with a sob of relief. "Thank God."

Derek hears Aaron murmuring to someone other than Daisy that moans in answer, or at least moans when he stops speaking. "It's a half hour or more to get help and rope, tell me how you ended up on the bus. Last I heard from the kids, Mrs. Collins got stabbed by a specialist when your vehicles broke down and the kids had to leave to deal with the 'bad mojo.'" *Talk to me, stay calm or you will kill us all. If Matteas was down here, he would know what to say.*

Shifting from down below as Aaron returns to the window keeps Derek breathless until he is once more settled in the bus window seat. He looks up at Derek once in a while. "We were all on the way to the community center where we were supposed to help set up a hospital. Then the engines cut out and Freaks and specialists were attacking. The guns didn't work, and everyone was running around yelling about the sentries."

"The sentries were taken out by magic. The five angels gave some warning but only one survived the battle, and she is pretty banged up. Fire still only works once in a while. The coven sent a Representative that says it will settle down in 6 months or 6 years." Derek's snort expresses his disgust to Aaron and Daisy listening in the bus, since they can't see the curl of his lips from inside.

"Well, Mrs. Collins got hit and the kids were darting here and there. They did more damage than the adults, truth be told. If it weren't for them, the initial shock would have finished all of us." Daisy speaks with pride and confusion.

"Derek, did you know about Angels, Dwarves, and Vampires living amongst us?" Aaron asks looking out the window trying to see Derek's head above him.

"I knew there were Vampires and magic users. The rest, well they seem to all be here in northern New Mexico and until now I have never been here." *Shit, I let my Pride down again. When Brother Lion and I are one again, we are going to have a long talk about what other things share the world with us.*

There's a long pause before Aaron resumes speaking. "The angel saved Peggy when a skinny man thing shot white light at her. Then the Freaks were chasing everyone else, and it was just us left behind. Peggy and Tommy got on the wolf before we could stop them and yelled, 'Belladonna protect them!' Then they disappeared on Sapphire, Belladonna never heard them because she was yelling at them to take us to the 'Center.' Then the angel flew off after the others."

Choking from inside the bus draws Daisy and Aaron from the windows for the moment, the bus doesn't shift anymore. The sun is nearing directly overhead when Aaron comes back to the window. "Derek, you still up there?"

He considers all the possible answers to that dumbest of questions and settles on, "No."

"Sabrina's hemorrhaging again. She can't shift into her natural state to heal right now."

Derek closes his eyes for a moment. "She needs to relax Aaron, until she relaxes she won't be able to change.

If I was close to her I could guide her into her change but I can't even sense her from here."

"That's my fault, magic doesn't work in the bus." Aaron sounds miserable.

"Have Daisy keep speaking to her, help should be here soon." Derek listens but can only hear murmurs and can't understand the words passing from Aaron to Daisy.

"Alexis needs to get back and take his royal furriness down a notch or three. That's from Daisy, we're doing what we can Derek. But we have had no water or food for two days. No bathroom either and since last night when the bus slid farther after the freaks hit it, well, we have not been willing to move farther away to relieve ourselves."

Derek's claws cut into the bus roof as his shoulders shake. "Understood. Continue the story."

"It was a long walk but there was never any doubt where everyone was. When we saw the first children_." There are several swallows before he can continue. "Well, we tried to get to where we could help. And we were hoping to find Peggy and Tommy. They think their magic makes them invincible, stupid kids." Aaron sounds like their Dad from birth not step dad of months.

"Anyway, we were too slow, carrying Mrs. Collins only made it worse. I couldn't leave her. Then we saw this bus moving, and an angel on the roof fighting freaks and those half men half robots you call specialists. When the bus stopped moving, we headed for it. When we got there, the Angel was inside the door, no longer on the roof, and fighting two Freaks."

"It killed one, Daisy and I put Mrs. Collins down and hacked into the other one from behind. The doorway was too narrow, and it couldn't turn to defend itself. Once it was dying, we stepped back and let it fall out of the door. The Angel was in the driver's seat."

Aaron let out a little sob, "He was so beautiful Derek. Perfect, like an angel should be, but he was cut and smashed too bad for even an angel to live. He told me to help him out of the bus to die. I said no, we would take him to help. We put him in a seat and Mrs. Collins across from him. Sabrina was in the middle of the bus unconscious. As I started the bus to drive away, the angel said we had to leave him because magic would not work anywhere near his dead body."

Derek's eyes widen. "He's in the bus, that's why I can't feel any of you in the pride bonds, no magic. Sabrina can't heal without magic like a Were should."

"Yes." Aaron's voice is low.

"Derek! We got rope, we can pull you out now!" Matteas' excited shouts startle Derek, who shifts too fast, and the bus loses two feet on the front end again. The new angle is making Derek hold on with his claws or roll off.

"The bus is slipping, Mrs. Collins and Aaron are inside and alive." *Can't tell him his mate is inside, possibly dying*

"They can't get out of the bus windows. We need a crane or something to pull the bus up!" Derek waits, not daring to move.

"A crane! Fuck man, I was lucky to find rope! Barb,

we have people trapped in the bus, the doors against the side of the sinkhole and the windows are too small for them." Matteas lowers the rope to Derek, who takes it and ties it around his chest.

"We have no crane, the regular reservation has a tow truck, though." Barbara sounds scared.

"That's no good, a tow truck wouldn't be able to lift a full-size school bus up thirty or forty feet." Matteas is braced holding the other end of the rope now tied around Derek.

"How much rope you got with you Matteas?" Derek looks down the side of the bus again seeing Aaron frozen against the window not moving.

"Just enough to reach you and tie to the tree up here."

Derek takes his index claw and cuts into the first layer of steel. *It will take too long to cut a hole big enough to get them out.* "Aaron, I'm going to cut a hole in the roof with my claws then carry you up the rope one at a time."

"Be careful." Aaron's words arrive with another sound of scraping metal.

Yeah, be careful Derek, why not say, Derek, why didn't you bring steak and beer? Derek's thoughts distract him so he can concentrate on making the hole. When he has a six inch round hole, he looks down and sees the angel's body inside the bus. He is aft with broad shoulders and pale skin. The sun is directly overhead. When Derek moves his head and looks up where Matteas is still standing. "Any chance Pedro has extension cords and a grinder or welding torch to cut this faster?"

"Just punch through it Derek, it can't be that much thicker than a car."

Before Derek can explain again that the bus is slipping, Aaron hollers. "The Angel's body is starting to smoke." Coughing follows his words.

Derek looks into the hole, but the smoke is spiraling up, black and bilious, too thick to see through. "Aaron, move Sabrina and Mrs. Collins away from the smoke!" Derek is coughing from just the small amount of smoke outside the bus.

Screams of "Fire!" and the sound of things being dragged followed by coughing are the only response.

The paint on the roof around the hole is blistering from heat. Then the metal begins melting in an expanding ring away from the hole Derek has made, forcing him back. Then flames shot skyward, brilliant white and silver flames, burning the fur off Derek's cheeks as he crawls as far as he can to the end of the bus.

"What the hell is going on?" Matteas yells down, hands gripping the rope tighter and following Derek's path so the rope will reach.

Derek is too busy coughing to answer before there is a loud whooshing sound and the flames fall away. The bus settles another inch but holds for the moment. As the smoke clears, Derek crawls to the five foot opening across the top of the bus. Looking down inside he sees another hole only four feet around where the Angel had been. Through the hole, he sees the flaming angel's body falling downward. The smoke rises but spreads out now that it is not funneled up the small hole.

Aaron shuffles over from the back end of the bus looking shocked. Red blisters and severe burns cover his face and hands. His clothing is smoking in places, and baked dirt falls off them with every step. "Get Mrs. Collins over here and have Daisy help you lift her up to me. Then I will come back down for the next person."

Derek speaks calmly and uses his restored Pride bonds with them to send reassurance and confidence he doesn't feel. Aaron looks up for a moment then turns away from the hole. When Daisy stumbles over with him, she has Mrs. Collins legs while Aaron has her arms. "I need 10 feet of slack Matteas! Bringing up Mrs. Collins, she's hurt badly."

The sound of vehicles arriving followed by more voices from the direction of Pedro's trailer. "A doctor is here now and more rope, one minute while they tie them together."

Derek closes his eyes, *anyone out there listening, thank you, now help me get my family out of this hell hole safe.* Opening his eyes, he draws a deep breath. "You got enough people to lower me down to Mrs. Collins? She's in no condition to go up on her own unconscious."

"We have Pedro's horses, raising you up now." Derek rises a few inches then they begin lowering him. It takes a few swings before he gets down through the hole into the bus. Tears fill his eyes as Aaron and Daisy pass Mrs. Collins' bloody and battered body into his arms. The lightness of her is startling.

"Pull us up! Easy now." Derek sees the silent stares from Daisy and Aaron, both burned severely and covered in filth, blood and in shock.

The rope pulls taut and Derek holds Mrs. Collins against him with one arm while holding the top of the rope tied around his waist. It is more of a walk up the side of the sinkhole than anything. The rope goes loose, and Derek loses a couple of feet before getting his feet back in place.

Shane comes over looking grim and accepts Mrs. Collins into his arms with a nod. The twenty other people clustered around the top are a blur to Derek as he starts to walk backward, looking down the sinkhole for Sabrina.

Halfway up with Sabrina, Matteas catches her scent and tries to climb down the rope he is supposed to be holding. Shane grabs Matteas by the shoulders and tosses him back into the arms of a pair of Delvers who hold the hissing Werelion in their thick arms. Derek manages to reach the top with Sabrina despite Matteas' frantic action.

"Matteas, she is hurt and needs to shift to a natural state." Matteas gets loose and runs to the edge where Derek stands swaying in the sudden wind. Shane is standing to the side, ready to hold the rope as Derek walks back down. "Shane, they have been without food or water for days and need medical care."

Shane nods, "Dr. Brown is seeing to them personally. An impromptu hospital is being set up in Pedro's trailer for now since they can't be moved for a while."

"Thank You." The Delvers approach standing

behind Matteas. "She needs rest, take her to Dr. Brown."

His face is streaked with tears and anguish. His shoulders are trembling and his hands shake as he accepts his mate into his arms. When he feels her thinness, he stumbles in shock. The Delvers follow him in case he loses it completely. Delvers mate for life or not at all, the grim set of their features attesting to their rage, not at the harm done to Sabrina but that she has been kept from her mate for months.

Derek turns, tears gone, leaving behind a dry rage smoldering beneath the surface. His next two trips are labored as his body complains to him at the over exertion. Every trip up, Shane offers water and food, he refuses.

At last, with Aaron in his arms, he makes it to the top again, his lips are cracked and bleeding. His breath comes in harsh bellows, recycling the dusty desert air over and over in heaving gasps. Rope still tied around him, he stumbles past Shane, Delvers and others offering to carry Aaron. He ignores them all, forcing one leaden leg to move after the other.

At the trailer he stops, staring in numb exhaustion at the five stairs leading to the open door. A woman in a white doctor's coat stops in the door looking him up and down. "You have my patient, bring him in or let someone else do so."

Looking up at her plain face, he doesn't notice the laugh lines by her thin lips. Or her black hair, oval eyes or the tattoo of a butterfly on her neck, all he sees is the clean tanned hands. Everything else he sees is covered in the blowing dust, sweat and filth. Moving his stiff legs up and onto the first step, he crashes to his knees. Holding Aaron up and safe from the ground, Derek gazes into his friend's face. Eyes closed, body relaxed.

Derek's heart speeds up to a frantic beat. "He's not breathing, help him." Another step on his knees and Dr. Brown takes him into her arms. Her back cracks as she turns without a word to Derek and carries Aaron inside. "Get an IV Rehydration Therapy in him. Rachel, find Ben and have him help you get that Werelion on the steps into a gown and feed him."

Derek crawls in the room fighting down the dizziness. "Heal. Be Well. Rest. I am Here." His words are a mixed roar and yell. The Lion in him pushes, adding its strength to his own. Blood runs from his ears, and eyes. His heart stammers for a moment as he forces the Pride magic to take all his strength and send it to his family.

"Dr. Brown, the Panther is awake!" Derek smiles as he loses consciousness. *That's right Sabrina, your home, heal. Revenge Sooooon..*

Derek's body folds into the fetal position in the Were healing hibernation.

"God damn Were Alphas playing God! Get that woman sedated, she pulled out her IV."

"My kids. Bring my children."

"Holy hell, there's a wolf with kids on its back in here!"

Even in hibernation, Derek feels a flush of warmth as his Pride gathers.

Chapter 18

Alexis slows as she reaches the last few steps. Brother Lion's breath on her neck tickles her neck. Knowing he's there, she still jumps as his hand brushes her side. "Something died a permanent death near us, I can feel the souls anguish as it fades." His words are soft, drawing her back from her thoughts.

Nodding, she draws a deep breath and starts to sing without words, pure harmonic melody. As her voice reaches the harmonic duality only she and her mom can, a pale pink glow begins in front of her. It lights her face in a soft questioning glow. Squinting in the light after the long walk down the dark stairs, her song stutters to a stop as she loses focus.

The stairs behind them groan and creak as if in pain. Mr. Armstrong cries out, "The stairs behind me are gone, there's a wind pulling me downward."

Shoulders stiffening, Alexis resumes the song taught to her all those years ago by her Mom. Forcing the use of both her vocal cords, the image of her Mom's face, full of pride, flashes in her mind and is gone. The glow deepens, not brightening but becoming richer. More colors flow from the now exposed door. The colors each produce a pure note as her exhaled breath reaches them. They join it running over her. Then a voice joins Alexis', blending harmonies.

Tears run down Alexis' face as she hears the voice. "Now the third set, embrace the pain, feed it to the music and feel it grow."

"Mother, I have come far from your womb. It is dark, and I am alone."

"Sweetest blessing, never fear the dark for you are light. Sing and delight in the sirens song."

The lights all swirl in musical delight, brightening and dimming to the melody.

Alexis' shoulders tremble as she forces another line of song past her tight throat. "Grandmothers hear my call, welcome me home."

The lights flare to new brightness as a warm breeze flows around Alexis, bringing the smell of spring and new growth. A chorus of voices ring out "Welcome daughter, we know thee." The stairwell vibrates to the song.

Natasha's voice deepens as a large thud reaches them from the top of the stairs. "Let those that trespass here feel the Sirens caaaaall."

Alexis inhales her mom's scent, salty like the sea one moment and dry Savannah with fresh grass the next. Never mixing, flowing around each of the group.

"Come play with us. Dance and play. Persephone awaits." Alexis' voice breaks as she finishes and stumbles through the opening at the bottom of the stairs. The light caresses her cheek before rising up the stairs where light can be seen flowing around a silhouette.

Brother Lion reaches behind him, pulling the others to get them moving. Mr. Armstrong turns to follow his wife's voice as sobs rack him. Brother Lion walks back up a few stairs and picks him up carrying him down the last stairs, each step away from the beautiful voice is harder than the one before.

Then the voice changes, hitting a note so high it brings Brother Lion to his knees. Mr. Armstrong falls when he drops him, and Marie slams the door at the bottom of the stairs cutting off the alternating beautiful song calling to the souls of all to follow it, and stabbing shrill notes leaving the mind lanced and bleeding ever more susceptible to the luring song.

Alexis' eyes widen in shock as she turns gazing at the room, "No, no this is the wrong room. We have to go back." Shoving past Mr. Armstrong sitting on his butt where Brother Lion has dropped him and rocking back and forth. She stumbles as she passes the others, opening the door a fraction.

The battle in the stairwell hits Alexis, raising the hair on her head with the energy being used. Inky blackness fills with loud static swamps the beautiful voice, reducing it to pain, moans before it comes back piercing and leading once more the static diminishing. The power that is unleashed in the stairwell rocks the house, like a ship in a storm. Alexis stumbles as Brother Lion slams the door shut.

Her eyes are staring at the closed door, "It's the safe

room where she always took me. Our place to sing and draw, the wrong room." Turning, she looks again at the row of now outdated recording equipment, the easel on the side with the last painting her mother had done before she died in the car wreck. The lighting is a fluctuating kaleidoscope of colors.

Mr. Armstrong is getting to his feet with Roger's help. Marie is looking around with wide eyes. "This is a special place of memories. It breathes magic in and out, the Siren is drawing on it to battle the damned out there." She gestures to the door.

"Alexis, we have to help her, that's your Mom out there." Mr. Armstrong is struggling against Roger to get to the door.

Alexis moves in front of him, wrapping her arms around him to still his wild exertions to break free of Roger's arms. "Mom's voice has never left, it sings for me when I am here. It did even before she was stolen from us." *I sound like the adult talking to the child. When did I change so much?*

Mr. Armstrong relaxes, Roger releases his arms standing tense behind him. "You and she share so much, I have always been on the outside." His haggard face is drawn and thinner than she has ever seen, he hugs her to him. "I am here. Never doubt that you have a father as well."

"I love you too Dad, when we get out of here you will explain everything to me or I will not have a Father." She hugs him tighter before stepping back so he can see the firmness in her eyes. *No more protecting me, those days are gone.* Turning from his nod, she moves to pass Roger whispering to Maria. "If the magic is dimming, how long before the defense spell is gone?"

Alexis keeps moving towards the projector. *It's the same room but different, like everything in this place. The lights, full-size door, Mom where is my message?*

Brother Lion is standing by the projector sorting through a pile of film strips. "Where did you find those?" Alexis asks rushing to his side.

He stands up dropping one of the film canisters and bumps the projector catching the film canister.

"Happy 16th Birthday!" Natasha Armstrong appears on the wall as the projector turns on and begins playing. "If you see this, then something has gone wrong, and I am not able to be here with you in my body." The image on the screen has tears in her eyes as she continues. "These films will guide you over the next years of your life as you grow into your birthright."

Alexis falls against Brother Lion's side as she watches her Mom on the projector. "Your Dad probably went ahead and got you the pink El Camino we picked out together. It's older than you but has character as your Dad puts it."

Roger turns away from looking at the film to watch the door with a tense Marie.

"If your Dad is not here with you let him know I followed his suggestion and put all your training on film so you would have it if something went wrong and one or both of us are not with you. Before I go on, I want you to know that your Dad and I love you very much. I'm

sure you already know that we have been working on a
way to allow Weres of all kinds to have children."

At this bombshell, everyone except Alexis turns to
stare at Mr. Armstrong, who is glued to the screen as
Natasha continues. "It's a tragedy that shifting from the
natural, relaxed state to human and back is too traumatic
for a fetus to survive in the womb. That is why our
ancestors lost their wings."

Alexis' back shivers, remembering years spent
dreaming of flying, so sure she had wings that when she
woke without them each time she was devastated. "You
see, we are descendants from the Sirens that are
Persephone's companions before Hades took her. You
may not know that many of the Mythological Gods are
not myths at all, they are actually Numen."

The image of Natasha cuts out to be replaced by
paintings of glowing beings with fangs feeding on people.
Unlike the vampires they resemble the Numen are
feeding on the soul not the blood of people either
terrified or in sexual bliss.

Natasha reappears on the screen. "Our gifts are
expressed in music and spirit. When the Numen's
children betrayed them and lured them into a millennium
of slumber, one of the Numen youngsters also kidnapped
Raidne, our many times removed Grandmother. All so
his kids, Wereanimals one and all, could have children."

The wall goes white as the film strip ends. The
snapping sound of the end of the film strip slapping
around the projector startles Alexis, who jerks. Brother
Lion turns off the projector and begins putting the film

back in the empty case labeled 'Happy Birthday film 1.'

Stepping toward Mr. Armstrong, trembling, tears drying up and face flashing from betrayal to anger, "Dad, you knew all of this? You let me go all this time thinking I was going crazy and said nothing?"

Shaking his head no, "No Alexis, I did not know all of it, some of it yes. Your mother was a stubborn woman, wonderful, but Gods was she stubborn." Alexis goes pale, clenching her fists. Mr. Armstrong continues, "Natasha refused to listen to me about the training films, she said she would be there, she had seen it." His voice breaks as he takes a deep breath.

Brother Lion steps behind Alexis, letting his shoulder brush her arm, but he doesn't interrupt. "So what, you thought she hadn't made the films, so you decided not to tell me who, or what I am?" Alexis' voice is shrill as the trembling starts to get worse.

Before Mr. Armstrong can respond the door rocks as something hits it. Marie spits on the door tracing a series of sigils across it that glow briefly before fading. "We must go, the damned has drowned out the spell defense. It will be in here soon, it is strong from the death of the Spirit Talker."

"I have to know." Alexis turns and grabs a film strip at random and begins loading it in the projector. Her eyes blur with tears as her hands shake. Brother Lion takes the film strip from her hands and finishes running it through the wheels. As he clicks it on the room rocks, the wall splits with an inch wide crack. The crack runs from the top of the door all around the room and back to the bottom of the door.

Brother Lion turns to the door tensing. Alexis pushes him out of the way and turns the projector on again.

"As you know your music is full of the magic of the Sirens. It can cloud minds, create illusions and at times kill. What we have not spoken about yet is the other side of your heritage."

The film goes from Natasha sitting in a blue gown in a high-backed wooden chair to a portrait of Grandma Armstrong. The thick arms and full eyebrows are red like Alexis' own. "You may remember Grandma Armstrong."

Alexis' mind fills with a memory of the stern woman wearing white, sitting with her in a garden. Alexis' memory of the moment is so powerful that she loses the sense of everything else around her. She smells the honeysuckle in bloom and the sickly sweet overripe grapes left too long on the vine.

The buzz of wasps moving from one sticky plant to the next fills her ears with static. "You must not use your power, Alexis. Only evil ever comes of it. My mother and her mother before her thought they could control the voices."

Alexi tries to speak, but she can't draw a breath. Grandma Armstrong gestures and a cloudy image of a stern visage woman with her gray hair in a tight bun. The chin and nose are eerily similar to Alexis' own. Then she fades to be replaced by an older faded and cracked painting of another Armstrong woman. Hanging in the air, it feels like she is viewing her down a long tunnel.

This woman is younger this time but still stern of face. The resemblance is just as striking.

Alexis runs her hand over her face, feeling the strong chin with the slight cleft. The eyes though, speak to her the most. The same hue as her own. Swirling green shimmers, flecks of gold floating through them like little golden clouds. "She loves you and would protect you. What she does not understand is that it's her own fear that weakens her." As the voice speaks in Alexis' mind, the paintings lips move silently to the words being spoken.

"All of them lost the battle of sanity and freedom to spirits they thought cared about them." Grandma Armstrong's eyes draw down as she sees Alexis staring at the painting. Turning, she hisses as the woman in the painting winks at her. A snap of her fingers and the painting shimmers, fading out of sight.

Turning to Alexis the lines around her mouth hard, lips bloodless, "Ignore me at your peril child. I have lived with insanity for longer than you have been in this world. Marry, have children and stay in large cities away from the places spirits still exist. When you hear them call to you, run away."

Alexis is falling backward, at last, she is able to get a breath and scream. "No! Help me, Grandma, help me!"

Blink, slap, blink tears are running. Cheeks on fire her eyes focus on Roger standing over her. His eyes are tight, he raises his hand again. Alexis' eye gazes into his. "Roger, I need to go back to speak to Grandma Armstrong. She has answers about the spirits."

"She's back!" Roger yells, making Alexis jump at the sudden bellow of his voice. He thrusts his hands under her armpits and heaves her onto her feet.

Alexis' ears pop and the sound of her father's pained crying reaches her. Turning her head, she sees Mr. Armstrong hysterical. "No, no you left me a note, don't teach her, it's safer. Burn the books you said and I did." A cold shiver runs up Alexis' back as Goosebumps pop up all over her.

The projector is on its side, broken. Brother lion is holding Mr. Armstrong's arms, grunting at the strain. "Alexis, if your back can you get through to your Dad?"

Walking closer she sees blood on the floor, smeared around the floor. Mr. Armstrong is heaving his body, throwing his head back and to the sides screaming, "No, take me with you!"

Stepping around them, she sees what her Dad is looking at, a pale image of her Mom shimmering, like a mirage in the desert. "Mom?"

Then the thing turns and looks into her soul. Where its eyes should have been is a pool of nothing. Black is the collection of all colors blended into one. This is the absence of all light and without light, there is no color. Feverish, hungry and welcoming her. Her mouth sags, a half step forward and she will be home, loved.

Marie screams, "Back to the damned lands unclean thing." A film canister flies through the image of her mom, bringing a harsh scream that fades as the image disappears.

Alexis jerks back as the thing's hold on her breaks.

Brother Lion loosens his grip on Mr. Armstrong as he sags in his arms. "Alexis, I am so sorry. I will tell you everything I know. I thought I was protecting you."

Alexis notices his bleeding wrist, steps to him and slaps him. "You are not leaving me like mom." She turns and begins walking toward the projector. Roger kneels down and begins gathering the scattered film canisters.

The door rocks as something massive hits it, the crack running across the room widens. "We need to get out of here, now." Brother Lion watches the crack and door.

Alexis' mouth tightens, her cheeks turning red as she bites them to contain her outburst. "How do we get out? I am not leaving without the films." As she reaches Roger, she begins gathering the ones farther away and adding them to the growing stack.

"You open the door from Limbo to your Mate in the mundane world. I can feel him even now. He wades through blood, lost in the lust of battle." Marie's eyes widened as they look from Alexis to Brother Lion's shocked faces.

Alexis mouths, "Derek?" She looks at the left-hand corner of the room.

Brother Lion follows her gaze with his eyes. As they both reach for Derek, they feel him in the Pride and Mate bond for the first time in months. The walls in the corner fade as an image of Derek covered in blood and gore appears in its place.

"Brother!" Brother Lion roars out as they see a tall, thin man swinging a glowing staff at Derek's back. Derek turns in time to leap aside and a gangly Werewolf leaps on the skinny man knocking him from view.

Derek turns squinting at them, "Brother Lion? Alexis!" Derek opens his arms and Alexis hesitates looking from the film canisters to Derek. Before she can decide what is more important, the thin man appears behind Derek, his staff now covered in white fire.

"Watch out!" Several voices scream but Derek never looks away from Alexis and the staff hits him in the side. He screams in terrible agony as flames spread over him and falls away. The corner shimmers and becomes just a corner again.

"Derek?" Alexis shakes, her body trembling from head to foot. "I can't feel him, he's gone."

"You said you could not feel him since you entered here except that he was alive and far away." Roger stutters to a stop as he hears his prophetic words.

Mr. Armstrong steps to Alexis about to wrap his arms around her, she turns to the canisters before he does. His arms drop to his sides, taking off his shirt he kneels and gathers the canisters in his shirt, tying as many as will fit inside his shirt and tying it into an impromptu bag.

Roger, seeing what they're doing goes to the row of cabinets and takes down a child's easel and backpack. He sets the easel down, bringing the backpack to Alexis. "Thank You." She says, her eyes dry as her voice throbs, breaking into three voices in those two words.

With the backpack, Roger and Mr. Armstrong's shirts they manage to get all but three film canisters ready to go. "He enters wounded, but the damned feed on pain and pleasure as one thing." Maria's words draw everyone's eyes to the crack splitting the room. Smoking black liquid drips from the ceiling and bubbles up from the crack in the floor.

"Carry the canisters." Alexis' voice sends tinkling echoes around the room. She moves toward the corner where they had seen Derek moments before. "Maria, tell me what to do."

Brother Lion hands his shirt, full of film canisters, to Roger as he follows behind Alexis and Maria. Mr. Armstrong struggles to his feet holding the backpack, and two shirts full of film canisters while juggling three loose ones. Following, he ignores Roger's offer of help.

Maria touches Alexis shoulder from behind. "You must sever the ties to this anchor. I cannot open a way out, it is too far from my home."

Alexis tenses, "How? Tell me what to DO."

"Sing to your Mate, pull on the bonds tying your body to his." Maria grips Brother Lion's arm and pulls him beside Alexis, "Reach for your body, it is as much yours as his. Together you can bring us there."

Alexis hisses as a black drop from the crack slides across the floor and burns through her left shoe. "Use the pain and begin. Time runs away from us."

The black goo is gathering into a puddle in front of the door. The silence thickens as Alexis closes her eyes, remembering Derek. His large, clumsy hands are massaging her leg when she wakes with a Charlie horse, even when he has only had an hour sleep in several days.

His breath always smelling of mint since they got to South Dakota and he had found mint growing wild all over the land. The shy boy showing himself in the lopsided flower he brings her from one of his patrols.

"Mate of my heart, hear my call." The words flow into music full of Derek's laughs, and kisses. After a few moments, the music drifts to Brother Lion and falls apart. *How can I call to my mate when one of them is already here?*

Tears start again, shifting her left foot brings a shot of pain-drenched adrenaline. "Maria, it's not working."

Maria turns her head, looking over her shoulder at the black acidic tar that is cutting the house loose to be lost in Limbo. Maria's breathing grows faster as their impending doom grows with every strand of reality being eaten away. "Lion Man do your part!" Her eyes are tight, new lines forming around them. Alexis looks at her over her shoulder and blinks. *Did she always have that little stomach bulge?*

As Maria turns back to her furious drawing with her fingers, Brother Lion steps up behind Alexis, wrapping his arms around her. "Try again, I will help."

Alexis leans against his broad furry chest. Without his shirt, his natural male cat musk is strong. His scent is relaxing, her shoulders tremble slower then stops as her breathing deepens. A rumbling purr vibrates from him into her.

Together? The gentle pressure of his mind against hers is enough. She lets her guard down and welcomes him in her mind and spirit.

Now, do what you were doing before. I will add my sense of Derek. Alexis nods her head and Brother Lion calls forth his memories of Derek.

The young man, just turned Werelion, running full tilt with his new Werelion body. Laughing as he runs faster and faster pushing the limits of his body. Then falling and rolling over and over with a stitch in his side.

The memories flow into Alexis faster and faster. Showing her the young man that never had a real family or girlfriend. Then he has the Unit that becomes the Pride. Then she sees the morning they met...

..."Lexi, I would like you to meet Derek Matthews. Derek served with honors in the army. He comes highly recommended," when Alexis fails to respond, Martin steps closer to Alexis. He puts his arm around Alexis and pulls her a step closer to Derek.

"This is my lovely daughter, Alexis Marie Armstrong. As we have already discussed Derek, you will escort her whenever she leaves the house." Martin glowers in irritation at the silent Derek, standing with his mouth slightly ajar.

Derek's mouth clicks shut as he speaks, "Pleasure to meet you, Miss Armstrong. I look forward to babysitting you." Derek smiles.

Alexis' heart skips a beat. Her body is on fire. *Wow, I wonder if he is that big everywhere? ...*

Her breath catches as her memories mingle with Brother Lion's. The music bursts out of her one octave then two. Memory after memory of Derek. Outside Sexy Kitties, pepper spraying him in the face followed by her breaking his nose. The hurt, betrayed look he gives her after.

As the memories build, Brother Lion and her's mingle as they both call out for the missing part of their Mating triangle, the music soars into three octaves. Painful, taking all of her breath to sustain, she grows lightheaded without being able to breathe.

Then the rainbow of lights plays over the walls in the corner. A breeze runs over her, tugging at her hair. The smells of night, before it rains, the charged feeling of an imminent lightning strike raising the hair on her arms. Still she sings on until the room they are in begins to fade.

Her feet are on wet grass, someone coughs behind her. Her eyes sting as something in the air burns them. Then a pop and she draws a breath and coughs on smoke filling the air. Gunshots sound from behind her, turning she sees the source of the flames. The Armstrong estate is on fire.

Smoke is filling the sky and in the distance, the sound of firetrucks and ambulances are getting closer. Brother Lion groans as he falls to the ground in convulsions, his entire body shaking as his eyes roll up into his head.

Alexis drops to her knees beside him, "Help him! He's been away from Derek for too long, we need to get him to Derek."

Roger scoops Brother Lion up in his arms "Lead the way, I can feel he's here but there's too much magic in the air for me to find him."

Everywhere Alexis looks there are bodies. The yard is large, several acres in the back and a generous acre and a half on the sides and front. Standing in the rear of the estate, looking toward the burning house, Alexis sees that the garage is gone. Where it had been is a large hole a couple of feet deep. Like something has scooped out the garage and the top two feet of dirt and taken it away.

The house explodes, knocking all of them off their feet. Then a scraggly Werewolf comes running from the front of the house. A winged woman following him carrying a large Werelion in her arms. The Werewolf and Winged woman slow as Roger and Mr. Armstrong step in front of Alexis.

"Derek?" Alexis shoves between Roger and Mr. Armstrong.

"You're Alexis, I can feel all of you in the Pride bonds. We have to go, the Mundane authorities are on their way." Shane slows as he draws even with Alexis.

"Here, put him here now." Her imperious command brings his shoulders into a hunch and a growl from his Wolf side. Alexis, seeing the Alpha response, instinctively sings out one harsh note, followed by a luring melody.

Shane's eyes glaze and he points to the ground beside Belladonna. The angel's eyes glow and a smile plays at the corners of her perfect alabaster mouth. Setting Derek down beside Brother Lion she runs a finger down his cheek before stepping back. Alexis' song turns cold at the gesture. Belladonna shakes her hand shaking small pieces of ice free.

Once on the ground, beside Brother Lion, Derek

moans as Brother Lion turns into mist and disappears. Roger looks from the now missing Brother Lion to Alexis and back to Derek. "What?"

The sounds of emergency vehicles are arriving and neighbors are demanding to know what is going on drawing Mr. Armstrong's attention. He takes a step toward the commotion when a gunshot rings out followed by a roar of anger from a Werewolf somewhere out front.

"Alexis, we love you. Home." Derek whispers out loud, but the shout in the minds of everyone for miles around breaks the few windows not broken by the explosion.

Maria falls into the angel's arms from the sky with a little shriek. The gun shots out front stop and voices and more yelling begin to drift closer. The sound of people and vehicles approaching the area behind the estate are also coming closer.

Belladonna sets Maria on her feet with a look of surprise on her face. "Carry him Roger, we have to go. Dad, there might be cameras, stay in the middle. You, winged girl, do you have a way out of here for all of us?"

Alexis' words have a crisp, no-nonsense, in command tone that she has learned from her Father over the years of going to work with him.

"The way out is beyond the treed area by the creek, we have transportation." Belladonna begins walking as she finishes speaking.

"We need to clean this up." Shane sounds lost. A glance around shows freaks, specialists, humans and

Weres dead or so close as to make no difference. And the calls from the Mundane authorities demanding to know who they are, tells them all that that ship has sailed.

Maria speaks very little on the long walk to the creek. She is burned in several places and Roger keeps looking at her in worry. Belladonna carries her after the third time she fell. Whatever Marie did so the Mundanes did not see them worked.

No one speaks until they reach the creek. The horses waiting for them are a mixed match but all have western saddles and standing watch over them is Bryan. Alexis runs into his arms and hugs, cries, then slaps him, followed by another hug.

"Horses?" Roger's incredulous gasp draws Bryan's attention to the comatose Derek in his arms.

"Is he, will he?" Bryan asks.

"He feels asleep but well. I think this is like the time in the house after they were apart too long. But how are we going to get out of here?" Alexis' voice is low as the occasional flashlight lighting up the dark woods behind them shows the Mundanes are out in force. The sound of helicopters arriving puts more urgency on their departure.

"Don't worry, once we're out of town we have trucks and trailers waiting." Shane shakes himself free of the befuddling effects of Alexis' song to him. Mounting up, they all look determined, worn out, beat up but far from out.

Belladonna places Maria on a horse but stays on her own feet. "I can outrun a horse, of course, I never have to." With a shrug, her wings spread to an impressive six-foot length. Bryan's smile of pride as he looks at her brings a frown to Alexis' face.

"A winged woman? All the Weres in the world and you pick a Winged woman bigger than you?" Alexis half teases half asks.

They walk the horses, Maria is too exhausted to hide them if they do too much to draw attention to themselves. They pause for long stretches of time to wait for mundane search parties, military and civilian authorities, seeking more clues to what has happened in the upscale neighborhood they are riding away from.

Hours later they reach the end of the creek and find the two pickups and horse trailers waiting. No sign of anyone around. Shane and Bryan share a look but don't question the absence of anyone. Alexis climbs into the back of the fancy horse trailer with the camper unit in the front.

Alexis shoos everyone out and lays down beside Derek and Brother Lion. Once they are alone, she kicks off her ruined shoes, one with a hole in it, and sprawls out beside them. "You're not leaving my sight for a long time, either of you."

The rumbling sound of the trucks engines firing draws Alexis into an exhausted sleep.

Chapter 19

"It was a long trip to get even this far. Brother Lion and Derek had to stay in the camper portion of the horse trailer all the way from California to here. They are awake more now, but their auras are too fragile to be around anyone else yet." Alexis is standing, looking over the New Mexico grasslands that looks more like scrub lands. What grass there is this late in the year is mostly tumbleweeds and dead brush on its way to becoming tumbleweeds.

Aaron and Daisy are standing together watching Alexis and holding hands. Aaron is still bruised and burned, he had tried to sneak into the trucks heading to California to rescue Alexis and passed out from his injuries. The two weeks since Derek and the others had left to get her has allowed Dr. Brown to put him together well enough that he can get around again.

"It all seems so amazing, are the filmstrips still safe in the horse trailer?" Aaron asks, wrapping his arm around Daisy.

Daisy leans against him, her face will have scars on the right side but other than a lingering cough from the smoke inhalation she is suffering no more than if she had a bad sunburn. "I wouldn't be able to wait to watch the films. Although, I even watch my families boring vacation slide shows at reunions."

Alexis turns and walks away, back toward the community center that is now seeing more use than ever before. "I was tempted to hold them up to the light, but Roger pointed out that it might ruin them. Now I'm stuck waiting on the projector Dad bought on E-bay. It's coming from England and will be here in a few weeks. Apparently the one that was destroyed is an antique and is the only model that will play the film strips. Until then, I have to wait."

As they draw closer to the parking lot, Sapphire runs up to Alexis rubbing against her legs almost knocking her down. She laughs, petting the large wolf. "Where are Peggy and Tommy?" All three stop, looking around the parking lot where several vehicles are scattered as Alexis finishes speaking.

Daisy sighs, her face resigned, "Somewhere, being kids again I imagine. Since Mad Coyote disappeared, while his Granddaughter was being cremated, they have acted more like kids again."

Aaron snorts as they resume walking toward the double doors of the brick building. "Yeah, kids from Escape from Witch Mountain maybe." He grunts as Daisy's elbow strikes his side. "Good kids, just a little strange having them tossing balls of light around."

When they reach the end of the gravel parking lot and start up the cobbled walk, they stop again. "Wait up!"

Turning, Alexis smiles as Bryan trots up, Belladonna waves as she watches Bryan walk away from her.

"Your girlfriend's not joining us?" Alexis teases, grinning as she waves back at Belladonna.

Bryan blushes like a school boy running his hand through his curly hair while not looking back at Belladonna. "Stop teasing Alexis. You know she cannot have a boyfriend. She is lonely and scared, being the last of her kind in existence will do that to a person."

Alexis flinches, "You know I don't mean anything by it. Besides, you said she hated the others and was relieved they would stop pestering her."

Aaron fidgets, watching Belladonna flare her wings once before walking away.

Bryan winks, a grin tugging at his lips, "Yeah, but this way you feel like shit for teasing me."

Alexis laughs, leading the way to the doors. "Any idea what they have decided?" Aaron asks, swallowing and looking ahead at the silence and grim looks on faces replacing the light-hearted happiness at being safe and together again, at least for the moment.

"No, Derek and Brother Lion would have been allowed in the meetings as Shane's Blood Brothers, but their fiancé doesn't rank that high." Alexis sounds peeved.

Bryan puts his hand on her shoulder, giving it a squeeze. Alexis flashes a warm smile his way taking a deep breath as Aaron opens the door. Shoulders tense, head high, she strides into the building. A glance shows a trio of people speaking in a doorway down the right-hand hallway.

Brother Lion, can you hear me from here? Pushing with her thoughts as he has taught her brings a flush to her cheeks as her pulse speeds.

HHhhhmmmmm long since one of you has spoken to me. Alexis stops moving, as her eyes close. The spirit speaking to her feels not just old but as ancient as time itself. The sense of dust being dislodged is so strong she sneezes.

"Gazoongtite," Aaron says before catching his balance on the wall as the ground shifts and a loud groan echoes through the building.

"Alexis?" Bryan asks, shaking her when she doesn't respond or move. Standing with her eyes closed, breathing rapid.

What do you want? Who are you?" Alexis asks the spirit.

The spirit pauses in shock, reaching out to roughly brush Alexis' thoughts and memories. *Arrogant gnat. Do you dare to demand my name, without naming the price you will pay for it?*

As the spirit laughs louder and louder the ground shifts again as a minor earthquake shakes the area. Breaking windows and setting off car alarms. "Alexis! Dammit, she's gone. We need Brother Lion, he can reach her." Before Bryan can leave, Alexis' nose and ears begin bleeding.

Bracchius is my name, be careful how you use it. I will take my price from you soon little gnat. For now, it's time for these other ants to remember whose skin they delve in. As he plants his name in her mind, Alexis feels a rushing of time slow to an infinite slowness. A year is a grain of sand on an endless beach of sand. Her body thrums with energy and connection to the earth under feet.

Opening her eyes, Alexis breathes, swaying on her feet. The earthquake draws to a close as Daisy slaps Alexis. "Come back here girl. You are not leaving us again so soon."

When Alexis looks in Daisy's eyes, Daisy steps back, her eyes going wide. Alexis' green eyes are haloed in brown, with gold lines connecting them. It looks like a terrible case of bloodshot eyes, only gold instead of red.

"I'm okay Daisy, right here. Shall we go?" Alexis begins walking as if nothing has happened while she is brushing away the blood from her ears and nose. Where it drops on the floor, it smokes.

"Go, get Belladonna and Maria," Bryan speaks in a rush before hurrying after Alexis.

The trio of Werewolves are representatives from the nearby packs. They stop speaking as Alexis walks by, with Aaron by her side and Bryan bringing up the rear. A couple of steps past them she turns, Aaron having to back pedal to keep from bumping into her.

"Your Alphas chose you to represent your packs. Why do you wait here on the doorstep instead of taking the positions reserved for you in council?" Her eyes move from one Werewolf to another. As her eyes meet each of theirs, they straighten and give a deep nod of obeisance to her.

The largest, at just over six-feet. Speaks after a long pause. "We are low in the pack hierarchy."

Alexis raises an eyebrow to him as her gaze returns to his. "You are the sole representatives of each of your packs. Your dominance should be equal to that sacred trust your packs placed in you by sending you to this meeting."

As she turns to go, the smallest Werewolf of the group snorts, "They sent us because they consider this a waste of time."

He steps back as Alexis turns, stepping toward him. Her brown rimmed eyes are latching onto his. "Then they have made a grievous error in disdaining the oaths shared between the North American packs for centuries. If you do not step up and be part of the decisions here your packs will be as dust in a decade or less." As her last word is breathed out the ground rumbles then settles.

Bryan and Aaron share a startled look before following Alexis into the large auditorium full of folding chairs set in a half circle before the raised stage area at the far end. The people present are a mix of Delvers attired in thick hide clothing cut and stitched with delicate precision, Werewolves are scattered around with an occasional Werebear from the Rockies.

The only Troll sits alone on the outer edge of the back row of chairs. Just over seven-feet in height his green skin, bulbous nose and odor of rotting swamp doing as much to ensure the chairs around him remain empty as his dour demeanor.

The humans in the room are an eclectic mix of races

and nationalities. The magic users are separate in two groups. One group is dressed immaculately in the latest fashions from the east and west coasts. Money and arrogance going hand in hand with the Coven's select few members to present.

The magic users that refuse or are denied admittance to the Coven are easy to spot. They are only five in number and all wear jeans and tee-shirts. Clean but apparently not prosperous and worried glances at the Coven members gives away their anxiety. The Coven dictate that it is morally wrong for any non-Coven member to use or possess magic of any kind. They are rumored to enforce this morality by helping those magic users that use their powers to disappear, permanently.

Bryan and Aaron watch the various groups as they stride behind Alexis. The voices of those on the stage are becoming clearer as they draw closer with each step. "The Coven will take those poor souls that are now left without guidance in the moral use of their powers to the Coventry's for training in their powers." Sebastian Renaldo Carmichael is standing at ease in his Armani suit.

The magic users who are not a member of the coven move closer together at his words, faces going harder. Alexis walks up the stairs on the side of the stage with Bryan and Aaron following behind her. They look around as the room grows quiet at Alexis' entrance. Bryan notices the three Werewolves from the doorway moving to follow them up the stairs.

"The Coven has no rights to anyone here. The People from Below have always trained their own in the uses of magic." Shane stands at the center seat. His face tight with dark bags under each of his eyes.

 Sebastian snorts, "That was acceptable when your Grandmother was here to supervise them. Now you are all homeless." He gestures over everyone in the room. "Nowhere is there anyone to take responsibility for the magic users here. The Coven will not allow Magic use without its supervision for the safety of all."

Shane growls low, his back arching as he shows his fangs in anger. "Try me, you will find we will defend our own."

Alexis glances over the Supernaturals in the room. She forces her attention ahead and on her goal, leaving them all a blur. The three Werewolves from the door stop beside her. Wide-eyed and tense, they take up positions by her, a half step behind.

"Boy, the dozen Coven members here with me could reduce all of you to nothing. You embarrass yourself and your pack with this pathetic posturing." Sebastian laughs as he finishes.

Alexis steps out of the shadows which were hiding the stairs and her small group from those in the spotlights on the stage. "The reason we are all here is to discuss our options now that the Mundanes are aware of our existence." All eyes on her, she steps forward, sitting in the chair set for Brother Lion and Derek beside Shane's. A place of power and respect as the only Pride of Werecats on the continent.

Between Shane and Derek, the two blood brothers have the respect of most of the packs of North America.

Or at least, fear on the part of Derek and The Unit, the legends of their exploits have grown over the decades of war.

Sebastian and the two women in his shadow jerk as if slapped as Alexis speaks and sits nonchalantly. The three Werewolves all take the seats around her as representatives of their packs. Bryan and Aaron stand behind Alexis on either side as her guards. Shane looks from her to the others with her and nods once to her taking his own seat.

"Shane, is this how you keep order among your own pack? You allow this child to speak for your pack?" Sebastian curls his lip in a derisive sneer.

Shane draws a breath, but Alexis touches his arm. "The meeting is about to begin, all representatives of their kind please take your seats." *Brother Lion, the plan is that you will be the soul riding me while I do this. Gods know that I never did well in debates.*

There's a pause as everyone waits, to see what will happen next. Then the other Werewolves, Delver, and the Troll all take seats prepared for them on the stage.

Sebastian turns red in the face glaring at everyone taking seats. The last man to take his seat is one of the magic users not affiliated with the Coven. He sits at the farthest end of the stage away from the Coven members.

Shane stands, "We all know that we are in turbulent times. I am not sure if you all have the most recent information so we will begin with the latest mundane news report and then go from there." Resuming his seat he gestures and the lights dim, the curtains at the back of the stage are drawn back, and a 65-inch screen TV is rolled out.

With the dimming of the lights, the TV turns on. A reporter stands outside of the cordon off exclusive community where the Armstrong estate had stood. Flames and smoke, as well as screams, sound in the background with sirens.

The woman facing the camera is a typical newscaster with years of experience, the fear on her face is palpable as she begins to speak. "We have now confirmed footage that the Army National Guard has confirmed the capture of what can only be called a Werewolf."

The screen goes blank. "I am sure you are all aware that the Mundanes have now, at last count, several dozen Weres and a pair of Freaks the Major left for them to find. The repercussions of this are still being realized. What you might not have heard, as we just learned this today, is that the mundane authorities have issued this proclamation and passed laws supporting it."

As Shane finishes speaking, the screen lights up again. This time, it's the White House press conference room and the President addresses the cameras. "We have in custody, beings that may once have been human. They claim to be Werewolves and Specialists. The third type of creature is referred to as Freaks by the others captured with them."

The President takes off his glasses as he continues looking into the cameras. "We know they were involved with Terrorist attacks on a home in an upscale part of Sacramento, CA. The medical examinations have proven, they are in fact, not human as we understand human DNA structure. They are being held at an undisclosed location and claim that there are many more of them among us."

"The United States of America has never bowed to Terrorists and will not begin doing so now. If there are, in fact, other Werewolves, Freaks, or Specialists or any other similar creatures out there, you are at this moment ordered to report to the nearest Fema Camp to your present location where you will be safe and treated humanely. Failure to report within the next 72 hours will constitute a threat to the sovereign security of the American people and you will be moved to one with all reasonable force. If you are aware of any of these people being in your community, call the hotline flashing on your screen now. Please do not panic the Marines and Army National Guard are being deployed to help with the safe moving of these people to the camps. God Bless America."

The screen goes blank as the TV rolls back, and the curtain closes. Even Sebastian looks pole-axed by the revelations.

Shane stands once more, "The Major is known to all of you, one way or another. He has given Werewolves, Specialists, Freaks and even a Coven member to the government. What none of us realized is that he also sent video footage and a Werewolf, Freak and Specialist to a national news conference so the government could not cover up our existence this time. Always before, we knew that some among them knew of our existence but we were able to deal with it quietly. This time, that is not an option."

He sits back down to the questions and demands for answers from the audience and the others on the stage. As things get louder Shane leans over to Alexis "About time for your move."

As Alexis draws a breath nodding, Sebastian steps forward, claps his hands together and releases a loud bang of sound with a flash of light. "By order of the Coven, I arrest Alexis Armstrong for plotting harm to the Coven and all Supernatural beings." He moves forward, shadowed by the two women with him.

Alexis and Shane stand in shock as Bryan moves in front of Alexis. Everyone else on the stage scurries to the back to get out of the line of fire. "You will arrest no one, this is People from Below Pack lands. You have no authority here." Shane sounds sure, but his eyes keep moving, looking for a way out.

"The Coven has authority wherever the good hold domain. Stand aside and turn over the traitors or you share their guilt." Sebastian draws himself up, his hands moving in the intricate motions of ceremonial magic, the smell of electricity begins to build.

Never fear the dark for you are the light. Sing out with delight and release the Sirens fright. Her Mom's voice echoes in her mind, seeming to open her mouth of its own volition as a blue electric whip knocks Bryan and Aaron down, leaving the smell of singed ozone in the air.

"Follow me to green delights. Bosoms heave, let go your weave." Alexis thrusts her large breasts out in challenge as she sings. Sebastian lowers his hands a few inches, as his face sags. The light and feeling of an electrical charge begins to fade.

"Bitch! How dare you_." Sebastian loses his usually calm demeanor, rage twisting his handsome face into an ugly mask of rage.

"I do hope you did not plan this show on my account?" The voice speaking from the shadows is low, male and sends goosebumps over Alexis' arms as she shivers. Bryan and Aaron scramble, putting themselves in front of her.

"You, why are you here?" Sebastian's mask of rage is still there, but now pale fear wars with the anger. His eyes flick from right to left as his two companions become five.

The man stepping forward is lean to the point of emaciation but moves with a fluid grace. Not quite reaching six feet, he holds himself in such a way that Bryan feels ungainly in his height and slouches to hide his size. The man moves forward with an arrogant stride.

"You children forget that Numen created most of you. And the rest well, you are like children to us. Now it seems we might need to spank some of you." As he finishes, his jovial tone turns dark and menacing.

Sebastian straightens, the fear on his face pushes down behind his haughty veneer. "Those Numen of which you speak are long gone, you were one of the children who saw to that, were you not Aloysius?"

The Numen flashes and suddenly is inches from Sebastian, who begins sweating. "Yes, I was there when the Ancient Numen ruled as Gods. I was among those with enough courage and power to bring such as them down." His quiet voice throbs with velvet power. "Now, it seems someone has brought one of the ancients from their sleep, would you know about that?"

Sebastian goes pale, his lips bloodless as a stir among the audience announces a new arrival. Alexis turns her head away from Aloysius with difficulty. Like looking away from a snake or spider on your chest, it is hard to turn away even for a moment.

Belladonna flies across the auditorium, people moving out of her way. Landing on the stage she moves to stand off to the side of Alexis' group. "So I was right, it is one of the Ancient Numen in the decaying body."

Aloysius' attention turns from Sebastian, who steps back breathing deeply as he straightens his suit. Aloysius eyes Belladonna, his face shifting from longing to loathing and back. "I thought the last of the consorts were long dead. Hello daughter, lover, does my Nightshade yet survive?"

Belladonna shakes her head no. "I am the last. Time escapes us, tell us what you know and I will tell you where to find her killer."

Ignoring Belladonna's words, Aloysius' attention shifts to Alexis. "I feel something familiar in you child. Where is your bond mate? I feel I may know him."

Bryan's fangs extend as he feels the questing thought to reach toward Alexis. Aaron, sensing something wrong reaches for the 44 in his new belt holster.

Stay out of my mind. Alexis holds her shields as

strongly as she can as Brother lion has tried to teach her.
The mind of Aloysius is toying with her, slowly applying
more pressure until her shield buckles, almost breaking.

Aloysius smiles, fangs showing for the first time as
his eyes light with a pale white light. "Yes, you have
something very old tied to you. I will enjoy rending the
both of you." Lust and drool play over his eyes. When
Bryan steps forward, two Vampires grab him while a
third holds a blade to his throat. Aaron's hand is held
behind him by the last Vampire.

Alexis feels tears begin as she fights. *No! Brother
Lion is mine, you cannot have him.* The instinctive fear
for her mate is fierce. Then she feels a stirring deep
below her feet. *So many little bugs think they are more
than they are.* Bracchius thoughts move slow but
inexorable like the turning of the centuries.

Reaching through Alexis as her shield crumbles,
Aloysius lunges to grab her mate bond to Brother Lion,
Bracchius buries Aloysius in his own powerful thoughts.
Aloysius pales, jerking back, his hands clench into fists as
his face tightens in pain.

Sending a flare of power into Bracchius results in a
shifting of the ground. Bracchius releases Aloysius,
laughing as his awareness fades from Alexis' mind. She
stands to breathe deeply, using the stabbing pain of a
migraine, left behind by Aloysius and Bracchius, to power
the third set of her vocals.

"Release my Pride, flow aside with the Tide. Glide
and move wide around those of my Pride." Her song
slips silken cords around the vampires. Drawing them

back in a daze, as the notes fade they snarl, baring fangs but don't leap to attack again.

Shaking his head, Aloysius draws back a step, "SheMiTali. This is unbelievable if not unforeseen. Hear me now, one and all." His voice deepens, growing louder to fill the auditorium as he continues. "The Mundanes now know of the Supernatural's existence among them. It will only be a matter of time before they know of all of you."

Shifting feet and nervous glances fill his pause. "I am leaving one of my children with the SheMiTali to assist with the tasks now before her. The mundane government must be made to see the Supernaturals as non-threatening and allow us to continue to exist among them. This idiocy of locking us up is dangerous to them, not us. The Numen give you one calendar year to accomplish this."

Alexis' mouth drops open, as she is about to protest, Sebastian beats her to it. "Now wait one minute, she is not a Were or anything other than an untrained Shamaness!"

Aloysius turns his gaze on Sebastian, a grin spreading over his face. "Good point. You will share her guilt if she fails in this task. Select someone to teach her what she needs to know so she is no longer untrained. You will, of course, be busy dealing with the mess in California. An Ancient Numen is trapped in the hole where a piece of this world and the spirit world once touched. When he gets out, and he will get out, he will be angry and more insane than ever. I believe you have named him The Other. That is as good a name as any. Your job will be to distract him until the Numen council can bring the trained SheMiTali to deal with him.”

Shane clears his throat. ”The Numen are not unknown to me.” Shane moves to stand beside Alexis as he speaks. “The days when the Numen had the power to force all the other races to do their bidding is millennia past.”

Sebastian catches himself nodding in agreement and glares at Shane as if he was tricked somehow into agreeing with him.

“Foolish Pup. This debacle you have helped to create with the Mundanes is nothing. If one of the Ancient Numen succeeds in cementing his ties to that Were body he is in now. If I am correct in which Ancient is awake in that body, this entire world will be no more if we fail to send him to the eternal sleep. If he was not insane from being bound in sleep too close to this realm for over a thousand years, he would already have destroyed or enslaved all of us.”

Turning, he walks back toward the curtained off backstage area. “One year, probably less and we will meet again, to live or die.” The vampires move, following him, when they reach the curtains a blast of frigid air blows the curtains out, and they stay out, frozen in sheets of ice. When everyone’s eyes clear the Numen and Vampires are gone.

The auditorium is silent for a long time after Aloysius leaves. Belladonna breaks the silence. “I have more reason than any here to hate the Numen and all they are, yet in this, we must all stand with them.” She stands trembling until Bryan moves to her side, leaning against her without saying anything. Her trembling eases and the tips of her right wing feathers brush his calves under his jean legs.

"The Coven will need to meet on these matters. Our decisions will be made known to all. SheMiTali, you will come with us for your instruction as suggested by Numen Aloysius." Sebastian gestures toward Alexis to come toward him.

Alexis shakes her head, regaining her composure. "He actually said you would provide a suitable teacher for me. You have to go to California." The three Werewolves step up to stand by Aaron, Belladonna and Bryan in silent support of Alexis.

Shane moves to his seat and sits back down. "Despite all the theatrics and orders that were given from the Vampire leaders, we still have Were business to discuss."

Sebastian laughs, "Come with me and I will see you are trained." When he say's "trained" the word sounds painful, the smile on his face as he speaks adds to the feeling.

"The first order of business is deciding what to do about the Major. He has sent another message that he is dealing with the Mundanes on our behalf. It has become more and more evident that he is unstable. How do we deal with the Mundanes and the Major, who still has significant political influence and is using it to further his own agenda?" Shane picks up a clipboard with a yellow legal pad on it from beside his chair as he resumes sitting after speaking.

The largest Werewolf from the doorway speaks, "The Colorado Basin pack feels that allowing the Major to speak for any Were pack in North America after his latest betrayal is unacceptable. Our Alpha will not go along with any action that doesn't first deal with the Major as a threat."

"That is easier said than done. The El Paso, Texas pack, has members on both sides of the border, and the Major has great influence in old Mexico. Not to mention no one knows where he is at the moment." The smallest Werewolf hesitates a moment then moves to resume his seat, the other two Werewolves from the doorway follow a moment later.

Alexis speaks evenly, "First, we need to decide which Pack or Pride is the most stable and is strong enough to avoid being forced into a FEMA camp. A DVD to the major news networks stating our position, and that the Major does not speak for us will need to happen right away."

Sebastian spreads his glare around the stage and auditorium when it is clear no one is going to pay him any attention, he turns and walks off the stage. Alexis' shoulders relax as he and his Coven members make their way to the door. Bryan and Aaron watch until the last of the Coven members leave the room, and the door closes behind them before turning their attention from them.

"I propose the Unit be the spokespeople for the Were and Supernatural Community. They have numerous medals, Purple Hearts, Congressional Medal of Honors and if they admit who they are that should really make a difference." Shane speaks evenly, only glancing at his notes once.

"That is all well and good, in the meantime, we all have a price on our heads." The speaker is one of the magic users in the auditorium in jeans and Def Leopard Tee-shirt from the 80's.

"No matter who is chosen as Pack or Pride speaker, we all will have prices on our heads. The Unit is prepared to be the face for now. We would like a member of the other supernatural groups to join us on our ranch in South Dakota to represent their group." Alexis speaks evenly, only sounding like a robot toward the end when her lips go numb.

"I will join you as the only living Consort if you will have me," Belladonna speaks in her usual voice of grinding rocks.

Shane draws in a breath standing, "I move that the Unit Pride of South Dakota is our designated spokes Pride."

The troll stands "I second the motion and will also join them there, as the only living troll in North America."

Alexis, Shane and the rest of the room turn to stare in shock at the troll. Bryan pulls himself together, "You will be welcome with us."

A gangly young man with a skull earing, not much past being a teenager with a few zits still lingering, steps away from the magic user group that is moving toward the door. "I will teach you and represent free magic users if you will have me." The shifting of his feet and the shocked stares from the others in the group that linger a moment before finishing their exit out the doors shows the impulsive decision was not without fear on his part.

"Thank you for your offer. I will hear your teachings, and welcome you as a representative of the magic users not affiliated with the Coven." Alexis reads the writing on her right forearm.

The other representatives begin moving around forming small groups, then breaking apart and forming new groups. Eyes are drawn to Alexis time after time. Shane moves to the rear of the theater, Alexis follows with Bryan close behind. Aaron moves to speak to Daisy, who just entered with Maria.

"Well, that went better than we expected. No official vote but no one objects and we will count those joining you as representatives as votes." Shane makes notes on his clipboard.

"I need answers, Shane. Brother Lion and Derek are still in limbo while their auras regenerate. Tell me what the fuck happened today." Alexis speaks with a fierce demand to know what is going on.

"Numen are the makers of Vampires, Werewolves, and many of the supernatural races. The ancient Numen anyway." When Alexis squeezes his arm in anger, he continues. "Look, I don't know all the answers. The ancient Greek and Roman gods were Numen."

Alexis gasps as Shane continues, "They don't feed on blood, but they do feed. Because they are not really alive as we understand living, no breathing or heartbeat.

They have no auras, nothing to hold their spirit to the shell of their bodies. So they steal auras from other living things. Usually human or humanoid anyway."

"I can add to that." Belladonna moves a few paces closer to Alexis before she continues. "They created my kind as lovers, consorts. The Werekin, they used as dogs to guard, entertain with dog fights and so forth. The Ancient Numen had so many worshipers that they had almost unlimited power. They almost destroyed the world in their petty dramas and games. Then the younger Numen and other Supernatural races worked together, luring them to millennia of sleep that we thought would never be broken."

"Are you telling me that Hades is going to wake up and start taking people to the underworld?" Bryan tries to be joking but the serious look on Belladonna's face stops his grin.

"Unlikely, the greater Gods Zeus, Hades, etc. are all buried deep, close to the edge of this world and the next. It is one of the lesser Gods or Goddesses that was entombed too close to this world that is The Other. I fought it in California. The smell of its rotting body and madness is overwhelming."

Maria steps onto the stage with Daisy's help. Alexis blinks at her in shock, Maria has a belly, not as large as Daisy's but larger than it had been a few days before. "The Other is trapped in Limbo where the anchor of the Armstrong Estate used to be. When I left my spirit home forever, I knotted the doors and windows as tightly as I could. It will not hold him back forever but will give the

SheMiTali time to learn to use her power."

Alexis stands to throw her hands in the air, "What do I have to do with it? With all the power the Coven has, wouldn't they be better suited to dealing with it? Or the other Numen?"

Belladonna shakes her head, "The younger Numen are not like the Ancients, and they lost most of their power putting their makers to sleep in limbo. The Coven would try and control the Other and use it to take more power over all of us. The SheMiTali is the only one with the power to lure the Other in song and the Shamanic power to untangle the magic holding the Ancient Numen Spirit to the mortal flesh of the Werewolf it is in."

The troll speaks from the floor in a monotone, "Or bind them together, forever freeing the Numen's power from limbo so it can destroy the Earth."

As if that is the cue, the doors open and some of the assembled Werewolves, magic users, and humans begin drifting out. Alexis' wide eyes move from one to another of the people on the stage with her finally stopping on Daisy.

"Hey, my kids ride a ghost wolf, cast magic, my daughter has a glowing dagger that cuts souls. You're not the only one with problems." Daisy shrugs as she finishes speaking, a wolf howls and the laughter of children reaches them.

Alexis' eyes shed a few tears as she and Daisy begin laughing a little hysterically.

"Well, we might as well go home. I hope that film projector gets here soon. Anyone seen my Dad or Mrs.

Collins?" Alexis asks looking around.

"They just came in together, looks like they're heading this way," Bryan says.

As Mr. Armstrong and Mrs. Collins walk up the stage stairs a few minutes later, all eyes turn to stare at the smiling and crying Mrs. Collins. Mr. Armstrong looks at Alexis, shifting his feet. *Something is going on, he is never this nervous, or never shows it anyway.*

"Alexis, we're getting married, isn't it wonderful?" Mrs. Collins holds her hand out to show Alexis, on it is a large diamond engagement ring. "Martin took me to Sturgis and well, we are getting married!" Mrs. Collins' face is beaming, Mr. Armstrong's face is uncertain as everyone watches Alexis for her reaction.

"Alexis, will you be my maid of honor?" Mrs. Collins' face shows the uncertainty of how she will react as everyone seems to stop breathing on the stage waiting for an answer from Alexis.

"Of Course, I would be honored to be your maid of honor." *I'm sure I can squeeze it in somewhere between learning what exactly a SheMiTali is, how to use my power, convince the US government that supernaturals are just ordinary people with fur, claws and magic. Oh and save the world from the Other that is really a Greek or possibly Roman God. No problem, I'm sure I can fit it in somehow.*

Daisy watches Alexis hug Mrs. Collins and her Dad. Then nods distractedly as they all chat about going home and the wedding. The young pimply faced magic user leans towards Daisy, "Are they really planning a wedding with, well everything going on?" He whispers to Daisy.

"Oh yeah. Stick around long and the gunshots, attacks, and magic disasters are just part of the day. No reason to put off a party or wedding. I need a cigarette." Daisy sounds wistful and proud at the same time.

"Mom, you stopped smoking!" The young man steps back as the large blue-eyed wolf materializes out of thin air in front of him with two kids on its back. "Tommy won't play right, he keeps changing my light globes blue and green instead of purple and pink!"

Tommy and Peggy's argument gets louder, as Daisy and Alexis share a look and start laughing.

Chapter 20

Aftermath

"No, you don't have to pull me in!" Joel puts his hands on his head groaning as he slides onto his back. "Maybe we should wait a few more days and have you practice with Brother Lion when he gets back."

Alexis stands, stretching her cramped muscles. "Yeah, that might be best. At least you didn't get sick this time." *I wish I was better at controlling my power. Every time, I either drag him into my mind and suck his energy dry or batter him with my thoughts. I really hope he doesn't get sick this time, those migraines I give him must really hurt.*

Walking over to the window, she pulls it open letting in the frosty winter air. The gray sky is teasing a white Christmas, but so far, that is all they have had since Thanksgiving, teasing. The sound of laughing and Holiday rock songs draws her eyes.

Roger and Bryan are busy stringing lights. "No! No, you have too many blue lights together! DO I have to do everything myself?" Alexis smiles as her Pride of Werecats move around the yard putting up holiday decorations. *Those Supra Agents better not ruin this holiday.*

"Fresh air helping or hurting today?" A glance back shows her that his eyes are closed and the swallowing every few minutes warns her that he might not be able to avoid being sick again after all.

"Leave it open, please. It's helping, I just need to zone out for a while." His nasal voice has become her bane over the last few months since they made it home.

"Okay, well I'm going Christmas shopping in town with Daisy. You promised to help the kids with their special Christmas show today." Alexis ignores his groan with a grin. *Serves you right, being shown up by kids less than half your age. Of course, you're my teacher so what does that say about me?*

Walking across the hall and down the stairs, she hears laughter from the dining room. Slowing, she looks from the stairs to see who is being so loud. "Martin, stop it! We're not alone." She slaps his arm but giggles like a school girl as he nuzzles her neck.

"Yeah Dad, you two need to get a room." Alexis continues down the stairs at a slower pace giving Mrs. Collins time to disentangle from Mr. Armstrong.

As she steps from the stairs, she dares to raise her eyes to the dining room proper. Mr. Armstrong is straightening his hair, as Mrs. Collins blushes gathering up the last of the dirty dishes from the afternoon cocoa and snack that has become a ritual since Thanksgiving.

"How did practice go today?" Mr. Armstrong asks, standing casually in his wardrobe. Rodeo shirts with shiny snaps and bright plaid colors paired with blue jeans.

The sound of Joel getting sick in the upstairs bathroom sounds as Alexis opens her mouth. When Mrs. Collins and Mr. Armstrong burst out laughing, Alexis grimaces. "Same as always. We've decided that we're going to wait for Brother Lion and Derek to return for more training."

Mrs. Collins sighs, "It's not right those G-men whistle and expect us to send someone off to deal with a problem they created." Raising her eyes from picking up the last cocoa cup, she notices she is now the center of attention. "Well, it's not."

Mr. Armstrong smiles warmly at her. "Well, all the same, I'm glad they finally admitted that dealing with Weres and Supernaturals takes more than guns."

Yeah, and it only took what, a couple hundred deaths? Locking up Supernaturals in FEMA camps only got them to work with each other. The memory of the satellite video the government had shown them still gives her nightmares.

The paper pushers had no idea that Weres need twenty to forty thousand calories a day. Sending what they considered adequate was slowly starving the Weres that had gone, of their own accord, in answer to the government's new laws.

The regular military base is understaffed with another war going on in the Middle East. The three magic users are probably an earth witch, sorcerer, and

Shatteuth blasting through the military base perimeter. The magic users had shut down fire so weapons wouldn't fire anymore. If the soldiers had just left, leaving the food behind, no one would have died. A few hundred soldiers with guns and machines that would not work were no match for starving Weres and three angry magic users.

Shivering, Alexis watches as Mrs. Collins pass into the kitchen. "Any word on the projector? If we could just play the films, Mom could teach me." Frustration fills her mouth with a rotten taste similar to milk a few days past expired.

"Want some cocoa and cookies? We managed to hide some, but when they come in from decorating this evening, they will all disappear again." Mr. Armstrong winces as the sound of Joel, groaning on his way from the bathroom to his bedroom, reaches them.

"No thanks. I'm heading out to go Christmas shopping in town with Daisy. I wish we could go to Sturgis, but it's probably a bad idea." Alexis watches the color drain from her Dads cheeks.

"You stay out of the city! Those pics of you and Derek have made the rounds, and you never know who might recognize you." Seeing her nod, his shoulders relax. "You have to stay safe. You're the maid of honor remember?"

Gods, how I wish I would have known I could tell truth and lies by listening to the song. She marvels again as she feels the music that even the most everyday words spoken create. Concentrating, she can see the swirl of color that is the music of their conversation. *I know now that you love me and never had anything to do with Mom's death.*

Stepping forward, she wraps her arms around him hugging him to her, "I love you, Dad."

A moment later his arms wrap around her. "I love you too."

Alexis sneezes as his Brute cologne tickles her nose. "Geesh Dad, take it easy on that cowboy cologne." Stepping back, she smiles at him before turning for the hall to the front door. "I have my cell if you need me. Daisy said something about wanting to eat at the cafe with her family."

Mr. Armstrong laughs, "Well, I will put a clean trash can out for you in your room. Have fun."

Alexis ignores the reminder of the last time she ate with Daisy's family. *Raccoon and possum stew might have been okay but who in their right mind throws in crawfish and clams just because they are about to go bad?*

In the yard, Roger walks over to Alexis, ignoring Amanda yelling. "Get back here and hold the ladder!"

"You're fine. I wasn't actually holding it anyway." Roger stops by Alexis looking her up and down with a raised eyebrow.

"The same as the last dozen times." Her frustration fills her voice with bitterness.

Roger grins, "Cool. I win the bet again today. Too bad you didn't break the new window, or Derek would be doing my share of the dishes for a month when he gets back."

372

Alexis sticks her tongue out at Roger looking around for Daisy.

"She's not here yet. She is with Marie, still taking baby stuff out to the cabin." Roger scuffs his foot looking at the ground.

Wow Roger, going to be a Dad. "So do you want a daisy or a rose for your first child?" Alexis holds onto the grave expression until Roger grins at her, his stiffness relaxing.

"You know we have a bet on whether it will be Derek or Brother Lion who knocks you up first." The bags under Roger's eyes deflect Alexis' anger.

Not fair Roger, you tease me then look scared and I can't tease back. Gods, what do I say? Will it even be remotely human? "Does Marie know when she will go into labor?"

Roger shrugs as his eyes fill but doesn't overflow. "She lost her memories of being a spirit when she left limbo in mortal form to be with me. She says she will know and that will be enough."

Yeah, like I don't have enough to be responsible for, remind me that Marie gave up immortality to be with you physically all because she was jealous of me. Me with Roger? Could that ever have been a possibility? Alexis shivers remembering that for that to happen, Brother Lion and Derek would both have died in limbo.

The kids yelling and charging around on Sapphire announce that Daisy is coming up the drive before Alexis hears the little car. As Sapphire runs by the ladder, knocking into it, "Roger get the ladder!" Amanda yells as she sways, Amanda grabs the string of lights she has been hanging along the gutters of the ranch house to hold the ladder upright. Roger darts over straightening the ladder.

Saved by the Wolf. "I'll remember the baby while I'm Christmas shopping Roger."

Sabrina glances out the window of the single-wide trailer across from the ranch house and Alexis' heart dips into her stomach as she waves, smiling. Sabrina raises her arm to waist height and half waves before dropping the curtain back into place.

Alexis strides to where Daisy is getting out of the car slowly. *Major, if I ever get my hands on you, I will show you what I have learned about using my power. At least she is looking out the window once in a while now. That's only taken a couple of months. Poor Matteas, he hates having to leave her but with Felix being a traitor only he and Bryan can handle the political mess to represent the Supernaturals in North America.*

"You kids get your butts inside to help Mrs. Collins! You better get those dishes done before dinner!" Daisy yells at the pair of kids running around who might or might not have heard by their response.

"Ho Ho Ho I know who gets no presents no mo no mo." Aaron's loud singsong is echoed by Dr. Michaels coming out of the barn with him. "Coal, shots and medicines for presents have I, for the naughty ones on my list."

"We will get the dishes done, don't have a coronary already," Tommy calls back as he blinks out of sight on

Sapphire only to reappear a moment later walking in the back kitchen door.

Daisy flashes a smile at Aaron before walking over to him and giving him a huge hug. Alexis buries the surge of jealousy beneath her happiness for her friends. "Hey Aaron, want to come have dinner with your in-laws with us?" Alexis calls as she stops beside the passenger door.

"No thanks Alexis, I haven't had my tetanus shot yet. I would say take Joel but we heard him in the bathroom and he sounded sick enough already for the sins of all of us in our past lives." Aaron grunts as Daisy steps out of his arms.

"Yeah, you would rather eat in Bangkok." Daisy smacks Aaron in the balls, he goes pale but laughs.

"Mom! You never hit boys there! He won't be able to give me a sister now!" Peggy is walking from the front door of the house while Joel stares wide eyed at her mom's red face. Aaron laughs and winces.

"I will do my best Peggy but you know if you end up with another brother it's all your mom's fault." Aaron limps away quickly as Daisy turns toward him.

"It's okay Peggy. I didn't hit him for real. We were just acting out That 70's Show. Do you want to see your Uncle Henry and Gramps?" Daisy asks as she walks to the car.

Peggy shakes her head no, grabbing Joel's hand and dragging him toward the pasture leading to the clubhouse the kids are building. "Joel has to put up our Christmas tree, he promised. And I have to help Mrs. Collins make tomorrow's brownies. Tell them I love them." She waves, hurrying away with Joel being dragged along behind.

Shaking her head, Daisy gets back in the driver's seat as Alexis shuts her door watching Sabrina's trailer. "Sabrina almost waved at me a moment ago." Alexis comments.

Backing up until she can turn the car around, Daisy sighs, "I went over with her breakfast tray this morning. The place is clean enough to eat off the floor." Turning the music on the radio she finishes. "I took her the CD's Matteas said are her favorites and she started to cry."

Alexis sighs, leaning back in the seat and watching the tree and winter bare grass go by. The radio weatherman says, "It's looking like we might get that white Christmas yet folks. In the meantime here's one to tide us over until then."

"Frosty the snowman...." Begins playing.

"The ones that were responsible have been dealt with and there will be no more incidents." Derek drops the folders on the desk in front of the middle-aged man in the department store suit.

Derek stands with stooped shoulders, mud to his calves and in his hair. Maintaining his human form is a strain. *He's not smart enough to understand that these Were's families have suffered enough.* Brother Lion snorts, calming them both with thoughts of Alexis and the Pride waiting for them to return.

"Supra has full authority to deal however it sees fit with those responsible. I will not accept that they have been dealt with." Spittle flies on the desk as he gesticulates and raises his voice.

"I didn't think you would. Matteas give the accused into his hands." As Derek finishes, Matteas steps up from where he is waiting by the door with a large black trash bag.

"The accused." Matteas in his natural form has a slight hiss to his words from his fangs. His glowing eyes and furred face have the man in the suit leaning away as he drops the bag on his desk with a wet splash. Turning, he salutes Derek before going to the door and holding it open.

"I have had enough of this bullshit. Make no mistake. Supernaturals have policed themselves for thousands of years while the rest of you learned to wash behind your ears." Throwing back his head, Brother Lion roars the Alpha roar of rage and loss at the senseless deaths of three teenage Weres in the wrong place and time.

"If you ever cause the deaths of another child, supernatural or mundane, I will hold you responsible." Golden eyes glowing, Brother Lion stares down the Supra Agent who was put in charge of policing the Supernaturals in the North East.

When the politician falls back into his chair from his half standing position, Derek drops the bombshell. "In three days a demonstration will occur showing that Supernaturals will not be the victims of Genocide by ANY government. Be sure that this death camp is empty by then or any deaths will be on your head."

Turning, he salutes Matteas as he marches out past the guards arriving in response to his roar. A large man wearing the MP insignia blocks Derek's path. "Halt!"

As Brother Lion slows, a thin woman in a silk pantsuit steps from the shadows, hand moving in a smooth swiping motion, the MP gently floats until he bumps into the ceiling, Derek catches his falling gun. Matteas crouches, glancing from Derek to the strange woman.

"Greetings, Arms of the SheMiTali. Tell her the Guardians of the Watch Towers of the East await her call." A green smoke funnels in a small tornado around the woman. When the smoke clears the woman is gone, and the hallway is full of soldiers and one woman in a pantsuit all hanging pressed against the ceiling.

Matteas walks past Derek heading for the exit as the man from the office looks out. "Come on Captain. I don't want to have to kill them when they start falling."

Brother Lion watches the woman in the pantsuit as they walk past her. *She's from Channel 19 evening news.*

Derek turns looking up at her. "I am Derek Mathews, Alpha of the South Dakota Pride. Designated ambassador of the Supernatural people of North America. A mourning for the passing of three teenage boys in the wrong place and time will happen here in three days. Be sure you and everyone else are a long way away. Set up your cameras and you will see the value we Supernaturals place on life. And the restraint we have shown to the nations which many of us have served.

Supra will treat us fairly, as a free people that have served this country, or they will not deal with us at all."

As Derek begins to turn away, she stops him. "Mr. Mathews, will you continue doing the dirty work for Supra? Does it not make the rest of the Were community distrust you?"

She is hanging from the ceiling and interviewing me. Gutsy woman. Appraising the Hispanic woman's courage and professionalism, as well as her attractive body, Derek responds. "I am not doing Supra's dirty work. In its rush to create an organization to police us, the government made mistakes, I and my Pride have been trying to help them correct the worst of those mistakes."

Derek lowers his head breathing deeply "That has proven to be impossible. Now the Supernaturals will show why we will continue to police ourselves. We will hold ourselves to the laws of this nation the same as any other citizen. But no longer will we allow our own rights to be voted away."

Turning, Derek ignores the questions shouted at him as he walks out the door held open by Matteas. The sound of a body striking the floor from the ceiling reaches them as the door closes. Walking to the red Jeep Wrangler, which Mr. Armstrong has given him as an engagement present after he sold his business, he reaches for Alexis.

Feeling her well and hundreds of miles away is reassuring and devastating all at once. "You need to get back to Alexis. You were staring far too long at that reporter." Matteas rolls his shoulders as they both feel eyes on them.

He's right. We need our mate. Let's go home.
"Let's get a room and you can call Sabrina then I can call Alexis. We both need to go home, as soon as this demonstration is over we will make a statement and then go home and we're not leaving again until after the New Year."

Derek doesn't need to comment to Brother Lion as they drive away through the open gate. The soldiers watching them leave salute, a first since they began going in and out of the camp a couple of months ago. Derek solemnly returns the salutes as he drives by.

The sun is a dim glow and the gray sky hides behind banks of clouds. Derek and Matteas are standing on a hill looking over the crowds of news crews and Supra-personal, once again supplemented by local Army National Guard Units. Sheriff Deputies are busy dealing with traffic and civilians, all a couple hundred yards from the barbed wire fenced camp.

"You tell Alexis what's going to happen today?" Matteas asks.

Derek shrugs, "I gave her enough information, I wasn't keeping her in the dark, but not enough that she hops on a plane to save us."

Matteas stiffens as he asks. "How do you know how much you can tell her before she does something that stupid?"

Brother Lion laughs answering "We'll find out if we got it right if she shows up today or not. Looking at the sky, so far so good, if she was coming I think she would have come on the first day not wait until the day of the demonstration." Seeing Matteas' grimace, the bags under his eyes testifying to his worry over Sabrina, Derek adds, "Daisy gave a bunch of CD's to Sabrina and she has been cleaning the trailer each day. Alexis mentioned that Sabrina has been watching the Christmas decorating and theatrics from the window every day."

Changing the subject as his throat tightens over worry for his mate, "It doesn't look like they are taking this seriously." Matteas says, breath steaming in the December Maine air.

"They will. I told Carmella to make sure there are no casualties. The idea is to show a fraction of what we can do, without scaring them into all out attacks." Derek ignores Brother Lion's snort of derision. "A combination of illusion and gathering the spirits of all those dead because of the stupid decisions made in fear on both sides should help."

Matteas glances over at Derek, both of them in their natural forms to show they are here as Weres not as part of Supra. "Who are you trying to convince, them or me?" He nods towards the camp where the American flag is being raised.

Shaking his head, Brother Lion begins loping down the hill with Matteas close behind. A young couple notices them first and starts pointing, the crowd pivots in what could have been a choreographed move to face

Derek and Matteas in Natural form, manes flowing, eyes glowing, as the fur, not covered in their old military uniforms covered with medals, steams in the early morning air.

As they pass, the crowd opens up for them, a light applause follows them. *Mr. Armstrong's publicist is working wonders, making us into furry war heroes.* Brother Lion nods in agreement, most of his attention feeling for the astral ripples that will give them a few moments warning before the magic begins.

As they near the front of the parked vehicles, the Sheriff notices them and heads their way. Matteas keeps going but Derek pauses at the edge of the road to wait for the pot-bellied Sheriff to arrive before continuing to the gate of the camp.

"You know anything about this Derek?" The Sheriff is only a little winded after his trot across the street and acreage that has become an impromptu parking lot. In his defense, the crowd never parted for him as it had for the Werelions with fangs and fur flashing in the morning light.

"You saw the news reports. That reporter got most of what I said correct." Derek and the Sheriff catch up to Matteas before the Sheriff can ask anything else.

"Empty the base or people will die." Matteas' voice is more growl than conversation. The two guards at the closed gate look miserable but shake their heads.

"Sorry Captain Derek, but the base is closed due to terrorist threats." He swallows as his eyes grow large at the medals hanging both on Derek and Matteas.

Derek shakes his head. "Not your fault, I imagine I will have to open the base so you can get out when the mourning ceremony begins."

Derek moves to the left end of the gate while Matteas moves to the right. The two guards look at each other while the Sheriff frowns after them. Once at the end of the gate, Matteas and Derek exchange a nod, bend, and grasp the gate with furred hands and heave upward. The metal gate posts resist but with some wiggling the ground gives up the cement blocks and electrical wires that power the gates opening and closing.

"Back!" Brother Lion's roar works, the guards scramble back giving room for Derek and Matteas to toss the gate onto the drive. "The base is now open so people can get out." Turning to the open mouthed sheriff he continues. "Get room made for the base personal. They will be coming out in a moment. The warning will be starting any time now."

Matteas and Derek move in a calm stride to the front row of spectators where the media has gathered. Lights flash as cameras snap pictures of the Werelions. Without answering any of their shouted questions.

The first waves are beginning. Brother Lion's excitement is palpable. At first, it's hard to tell what is happening in the base. The gray clouds lower over the camp, then thicken until you can no longer see the camp. The brick and block buildings are soon covered in a moving gray blanket.

Then the screams begin, they're horrible screams of terror. A few gun shots sound but not as many as Matteas has predicted. The crowd grows silent. Even the reporters stop shouting questions from behind the sheriff deputies' line. The Sheriff, who has been standing watching the guards on their radios and the growing crowd of MPs surrounding the downed gate, moves briskly away from the camp as the gray wall of clouds descends to swallow the base.

"Move those people back! Make room for the camp personnel. Make room now, come on, move." Derek buries his grin behind his hand as he watches the Sheriff doing what he had suggested minutes before.

Then the groaning, sounds of people in pain begin to drift out of the enshrouded camp. "Someone should help them. Those people are in pain. The police should do something." The voices from the crowd stop as the first uniformed camp personnel begin to stumble out of the base.

The paramedics rush forward to help the first few to the ambulances. "I am sorry. You have to believe me I didn't know they would die." He grabs the paramedic's arms and shakes him. "Believe me, damn you!" The paramedics reply is drowned out by the screaming of the next group to stumble out of the gray wall.

The crowd begins moving back of its own accord at this point. The sky grows darker as more clouds replace the ones swirling around the camp. The gloomy midday is sunk in a twilight gloom. More uniformed and civilian clothed people are arriving.

"The fog is eating them alive!" The reporter has forgotten himself, lowering his camera to film the ground. Shapes are now visible, arms and torsos push out of the cloud only to sink back in with a ripple of the gray fog. People move back several more steps.

"How many do you reckon are still in there?" Derek asks softly.

"The records say that a hundred and fifty were assigned here after Supra started. Stupid name, makes CIA and FBI sound intelligent." Matteas grimaces in distaste as he speaks the despised name.

"Well, they were in a hurry to stop the hysteria. The politicians in charge are all over sixty and they don't understand that Zombies, Werewolves and aliens are believed to be among us. The fact that they exist is actually less of a shock to the average Joe than it is to the politicians in charge." Derek's head goes up watching the first shooting light descend toward the camp.

"Yeah, well it's still a stupid name." Matteas sounds peeved that Derek has not agreed.

The people leaving the camp in twos and threes become a solid wall of people fleeing. Most in tears, some with scratches around their eyes. All of them in a hurry to leave the base. "Reckon the show is about to begin."

Brother Lion smiles in grim pleasure as the lights begin flashing up from the wall of clouds. *Bit dramatic.*

Derek replies, *They understand the people in charge have no imagination. Or they should, we told them often enough.*

As the last few people are escorted away from the base, the gray clouds swirl up into the sky. Then the illusion begins. Warm, red, salty rain falls and it only takes a few moments for people to realize it's raining blood all over them, then they begin screaming and pointing.

Almost at the same moment that the people are all in a panic over the blood rain, it stops. Then the sores begin to appear. Puss filled oozing sores, coughing, patches of hair falling out. People losing teeth and pieces of flesh fall off to leave oozing puss filled sores. Then the screams become moans and pleas for help.

Then the swarms of bugs descended from all directions. They swarm up legs, under pants, falling in swarms from the sky. They devour the sores, puss and all the drops of blood in moments. "You know, with all those movies, someone should remember to keep their mouths shut." Matteas curses as a thumb sized wasp flies into his open mouth.

Derek grins at Matteas, keeping his own mouth shut. Matteas flips Derek off with his free hand while he digs the wasp stinger from his tongue with his other.

Then the ground churns, illusional bodies rising as the bugs leave. They are the dead Weres, Supernaturals of all types with a few mundane humans as well. All those that had died as part of the government's panicked attempts to deal with the Supernatural population that has been among them from the beginning.

As people grow sick, seeing the death surrounding them on all sides. Children with fur and fangs are still children. Tears become groans as people grab stomachs in hunger. Shirts raised show stomachs flat, in the extreme stages of starvation.

"You have used us to fight in your wars." The voice

speaks from a roughly humanoid shape made of clouds and fog towering above the center of the camp. "We have been patient, talking to your leaders and assigning an ambassador. Yet, you starved and killed us." The bodies moan, eyes opening to stare in accusation at the horrified people trapped among the sea of bodies.

"Now you see, we will not give up and die. If you push us, you will find Death, Plague, Pestilence and Famine beyond your worst fears." The last words are a shout as the bodies created in the illusion rise and shuffle into the camp. "Deal with us fairly and we will be your neighbors, family and friends as we have for generations. Grieve with us this day for the senseless loss of lives too soon gone from us."

The fog man settles back into the camp, still covered in fog. Derek and Matteas turn with military precision. Matteas helps a cameraman right his camera and point it at Derek.

"I am Derek Mathews, Alpha of the South Dakota Pride and Ambassador for the Supernatural Peoples of North America. Today, we all should grieve for the senseless loss of life that confusion and lack of communication has caused us."

He bows his head as does Matteas in a moment of silence before continuing. "I am going home to my fiancé and family for the holidays. The Supernatural Peoples thank the United States Government for the camps and land they sit on gifted to us. We accept them but do not need the servant's placed in them for our convenience by the government. Let these people take their things and go home to be with their families for Christmas."

Other reporters are now recording the speech. "This camp will remain a gift to the lost and too soon dead. Those who enter will join them for eternity. I will return to my duties as ambassador after the New Year. Please remember that what you experienced today is only an illusion of the smallest part of the very real atrocities visited on the Supernatural Peoples by blind and uncaring policy makers safe in air-conditioned cubicles. Write, call, march in protest against the senseless loss of life experienced by the American people." Derek turns, trotting with Matteas behind him with the dim lighting only beginning to return to normal. They are soon lost to sight.

Hours later, Derek answers his cell while Matteas drives the SUV. "Hello?"

"We all saw the speech and your report." Alexis' voice is full of excitement.

"Good." Derek holds his breath waiting.

"We're, I uhhmm am proud of you." Her breath is fast as she speaks.

"I will be home soon, remember I am Alpha, I get to put the topper on the tree."

Alexis smiles "The projector is here, I am trying to wait for you as we planned."

Brother Lion speaks, "Please wait for us, it is a delicate thing using items made in Limbo in the mundane world."

"I will wait. Oh and boys, my Dad let slip that you will be his best men." There is a warning edge to Alexis' voice.

"Yes." *Is that the right answer?* Derek asks.

Why are you asking me? Things are simpler with Werelions.

"I expect us to set a date when you get here." Alexis' voice is firm.

"Of course dear." *Why do I feel like we are driving to be sentenced for our crimes?*

Matteas laughs, showing that Brother Lion has asked him as well as Derek.

"I think I will stop and get a Christmas tree on the way home for the trailer. Might cheer Sabrina up." Matteas turns south onto the highway as he finishes speaking.

"That's a great idea, I know everyone got you both presents or made you something. One person at a time will be stopping by and staying across the room while she opens their gifts and she can give the gifts she ordered from the internet. It will help her to remember that she's home with her family."

Matteas nods as his face goes grim. "And after the holidays?"

Derek and Brother Lion speak as one, "The Pride Goes to War."

Somehow, that simple declaration that blood will spill for the crimes of the Major and the Other makes them treasure the Holiday rock music all the more on the long ride home to the Ranch.

Other Books By Mary Leihsing and Aden Lewis

Book 1: ***Heart of the Pride*** : *Fur, Lust & Magic* series.

Kindle Edition: http://www.amazon.com/Heart-Pride-Lust-Magic-Book-ebook/dp/B01DMS8HE2

Print Edition: http://www.amazon.com/Heart-Pride-Lust-Magic-Book/dp/1530493617/

Large Print Edition: http://www.amazon.com/Heart-Pride-Lust-Magic-Book/dp/1532757425/

Did you enjoy this book?

We want to thank you for purchasing and reading this book. We really hope you got a lot out of it.

Can we ask a quick favor though?

If you enjoyed this book we would really appreciate it if you could leave us a positive review on Amazon.

We love getting feedback from our customers and reviews on Amazon really do make a difference. We read all our reviews and would really appreciate your thoughts.

Thanks so much.

Mary Leihsing & Aden Lewis

Printed in Great Britain
by Amazon

25225427R00229